MW00857007

ALSO BY KAREN RUSSELL

Sleep Donation
Orange World and Other Stories
Vampires in the Lemon Grove
Swamplandia!
St. Lucy's Home for Girls Raised by Wolves

The
ANTIDOTE

The
ANTIDOTE

Karen Russell

ALFRED A. KNOPF
New York
2025

A BORZOI BOOK
FIRST HARDCOVER EDITION
PUBLISHED BY ALFRED A. KNOPF 2025

Copyright © 2025 by Karen Russell

Penguin Random House values and supports copyright.
Copyright fuels creativity, encourages diverse voices, promotes
free speech, and creates a vibrant culture. Thank you for buying
an authorized edition of this book and for complying with copyright laws
by not reproducing, scanning, or distributing any part of it in any
form without permission. You are supporting writers and allowing
Penguin Random House to continue to publish books for every reader.
Please note that no part of this book may be used or reproduced
in any manner for the purpose of training artificial
intelligence technologies or systems.

Published by Alfred A. Knopf, a division of Penguin Random House LLC,
1745 Broadway, New York, NY 10019.

Knopf, Borzoi Books, and the colophon are registered trademarks
of Penguin Random House LLC.

Marie Howe, excerpt from "Gretel, from a sudden clearing"
from *The Good Thief.* Copyright © 1988 by Marie Howe.
Reprinted with the permission of Persea Books, Inc. (New York).
All rights reserved by Persea Books, Inc.

Library of Congress Cataloging-in-Publication Data
Names: Russell, Karen, [date] author. Title: The antidote / Karen Russell.
Description: First edition. | New York : Alfred A. Knopf, 2025.
Identifiers: LCCN 2024031643 (print) | LCCN 2024031644 (ebook) |
ISBN 9780593802250 (hardcover) | ISBN 9780593802267 (ebook) |
ISBN 9781524712822 (open market)
Subjects: LCGFT: Novels.
Classification: LCC PS3618.U755 A84 2025 (print) |
LCC PS3618.U755 (ebook) | DDC 813/.6—dc23/eng/20240712
LC record available at https://lccn.loc.gov/2024031643
LC ebook record available at https://lccn.loc.gov/2024031644

penguinrandomhouse.com | aaknopf.com

Printed in the United States of America

The authorized representative in the EU for product safety and
compliance is Penguin Random House Ireland, Morrison Chambers,
32 Nassau Street, Dublin D02 YH68, Ireland,
https://eu-contact.penguin.ie.

But I remember you before you became
a story. Sometimes, I feel a thorn in my foot

when there is no thorn. They tell me,
not unkindly, that I should imagine nothing here.

But I believe you are still alive.

—MARIE HOWE,
    From "Gretel, from a sudden clearing"

The
ANTIDOTE

Prologue

Deposit 69818060-1-77
Harp Oletsky's First Memory

It is nowhere you chose to be, and yet here you are. Papa steers your shoulders into the heart of the jack drive. Hundreds of rabbits stare at you through the wire around the fence posts. It feels like looking into the mirror. They do not want to be in this story either. Men have been working since dawn to herd the wild jacks into this pen. The town has gathered to solve the problem of the rabbits, who chew through rangeland and cropland, who eat the golden wheat your papa turns into money. Worse than the locusts, says Papa. Every hide brings a penny bounty. So many turnipy sweating bodies and a festive feeling in the air like a penny rubbed between two fingers, like blood shocked into a socket. A smell that reminds you of the room where babies are born. When you try to turn and run away, Papa grabs you. There's Mr. O'Malley, Mr. Waldowko, Mr. Zalewski, Mrs. Haage. You can't remember any more names. A hundred jointed arms come swinging into the pen that is alive with jackrabbits, the place of no escape. Now there is only madness. Terror of cudgels, terror of ax handles and hammers, terror of being trampled. "Papa! Help! Stop!" Rabbits run over your feet. "Settle down, Harp—" Papa is angry. He pours your name over your head like scalding water. The rabbits are angry. The rabbits are crying and dying, the clubs coming down, down, down. "If you ain't gonna help, stay clear of us, boy—" You are six today. Your family will have a party after supper. The cake was cooling when you left for town. You feel sick thinking about it. Cherries come slopping out of the rabbits. Gray skins are splitting, slipping under bootheels and wooden bats. Papa shows you what to target: the skulls and the spines of the screaming jacks. It's the fastest way to stop their screaming. *There is another way*, a voice cries out inside you. Smash it flat. You watch Papa click into his rhythm and begin to kill alongside the rest of the men.

You meet your baby sister's gaze through the fan of her clean fingers. Lada is sitting on your mother's lap. Three girls you know are watching from outside the fence. The girls are allowed to squeal and shield their faces. You wish you were a girl with them. Down, down, down come the clubs and the planks. Your stomach bulges and flattens. You are screaming with the rabbits. Your birthday wish is to get to the end of this sound. Quiet comes at last. The men's arms rest against their sides like tools in a shed. Women are hanging the dead jacks to dry by their long ears. Every twitching rabbit's foot has stilled. Inside of you, the screaming continues. It goes on and on and on. Papa finds you where you have hidden your eyes behind your hands, your tears inside your palms. "We can't let the jacks overrun the whole prairie. No one likes it, Son." This is a lie. Many had liked it. You shut your eyes along with the dead rabbits, because you did not want to see whose faces were smiling.

"Here," says Papa. "One is still living. You cannot be softhearted, Harp."

Your father puts the club in your hands. And after that, you are always afraid.

Section I

Collapse

The Prairie Witch

Aperson can lose everything in an instant. A fortune, a family, the sun. I've had to learn this lesson twice in my life. The first time it happened, I was a fifteen-year-old fugitive from the Home for Unwed Mothers. The second time, I was a prairie witch chained to my cot in a cinder-block jailhouse. "Your second home," the Sheriff liked to say. Officially, I do not exist in his West; nevertheless, it is a crime to pay me a visit.

On Black Sunday, before anybody knew to call it Black Sunday, I woke up in the jailhouse to a sound like a freight train tunneling through me. An earsplitting howl that seemed to shake the stone walls. My body trembled like a husk on the cot. My fingers clawed into the mattress. For those early moments in the dark I was nothing but the fear of floating off. What had happened to me while I slept? It felt as if a knife had scraped the marrow from my bones. Something vital inside me had liquefied and drained away, and in its place was this new weightlessness. Lightness and wrongness, a blanketing whiteness that ran up my spine and seeped out of my mouth. *Bankrupt* was the word that rose in my mind. At first, I did not recognize the voice crying out for help as my own. I clamped down on the sound, panicked—I could not afford to lose any more ballast. My numb limbs began to prickle with feeling, pins and needles stitching them back to my brain. It was not a happy reunion. Ten white toes sprouted like mushrooms on the edge of a filthy green blanket, waving to me from the outermost limit of what I could make out. A kerosene lantern in the hallway gave off a feeble emerald glow, beyond which the cell plunged into shadow. Not even the pain was mine. It came and went like the wind. Then it drilled through my skin and swallowed the world.

Or perhaps the black blizzard was already well under way when I woke up. Choking heat filled the jailhouse, along with lashing tails of dust. It occurred to me that I might be buried here before I could recollect who I was. Minutes and hours lost all meaning for me; I balled up on the cot and prepared to be pulled apart by a cyclone. Eventually the winds began to weaken. Light cut a pathway across the turbulent sky—I watched a pale line brightening and widening through the small cell window. A greenish disc hung above the cloud wall, and it took me ages to recognize the sun. It was not midnight after all, but well past noon.

I began to remember more about the land beyond this cell, the edgeless prairie. The name of the town where I worked returned to me: Uz, Nebraska, southeast of the Sandhills and west of the Platte River. We were four years into the worst drought that any newcomer to the Great Plains had ever experienced. Other beings kept older diaries. Cored cottonwood trees told a millennial story written in wavy circles that no politician had cared to read. Congressmen train themselves to think in election cycles, not planetary ones. They see spiking market highs and lows, and forget how to read in circles. Uz had been having brownouts for months. Plagues of jaws and mandibles. Grasshoppers rattled down on the tractor cabs from hissing clouds. Thousands of jackrabbits fanned over the Plains, chewing through anything green. Winged indigo beetles blew in from God alone knew where, husks shaped like hourglasses that nobody on the High Plains had ever seen before 1931. Red sand from Oklahoma and black dirt from Kansas and dove gray earth from the eastern plains of Colorado formed a rolling ceiling of dust above Uz that flashed with heat lightning.

The Sheriff and his family lived in a two-story brick frame house facing the jail, parts and blueprint purchased from the Sears, Roebuck catalog. It sat on the free side of the property, five hundred yards beyond the bars of my two-foot-by-two-foot window. As the dust blew into my cell, outside things became less and less real. The Sheriff's house slimmed to a charcoal sketch. Erased, redrawn, and finally lost to sight. The sky was well and truly falling.

At last I forced myself to scream for help. It felt terrifying to release so much breath at once—the lightness rushed into my head. No one responded. How long had I been trapped here? The cell was seven feet by eight feet, and furnished with nothing but the cot and a tin bucket half-filled with the previous inmate's piss. Or my own, perhaps. It seemed I was the only prisoner left inside the jailhouse. But I was wrong about that. Something pounced lightly onto my chest, then launched up to the ledge of the cell window—a huge bristling cat, whose carroty fur seemed absurdly bright. Her ears pitched forward, her claws tensing on the ledge. Her golden eyes regarded me serenely. Nothing called to the animal that I could hear. But a moment later, the cat slipped through the bars and jumped nimbly into the whirlwind.

Just as she leapt, I recognized her—the Sheriff's cat, a flatulent tabby who often slept on my chest during my stays in the jailhouse. The Sheriff, out of stupidity or laziness, called her nothing at all, not even Cat. A memory wailed awake inside me: the Sheriff had once drowned a litter of her kittens in a washbasin within earshot of my cell. Five infant voices flooded through me, clawing at the soft walls within the walls. Again I heard the splash as the bag went under. Displaced water had come trickling down the hall while their silence deepened to permanence. The Sheriff had caged the mother cat in a nearby closet, locking us both into impotent witness. Her angry cries had blended with her children's dissolving ones. The last voices in the world could not have sounded more forlorn.

A stupid man can still be a savant at torture. The Sheriff had squatted on his haunches in front of Cell 8, grinning through the bars at me as he poured fresh milk into a bowl for the dead kittens' mother. "What a racket, eh? You'll forget that nasty business in a snap. A powerful witch like you . . ."

My job returned to me before my name did. *Yes, I am the Antidote* I learned, and remembered. *I am a prairie witch.* A door swung open onto my life. Now I could picture my rented room in the boardinghouse. My poster facing the street from the third-floor window, hand-lettered for me by the calligrapher in Kinkaid gold: THE ANTIDOTE OF UZ! NOW ACCEPTING DEPOSITS. I advertised my banking services as a panacea for every ailment from heartburn to nightmares. Some of my customers, I recalled, had made up a little jingle about me, taking the lyrics from my poster:

"The Antidote to lovesickness! The Antidote to grief! The Antidote to gas pains! The Antidote to guilt! The Antidote to sleepless nights! The Antidote to sweaty palms! The Antidote to daydreaming! The Antidote to shame!"

Most everyone on the Great Plains knew about us, even those who denied our existence. The Vaults, some called us. The prairie witches. Now I remembered what I did to earn my bread—what I had been doing since I was a much younger woman. Absorbing and storing my customers' memories. Banking secrets for the townspeople of Uz. Sins and crimes, first and last times, nights of unspeakable horror and dewdrop blue mornings—or who knew what my customers had transferred from their bodies into mine? These were only my guesses. I disappeared into a spacious blankness during my transfers. A prairie witch's body is a room for rent. A vault to store the things people cannot stand to know, or bear to forget.

Half the town of Uz banked with me, and even those who denounced me as a fraud and a blackmailer knew that I was open for business in Room 11. People came and paid me to store some portion of their lives. A memory that felt too heavy to carry into the future, or too precious for daily reminiscence. As they whispered their stories into my green earhorn, memories lifted out of their bodies and into mine. It was a painless exchange. Nothing my customers told me had ever disturbed me, because I was not awake to hear them. Cocooned in blue trance, I could dilate to absorb anything. I did not return to my waking mind until a transfer was completed. "I know as little about what I contain," I reassured my customers, "as a safety deposit box knows about its rocks. As a jar of pickling vinegar knows about its floating roots." *As an attic knows about its ghosts.* Their dead were alive inside me, patiently waiting to be recollected. The weight of these deposits refreighted me. After a transfer, I often felt a heavy ache in my rib cage or my pelvis—sometimes a swimmy brightness like goldfish circling my chest—and in this way I knew that our exchange had been a success. My new customers would smile sheepishly at me and say, "I wonder what I just told you, ma'am? It's gone clean out of my head!"

Now I understood why my body felt so frighteningly light, why the word *bankruptcy* kept running through my mind. Something had happened to me that I had not known to fear.

Fifteen years of deposits, somehow, had been siphoned from me while I slept. Drawn from my flesh, like vapor from a leaf. Where had they all gone? Out of my body and into the whirlwind? Were they still intact somewhere? Or had they dispersed with the dust? With each roomy breath, I learned more about the shape and the scale of what I'd lost. I rolled onto my side and pulled up my night-gown—a repurposed sackcloth from GROVER'S ORCHARDS, too short for a woman my height, printed with repeating sandy peaches that seemed to shrivel and ripen with each breath. I palpated my stomach with my fists, as if the thousands of secrets I'd housed might merely be misplaced.

To be clear, I hadn't forgotten these secrets, because I'd never known them in the first place. Or perhaps that's not entirely true. I knew them the way I knew you, my Son, before you were born. Nestled in my body, as pressure and weight. Memories are living things. When you house as many as I did, your bones begin to creak. Now I felt in danger of evaporating myself.

As it turned out, I was not alone. Farmers all over the Plains were losing their entire harvests at this very moment. Families hid in their cellars while the clouds grew fat with black earth. The sky became a growling belly. Uzians caught out in their fields when the darkness eclipsed the sun believed they'd gone blind.

Many of these same farmers and ranchers had also—unbeknownst to them—just lost huge tracts of the past. The days and the nights I'd held in reserve for them while they went about the business of living. My customers who had banked with me loyally since my arrival in Uz would soon learn about my crash—how could I prevent it? They'd come to make their withdrawals, and I'd have nothing to return to them. I had retained only a palmful of facts about my solitary life.

I have always kept scrupulous records. I could tell you who visited me on July 12 of 1927, and the duration of the visit. I could tell you to the penny how much money I made in Uz County between the years of 1920 and 1935. But what did it matter if I'd charged this client two dollars, and this one two hundred? None of the numbers I'd inked into my ledger had anything real to say about the vastness of what I'd just lost. It was spasms in my belly and the clawing grief.

Black Sunday, before the newspapermen named it and swept it into history, pulverized the region now known as the "Great Dust

Bowl." Like so many of my neighbors, I woke to ruin. In the center of the storm, I believed that the worst had happened. But I was wrong about that. The dust had another lesson to teach me: so long as you're still drawing breath, there's always more to lose.

Home. Home. I tugged at the word until a world rose up. Chained to the cot, dirt inflaming my nostrils, I smiled in the dark. I believed I'd lost everything, but I hadn't after all. I remember You. Hope grew inside me then. Unstoppably, as You once grew. I pictured green leaves twining around my rib cage, tethering me to my memories of You. Your slippery, seven-pound body and your strong wail. Every kick and twist, I rehearsed in my mind. Even the ache of losing You, I welcomed home. It was the weight I needed to sit up and plant my feet on the floor of the cell. As long as there's a chance of our reunion, Son, I promise You that I will go on living.

On the night that You were born, one of the nurses at the Milford Home for Unwed Mothers risked her job to let me hold You. *Lie back*, she said, and *let your baby drink. He knows what to do, honey. See that? He was born for this.* I had never met such a hungry creature, so eager to live. I hadn't guessed my body could meet another being's needs so completely. You cried out, and I realized with wonder that I was the one You were calling for. I was the answer to your question. The antidote to your distress, your fear, your ravening hunger, your life-thirst. I stared into your fierce, dark eyes, born open. We fluttered in and out of sleep together, in a dream of milk and heat and love. Then came the block of hours which were stolen from me—I believe now that I was drugged. *We are sorry, but you lost your baby*, a new nurse told me when I awoke. The sensation of my milk lifting through my breasts to flood your mouth was barely a memory when a doctor I had never seen before handed me your death certificate. Those monsters with their sad smiles lied to me. I knew You were alive.

Are You still?

Asphodel Oletsky

You know, if you sync up your breath with the thing breathing behind you, you can barely hear it at all.

On the morning of April 14, I was the only girl on the prairie court. I liked to play two-on-two with Valeria and Pazi and Nell whenever they could sneak away, but that afternoon I was alone. I'd refused to go to Mass with my uncle that morning, our Sunday ritual. When I first arrived in Uz, I went to the Polish church with him for a solid three months. So many whiskery parishioners felt compelled to tell me that if my mother hadn't eloped with that deviant, that swindler—my father, a man unknown to me—she would never have been murdered.

"Lada was such a timid little flower. Such a sweet girl, before she run off with that roustabout," said one Polish grandmother who smelled like borax and Grape Sparkle. "She'd be alive, had she only stayed in Uz—"

"Well, buscia," my uncle had interrupted. "That's true. But if she'd stayed with us, her daughter wouldn't be alive. It's the killer we must blame for his crime, eh? Not my sister." For an instant, I felt pure love for my uncle; then my face went hot with shame. What was I doing here, breathing? Using up the air that had been earmarked for her? For the next few weeks, I prayed intently for my mother's soul, genuflecting on the wavy yellow risers that someone had made out of a forest's kneecaps. Who knew that prayer could give you splinters? I could not keep it up. Going to Mass at St. Agnieszka feels like attending a headache with fifty strangers. The bells! The holy smoke! Like a hangover without the party. Too many eyes staring at me with pity and superiority. The only gaze I liked to meet belonged to Veronica in the Sixth Station of the Cross, whose onyx eyes were cool and pupilless and capable. Veronica was a great teammate to Jesus, wiping the blood and crud from his face. Once I made varsity, I discovered my own way of worshipping—under the fiery sky, with my basketball. I would rather leap than kneel. I pray to the God who loves to win.

"Maybe next Sunday," Uncle Harp had muttered, taking my hand through the driver's side window before releasing the clutch. He shouted a reminder to me that my soul was in jeopardy, then reversed down the sandy cow path to the main highway, the baked ground under his tires coughing yellow dust. This was exactly what *his* God had done, if you thought about it—disappearing into that remoteness my uncle called heaven, leaving the rest of us poor rubes to rake up the ashes. Uncle Harp prayed for rain every morning, and then he used the wheat comb to dig out the porch. At the start of our last basketball season, Dagmara's mother gave every player a Red Cross dust mask dyed in our team colors.

When I first came to Uz, coughing woke me every night. I'd sit up in bed with my face in my hands and think for a good moment that my mother was still alive. That we were living in the yellow house in Hubbell. Then I'd remember: she'd been murdered and I'd been sent to live with her gray-haired brother. Every morning that I wake up here, I enter and exit that same tunnel of facts. I wake to a view of the fallowland, tangled in my dead mother's blue cotton sheets in my dead mother's bed, a bad dream that has continued for almost two years without interruption.

The detectives in our town never found my mother's killer, but they did manage to locate her living brother. They shipped me to Uz on August 4, 1933, in the middle of the hottest summer on record. It was 104 degrees on the afternoon my train pulled in. My uncle seemed to feel this record-breaking heat was no coincidence—not that he blamed me, exactly, just saw me as more bad luck.

My hopes had no shape when I stepped onto the train platform at the Uz depot, looking for this uncle I'd never met. When I found him, the fog of hope cinched itself into a disappointment that was exactly Harp Oletsky's height and shape. This rat-gnawed corncob of a man took my satchel and brushed my hair out of my face as if he were pulling back the curtains—a gesture that made me want to bite him. "Well, you don't look a thing like her!" he told me. "Your mother was a very pretty child."

Disappointment was the first thing we ever shared. Harp Oletsky, I realized, had no idea who my mother was. When he said "Lada Oletsky," he was picturing a baby sister. The youngest mother in my memory is twenty-seven, with her ruby lipstick on at night and her sun-colored freckles. Harp Oletsky had no awareness of my mother's best qualities, and her other qualities—her very poor judgment of men's characters; her love of polka music and any kind of party; her struggles to keep hold of jobs and money; her gift for reviving sick birds and bald plants; her laughter that fell like rain inside our house, washing the sticky sadness from the walls; her habit of sticking out her tongue when she was reading or sewing. Right from the start, I understood that I was going to be alone with her. My mama's only pallbearer. Even dead, she needs my care. I had hoped that Harp Oletsky would help me to remember her. Her real voice was slipping away from me, sounding more and more like my bad ventriloquy. But this stranger could only tell his silly stories about a toddler.

Hopes soar and teach you what a fool you are—Mama used to say this after a new job or a new man disappointed her. Staring into my uncle's wrinkled face, I felt embarrassed by my hopes. Never once did my uncle come looking for his sister, even though he claimed to be heartbroken when she ran off. "Well, she didn't run far," I'd pointed out. The town where we lived on the Kansas border was a three-hour train ride from Uz.

"Lada didn't want us to find her," he'd said curtly. "I can show you her letters."

On my first day in Uz, my uncle toured me around the Oletsky house. He led me to a faded family portrait hanging in the parlor. "This was Lada—" He pointed to a blurry child with a shy expression, clutching a tin watering can. Frozen there forever, never to be liberated, between my custard-colored grandparents and her two unsmiling brothers.

"You Poles all look bewildered or constipated," I told my uncle.

"You're a Pole, Dell."

He followed me throughout the house, saying very little. I could feel his eyes drilling into me like two woodpeckers. He took me upstairs and opened the door onto Mama's childhood bedroom—my room, now. "Well, Dell," he said at last. "I can see this ain't what you pictured. You tell me what's missing. What would it take to make this place feel like home?"

"My bones in the ground," I told him. "And even then, I'd just be visiting."

On Black Sunday, before I knew it was Black Sunday, I picked up my ball and stepped back into the furnace. It had been ninety degrees every day for three weeks. My uncle's truck bulged on the horizon, twin beams shining up the sparkling mineral inside the dust. It was no longer unusual to see cars driving with their headlights on at noon.

I would have liked a ride into town, but not enough to ask for one. I walked four miles into the once-grassy hills. The creek had run dry last summer. A foot of earth was missing. More blew off every time the wind picked up. The bankers worried themselves sick about their money flying off, but my uncle said that gold was small potatoes compared to what the High Plains had lost during this drought: soil. "Six inches of topsoil is what makes everything happen, Dell. All the food you've ever eaten depends on those six inches."

Hardpan is what remains after the soil has vanished. Bony earth so dry you could bounce a basketball off it.

I was only alive to play basketball. It got me out of bed and it gave me a reason to keep breathing. Alone on Black Sunday, I pretended Coach was watching me. I ran downcourt while the dust scraped my calves raw, missing shot after shot, screaming whenever a gust came at me headlong. To move at all was a struggle. To breathe through my mask. To push a ball through the wind took enormous strength. The backstop shuddered *almost, almost. Down-down-down*, repeated the basketball to the ground.

We played on a secret court a mile west of downtown, on concrete that Coach had personally poured onto the prairie. Land that had been abandoned, too sandy to turn a profit. "Nobody will ever pay a nickel to watch girls play ball," Dottie Iscoe once told me. "Female basketball is a freak show." Dottie Iscoe clearly did not know about Babe Didrikson and the Barnstorming Reds, or the AAU tournaments with their prize money and college scholarships. We all held on to the prospect of being a prospect. Scoped by recruiters and sent to play for real money. But it was love that drove us outside in all seasons. A crazy love that pitched us against the dust, that hurled our bodies into the inferno that Coach was still calling Spring Training. "Who needs a rival team, girls," Coach shouted from the sidelines, "when you can play against this wind?" Later was better, to beat the heat. When possible—not every girl could get away from her family so easily—several of us met to practice by moonlight. Coach was a gruff voice in our heads, directing our movements. At our afternoon practices, when attendance was mandatory, the whole team assembled and awaited Coach's instructions. He'd blow his whistle and scream criticism of everything I was doing, his voice raking through me and drawing secret blood. It felt wonderful. Coach didn't love me. He didn't much like any of us. He never bothered with our names during practices and games. He called us by the numbers stitched onto our jerseys. We were like a math problem that Coach was continually solving. He wanted the same thing I did, which was to win.

Coach would stand under the basket barking insults at us, his snouty green car parked at the edge of the court with its headlights burning. He angled the lights so we could see the center line. We practiced half-blind, running through swirling corollas of dust. Pink shorts ballooned above our knees, floating through the twin beams as we ran, and I saw this again in my dreams at night, where I was still practicing, always practicing. Downcourt, upcourt. Coach honking three times for each basket, flashing the lights on us. Basketball turned me into something so much larger than a girl. All the legs on the court belonged to a single unstoppable animal.

The land here is so flat that it's easy to lose your bearings. When the sun begins to sink, even veteran Plainsmen consult their compasses. I've heard that it feels like being lost at sea. I have never seen the ocean, but I know what it means to live without landmarks. I turned to find the road. When I looked to the southeast, I saw a black bar, floating midair. This was not such an unusual sight. The dust played tricks on our eyes. A city might seem to ripple into focus on the horizon and then collapse again. This had happened, said my uncle, even before the drought. He took me to see the "Mirage Flats" in the Sandhills, where the light and the grassy dunes cast up all sorts of illusions in people's minds. One of them was that this sandy country could be profitably farmed. These vintage mirages decorate the Grange Hall. An entire wall is covered with the posters from the railroads that advertised Uz, Nebraska, to people like my grandparents as an "American Eden": WHEAT PILES UP LIKE GOLD IN SOUTHERN NEBRASKA! RAIN FOLLOWS THE PLOW!

Staring out at the thirsty prairie made me feel lonely and important. The country needed me. It needed my teammates, the high school warriors who played ball in Region 7 of the Western Plains High School Girls' Basketball League. Our team name, unfortunately, had come from our sponsor: Uz Poultry & Eggs. We were three games away from becoming the Region 7 Champions for the second year in a row. The farmers and the ranchers were sunk in a losing season, but Uz Poultry & Eggs kept winning. Very few people were turning out to watch our games in the early months of 1935, but the scores got reported in the local papers and I knew that they mattered—certainly more than the mostly empty gymnasium suggested. When we won, I believed it shored up everyone in our disintegrating town.

I was the starting point guard of Poultry & Eggs this season, owing to my natural playmaking skills and also because I had nothing to do but practice. Other girls had homes to which they longed to return, water to pump and chickens to feed, mothers to chide them and to kiss them, fathers to scream at them to haul ass, what seemed like thousands of younger siblings to burp and diaper and bounce to sleep. Love wore them out. I had nothing to burn off the reserves of my anger but basketball. I needed rivals to wring it out of me. Game day was the greatest release, the one day of the week when I felt anything like peace. Coach told me what to do and the scoreboard told me what to feel. My feet left the ground, the ball left my fingers, and I could tell in that instant whether I'd made my shot. *Into and through.* I played under the moon, straight through the summer months, when every other girl my age was helping with harvest. Uncle Harp did not expect help to come from me. He'd given up on asking me to do much of anything (although he often left his bedroom door open so that I could hear him praying loudly for my salvation). There was no one to stop me from doing whatever the hell I wanted. My murdered mom was dying a second time—fraying and fading inside me—the earth was attacking us from the sky, and the only consolation I still believed in was that all weather is temporary. Weather could change in an instant.

The black cloud, I noticed, had started moving inland. Racing toward me—toward *us*. The dust began to lift and curtain. The wind bansheed across the prairie with nothing to split its tall loony cry. Even then, I knew I had to keep dribbling. My ball was the only thing nailing me to Earth. Thud! Thud! Thud! I kept my eyes on my hands and sprinted up and down the court while the wind tried to steal my ball.

A Dodge truck was making its slow, boxy way down the road. It was another five minutes before my uncle's frightened face came into view, a gray pebble behind the windshield.

"I was gonna walk."

"Are you crazy? There is a storm about to hit. Get in."

The Dryland Farmer, Harp Oletsky

B lack Sunday began as a gash in the western sky, growing wider and wider and spilling down dirt instead of blood. Sometimes I imagine the glee of those journalists at the New York City papers—typing up the story of our worst day in their fancy language. Adjusting the margins and pushing our tragedy into a skinny column, just like old Marvin at the funeral home shoving a tall corpse into a tight suit.

DUST VICTIMS IN NEBRASKA PRAY FOR RAIN!
"MESSIAH" SUNG IN THE SANDHILLS

Poor ignorant farmers! Is that what the reporters think?
Poor gamblers, putting it all on wheat.
Imagine every ghost rising up to hurl their cemetery earth at the

living. That was the sound we heard last Sunday afternoon. At 3:00 p.m. the sun was murdered in cold blood, in full view of every woman and child. The sun sank into black cloud. Buried alive, at a shocking altitude, by the duster to end all dusters.

But at a quarter past 2:00 p.m., the skies were blue and I'd felt almost cheerful. Driving home from Mass, I passed Ed Leedskalin and stopped to chat with him. Ed was doubled over on the side of the road, gathering thistle. Pulling the plant while it was green and young, before the prickles form. Plenty of ranchers in Uz were keeping their famished cattle alive with tumbleweeds, but Ed told me he'd been giving them to his four hungry kids, boiling them with lard and salt. It broke my heart to picture a meal of thistle. It sounded like a scene straight out of that fellow's doomsday film.

A couple months back, a tall Yankee came to the Grange to lecture us on our part in the catastrophe. A New Dealer employed by one of Roosevelt's alphabet soup agencies, sent to reform us. A college boy, we'd assumed, because he had one of those starchy accents from no-place. He had come to Uz directly from some fancy summit about dirt. Scientists from all over the world had attended, he said. Palestine, Ceylon! Places where colonists had plowed up the land. Places that also had dust bowls. "America is not the only country dealing with soil erosion!" he'd shouted from the podium. He had a bad sunburn and canary yellow hair. I'd wondered how the kid got this government job at twenty, if he'd grown up in a farming family.

The boy scolded us for uprooting all the native grasses, exposing the soil to the elements. He wanted us to plant cover crops, perennials. To leave more living roots in the ground. He screened an early copy of a film for us—*The Plow That Broke the Plains*. The filmmaker had made farmers into the villains of the story, or so it seemed to me. Were we? "What is this hooey?" my friend Otto had shouted. Others used nastier names. As the credits rolled, the young man had pitched his voice low, like he was trying to impersonate the tenor in the film: "You need to change the way you farm this land. Thousands of years of fertility is banked in topsoil. You people are losing tons of it every minute."

"How do we get the soil back?" I asked.

"You can't, sir," said this baby-faced expert. "It takes five hundred years to build an inch of topsoil. You've gotta protect what's left." Then he hiccuped at the podium and never quite regained his composure. The boy's presentation had riled us, but it wasn't exactly news. The more sod we plowed up, the less water we had. Nature's sponge was gone. We had tilled the soil to powder. We had pulled up all the anchors. Now everything was blowing.

Tassels, leaves, stalks. Houses, trees, hearts.

The driest April in the history of the Weather Bureau. The windiest in living memory.

April 14 broke without augury, and then at 3:00 p.m., not half an hour after I said goodbye to Ed and got back on the road, midnight ran over the sun. It was darker and louder than any moonless night has ever been. The soil rose in mutiny against the farmer. Nobody who didn't live through it can ever understand it. By some grace, I was able to reach Dell before the dust wall covered us. "It sounds like a thousand tornadoes," said my niece. Did I take some satisfaction in the fear seeping into her voice? Yes I did. I had risked my own life to come save hers. Lada's girl came to Uz with a little smirk tied to her face. Not a smile. More like a bowline knot. I confess that I enjoyed watching it unravel. It proved to me that my niece was a child after all. Dell never joined me in prayers, and I felt a rush of gratitude to my stubborn niece when she joined me in my terror. It only took Armageddon to get her jawline to relax. We crossed into the wrong lane as I swerved to avoid the dust wall.

The girl was breathing along with me all of a sudden, no longer alone in her own dark. We were feeling the sprawl of it. Awe, if you want to call it that. A windmill on Sender's property caught fire as we sped past, wheeling scarlet flames under the angry clouds. Dirt rained across the windshield, blood roared between my ears, until there was no fence in my mind between inside and outside sounds. The flat horizon rose and stretched into one great swallowing mouth. It flew toward us, round and open.

"Can't you go any faster?" Dell yelled at me. "I don't want my obituary to read that I got buried alive on the passenger side."

"You think your death would make the papers?"

I had on my driving goggles, and I'd had the foresight to soak a rag in water from the radiator. The girl pushed the rag against her face, silent at last.

It was a miracle that we made it home, with only a few feet of visibility and the earth pounding on the truck cab. A screen of darkness advanced toward the northeast, thousands of birds flying before it. I could not hear even one of them over the screaming wind. But that is a sight that will never leave me. The waves of earth crashing over the prairie. The sky exhaling all her birds.

The Scarecrow

I was not annihilated. Whatever "I" was.

The Prairie Witch

L ucky you," the Sheriff's wife said flatly when she found me alive. I have the cat to thank for my rescue. Dottie Iscoe had brought her middle daughter, Gladys, to call for the tabby underneath the windows of the jailhouse. The child's cries sailed up like birds while her mother's tongue spaded at the thick air like an undertaker. "Caaaat!"

I don't think either woman was expecting my voice to call back.

Mrs. Sheriff came coughing down the hallway toward my cell. Carrying a lantern, for all the good that did her—the joke in Uz was that you needed electric light to know if your kerosene lamp was still burning. Dottie had a red bandanna tied over her mouth, her tiny eyes enlarged by a pair of motorist's goggles that she kept pausing to wipe clear as she groped along the walls.

"Jed! Red! Bring the key ring for the Yale lock!"

Jed and Red were her two boulder-faced sons. There was something funny to me, on a good day, about the contrast between the brothers' blank expressions and their cowlicked red hair. But perhaps I misjudge them, Son. For all I know, the Iscoe brothers are geniuses in hibernation.

"I'm alive!" I called to them, somewhat unconvincingly. "Help!"

Down the hall, Dottie screamed. She jumped back as if she'd stepped on a rat. Her large son let out a yodel of terror. For the first time since I woke up to the hideous lightness, I was able to laugh. It felt wonderful to laugh again, like remembering how to blink and swallow. For hours I'd been lying stiff under the dust, gritting my sandy teeth, afraid to release a breath and weigh even less.

I heard a key biting iron. The cell door scraped open, rousing the dust from where it had gathered into hummocks along the walls like fat brown serpents. I laughed even harder, because this joke was not lost on me. The same people who had trapped me in the first place had come to free me. And tell me I was lucky.

Women like Dottie Iscoe often insist that people like me should feel grateful to them, Son. As if we are lucky to be alive at all in the world that they control. Ask any stone or flower if it feels grateful to be here. Your mother does not have much advice to pass on, but I can tell you when to be wary. *You should be grateful* is a sentence that the powerful wield like a cudgel. I heard it night after night in the Home for Unwed Mothers.

Dottie knelt over me on the cot, both of us coughing. She freed my arms and got me onto my feet. "Did you forget how to walk?" She grunted. Indeed I had. I felt like a corn husk, like a doll without its stuffing. We moved carefully down the narrow hallway where the dust lay thick enough to ripple. Jed and Red were waiting at the entrance. Jed lifted his mother by the waist, while Red hoisted me under my armpits. The boys spun us around, very formally, and set us down in daylight.

As I stood staring out at the buried garden, my vision swam.

Hollow-boned, bird-light—

The hideous lightness—

Bankrupt.

The word rose inside me again and attached itself to my condition.

I shuffled along behind her sons, fighting down an impulse to run back into the jailhouse. It seemed like the next gust of wind would lift me like a paper wrapper or dash me against the stones.

"How did you and the kids make out?" I asked Dottie. My voice sounded thin and faraway.

"Better than most. The obituaries ran three pages in the *Register* today. Vick telephoned from the hospital in Kearney, he says it will be twice as long tomorrow . . ."

The Sheriff had left before sunup, as soon as the winds died down, Dottie told me. He and Cam Yernhoff spent the morning digging people out along the highway. He had neglected to tell her that I was in the holding pen, she said with irritation. "You spooked me good."

There is a log of prisoners that Sheriff Iscoe keeps for the state of Nebraska in which I'm sure my name has never once appeared. Unlike me, the Sheriff has no discipline when it comes to record keeping.

From Mrs. Sheriff, I learned that the storm had attacked towns and cities from west Texas to the Dakotas. Jackrabbits electrocuted near Kearney. A field of exploded watermelons. Cars shorted out on Route 20 and were abandoned by their drivers, two of whom collapsed and got buried by five-foot drifts not a hundred yards from the highway. I did not want to hear any more, and I said as much, but that only made Mrs. Sheriff pour these horrors into me with greater relish. In Uz people call her the town gossip. But Dottie is a scavenger bird. She perches on the Party Line collecting horror stories. She has an archive of bones to rival my own.

"Gesundheit," said Dottie as I sneezed up bits of her atomized property. The air scraped our throats and our nostrils. We were inhaling farmland and ranchland. We were choking on the harvests of our neighbors. Dust tinted the sky a hazy red. Across the yard, the gateposts to Dottie's garden rose out of pale sand; the garden plot was a new beach. You could see where the wind had left its autograph. Dust lapped over the Iscoes' third porch step. Dozens of tumbleweeds had gotten pinioned to the barbed wire around the jailhouse. Snarls of green hid inside the dead thistle. A shovel-faced yellow pony nosed around them, her lips moving like those of a woman in church.

The Sheriff's house looked like a shard of bone someone had dug out of the sand. Two ghostly faces stared at me through the gum-taped windows, and I was relieved to find I recognized them. Luyenne and Bettle, the tiniest Iscoes, three and four years old. So new to Earth they wouldn't know how wrong the world was today. I wondered how old they would be when they figured out what they had survived out here. I wondered if they would ever know that their daddy was evil. Perhaps love would block the knowledge like an eclipse.

It was the worst dust storm to hit the southern Plains in living memory, Dottie told me, with something like glee. The Red Cross had set up in McCook and Hastings, treating eighteen babies and twelve elders with dust pneumonia. A dozen barns and farmhouses had been caved in by the black roller. Half the county buildings were damaged so bad they were not worth repairing. Her happy tone confused me until I realized she was celebrating her family's fortune relative to all these smited neighbors.

"Lucky you," I said.

"Ca-at—" Gladys Iscoe kept calling for the animal. Her worried cries were so rhythmic that her mother seemed to have stopped hearing them, the way living music can fade to the background of one's own dramatic thoughts. "Ca-at—"

Before Dottie could stop me, I knelt and took the girl's hand. Cruel words flooded my mouth: *May the cat escape your family forever and never return. May the cat make it safely to the land of milk and mice and honey.* The frostiness of the child's dark eyes stopped me from saying them out loud. Gladys Iscoe was ten or eleven—too young to have that deadness already spreading through her.

"Take heart, Gladys," I whispered. "Your cat will turn up alive."

She looked up at me solemnly and squeezed my hand.

Over her daughter's head, Dottie stared at me. We were both shading our eyes against the tiny knives hidden in the air. The hole in the sky that had screamed at us for hours had been replaced by a dull yellow haze. Dottie broke our gaze first, coughing into her sleeve.

"You must be wanting to get back to town, Miss Witch. It's the Sahara from here to the windmill, but they've got the main road just about clear. Red can give you a ride."

I refused to feel grateful to Dottie. But I did feel a jolt of sky-blue surprise. Kindness has its own electric current. I am almost never expecting it. She touched my wrist where the cuffs had been and handed her boy the key to his father's car.

⚞⚟

Red Iscoe was a terrifying driver. After twenty minutes of slamming the Sheriff's tires into the dunes and then reversing into buried shoals of fence line, he sheepishly asked me to take the wheel. We were lucky the Ford didn't short out. Dust was piled on either side of the road like bleak snowbanks. Miles of gray, impaled thistle and toppled fencing raced the road into town. The rows of tillering wheat were crushed and buried. In the northwest, Miguel Herrera's ruined fields shrugged darkly at us. A dozen saplings from his newly planted shelterbelt lay stunned around the road. Perhaps he was relieved to find his trees destroyed. Plenty of people in Uz and the surrounding country had planted shelterbelts to get their checks from Roosevelt's relief program, the so-called New Deal. Men talked openly about how they intended to cut down their freshly planted saplings as soon as their government money arrived. "I doze 'em off faster than I plant 'em," one of my loyal customers, Wade Immey, had bragged to me. The New Deal ran into old habits out here.

Red and I dragged the trees by their roots, locking eyes over our dust masks. It was a strange intimacy to have with the son of my enemy. The Sheriff's boy cleared a way for me to get to Uz.

At last we saw the right angles of the town spearing out of the murky light. A huddle of buildings that look frightened and conspiratorial, their backs to the immense prairie sky. "Uz is just a wide place in the road," I once heard a lineman complaining to his friend. Red's headlights lit up the shattered windows of Smallfry's Eats; a rotting pineboard marquee; Easter's Feed and Seed; the shuttered Bank of the Prairie. Every storefront was coated with black mitts of dust.

Beyond these respectable enterprises, at the abrupt, ungraded end of the main street that leads like a gangplank directly into a sea of treeless sand, You will find my window with its view of ruination. I lived on the third floor of one of the tallest structures in Uz, a three-story boardinghouse and saloon which leased rooms to spinsters like me, traveling salesmen, traveling preachers, traveling killers—let's assume—although so far I had not encountered one. Suitcase farmers, rainmakers, drunks who lost their keys and their way home.

The Country Jentleman operated on the ground floor, serving "non-intoxicating liquor" to a dozen veteran alcoholics. Two years after Prohibition, Uz remained committed to its reputation as a dry county, a place of decency and virtue. They kept the "non-intoxicating" claim on the label and the whiskey hidden in those salubrious blue bottles. You'd often find the drunkest person playing a battered Steinway that turned every note into a plea for a piano tuner. The piano had come from a pirate ship with a mermaid hidden inside it, according to Rasmussen. My landlord was an unusually cheerful Swede, formerly of the circus Swedes, the "Rolla Rolla Rasmussens," who still perform in Gordon; I think that sequined branch of his family gave him a soft spot for witches. He let me put my poster up in the window of the Country Jentleman, and he got on very well with me when nobody else was around. He charged White farmers flophouse rates: fifteen cents for a bed in the shared dormitory, twenty-five cents for a private room. Married men traveling with their wives got a discount. I paid twice as much as any other guest except for Charles Evans, a homesteader who had relocated here from the all-Black settlement of Audacious. Rasmussen had been charging Mr. Evans a dollar a night, the same rate they charged for the president's suite in the Wheatgrower's Hotel in Kimball. The poorer you were the more expensive things became, and if you were a Black man or woman, the White proprietors in Uz would overcharge you without shame, then go to bed feeling they'd done you a kindness by serving you at all. When I complained about my rent, Rasmussen told me that I should be grateful. "Think of the risk I run, letting a Vault operate above the Jentleman!" In truth, I must have tripled his income; my customers often drank a pitcher or two of his non-intoxicating liquor while they waited downstairs for their appointments. I watched Red Iscoe gulp water from the Sheriff's battered canteen, his Adam's apple jumping, as we made our way down the graded road into town. He had a sweeter version of his father's face.

Without warning, time pulled into a line. An awful memory returned to me—now I remembered why the Sheriff had dragged me to the jailhouse in the middle of the night. On the Saturday evening before the Black Sunday storm, the Sheriff had forced me to take a deposit from the sozzled doctor who ran the State Asylum in Hastings. A slab-tongued fellow whose glasses were sliding off his face, swaying on his feet in front of my earhorn. Vick had pulled him out of the drunk tank and dragged him to Cell 8. I recognized the doctor's ruddy face. He'd been all over the newspapers when he testified in the trial of "The Lucky Rabbit's Foot Killer." The doctor, shaved and sober, took the stand and told the jury box that Clemson Louis Dew—a skinny, trembling vagrant of seventeen—had a "mental defect" that caused him to murder seven women in four different Nebraska counties. What testimony had this doctor slurred into my earhorn two nights ago? He'd been hiccuping uncontrollably above me, and this was the last sound I heard before I blacked out ("Pardon—hup!—Me!—hup—Miss—hup!—Witch!").

The Sheriff never pays me for taking these strangers' deposits. He comes to the boardinghouse without warning and drags me to Cell 8. Once I saw his wife sponging blood off a wall, and I thought: *That is all I am to Victor Iscoe.* He needs me to sponge up people's dangerous recollections. *Think of it as a tax*, he told me once. *A tax on witchcraft.* A few of these people the Sheriff brings to my cell have been formally arrested. Most have not. I've taken midnight deposits from two Filipino brothers with purple shiners, an Irish farmhand in a bloodstained apron, two agitated Polish women who winced each time the Sheriff spoke. *You can thank the witch for saving us a world of trouble*, he liked to joke with these frightened people, nudging them toward my earhorn in the dim cell. *You don't have to skip town, and I don't have to kill anyone.*

All at once, I remembered the vertigo of rolling into my trance on the night before Black Sunday—releasing my grip on my name and falling backward from a great height, dissolving into waves of blankness. When I returned to consciousness, the drunk doctor was smiling just above me, his hairy face floating over the earhorn, his crystal blue eyes sparkling like plates on the drying rack. "Thank you, Miss Witch," he said. "I feel like a sunbeam, so light—what a marvelous gift!" The Sheriff watched us from the corner, where he had chaperoned the transfer. His face was stiff as a broom, but I watched his shoulders relax. From the doctor's bright, empty eyes and the ache in my chest, I knew that the transfer had been a success. "Your secret is safe with me, sir," I'd promised him. A guarantee I offer every customer mechanically, the way you'd hold a kerchief to a running nose. "And secret *from* me also." Where had it gone?

The lurching sensation of lightness had not left me. Even more frightening was the crust of resignation forming around it. Staring out the windshield at the toppled fences and saplings, I tried to guess where—to what other world or realm—the memories I once held had been transferred. Perhaps the vacuum in the sky had pulled them out of me. Perhaps the great scouring winds had swept them into the clouds. But dust settles back to earth, doesn't it? Dew lifts from the leaves and returns as rainfall. Why shouldn't my customers' memories be restored to me as suddenly and completely as they vanished? This was my prayer. Dead cattle covered the fields like inky holes. We crawled past the Bakowskis' ruined grain, Iverson's half-buried barn. Leghorn chickens wandered into the road, looking as stunned as I felt.

On the radio, Red and I listened to grim news from neighboring counties and states. Hundreds of farmers had lost their entire year's crop to the dust. Some of my clients were certainly among them. What was I going to do when a customer came to make a withdrawal of their past and was met with an empty hiss?

Three men were clearing the main street, waving us on with their shovels. Mr. Grigalunas gave me a curt nod as we rolled by. He'd been banking with me since the boom years, and I felt a pang in my gut. Did he guess from my face that I was bankrupt?

Now the lolling tongue of Main Street came into view, the train tracks curving off into the dust like buried teeth. I could have walked the rest of the way to the Country Jentleman, and should have done so.

Instead, I held a dry rag to my face.

"Do you know what your father does to me in Cell Eight, Red?"

"He brings you in for questioning. I imagine he asks you questions."

"How do you imagine it? The two of us sitting on the cot, having a chat?"

"It can't be easy work," he said. "Getting an honest answer from the likes of you."

It had worked; I heard it in his voice. A suspicion had taken root in the boy. I'd begun to cultivate my revenge against his father.

"I'm going to tell you something that will haunt you for the rest of your days, Red. Whether or not you want to believe it, you will hear the ring of truth and . . ."

His stony face cracked apart. "*Stop—*"

I did not stop. I raised my voice over his protestations. Cataloged every cruelty that I had suffered at the Sheriff's hands, every gruesome and despicable act. I watched the struggle on the boy's face. His brows and lips hardened into a sneer, but my words were reaching him, stirring color into his flush-red skin. He could not reject my story as a falsehood. The tiniest details had breached his defenses. Something as irrefutably small as the white mole on his father's back, the dead kittens floating in a flour sack.

Red was sobbing by the time I finished.

Shame flooded through me then, watching the boy cry into his hands. I had an urge to remove the splinter I'd just driven into him.

"Don't fret," I said. "I can take it all back. Come upstairs with me, and make a deposit . . ."

In our treeless prairie, lost winter migrants sometimes fly in circles until they drop like stones from exhaustion. Having nowhere else to rest, Red eventually lay his head on my shoulder. My hand lifted to stroke his sweaty hair. I had an overwhelming urge to shut my eyes and sleep beside him. I wanted to dream about the earlier heaven, when I was still a young woman and heavy with You.

"My father isn't who you say he is."

"Red," I said. "What if I tell you it was all lies? Pure invention."

"Get out of my car."

It's rarely the truth itself that people can't accept. It's how they feel about it.

I stood on the street and watched as Red Iscoe disappeared in the Ford, moving ant-like down the curl of road. Son, I struggle to believe that today You are older than Red—a man of twenty-six. I pray You landed with people who love You. If You call someone papa or daddy, I pray he is nothing like Vick Iscoe.

I often wonder if I would have been a good mother to You. I want You to know me, baby, but I also want You to love me. I worry that success at one aim will mean failure at the other. Still, I will do my best to be honest with You here. The truth is that I hurt Red Iscoe out of rage at his father. And I fear that, in this line of work, I have done far worse.

⌐§§⌐

In the boardinghouse, I found an inch of dust on the floor, and my red shoes were filled with the stuff. Every cup and vase had become an hourglass. Rasmussen's daughter-in-law must have come into my room, because there were damp sheets pasted to the windows and fingerprints were visible on the dust-covered table. The mirror glass was crusted over, and my shocked face gazed out at me through the scrim. My age always startles me—the lines webbing my eyes, the new gray in my braid. I was fifteen when I fled the Home for Unwed

Mothers in Milford, and somehow that's still the face I expect to see in the glass. I'd prepared to be your mother, and then I woke in leather restraints to the doctor's lies. Milk wept out of me. My body did not believe him. My body knew you were alive.

I turned from the powdery mirror and spent a quarter hour polishing my earhorn. My earhorn is my conduit—the only object I have ever cared about. It was a gift from my teacher, Kettle. A valuable antique she had received as payment from a San Francisco dowager. Painted emerald-blue, the prettiest color in this West. "Modestly enchanted," Kettle had told me with a smile. "Now you will be a proper prairie witch."

Every Vault I've ever met has her own conduit. The Jewel Box of Gordon receives deposits through a dented old trumpet studded with sapphires. A young Vault I know who lives along the Elkhorn River uses a hollow antler. But in a true emergency, a witch can make do with whatever pipe or horn or tin cup is available. An older memory flashed through me: yes, I had once taken a deposit from a laboring mother using the doctor's pinard horn. She was birthing and dying at the same time, bleeding unstoppably as she pushed her breech baby down the canal. She'd used her last breaths to make a deposit. She wanted to leave her child a memory of love—to deposit it in me for safekeeping, before she died. On another dire night, I took a deposit from a fellow runaway in the back of a boxcar, her slim, dark hands around my burning ear. I've lost whatever I promised them would be protected inside my body.

The first thing I did was swab the dust from my earhorn. With each twist of my rag, it seemed to exhume itself from the dark, like a tusk from the Chadron dinosaur pit. I felt relief when it was clean again. In the moonlight, my earhorn looked like an enormous seashell, humming an undersea green. A customer from the university once told me that there are shards of prehistoric shells buried all around the Plains, the fossils from a vanished ocean. I was glad to learn this. Some nights, I swear, I can hear it lapping.

Rasmussen's daughter had used old newspapers as insulation, stuffing them into the cracks of the walls and papering the window. She left a stack of them on the bedside table, next to the broken pieces of a ceramic vase that must have fallen off the windowsill during the storm. Then I saw it, among the shards: a real rabbit's foot. Its claws curled toward the ceiling, as if it were begging for something. A chill ran up my leg. What a nasty prank. Had the Sheriff left it to taunt me? Or was this someone's idea of a joke? My mind went to the men who had visited me last week. Then, running like a blur through the bristling grass, came a new fear.

I walked from the desk to the window and peeled back the newspaper—as if whoever had left the rabbit's foot might still be visible, staring up at me. The street was almost empty. Two men were shoveling dust in the greenish beams of a truck's headlights. Bile flooded my mouth, and I clutched at my sides as I walked. My fist squeezed around the little claws, which seemed to squeeze me back. The sun had set, and moonlight filtered through the heavy dust on the window glass. I took off the sackcloth gown from Cell 8. Naked and feeling half-mad, I crawled onto my mattress and lay flat. I placed the furry gray charm on my chest, lifting and lowering it with my breaths. *Something wants me to remember it.*

❧❧

Son, I don't know what part of the world you call home. If you live anywhere near the state of Nebraska, you've probably heard about the Lucky Rabbit's Foot Killer.

It was sensational news here in Uz County—a murderer terrorizing southwestern Nebraska. Newspapers spread the local fear like wildfire. That gruesome prop, the bloody rabbit's foot, captured everyone's imagination. It was very good for business, if you were a prairie witch. I took dozens of deposits from first-time customers during the months when the "Lucky Rabbit's Foot Killer" was loose inside of people's minds.

In the summer of 1933, while Uz prepared for another bust of a harvest, two women's bodies were discovered in the sandhills west of Thedford. They were identified as nursing students who had grown up together in Uz. Olga Kucera and Nina Rose, on their way back to Lincoln after the spring holiday. They were last seen at the train depot. Someone had left a rabbit's foot at the crime site, "the silver fur matted with their blood."

Reporters had a field day with that detail. Two brutal murders, no suspects. A clue that felt like a cruel joke. Three more women went missing in southern Nebraska between harvest and planting. By the start of 1934, everyone was bolting up their houses like a bank at night. If you saw a woman running down Main Street at dusk, with no one pursuing her, you understood what she was running from—the threat was everywhere. Like the dust. Like tinder in the air. In addition to terrifying everyone in a five-county radius, these murders and disappearances were terrible publicity for the God-fearing town of Uz. People started to complain angrily about Sheriff Iscoe, "the lawman who couldn't catch a cold." Months passed without a drop of moisture, and the suffocating air came to feel inseparable from the blanketing fear throughout western Nebraska. In mid-March, the strangled body of Allene Adams, the pharmacist's assistant, was discovered behind the grain elevator with a blood-wet rabbit's foot on her chest. The Sheriff informed the reporters that he was now hunting for a mass murderer.

On Easter Sunday, the Sheriff found Minnie Guzik's body dumped behind the Hooverville five blocks from the train station. Minnie had been the wife of a prominent rancher, a granddaughter of one of the town's founders. Rumors spread that the killer had once again left his signature: the curled gray foot stained with the victim's blood. Panic spiked throughout Uz.

In under twelve hours, Sheriff Iscoe had made an arrest.

The Sheriff picked up Clemson Louis Dew in the hobo camp behind the train depot. A young White boy from Indiana, who had been hopping trains and following the harvest—apples in Yakima, sugar beets in Grand Island—doing odd jobs between seasons. He'd been in Uz for three weeks, according to the newspaper story that ran after his arrest—long enough to earn a reputation for his beautiful violin playing at the campfire. "The boy sounded like an angel," someone from the Uz homeless camp was quoted as saying in *The Gazette*. "People too sad to move all day got up to dance when he played. It was how we knew Clemson, his music. It's *all* we really knew about him."

In the next paragraph, the journalist recorded the Sheriff's first impression of Dew:

"The young killer was fiddling away in the firelight mere hours after the murder, a remorseless smile on his face . . ."

"Do you know what this is?" Sheriff Iscoe had reportedly asked Clemson Louis Dew that night, holding up a bloody rabbit's foot.

And this boy had made the mistake of answering the Sheriff honestly, and naming the tiny amputation: "Yes, sir," Clemson had answered. "That's a rabbit's foot."

Sometime that same evening, behind locked doors, Clemson confessed to the murder of Minnie Guzik and six additional women—five in Uz, and two in neighboring Hayes County. (I can imagine what might have happened to the boy that night; I have been shut up in those rooms with Vick. Under the fear, there is a bottomless loneliness.) Sheriff Iscoe emerged from the interrogation room and drove straight to the Grange Hall, interrupting the monthly meeting to inform everyone that Uz was safe at last—he had the Lucky Rabbit's Foot Killer in custody.

Did anyone truly believe this gentle boy was a mass murderer?

Journalists from as far away as Chicago took the train to make the trial.

Q: Was he the man? A: Well . . .

Q: Was he the man? A: Well . . .

Q: Was he the man? A: I don't want to say . . .

Who were the other three women that this young man had confessed to killing? Luz Arrow, a Mexican mother of three who lived on the outskirts of Uz; Enesta Risingsun, a woman in her seventies traveling through Hubbell on her way to visit her granddaughter; and Lada Oletsky, who according to *The Gazette* was "an unwed mother living in Hayes County at the time of her death." These murders were cold cases when the Sheriff arrested Clemson, crimes that had occurred in the months before Olga and Nina were killed without provoking the same rippling panic. Luz had been married to a hot-tempered pawnbroker, Al Arrow. Al had a nasty reputation, and plenty of folks in Uz believed he'd killed Luz himself, though no charges were brought against him. After Luz's body was discovered, Al Arrow had her buried without services and moved to Gordon with his new wife. Enesta Risingsun's murder, as far as I know, went uninvestigated and unreported in the newspapers. Some had speculated that Enesta must have stolen the money for the train ticket.

I hate to say it, but an Indian woman traveling alone, what did she think would happen?

Al Arrow is a rat bastard. But if he did it, he may have had a reason.

Dottie told me that Luz was stepping out on him—

It's awful what happened, but Jed says that Lada Oletsky was a loose woman and everybody knew it—

I heard the men of Uz croaking about these murders on their barstools at the Jentleman. The rhythms of their conversations were as familiar as frog song on the Platte. Many in Uz were upset that these earlier murders had happened in their backyard, but their concern seemed to spoke around the town's soiled reputation. The women had not deserved to die; nobody was suggesting *that*, the men reassured themselves. It was a pity that they were dead.

When Olga's and Nina's bodies were found with the twisted charm on them, all of Uz had joined the search party. The nursing students, it seemed to me, were "more dead" to most Uzians. If the murders of Enesta Risingsun and Luz Arrow and Lada Oletsky had been a pity, these new murders were a tragedy. An emergency. I took care to double-bolt my own door; a prairie witch is always "less dead" than a townswoman, a fact of life known to both killers and lawmen.

At his trial, Clemson Louis Dew had on cheap reading glasses that were far too big for his narrow face, a piece of green string knotted at the bridge, and a boxy aubergine suit donated to him by the Sisters of Charity that made him look like a child playing dress-up. Some Uzians did raise an eyebrow. Could such a frail-looking young man overpower seven women? In *The Gazette*, he wore a hopeful, bewildered expression—a shy, obedient smile that told anyone who cared enough to really look that he did not understand what was happening to him.

It hurt me to look at the newspaper photograph of Clemson's smile. Before my nonna died, I was very docile myself, and eager to please. Very "well behaved." I had a good girl's conviction that good behavior would bring about a good outcome. On the stand, wrote one reporter, "Clemson Louis Dew nodded eagerly even before the lawyer asked a question." How could this habit move anyone toward a guilty verdict? Somehow it did. There was talk at the Jentleman of Clemson being "a slow study," but this only seemed to solidify the general theory that Dew was indeed the Lucky Rabbit's Foot Killer. The Sheriff rounded up other hobos from the camps, some he pulled out of the drunk tank, and they testified that this young vagabond had a screw loose, an "alarming innocence." One witness was quoted in the papers as musing, "Stupid and evil go hand in hand, don't they?"

As a veteran eavesdropper, I knew well how the same set of facts could spin people toward or away from an idea. After the trial, there was near unanimity on the question of Dew's guilt. A conviction that seemed to wrap every new fact around it. The journalists who called the guilty verdict a "triumph of Lady Justice" cited Clemson's gentleness, somehow, as evidence of his derangement.

The press, naturally, wanted to know: "Were rabbits' feet also found on the bodies of Lada Oletsky, Enesta Risingsun, and Luz Arrow?"

"At this time, we cannot rule out the possibility that a rabbit's foot or rabbit feet had—at some point—been in the vicinity of these victims' bodies," a sweating bald prosecutor suggested, rubbing his shiny head as if to summon the genie from its lantern. No physical evidence linked the defendant to any of the murders. Still, a guilty verdict was swiftly returned, and Clemson Louis Dew was sentenced to death.

Some may be sleeping easier since his conviction, but I'm not among them.

The rabbits' feet, I learned from chatter at the Jentleman, are presently on display at the Lincoln penitentiary. A store in downtown Uz is hawking replicas. After the sentencing hearing, the Sheriff took out a gloating advertisement that read BETTER LUCK NEXT TIME above a picture of a rabbit's foot.

Son, I've witnessed seemingly kind people do horrendous things. I've done some myself. Is it possible that this young transient killed seven women in neighboring counties and decorated each of their bodies with a tiny foot? The grim memento of a rabbit's very bad luck? I can't disprove it.

But I also know that the Sheriff is up for reelection this year. I know that Vick and his putty-faced deputy would have arrested Clemson Louis Dew just for breathing night air.

I floated on my mattress, watching the rabbit's foot rise and fall like a metronome. Afraid to shut my eyes, Son. Afraid of losing my memories of You. As the sky began to lighten over the spires of the grain elevators, I was still awake. The black clouds waited for me wherever I let my mind drift. Had I caused my bankruptcy, somehow? Taking on too many new customers, to survive the lean years? Absorbing deposits six days a week until I ripped at the seams like an overstuffed grain sack? I'd seen the farmers running their tractors after midnight to make up for lost harvests, pushing against an invisible debt. I understood what lashed at them. It was at my back too.

Am I the only Vault who lost everything in the storm? I pictured a black funnel moving across the prairie, howling over other witches' bodies, spinning their deposits out of them and into the dust wall. A new fear opened under my navel and caved into itself, revealing layer after layer of inky terror: what if other prairie witches had woken up to the same emptiness during the storm? I watched the little gray comma of the rabbit's foot rise and fall on my chest, trying to fathom the scale of such a loss. What would it mean, if every prairie witch who survived the Black Sunday dust storm had gone bankrupt? Could such a crash be reversed? I had no answers, no ideas, only the howling lightness still ringing in my body.

I recalled a line that had captioned a newspaper story about Wall Street on Black Tuesday:

Businessmen, in trying to save themselves, could only wreck their system; in trying to avoid the worst, they rendered the worst inevitable.

The photograph was what I remembered best. A hundred dapper hats floating over the men's shocked faces, serene as clouds.

When the market collapsed in 1929, billions of dollars vanished in a few hours. Then the drought years came, and the soil flew off. Dust blots out the sun at noon. Perhaps this is the next calamity—a collapse of memory.

If that's the case, I'm sure there will be a run on witches—just as there was a run on the banks. We will be hunted, Son. "Held to account": what our customers will call it while they try to torture their deposits out of our mouths. For all I know, this is already happening in other western towns and cities that were engulfed by the black blizzard.

Or maybe I'm wrong, and I am alone with my disaster.

I waited two days to telegram Cherry Le Foy, my friend and fellow prairie witch, known to her customers as Madame Quicksand. Cherry, as far as I know, is still working out of her cabin on the Republican River in southwestern Nebraska. Uz was hard hit on Black Sunday. But maybe Vaults on the periphery of the storm came through unscathed. Perhaps it is still business as usual for Cherry in Hayes County.

It's a good thing I am not a Navy spy, Son. Until Black Sunday, your mother excelled at keeping secrets. But I lack the imagination for codes and riddles. MY AQUIFER IS EMPTY was the telegram I sent to her. No Vault who woke up bankrupt after the Black Sunday storm could mistake my meaning. Either it would be nonsense to Cherry or she would understand instantly. The heavy sound of the typist's fingers pounded into my ears.

Last night the sound returned to me in dreams, growing louder and louder until my eyes flew open on the pillow. Someone was banging on my door, cursing at me through the wood. The Closed for Business sign hung from my knob, but words have never stopped certain customers from trying to rouse me with their fists. No one has ever broken the door, but plenty have tried.

"Open up, you lazy bitch! This is no time to take a holiday—"

It was two in the morning, and the saloon on the first floor was in full ferment. I recognized the liquor-thickened voice of Grayson, one of my best customers. His anger had that giddy edge that I know well—the wobble before an explosion. Eventually he left. I was too rattled to sleep. I may never sleep again, Son. I studied the train schedules and contemplated running. If it weren't for You, I would make darker escape plans. How long can I hide my bankruptcy from these fists hammering at my door?

Asphodel Oletsky

Two newlyweds in Olaf got out of their car and suffocated six hundred yards from the courthouse—"

"No! Dottie! How awful!"

After Black Sunday, the Party Line came alive with horror stories. The line connects us to ten other families, including the Iscoes. Dottie Iscoe is better than the radio for drama.

"A fellow on the road crew spotted the bride's corsage sticking out of the dust. Saw those gardenias and thought, *What flower could grow here . . .* "

"Oh, Lord! That gives me a chill . . ."

"Get off that telephone, big ears," my uncle shouted at me from the kitchen. "I should have never gotten wired up."

"Doomsday is everybody's business, Uncle!" I said. Mostly to needle him. I agree that people have a right to private conversations. Eavesdropping was one of my favorite pastimes at the lunch counters with Mama. It's a bad habit, and it's getting worse. Too much time spent listening feels like gorging on penny candy.

"Eleven eggs today!" my uncle called to me from behind the porch screen. "The most we've had since last May!" This is what constitutes gossip in the Oletsky place. "Come give me a hand—"

I pretended not to hear my uncle; I could not afford to get off the Line today. For the better part of an hour, I'd been listening to our neighbors' chatter and waiting for someone to mention the electrocution of Clemson Louis Dew. It had been scheduled to take place last Monday evening, "a minute after midnight" on April 15, according to the warden's invitation—smack in the middle of the Black Sunday duster. Our radio battery was dead, and we couldn't get downtown to buy a newspaper—assuming anyone was still printing and selling them. The Party Line was my only hope of learning anything about Dew's execution. I wanted nothing to do with the town's morbid celebration, but I did want to be free of my wondering. Prior to Black Sunday, people in Uz had been counting down for weeks, treating the electrocution of "the Lucky Rabbit's Foot Killer" like a holiday. Even Coach had tried to celebrate with me ("Oletsky, soon the scoreboard will show a zero next to that killer's name"). I'd retreated from his smile, and from every conversation about Dew's death date.

But now that date had passed, and I felt desperate to hear how it had gone. To know that it was done. I needed the cold facts. Then I'd have a box of pins to pop the fiery visions that kept swelling in my head, driving me mad. Sure enough, Mr. Albertson jumped onto the Line a few minutes later and started in on "the Lucky Rabbit's Foot Killer." Who was not dead. Whose electrocution—I learned—had failed to kill him.

Outside the window, I could hear my uncle grumbling as he candled the eggs. A curse told me that he had cracked one. He swears more softly than any man I've ever known. *Hang up*, I heard inside my head, in my mother's firm voice. *Don't listen to these men. These words are like poison.* And I wish I had listened to her, instead of the voices that crackled over the Party Line. Instead I pinned my earlobe to my skull with the bowl of the receiver.

"Something went wrong with the Chair. I guess the dust interfered with the wires—"

"I just read about that!"

"The Lucky Rabbit's Foot Killer—he's still alive!"

"The warden blamed that black roller. The whole penitentiary damn near caught fire."

"Did the Chair burn?"

"Nah, just the sack over the kid's head. He was screaming and straining against the straps and finally they cut him free. The flames jumped six feet from the helmet. The whole room went smoky—"

"Dew had a bad stutter, didn't he? Can you imagine him screaming through that sack? *N-N-Not dead!*"

One man laughed hysterically. The other waited patiently for him to finish.

"I can't believe they let him live."

"They gotta fix the Chair. They're sending it down to Amarillo for repairs."

"That's a laugh, ain't it? Nebraska needs Texas to help us with our barbecue . . ."

Muffled laughter boomed into my left ear. Wheezing and coughing. Outside the window screen, I could hear my uncle humming as he worked. My cheeks were wet.

"So what now? He's just sitting in the coop, waiting to fry?"

"His electrocution is 'postponed indefinitely.' A dust delay. Could be a couple weeks, or a couple months—they only got the one Chair."

"A lucky break for the Lucky Rabbit's Foot Killer."

"Unlucky, if you ask me. Why draw it out? Get a firing squad. String up some rope. Get a brick and finish what you started, Warden—"

"Two deaths feels too cruel to me. We kill animals with more mercy!"

"Dew is a mass murderer! Not some porker you put out of its misery. He killed seven women, and probably more besides! He's getting his just deserts with a cherry on top . . ."

Uncle Harp leaned in and pried the receiver from my ear. How long had he been standing there, staring at me? Pictures sparked and smoked behind my eyelids. I was thinking about my mother. How much she must have suffered in the minutes before she died. The only person near enough to help had been her killer. I can't imagine a worse loneliness than that.

⧉

We had been invited to attend the electrocution. Back in February, the Sheriff drove out to hand-deliver a letter from the warden. "Good news, Oletskys!" He barged onto the porch in a coppery veil of dust. My mother's killer, he said with childish excitement, would be electrocuted on April 15, 1935. Two days prior, the governor had signed Clemson Louis Dew's death warrant. Sheriff Iscoe handed me the invitation to the execution. "Go on and read it, honey." He smiled down at me, as if he were giving me permission to unwrap a candy. The slope of the word *electricity* in the warden's sprawling handwriting had carried me out of my body; my vision blurred and I handed the letter back before I finished reading it. My uncle held me while I coughed bile into his shirtsleeve, the Sheriff watching us impatiently from across the table. My uncle turned the invitation onto its blank side. "I wish that Lada's killer had never been born," he told the Sheriff. "But I have no wish to see a man shocked to death." When he heard my uncle's tone, the Sheriff puffed up with offense. He went from pink to red to purple, right there at the table—as if he'd spent hours baking and icing a cake for us, only to have us refuse to lift our forks. "Plenty have already said yes. The Kuceras. The Roses. Minnie's husband and sister. Change your mind before April, and I will give you a ride to Lincoln. I intend to be front and center to watch that monster meet his Maker."

"He's thinking of the cameras," my uncle had told me after the Sheriff left. "He wants the victims' families to be in the photographs. The Sheriff can pretend this is a celebration if he likes. You and I know better."

When I got on the Line, I believed that I'd be cured of my nightmares by learning the truth of what happened at an electrocution. But now my visions became even more terrible—I saw tongues of fire, I heard Clemson crying out for help. I could not stop myself from imagining his pain and his terror. I felt no relief. "Clemson Louis Dew is still alive," I told my uncle. I gave him a bare-bones description of what I'd overheard. The taste of ash was on my tongue. He was locked in solitary confinement, waiting to die a second time. The quiet boy from the hobo camp who had been convicted of seven murders. The young violinist with cracked glasses and a dopey smile who had confessed to killing my mother.

⊰⊱

"Do you think that boy killed Mama?" I asked my uncle after he pulled me off the Party Line. He stared out the window for a full minute, as if the answer was floating somewhere over the scarecrow's hat. "Well, the boy confessed," he said at last. "I don't know, Dell."

Then my uncle did something unusual. He stood and walked onto the porch and returned with my basketball. "Let's shoot a little." Long after sunset, he followed me in a creaky clockwork under the hoop that he'd nailed to the barn door for me. Dust turned the crescent moon a reddish color, and the tillering wheat shivered in the field. The temperature kept falling, and soon my hands burned inside my gloves. My muscles screamed like machinery as I ran, and I forgot about everything except the distance between my hands and the round basket. The gold fire that eats every other feeling spread through my chest, lifting me off my feet. I made jump shot after jump shot. Sweat sheeted into my uncle's crystal blue eyes and he made his shots blind. Talking stopped. Thinking stopped. The ball flew between our hands, and for an hour I felt closer to my uncle than I did to anyone living. We didn't stop shooting until the Dipper came out. My uncle missed his last layup and cursed in Polish with a fury that shocked us both. I laughed at him and he laughed at me, until our laughter pooled into a kind of howl.

When my mother was murdered, everybody wanted to pretend to be sad about it. Neighbors who had ridiculed us embraced me, crying into my hair. "Can't you people afford a tissue?" I'd grumbled. I heard a lot about God's mysterious workings. Church ladies threw Bible verses at me with the same frenzy that they tossed lilies and clumps of sod at the open graves, eager to seal up a hole. I got the sense they would have loved to bury me, too. Tidier that way. In the hours and weeks following her death, people crossed the street to hug me and offer me their condolences, shoving them my way with potluck flair. A month later, these same people crossed the street to avoid me. Like I was a little hatchet walking around town. A reminder that a killer was still on the loose.

If my mother had been married, I know her murder would have been a tragedy. If she'd been someone with money, her death would have counted for more. Instead, my mother was a pathetic drunk who bought her groceries with promissory notes. Some people seemed sad that she'd been killed, but nobody but me seemed to feel angry, or surprised.

Two days after they found her body in the ditch, I spent hours at the station describing my mother's ex-lovers, ex-employers, and drinking friends. Joe Lacy, the friendly, useless Sheriff of Hayes County, did not seem especially interested in following the leads I laid out for him. He did a much better job of locating my uncle. After Clemson Louis Dew's arrest, Joe Lacy had been quoted in the papers: "I am grateful to Sheriff Iscoe for bringing this fiendish killer to justice."

Last spring, the Sheriff had pushed me to testify in the trial of the Lucky Rabbit's Foot Killer. He kept trying to cajole me into a memory I didn't have. "You don't recognize this ugly mug?" Clemson Louis Dew had a cowlick and crooked teeth grinning out of a pale face. He was smiling so hard his eyes bulged. He looked terrified. It would have been a funny picture, in another situation. Someone who loved him could have teased him: "Were you storing nuts for the winter in those cheeks, Clemson? Did you see a ghost behind the cameraman?" Nobody like that, I realized, would ever look at this photograph. The Sheriff told us he was a tramp "without kin or kind." *Did you kill my mother?* I asked the young face in the photograph. "I don't know this boy," I'd said to the irritated Sheriff. "Sure you're sure? I hear your mama had plenty of male acquaintances." He'd winked at me then, a terrible sight. "Barrooms and bedrooms, those are dark places, aren't they?"

My uncle and I barely spoke about the botched electrocution. We came inside drenched in sweat and smelling of leather. "You wore me out," my uncle grunted, tossing me the ball. We agreed to skip dinner that night. Once I stopped moving, running and shooting, I was in trouble again. The men's laughter swelled in my mind, along with pictures of the smoky room. The flames leaping six feet above the helmet. Mr. Albertson's squeaky parody of Dew screaming inside the sack, *N-N-Not Dead!* It kept running through my head until I wanted to scream myself. I started to tell my uncle about it.

"Quit eavesdropping, Dell. We sure don't need any more nightmare fodder around here."

Uncle Harp began blinking like a hog in hard rain. His face turned bright pink, and sweat streamed down his cheeks. I wondered what age my mother was in his mind just then, if she was a living child of seven or a body in a ditch in Hubbell. I saw that he wanted to help me out of the hole into which I kept falling. I saw, also, that his weak gray eyes could not summon a sunbeam, and his old ears could barely pick up my voice in the same room.

So once again I learned to keep my mouth shut.

Whatever is happening here, I am alone with it.

The Dryland Farmer, Harp Oletsky

Uz is a good name for a town like ours. When the Fourteen Founding Families came to establish a new settlement, they borrowed the name from the Book of Job: The Land of Uz. Sometimes translated as the Land of Counsel.

"Sounds like a fun-loving bunch," my niece said.

"Those Poles crossed an ocean and half a continent to escape persecution," I told her. "Look how Job's patience is rewarded. Your grandparents left everything they loved and knew. They lost everything when they came to Nebraska. They saw themselves in his story."

There was a man in the land of Uz, whose name was Job; and that man was perfect and upright, and one that feared God, and eschewed evil . . .

My niece is impossible to educate. She'd interrupted me, wrinkling her nose.

"Uz sounds like a sneeze, Uncle."

"That's enough. Go blaspheme under someone else's roof."

When I returned from the fields at dusk, I found my Bible open on the kitchen table, Job 42:12 circled in pencil: *Nothing says you are God's beloved like the gift of a thousand she-asses!* My niece began laughing hysterically.

"You think this is a funny story?" I'd asked her. "Look outside the window, girl. Look what chapter and verse we are living in . . ."

It's a terrifying story, of course. A mystery like the inkblot of crows that spills through the inexplicable blue sky. After trial heaped upon trial, Job accuses God. God answers Job—a Voice speaking out of the whirlwind. The Lord bestows upon Job a holy vision that is only ever alluded to in the Bible story. A vision of wonders that go mostly unwritten.

In the end, the Lord blesses Job with twice his former prosperity. This was what inspired my parents and the other Kinkaiders. Job's homeland held up a mirror to what they had lost to become Americans, and a promise for their future, if they could simply hold on through the droughts and the locusts, the hailed-out crops and the market crashes:

> So the Lord blessed the latter end of Job more than his beginning.
> After this lived Job one hundred and forty years, and saw his sons, and his sons' sons, even four generations.
> So Job died, being old and full of days.

Full of days. That line always struck me. Even as a boy, I felt a heaviness when Papa read it. Some premonition of age. Old Uzians seemed as arid as the land to me, wrinkled and brittle. Yet I heard that line and I understood that in some secret region their rivers ran full of days. Soon enough, their life's time would overrun its banks. Death felt less frightening to me when I thought of it that way. When I was a boy, the schoolteacher told us that every droplet of water that has ever been in this world is still here. His claim felt no less incredible to me than the eternal life we were promised on Sunday mornings.

Now we are glutted on months of dust, years of sun. We have entered the fourth year of drought and failure. A great exodus is under way in Uz. People are blowing off the land, faster and faster. "Okies" is how they get written up. But Nebraska has lost entire towns to this drought and this dust. Since the bottom fell out of the market, Uz is down a hundred residents. The chorus at the Grange Hall grows thinner and hoarser at each monthly meeting.

I was already up to my hat brim in debt when the Deere man showed up, offering me a line of credit, making his grand promises. "Once you try a Spider, you'll never go back . . ." My father used a moldboard plow and raised me on horses. I had my doubts about the Spiders. A smoking, shining cavalry of machines that ran on diesel. But I could not afford to hire help. I could barely keep my horses fed. And this new tractor could plow an acre in a quarter hour! Unlike my horses, a Spider would never get cold or hot or tired. Unlike hired hands, the salesman joked, you only feed a tractor when it's working. At the Grange Hall, the jug-eared salesman made his pitch to hundreds of us. He said that Uz was very lucky—we had been selected as a "test community" for the Spider prototype. Fifty of us signed up that morning. And where did "the tractor of the future" get us? I buy my gas on credit. I'm still working to pay off that hungry machine.

Tumbleweeds blew up against my fence, knocked the damn thing over, post by post, and by morning you'd never guess there had ever been a boundary between the homeplace and anywhere else. Otto's land dumped on top of my land when the wind blew from the southeast. My land dumped on Otto's when the wind changed direction. Turns out, these lines we'd drawn so painstakingly around what we owned, they only existed on paper. There was some excitement in that, I'll admit. Everything mixing with everything else, as dust does.

The bank owned me, as it did most everybody in Uz County. I worked sixteen-hour days, gambling against the weather—in 1922, I got twenty-two bushels an acre; in 1926, I was hailed out entirely. Then the rain vanished and never returned. I started working to pay down the loans I'd taken out to buy the Spider, whose joints were already rusting in the sun. By 1934, I was living on the runoff of my labor. Do that for long enough, you start to feel like a man trying to quench his thirst with his own sweat. You're paying the bank for the privilege of working your land. That's the whole trap of it. You take out a loan or a line of credit. Your seed money cooks in the ground. Now you're breaking sod to stay ahead of your debt, water pouring down your back at midnight. All across the Plains you could see the headlights of the demon-machinery we'd mortgaged our farms to buy, lighting the way clear to this present disaster.

Hindsight is never a flattering mirror. Not for me, anyways—shows me what a fool I am. I don't know what I could have done differently. Or to put it another way, I know I could have done *something* differently. I never have the time, it seems, to figure out what that might have been. This contest was up and running when I was born. You could win or you could lose, but the rules were set. The salesman said as much, and nearly every Granger bit. What choice did we have? Sometimes I wonder about that, tipping the funnel into the tank of the Deere prototype.

Last year, I was a zero-yield man. The same as just about every other Uzian. Even so, I kept hoping that my luck might change. On Black Sunday, I thought I'd come to the end of the line. On the crazy ride through that blizzard of earth, piloting the poor one-eyed Dodge through the gales, unable to see the road, I had prayed without pause. Those winds tossed road signs around like dominoes. They tore wheat out of the fields faster than any machine. They raked the sight out of my eyes. The headlights only made things worse. Dust in the air threw their glare right back at us. It was my niece who spotted the bulk of the house and yelled, "Uncle Harp, stop! We're home!"

And even in the middle of my terror, I was pleased to hear her call it that. Home.

It wasn't until I struck a match and lit the indoor lamps that I began to feel uneasy. The relief I'd expected never came. The fear I'd felt on the road, swerving ahead of the black roller—that fear made sense to me. The dirt cloud, the green lightning, even the rolling carpet of sod coming to kill us had made a terrible sense. Nothing I saw inside the parlor did.

Strange stories percolated in the aftermath of Black Sunday. There was an abandoned house full of a thousand black rabbits in the oil ghost town of Slick, Oklahoma. There was a creature that looked like a rhinoceros glimpsed through the dust on the new highway between Oshkosh and Broadwater. A girl in Valentine with tuberculosis of the bone had been cured by a sandhill crane that descended from the dust wall and alighted on her shoulders. I felt a tightness in my throat, hearing that fairy tale about the sick child. Of course we were all in the market for miracles.

Here's a miracle that never got around—one that even my nosy niece seemed to mistake for mere luck. When we ran for the house that night, we did not slide or fall or lose our way. My eyes were shut against the raking claws of the wind, but my hands somehow closed on the doorknob. Inside the house, I heard my niece draw a long breath. Air filled and fled my lungs, I could breathe again without pain. My match caught on the first strike. When I lit the kerosene lantern, its blue flame revealed my stunned face in the hall mirror. The glass was perfectly clear.

There was not a speck of dust anywhere.

The Scarecrow

I ...I...I...I...I..."

A stuttering, a shattering. All names escaping me. Firstname, skyflung. Lastname, abandoned. Waist-high bluestem crumpling into years of dust. A wrong turn on the long drive home. Fireflies collecting on a windshield and bouncing by the thousands down the low blue hood. Froth of earth and fizzing light inside it. A silhouette in the driver's seat. A body crashing through the glass. No hands on the wheel. No one seated nowhere.

This is my only memory.

I watch a man walking toward me through an empty field.

He is not me. This is clarifying.

"My Lord," says a voice I do not know. A voice I am not making. "How did a scarecrow come through that duster intact?"

The Prairie Witch

T hree days passed. Red did not return with his father to kill me. The Iscoes likely had their hands full. The aftershocks from the Black Sunday roller continued to multiply. Dozens of bodies were recovered. Every third building around Uz had been wrecked beyond repairing. People were packing up mattresses and rocking chairs and forlorn family treasures. Into the night, long caravans of families drove off, fleeing their debt and their ruined crops. I watched a truck driving slowly down the desolate Main Street. Lashed to the bed was a calamitously unbalanced tower of crib frames and dressers. The dented gray running board made the truck look like a whale with a withered fin.

After a week of waiting, I could not stand to hide another minute. I decided it was time to ride out to Cherry. Fred Raffles—one of my poorest clients—unhappily loaned me Angel, his beloved Appaloosa. Angel looks like the daughter of a pegasus and a dalmatian. She moves that way too, spreading invisible wings as her hoofs wake the dust. I always cut Fred Raffles a deal, because I like him and because I love his horses. Fred chewed his lip as I rode off.

The day's ride to Cherry would have taken less than an hour by train, but I was afraid of getting trapped in the passenger car with a customer. On horseback, I can always leave the main road and disappear. I woke before dawn and dressed like a man in denim coveralls and a straw hat. By noon it was ninety degrees and climbing. Sweat stuck my shirt to my armpits and darkened the horse's flanks. Our centaur shadow on the road had vanished. We rode along a burning gangplank of asphalt, passing half a dozen eerily quiet farms as we crossed into Sheridan County. Hawks wheeled overhead, our only companions for the next twelve miles over the hissing brittle grasses.

Cherry would have hot soup and a soft bed for me. Soap for bathing in the river and a clean towel and a change of clothes. Even if she had lost every deposit, she'd still greet me with her rich, cigarette-thickened laugh. She would anchor me, and I would anchor her—just as we did for most of our youth, traveling the railways from Omaha to Chadron.

We met as teenage runaways on the spur line to Beatrice. We had the same teacher, Kettle. At first, I'd felt jealous of Cherry Le Foy. Cherry was a natural. She understood Kettle's lessons effortlessly, whereas I needed a hundred repetitions before the same instruction began to make sense to my body. *One by one, the stars wink out*, said Kettle in her sleepy drawl. This statement actually meant something to Cherry, whereas for months I gave myself a headache trying to clear the stars inside my mind. I could not black out on command, and when I did finally manage it, I could not wake up again without Kettle there to shake me back into the room. Cherry began rolling into and out of her trances almost instantly. "Oh, I worked in a brothel," she told me. "I'm just refining a trick I learned on my back. I've got years of 'going blank' and blinking back to life under my belt. Kettle is just teaching me vocabulary. I already knew how to do it, I just didn't know to call it witchcraft. You'll get it. It just takes practice."

I was jealous of Cherry's chosen name, too. Madame Quicksand sounded like the star of a high-end burlesque show to me. "What about 'The Pit'?" I asked Cherry and Kettle when we stopped to take deposits from the dig crew in Royal. They laughed as if I were making a joke; I laughed too, mortified. All the good names had been taken. The Sword Swallower had been snapped up by an enterprising young Vault in Antelope County; Fort Knox operated out of a road ranch in Gering. For months, I referred to myself only as Kettle's apprentice. Then one night, while we were working the fairgrounds of the Summer Moon Circus, I saw a poster advertising Pauline's Panacea. Glowing orange "medicine" in what appeared to be a crystal-cut perfume bottle, pitched to a hopeful, curious crowd as "The Antidote to All that Ails You!" A chill ran up my legs. *This is what I can do for people*, I thought. *This is my new purpose. I will take whatever they cannot stand to know. The memories that make them chase impossible dreams, that make them sick with regret and grief. Whatever they hope to preserve for the future. Whatever cargo unbalances the cart. Whatever days and nights they cannot absorb into their living. Whatever they wish to forget for a morning or a decade. I can hold on to anything for anyone. Milk, honey, rainwater, venom, blood. Horror, happiness, sorrow, regret—pour it all into me. I am the empty bottle. I am a new kind of antidote to all that ails you.*

"What do you think of 'The Antidote,' Cherry?" I'd asked.

She'd smiled at me. "I like it. Makes a big, dumb promise."

I was still tingling from the apprehension of what my life could be, helping so many with my new power.

"You're the Antidote! You can fix it all." She grinned at me, her dark eyes holding glowing twin Ferris wheels. "Sort of like how death is the antidote to living."

That night, for the first time, I had a recurring dream that still afflicts me—I am seated at my booth at the fairground, under THE ANTIDOTE in lighted pink and green bulbs, staring at two Ferris wheels. On one, every seat is full, and on its spinning double every swaying cart is empty.

Cherry was foulmouthed and funny and excellent at concealing whatever wounding had turned her into a Vault-in-training. Her howls of pain became howls of laughter—it happened before they hit your ear. For our first three months traveling together, I felt so jealous of Cherry that it hurt me to share a flask with her, a bench at the depot, a smile from our mentor. It took half a year of working side by side before we moved from rivals to friends. I have not heard from Kettle for eight years, but Cherry and I visit once a season. She is the closest thing I have to a blood sister.

In our early twenties we worked the main line together, traveling the Northwest Corridor. Cherry wore men's trousers, wool gloves, and a hat to shade her face. Her skin was two shades darker than my own, which, in certain towns, could mean a death sentence after sundown. We traveled together for safety. "My little brother," Cherry teased me. Cherry is six foot one in stocking feet. I bought a pair of bib overalls from a freight hopper who could not have been older than twelve or thirteen, fresh off harvest in Spokane, Washington; for a month I smelled like apples. "I got paid a penny a box," he complained, "and somehow I owed them two quarters at the end of the week!" We introduced ourselves as brothers at a pool hall in Superior, Nebraska, and endured some of the ugliest jokes I've ever heard about our imaginary mother. We were two bums riding to California orchards together, or we were two young soldiers who had met in the barracks at Fort Omaha. Often I had to restrain Cherry from amusing herself with even wilder stories and putting our lives at risk. Lies did not come naturally to me. I could hide the truth, but I could not invent with her confidence.

How does a woman become a witch? I don't know, Son. I have my theories, and I have my doubts about all of them. I can tell You what happened to me: You were stolen from my arms. The pain of losing You was all I had left, and I clung to it. I did not want to forget a minute of the short time we lived together. My body betrayed me, slyly returning to its original weight and shape with each passing week. My milk had dried up by the time I reached Alliance. Six months after I ran, I'd remade myself into Kettle's sixteen-year-old assistant. No one would ever guess that I had once carried a baby to term. But the space You left in me remained open. With each passing day, it seemed to deepen and widen. Every witch I've ever met has experienced a shock from which she never recovered, a loss that is ongoing—the way I lost You. I scan every crowd for a face that might be yours. I see your absence everywhere. So You see, Son, in this strange way, You birthed me. When You vanished from my arms, I became a prairie witch.

Why me? Why us? Cherry teases me for speculating about it. She says it's the wrong question. "Freak luck, Ant. The way a bone will sometimes set crooked. That's what made you a witch." Cherry takes a mechanical view of what happened inside us. We survived a blast that opened a door. In most people, the door becomes a wall again. Time heals it. Time seals it shut. For us, there is no more door. There is a permanent opening—a vacancy. *Space for rent.*

It was Kettle who taught us how to use these open wounds of ours to turn a profit.

Once, and only once, I made the mistake of telling a lover about You, Son. This was when I was still a young Vault, and less accustomed to my loneliness. I sometimes invited a customer into my bed. This particular man had such kind eyes, bright as red cedar. I told him that I was a mother, but that I did not know where my son was living. My newborn son, I said, had been stolen from my arms. He whistled and shook his head, fixing a sad look on his face. "Damn. I bet whoever took him makes a killing selling babies." To my horror, I heard a door shut and settle on its hinges inside him. Your abduction made *sense* to him. Money had made sense of it. His face puckered effortfully in unconvincing sympathy, but was he outraged? Was he surprised? No, "it all added up."

Why should money make evil comprehensible to anyone? But it does precisely this. Greed, violence, cruelty—money can explain them. Money can make the most heinous act seem like a sane one. A business decision, a necessary calculation. Evil's genius is to costume itself as sense. The "reasonable choice."

Cherry's cabin is hidden by four aspen trees beside an ancient tin windmill. The property was a gift from a wealthy customer, complete with a tufted chenille bedspread and the handsomest cherrywood headboard ever to support a sleeping witch. I nudged Angel onward, dreaming only of sleep. Sleep is a relief and release, and the things I see and do in dreams nearly always sieve away with the morning light.

We reached the cabin an hour ahead of nightfall. The windmill blades were swinging sunset around and around. Tin blue and fiery pinks and golds. The wind was almost unbelievably gentle that night. It felt strange to use the same name for both the warm breath gliding through this forest, and the annihilating force behind the dust storms.

I knocked on the door five times before trying the knob. The place was bare and quiet, every surface cleared of any living sign of Cherry Le Foy. The linens had been stripped from the cherrywood bed frame. The cupboard and the pantry were empty. There was no suggestion that anyone had lived here in recent times. No evidence that the cabin had hosted dozens of Madame Quicksand's customers. No paper, no ink, no note. Through the window I could see Angel looking at something invisible to me in the trees, her ears flattened.

An eerie feeling moved from the four trees outside the windows into my body. The green leaked out of the aspens' leaves while I sat on Cherry's bed waiting for her to return. When I next looked outside, the filtered gold of sunset had deepened to blue. The aspens were silhouettes, their branches folding shadows around Angel. The horse stood stiffly in the darkening woods, staring straight at me through the glass. "Cherry?" I called, long after it was clear that my only friend in the world was gone. My nonna died thirty years ago. My friends at the Home for Unwed Mothers all scattered to the winds. Kettle vanished from our lives. The barkeep at the Country Jentleman is kind to me, but we remain strangers in all the ways that matter after fifteen years of hellos. If I went missing like Cherry, my customers would mourn only the loss of their treasure. You are my greatest love, Son. But you may not know that I exist. If Cherry is gone, who can help me now?

Asphodel Oletsky

I am not a confident driver. I do not let that stop me from bor-
rowing the keys to my uncle's wheezy green Dodge. A week after
Black Sunday, when the roads were mostly clear again and the
air didn't scrape your throat going down, I drove to meet Valeria Ramos in the parts graveyard behind her house. The low reddish moon followed me around dunes and potholes, onto the old
bridge that crossed the dry riverbed. The bridge felt like a tombstone
for the vanished water, which I could still hear running through my
mind. East of the train tracks, I could see the sloping roof of the
Ramoses' tidy porch, their sparkling pyramid of junked machines.
Val was waiting for me in the cab of a wrecked tractor. She'd brought
a flask of whiskey and we grew warm and silly, sitting in the middle
of the rusted junk that hummed with so much moon. I loved it out
there. It felt scary, in a good way: the old jaws of the threshers grinning at us and nobody awake for miles and miles of night. I felt like
we were stargazing on dinosaur bones.

Val's mother seems to disapprove of me, although Valeria says
that's all in my head. Sometimes her mother came out to stand on
the porch, watching us play basketball with folded arms. Mrs. and
Mr. Ramos and their sons were asleep inside the dark house, which
looked so small from our perch in the cab. I felt grateful to be alone
with their daughter in the dead tractor.

I could live out the rest of my days happily playing basketball with
Valeria. Making shot after shot. Shutting down our opponents. Val
is our center. She's my center here too, my best friend on the team.
Taller than her brothers and growing right before our eyes, always

needing new clothes and new sneakers. Last season, Thelma tried to nickname her the Beanstalk. Val retaliated by spiking the ball square at Thelma's face. Nobody knew who to defend. That's the tricky part of belonging to a team as close as ours—when a fight breaks out, nobody wants to take sides.

Val scooted closer to me in the quiet cab, reaching a hand out for the flask. She's a head taller than me, but when I kneel on the cab seat we are the same height. I don't have to crane up at my best friend like a leprechaun. Val's brown eyes are actually plum-colored and veined with gold, but I can only see this when we are facing each other in the moonlight. The flask sat between us on the seat. Val started teasing me about my lousy playing—all week I had been missing easy layups, making sloppy passes. Fear leaked into her jokes, clear as yolk. We were both worried about losing, and I felt surprised to discover that my friend was also worried about me.

"I have been dreaming about the ditch again," I told her, staring through the cracked tractor windshield to that point where land and sky became a single black sheet. My mother was down there, calling for me. "It doesn't help that I have to sleep in her bed," I said. My fingers were clutching the wheel, which made me feel less drunk.

"Why don't you go to the Antidote? I have money, if you need it," Valeria offered. "If ever there was a reason to visit a Vault, this is it . . ."

Valeria had visited the Antidote twice, she said, although she had no idea why.

"That's how good the magic works, Dell. You'll sleep like a baby."

"Babies are up every two hours, screaming."

She punched my arm. "You'll play better. We have a big game coming up—"

If I visited a prairie witch, I told Valeria, curiosity would get the better of me. I'd be back within the hour. Even a dog knows the shape of the bone it buries. Not-knowing sounded like torture. Who could stand that suspense?

"You think that *now*." Val yawned. "But just wait until you see how much *better* you feel."

"You plan to leave your secrets inside her?"

I thought of the cobwebbed red hymnal I'd found inside the piano bench. All those expiring Polish songs, unsung by any Oletsky for half a century. Glue stuck half the pages together. It hurt my stomach to think about the trapped notes.

Valeria licked a bead of moonshine from the flask and made a sour face. "Later in life. When I am settled. *Then* I will go retrieve them. Not midseason, when we have a championship to win. Right now I need to stay light on my feet. Like you, Captain."

She hiccuped behind her hand and handed me the flask.

"Let me loan you the money. Don't be proud."

"Why should I pay a witch? You listen to my secrets for free." My laugh spooked me a little, so syrupy and far away. I unbent my knees and slid low in the cab, watching the stars above the bare field ripple like water.

Val shook out her curls and stretched her long body onto the seat beside me. Her black hair brushed the floorboards. Her voice sounded drowsy, so close to sleep. I wondered if I'd be strong enough to carry her to her house. Maybe we could sleep out here, under the moon. Her head was resting in my lap, and I did not know what to do with my hands. It felt strange to go on holding the rusted wheel. I folded them under my chest, watching her watching me.

"Maybe you're a witch yourself, Oletsky."

It was as if Valeria had read my mind. Out of embarrassment, I lied:

"I'm no witch."

"How do you know? You weren't a basketball player when you started eighth grade, and now you're our star point guard. If you were a witch, think how much money you'd make. More than Babe Didrikson, that's for sure."

This surprised me. The lady who calls herself the Antidote lives in a rented room above the Jentleman. I did not think of Vaults as wealthy women.

"You think the prairie witches are raking it in? I've never heard of one living in a mansion, or even a regular house."

"Well, nobody wants a prairie witch for a neighbor, but they're the only ones who have steady work during this Depression. That's what my papa says. I hear the linemen complaining about how much the Antidote charges—five dollars for a half hour deposit! And she claims she's giving them a special rate."

I whistled. "She must make a hundred dollars a week, easy."

Valeria laughed and pulled her eyes wide open, imitating me I guess.

"See that? Do the math, Oletsky. You might decide that you're a witch after all."

We both laughed, but I could hear something like fear bubbling under Val's giddiness, Val's genuine uncertainty about who or what I might be. Heat flooded into my face. Why did it make me so happy that Val thought I could be a witch? She yawned and rolled up on the seat. I rubbed the back of her neck, checking to see if she liked it, if she wanted me to stop. "Wise counsel," I muttered. "I'd rather be a prairie witch than a farmer, that's for sure."

Valeria was looking past me to the hanging moon. She stretched and curled against my side, her whole body yawning. My body stiffened with surprise and happiness. Our fingers laced together on the seat, question and answer. I wouldn't admit this to Val or anybody, but I am often embarrassed when I shake hands with people—Coach once joked, "Oletsky has hands like a lumberjack." But Val's palm was like mine, a blistered mitt. Her thumb circled my bruised knuckle. I felt electrified, no longer groggy; Val, meanwhile, snored once into my shoulder and startled herself awake. We watched the stars for a long time, our clasped hands resting on my knee. It made me think of a stone underwater, flashing dark and pale while the water flowed around it. My eyes shut and I could still see the night sky. I felt the heat of our single fist on my thigh, parting a river of stars. Which of us had moved our hands there? Could we sit like this forever? It would break the spell to ask this out loud. I squeezed my wish into Val's palm. *Stay?* It felt so good to breathe together in the cab, wishing only for more breaths.

"It's late, Oletsky." Val yawned and straightened. "I'll see you at practice."

"See you," I said. We came unstitched, her fingers pulling free of mine as she jumped down from the tractor. She went lurching across the moonlit field and vanished into the block of shadows on her porch. I felt a shock like I'd been cut in half, our sweat cold on my skin. *Come back?*

᚛᚜

When I saw Valeria at our Tuesday practice, I didn't mention that I'd spent the night in her tractor. I didn't say a word to anyone. I threw the ball to Pazi and started running. I had terrible news to share, but I wanted to drill first. I did not want us to get slack before we took on the Gordon Lady Grouses. The Gordon Greaseballs, Val called them. We needed the practice. If we won our next game, we would advance to the semifinals.

When we win. *When* we win.

I had to be vigilant in my repetitions. An *if* kept trying to needle in there and undo my *when*.

Our last Away game had been one of the happiest nights of my life. Coach had accompanied us on a train ride to Kimball. We got to stay in a motel paid for by our sponsor, Uz Poultry & Eggs. We ordered hamburgers and milk at the diner and sat in leatherette chairs facing the huge plate-glass window while snow spun under the electric streetlights outside. "A good veterinarian could still save this cow," Valeria had said in a low voice, imitating Coach, and I'd laughed for so long that I got the hiccups. In the morning, we faced off against the fearsome Kimball Krusaders. By halftime, the skin of my hands was coming off in ribbons. I did not want the burning feeling to ever leave my palms. With seconds left in overtime, I took three dribbles, lunged past my defender, and sank the winning basket. I thought I would die of happiness.

Elsewhere in America, girls' basketball teams play low-scoring, methodical games. Pass-dribble-pass—guards and forwards confined to one of three sections, prisoners of their assigned zones. Players get two dribbles, then have to pass. They cannot touch the opposing player. They are not allowed to block shots. We had no such prohibitions in Region 7. We played six on six, full court. "Girls' Basketball" had evolved into a warlike sport in our pocket of rural Nebraska. Its speed and its violence would have stunned Dr. Naismith.

Only nine of us had showed up to practice that afternoon. We had started the season with seventeen on the roster. Players had been dropping like flies all year. Bea Gratz was the latest to turn in her jersey—her family was going "home" to her mother's people in eastern Ohio. "Three crop failures and your port of departure starts looking like home again," Bea's mother had told me, "but I guess you Oletskys can't go back to Poland though, can you?" I tried to think of an answer. *I sleep in my dead mother's childhood bedroom. Every morning I wake up and I don't know where I am. Then I remember and I wonder, Where is my mother? Then I remember more and I want to be dead. Then I go outside and I play basketball.* My eyes had sealed themselves off. "Not everybody knows how to get home, Mrs. Gratz." I respected Bea or I might have said something else.

It's a shame that nothing is growing this year. I can almost imagine the secret court in another sort of April, with everything fragrant and green. When I lived in the yellow house in Hubbell, April smelled like the beginning of the world. Even in Uz, it can still feel like paradise on the rare evenings when the sky is clear and the dust does not stick to your lungs. Brown clouds ridged the sky, and I thought of the truck-flattened armadillos on the way into town. Already the wind was picking up. We'd grown accustomed to practicing in these conditions, with the dust blinding us, erasing the lines we chalked onto the court. It felt like love, to play against the weather together—to run drills in hundred-degree temperatures, to wear masks over our noses, to spit out dirt and blood. I caught Sofia's pass with squints for eyes, jumped through the shrinking gap between Thelma and Pazi, pitched the ball at the backboard. It fell through the net and rolled right back to my sneakers. My ball is more loyal to me than any person or animal has ever been. More predictable also. My small sun.

The Coach's whistle split our ears. "Good work, Oletsky," he said as I paused to get a drink of water from the team canteen. Coach did not look well at all. His voice was just a hiss today, as if his mind had sprung a leak. His grimace twisted his long, handsome face into a melting horseshoe.

"Where is Balbina? Oletsky, do you know?"

I shook my head.

Coach looked irritated.

"All right. Where is Maria Elena?"

"Watching the twins, Coach."

"Where is Lulu?"

"Doing the ironing for Mr. Kimberly."

"Where is Abby? Abby Ohrn?" Coach asked.

Several players looked my way. I have a reputation for knowing things first. I spend too much time on the Party Line, listening.

"Abby Ohrn died, Coach," I said. "Two nights ago."

Valeria shot me a look. I hadn't mentioned this to her, or anyone. Half of my teammates looked at the ground and the others looked at me as if I had killed Abby. I hadn't intended to keep her death a secret—I'd just been waiting for the right moment to share this sorrowful news. Morale was already on the floor. The dust was trying to suffocate us. Now these bad feelings were going to choke all the joy out of us, and slow us down. Was it so terrible of me to want to have a goddamn practice?

I had tried my best to cry for Abby when I first heard the news. I learned about it on the Party Line. The fact of her death bobbed on the surface of my mind—somehow I couldn't bring it any closer or deeper into myself. I found it unbelievable, even after I tried very hard to believe it. So many kids had disappeared from Uz that year, pulling up stakes and moving elsewhere. In my mind, she'd simply vanished with the rest. Abby looks like a crane, with her long neck and legs. Graceful like a bird, even with her head buried in her arms on the school desk. Abby is shy, never answers the teacher's questions. We eat lunch together sometimes without exchanging a word. When someone fouls her, she's just as quiet. And then she will ferociously attack, soundless like a lioness, and get her revenge. She is dead now. I keep forgetting. She is not our forward. She is not Abby any longer.

"It was the dust that killed her. The silicosis. She had bad asthma, from the time she was a baby. They tried to get her to the hospital in Hastings but the roads were bad."

"She died *on the road*? In the backseat?"

"She died in her sleep," I lied. "Before they were able to leave. Very peaceful."

Thelma was crying soundlessly into her fists. Dagmara blew her nose into her dust mask. Valeria shoved a third green gumball into her mouth. I started dribbling the ball, cutting a pattern into the heavy silence.

"Stop that, Oletsky," Coach snapped. "I have an announcement myself."

Even the grass seemed to stand up straighter. A crow preening his friend on the branch of the lone willow tree turned to stare at him.

"Uz Poultry and Eggs has discontinued their sponsorship. Miss Irene has gone bust."

"Oh! No!"

We all love Miss Irene. This was sorry news to receive, although nobody looked surprised. She was the local chicken empress who had backed the team through three years of drought. She came to every game, Home and Away. She had many egg metaphors for the game of basketball, and some were even helpful. You *did* have to break quite a few to make an omelet, for example. When Pazi twisted her ankle and played through it, winning us our regional championship, Miss Irene gave us each a dozen of the world's yolkiest chocolate chip cookies.

Coach was still frowning at us. "There's more, ladies," he said.

And once again, I failed to guess how bad things can get from one minute to the next.

"Unfortunately, I cannot continue to coach you this season." He paused to lick his lips. "This will be our final practice. I'm leaving Uz, girls."

"No," said Nell, with lightning forking through her auburn eyes. She spoke to Coach in the same level tone that I'd heard her use on skittish dogs and horses. She turned her fury into a calm command: "That cannot be."

A smile was agitating my lips. A smile I was failing to suppress. Laughter bubbled through me like boiling water. Like the fizz of summer nights in Hubbell when Mama was drunk and talking in her loudest voice to strangers. I'd never heard any girl speak to Coach this way.

Coach was often praised by other light-skinned men at our games, within earshot of Nell, for coaching her. It happened at every game we played, Home and Away. Other White people called Coach "an enlightened man" for doing what any child of five does naturally. Nobody had to teach us how to play together.

Our team is unusual in the Western Plains League because Coach let any girl in Uz who wanted to play try out. Even girls who did not attend the high school. Thelma dropped out last December to help her mother with the babies and she still plays with us.

"Nell. You keep practicing, honey. You're gonna shoot up this summer and then you'll be truly unstoppable in the post—"

"Stay," said Nell. "We are two games away from the championship."

Coach coughed, and we watched it become a fit.

The wind changed direction, and we all shuffled around with it. It made me think of the way my uncle's chickens fanned out after scattered seed, turning with his fist. Without quite realizing it, I noticed that we were tightening our circle around Coach.

"I am leaving Uz in the morning," he said. "Going home to Ohio where they still have water. I'd like to get out of this with my hat on."

"Stay," I said. "Stay, Coach," we all chimed in.

Demanded, begged: "Stay with us. Be our Coach."

"Please . . . ?"

It was the closest we'd come to singing.

Every girl was staring up at Coach with identically wounded eyes. He lifted a hand as he stumbled backward—a goodbye, I guess, although it looked to me like he raised the hand in defense. He wore a bewildered look on his face, as if he, too, was shocked by his announcement. I tasted blood and realized I'd been biting down on my tongue.

"I am proud to have been your coach, ladies. Goodbyes are not my forte . . ."

He gave each head a rough pat as he pushed through the knot of us, tossing out praise with a note of panic in his voice.

"Take more shots, Valeria . . ."

"Don't be afraid to get chippy with the bigger girls, Pazi . . ."

"Stick with it, Oletsky," Coach said, pausing to scratch my head. "You have real talent." It felt so good to hear it. I hated how much I loved hearing it. Already he was vanishing from sight. Moving like a drunk barging through chairs, fumbling for the exit.

In the far distance, behind the glittering fence where the grassland became the Johnsons' ranch, you could see the black shapes of horses at dusk. Only their mouths were moving, chewing a few last stalks of fodder before nightfall. We watched Coach climb into his car and drive down the sandy path that connected with the main road, and whatever new life was waiting for him beyond Uz.

No one spoke for what felt like a very long time. I hugged the ball to my chest, letting the wind scour my eyes. We could still make out his headlights, traveling parallel to the secret court. Someone lit a tulip-colored lamp, which warred with the steadier burn of someone else's flashlight. Night seemed to fall in large, jagged pieces all around us. Dust obscured the frog's belly moon. It swam through thick clouds to reach us, leaking pale gray light onto the court. Behind me, I felt Val trying to start a fire. When it was ten degrees cooler than it had been for Coach's announcement, and what felt like a thousand years later, Sofia finally spoke. What she said was "I'm quitting."

It was a funny way to phrase it.

"Let us know when you're finished. We can wait."

"I quit."

"No," I said, trying to imitate Nell's tone of authority. "We need you."

"I quit too," said Daniela.

We watched them walking together back toward the main road. There were seven of us present: Valeria, Pazi, Dagmara, Thelma, Ellda, Nell, and myself. Enough to field a team with one sub.

"Okay," I said. "Let's take a vote. All those who want to keep playing, raise their hands."

We voted to complete the season.

We voted to keep to the ordinary schedule of practices.

Only Ellda objected, waving her thin arm.

"How are we going to travel without Coach? A team of girls, and no chaperone? Our last game was a six-hour drive from Uz. Think about all the dangers!"

Ellda was outnumbered.

"We need a new name," said Pazi. "We can't be Uz Poultry and Eggs anymore, can we?"

"There is nothing less intimidating than an egg," said Dagmara. "People break eggs. They scramble them."

"Eggs are powerful, you fools. Eggs are the future of chickens!"

Tiny Ellda was outraged at us. Her mother raised broilers and laying hens.

"Who should we be?"

Girls called out suggestions:

"The Lynxes?"

"The Porcupettes?"

"The Prairie Roses?"

Valeria stared at Ellda. "The Dangers."

The Dangers. Only Ellda voted nay.

What about a new coach? Should we ask our teacher Jan Castle?

One of Valeria's brothers? Everyone wrote down a name and piled the slips in Dagmara's hat. Valeria tallied the votes: "One for Carlos Ramos. Two for Jan. Four for Asphodel.

"Congratulations. It's you, Oletsky. You're our player-captain."

"Oh." I felt my brow descending. "It's me? Why me?"

"Because . . ." said Val almost angrily—as if she were embarrassed by my question—"because, Oletsky, it's just you and your uncle, and you have nothing else to do."

"Because you won't let us lose," added Nell. "For your own sake, you won't."

"Thank you," I said. What was I supposed to say? I did not know the etiquette for this strange moment. *For your own sake . . .* It stung because Nell was right. I was done with losing. Last week, we lost Abby for eternity. In the last hour, we'd lost Coach and Sofia and Daniela.

"We are not going to lose anybody else," I said. "We are going to hold tight to each other. We are the Dangers. We are the winning team."

I looked from face to face and felt slow-motion lightning strike me, a very delayed understanding of our new status. Inside of me, a tree went up in flames. I let out a heavy exhalation and with it my hope that Coach would turn his car around. Coach was gone. I was our Coach.

"We have a quarter hour of light left. Let's finish practice with an intensity drill."

Coach started every drill the same way, calling: "Ready, Set, Lightning!" I did my best imitation of him, feeling a little silly. Once we were moving as a team, everything came more naturally. We formed two lines, reeling off ten passes to our partner and stepping a foot apart, reeling off another ten, widening the distance. Nobody missed. In pairs, we reached the rim and returned to run the passing drill again.

A happy feeling began spreading through me: I was the *Captain* of the *Dangers*. My teammates had voted me in. My friends. When I looked to the west, the horses were gone; Johnson must have brought them in for the night. The red sun had stretched itself from end to end of the horizon. I wanted my mother to hear what was happening. I wanted my sober and wide-awake mother right here, wide alive, back in her body, to watch me win. The triumphant feeling shaded into a lonely one, just as the sun slipped out of sight and blue sang its way outward across the flatlands.

At the end of practice, Thelma started complaining loudly about how stupid we all looked in our Poultry & Eggs jerseys. Personally, I had always loved them, with their scarlet trim across the soft gray cotton.

"Gawd," said Val, knocking me backward with her chest pass. "We can't wear these egg uniforms, Captain. We look like a team of zeroes."

"Okay, sure," I nodded. "We need new uniforms. We also need money, do any of you have that?"

Clothes were the least of our worries. We had to prepare for our own rogue season. We had to find the means to get to the Away game. We had no transportation, no money for motels and food.

"Maybe we could ask a new sponsor . . ."

"We don't need a sponsor," I said. "We can fund ourselves."

All six of my teammates looked at me skeptically.

"We can sponsor ourselves. Govern ourselves, and organize ourselves, and chaperone ourselves. The Dangers sponsor the Dangers."

I have a plan, but I can't share it with them. I know a way to get real money in a hurry, a lot faster than it takes wheat to head out and flower. I am going to visit the Antidote. Valeria was right—I might be a witch myself. Or I think I could become one.

The Dryland Farmer, Harp Oletsky

Two days after the black blizzard, my closest neighbor and friend, Otto Goerentz, came over for supper. Black Sunday had killed two of his lambing ewes and shorted out his Spider. He'd watched the tops of his plants turn red, burned by the electricity in the air.

"Some of the wheat in my northern field was still alive," he said. "I tried to ridge it up solid, and I swear to you before I could get that first field listed three others were moving—"

Sand had blown into his kitchen, he told me. He'd found a beach inside his larder. His kids were living out of cans.

I am not a cook. I confess I had been hoping for a little help in that department. As it turns out, Asphodel can't boil a potato. Lord knows how she and Lada got on in Hubbell. An orphan and a bachelor make an interesting pair in the kitchen. Most nights we eat a fair bit worse than those CCC boys at the chow hall, going back for gristly seconds of stewed chicken thighs and snot-green pea soup.

I told Otto that he and Bettina could use my stove anytime. From his red-faced *no thank you* I gathered that they had nothing left to cook.

"Otto, there's some turkey in the icebox. Take it, before it spoils on me. My stomach is off and my niece turns up her nose at my cooking . . ."

I started gathering bunches of toothy carrots and spring onions, a box of saltines, last week's milk, seven eggs. Something smelled off. Tendrils of rot curling up around the carrots. Shame pressed on my heart. I did not let it stop me from handing the box to Otto, and

Otto did not let shame stop him from accepting it for his kids. Easily it might have gone the other way. By the time we got the food out to Otto's truck we were both breathing harder than hefting groceries should ever require.

"Thank you, Oletsky."

"You're doing me a favor. I hate to see food go to waste."

We bent and straightened, loading up Otto's truck. When we finished he turned to face me with a stiff sideways grin. I had to smile at Otto, who was trying so hard to smile at me—like a man straightening a bow tie.

"I heard about the mess they made of that killer's electrocution last week. Is there nothing this dust can't screw up? Well, I guess the good Lord must have wanted to punish him twice—"

I chewed my lip until I pulled the blister off.

"They'll finish the job soon," he said, misunderstanding my quiet.

"I don't know how to feel about it, Otto. My sister is still dead, along with all the others."

"*When justice is done, it brings joy to the righteous but terror to evildoers . . .*"

Otto mumbled the verse, sounding embarrassed. Neither of us felt joyful, that much was clear. His smile slid into a grimace, and I figured we were both picturing the tall flames jumping from the boy's head in that Chair.

Joy to the righteous. Terror to evildoers. I just felt sick in my gut. Did that make me an evildoer? Hell on earth exists, nobody needs faith to know it. That's where we'd sent Dew. It brings me no joy to contemplate anybody burning anywhere—here or below.

Otto was reaching for his keys when I took his long arm.

"Can I get your eyes on something, before you split?"

I wanted him to see it:

The marvelous thing.

The joyful thing.

The terrifying thing. The thing I cannot explain.

I pulled ahead with Otto's arm in mine, like a dog tugging at its lead.

"Are we late to see the Queen?" Otto grumbled, trotting to keep pace. He stared without interest at the miracle in front of him. Wide eyes empty as a pantry.

"Harp. I will confess that I do not know what I am supposed to be looking at."

"Look again. Look harder."

My hands gripped onto Otto's shoulders, turning him like a periscope. His boot toes swiveled toward the doll. You can buy a head from the Sears catalog with a machine-stitched face. Our scarecrow was hand-sewn by my mother, Ania, who retired a pair of our papa's long johns, stuffed them with straw, and stitched the soft lump up in burlap. Otto squinted at the scarecrow's tiny button eyes. Otto's lips pressed thinner than my scarecrow's thready grin. I lost my temper then—how dare Otto pretend any of this was ordinary?

"Not a lick of stuffing missing. Not a speck of dust on him. Tell me, how does a scarecrow come through the worst roller in history in one piece?"

I wasn't trying to sing my own note higher than anybody else's. I just needed somebody to see what I was seeing.

Otto forced a laugh. "With all due respect for your luck, my friend, I am not sure this constitutes a miracle."

"Is that so?" I snapped. *Miracle* was a word I myself would have scoffed at this same time last Saturday. But as we crossed the fallowland to the adjacent field, Otto whistled. "Now that *is* miraculous."

My wheat field shimmered like a shallow lake in the afternoon light. Green piled on green from the barn to the road, the even stands shifting with the dry wind. City people think that blue is the color of water, but farmers know otherwise. Plants are where the water goes and grows—and green is the color water wears all spring.

"Congratulations, my friend. You'll be the only dryland wheat farmer in three counties to make a good crop this year." I was touched to hear this came from the heart. Otto wasn't bullshitting me. He was hurting, but he was happy for me.

The seed I planted in October never emerged. Last fall, it scarcely rained. Yet somehow my winter wheat had broken dormancy. My crop was greening up during the hottest, driest month on record. I wanted Otto to tell me how this was possible.

"Maybe you got a perched water table," Otto said in his slow way. "Underground springs . . ."

"If I do, this is the first I'm catching wind of it, Otto."

Some explanations men offer to each other like hardtack, to sober up a buddy who is teetering on the edge. *Underground springs*. Neither of us believed it.

Otto tickled my rib with a sharp elbow. "Would it kill you to smile, Harp? Most of us would love a U-turn in our luck. Maybe that Oletsky family curse is lifting."

"Maybe so." My brow felt so heavy. "Maybe our curse blew off with all this dust."

Otto started humming a patriotic song. "Anchors aweigh, my boys . . ."

I hate that damn song. It makes me think of the boys who never returned from the war. It makes me think of my brother, Frank.

"Aww, Harp." Otto was looking at me with amusement. "Laugh a little. You are just unused to luck running uphill."

We stood for a quiet moment watching the scarecrow sway slightly on its frame.

"Why does everything have to be *good* or *bad*? Maybe it's just strange luck."

I hollered and jumped at the sound of Dell's voice. My niece thinks it's funny to sneak up on me. It won't be so funny when I have a heart attack and she's responsible for the funeral expenses. She ducked under my raised arms, snapping her nasty gum. Otto was still laughing at my reaction.

"Who asked you?" My niece is like a barn cat living on my largesse. She skulks around and demands to know everything and offers very little in return.

"Did you spend my money on that candy?"

She answered me with another pink bubble. I wish my sister had taught her daughter better manners. Gum chewing is coarse and unladylike, probably why my niece enjoys it. She inhaled the color like a magic trick and turned to Otto.

"Uncle Harp is always after me for being *profligate*. He acts like I'm some whore from the Bible if I buy myself root beer after basketball practice."

"She'll buy it with my money, take two sips, and toss it. What would you call that, Otto?"

Otto looked with alarm from my face to hers.

"Well, Asphodel," he said. "I guess you're entitled to some profligacy after a storm like that one. You and the scarecrow survived Black Sunday."

He winked at me, and I could feel Otto trying to draw me inside the joke. He didn't want to deal with a miracle next door and who could blame him? Ordinary life had become impossible to comprehend.

"It is good to see you Oletskys come through this storm with your hats on."

"Did my uncle tell you he thinks God intervened?" Dell rolled her eyes at me. "Oh heavenly Father, thank you for saving the scarecrow from perdition. Thank you for delivering all the dogs and the horses and Monsieur Combs, the world's stupidest rooster, from the black blizzard. Clearly we are your chosen people . . ."

I used to think of myself as an easygoing person before Dell arrived. She popped another bubble, and my hands balled up at my sides. It took my fifteen-year-old niece to introduce me to this ancient rage. It feels much older and stronger than I am.

"That's enough," I said. "You oughtn't mock the God that saved you—"

My fists unclenched into palms. I regretted what I'd said. I knew we were both thinking about Lada, who had died in a ditch all alone. If God could save us, why not Lada? "The will of God is a mystery!" the priest tells me irritably, smoothing the wrinkles in his purple dress. But I keep asking the question. I can't seem to stop.

Asphodel turned abruptly and mowed a slant line back toward the house. Angry at me, or at the God she claims not to believe in. We watched her slam a fist into the scarecrow as she passed it.

"Dell has her strong moods. I fear I will never get used to them."

"She's a weather vane," said Otto. "Like her mother."

That surprised me to hear. I do not remember my sister that way at all. Dell is so short and solid and quick to anger, whereas my sister was pretty and pleasing as blue phlox, always smiling, always singing to her dolls. But I suppose a sister who runs away from home is also possessed by a strong mood.

Otto put a hand on my shoulder, and he gestured to the shrouded red sun in the northwest.

"Fortune brings in some boats that are not steered, Harp." He paused and looked at the scarecrow and me as if waiting for applause.

Otto did two years of schooling at the Ag College, but he always wanted to be an actor.

"What the heck is *that* supposed to mean?"

"Harp Oletsky. You have got the best-looking wheat field in three counties. Just keep a hold of your aces and don't make any fuss about it."

⫷⫸

God invented a thousand clocks, and winter wheat is one of the most beautiful. Green in its infancy becomes the husky red-gold of a mature crop in a matter of weeks. At first a shimmering of tiny shoots, just a rumor of green really, invisible from the roof of the farmhouse but evident to any man who drops to his knees. Crush a wheat kernel in April, and it should give off a clear liquid; by May this sap grows milky, then mealy. Soon the kernel gets too tough to split with a fingernail. Then you know your wheat is ready. Otto was right. If my strange luck held, I might be the only farmer in Nebraska to harvest a bumper wheat crop this June.

Just before dusk, while walking the rows, I knelt and pulled up a cluster of tillers, roots and all. "What water are you plumping on?" I asked the mute and trembling stalks. "What is keeping you alive?"

⫷⫸

As a boy, I felt certain that my family was cursed.

Now that I've been alive for nearly half a century, I know how commonplace the most outrageous tragedies turn out to be. But for many years, I thought my family was special. Long before Lada's murder, I learned it was possible to suffer the unthinkable.

Wake up in the same bed as always and continue.

When he registered for the draft, Frank had described himself as "a male of substantial build." We'd all teased him about that word, *substantial*—Frankie was skinny as a hay rake. Once mobilized, my brother joined Company D of the 136th Infantry and shipped out to France as a private. I felt jealous and relieved when I got my exemption to stay in Uz and help with the harvest. WHEAT WINS THE WAR! had been painted on the side of the grain elevator that year, the ripe

ears standing at attention below an American flag. The Army advertised for recruits in the English newspapers with a promise of free
irrigated lands. Veterans were to receive first preference from the
General Land Office, and Frank had decided to homestead in Wyoming on his return. He had this idea that he would prove up on a
homestead with water. Wyoming sounded like Eden to him. "I am
sick of trying to grow wheat on ground that don't want it," he told us.

Frank came home in 1919 with a medal that Mama hung around
his neck for all our neighbors to see, declaring, "My Franciszek is a
hero!"

He killed himself eight months later.

I couldn't understand it. One morning, Frank had been pitching
hay, breaking ice so the cattle could get water. The next morning, he
was dead.

The story we told everybody at St. Agnieszka was that the rifle
discharged while he was cleaning it. My parents decided to believe it,
so that they could imagine Frank in heaven. It was prudent to believe
this lie—but I could not do it. I refused to forget that Frank put the
barrel to his temple.

My brother survived the fighting, but it kept on going in his head.
He may have been sleeping in his old bed, but he was not "all in
one piece" like the neighbors said with relief. The Army turned the
whole world into a war for him. It didn't stop when he came home.

When my brother died I thought I couldn't bear it, couldn't take
another minute of that searing pain. I was furious at Frank for leaving us the way he did, with no farewells. I tried to imagine a hurt that
was bigger than the one he'd left for our mother to sponge off the
walls. Yet in the end we did bear it. Even our pa, who was unable to
cry, who instead shouted at me and Lada and Mama for years of bad
nights, his gray eyes spinning behind his glasses like shot quail. Even
our mother, who at the funeral had begged God to let her join her
son in heaven.

Was it a relief to hit the breaking point? Did Frankie feel a
moment's peace, before he squeezed the trigger? I wish I could ask
him. Frank was less rubbery than me. My brother had integrity.
What teachers called a strong character. Frank shattered. Whereas I
have bent so far away from the boy I used to be.

Still, I won't forget the true story of how my brother died. I won't pay a prairie witch to put Frank out of my mind. He still draws breaths inside me. I do not want to lose my brother a second time.

I only visited a Vault once in my life—back when I was just a boy—and what I remember best is the ride home to Uz with Papa, how light I felt, holding on to the saddle horn for dear life. Once was enough to convince me that I never wanted to make another deposit to any witch. To this day, I have no idea where this Vault was located—I remember that we rode for hours outside of Uz, at one point wading through a cold mud-colored creek. I don't know why Papa took me to a Vault, or what I entrusted to that stranger. He burned my deposit slip as soon as we got back to the house, stirring the ashes in the grate. The truth is that I would be terrified to withdraw it now, even if I could locate this Vault. Who wants to be reunited with a ghost whose name you have forgotten?

My sister had left Uz, and now my brother was in the ground. The summer after Frankie killed himself, the silence in our house seemed to bellow at us: *I cannot bear it. I cannot go on. This has to be a mistake*, I thought. It had to be the Oletsky family curse. The pain I felt seemed supernatural to me. I could not explain it any other way.

When I lost Lada a second time, the pain was no less excruciating. The only difference is that I'm older now, and I know many people who have survived pain like this, and worse. At forty-five, I have witnessed the extraordinary sorrows that ordinary people must bear. Carina Reinholt lost her twin girls in the same week; Paulson Nilley had a meaningless accident with his brand-new thresher that cost him his right leg; Otto buried his first wife when he was twenty. My neighbors are not cursed by God. They are like me: alive.

The Scarecrow

The man who is not me comes out here every day to scowl at the ground. He mutters to himself. Does he know my name?

It's strange detective work, piecing together the Universe.

My new eyes reach out, but only so far. Grass flows right up to the gray horizon. I watch a plant catch on the barbed wire. It looks like a mind drained of thoughts. Like this one.

Plants keep collecting on the wire until it topples over. The name enters me: *tumbleweed*. More names tumble into my awareness. *Russian thistle*. *Wind Witches*.

Names are memories. Names return to me like gifts.

What am I?

Why am I?

Or did I simply snag here, accidental as a tumbleweed?

The Prairie Witch

I spent the night in the empty cabin and left for Uz an hour before sunrise. I felt guilty I hadn't searched harder for Cherry, who might be alive somewhere and in trouble. I knew the worst may have already happened. I was afraid for us both.

When I returned to the Country Jentleman, the sun was low in the sky. Climbing the last flight of stairs felt like summiting Scottsbluff, going hand over hand as the wavy stones seem to endlessly recede. All I wanted was to collapse in my bed. At last I reached the third floor. Then I looked down the flickering hallway and saw her.

A girl was sitting on the rug outside my door, sucking on a dirty strand of hair.

Current rode up my spine when our eyes met. The girl had the golden eyes of the jackrabbits I see everywhere around Uz, resting under the skeletal hedgerows. Imagine that sort of twitchy paradox—a jackrabbit at rest—and you'll have a sense of the young person who I found hunched outside my door. She was underdressed in boys' shorts and a basketball jersey. A necklace of small, sharp teeth was strung around her neck. Her shrewd eyes in a face still round with baby fat made her look like a hundred-year-old girl. I wondered what she was doing here alone.

"Who are you?"

"Asphodel Oletsky."

"Miss Oletsky, I am not seeing customers tonight."

"I'm not a customer. Don't you remember me?"

The current spiked again.

"No," I said. For a disorienting moment, I wondered if she was someone I'd roomed with at the Home for Unwed Mothers, but, of course, she would not have been born yet. At her age, had I looked this wild?

"I helped you with your horse on Saturday. At the market downtown."

"Ah. You were cleaner then. And dressed like a girl."

"I came here straight from basketball practice."

I pointed to her necklace.

"I bet that smile you wear scares your rivals."

"That's the idea."

"Did those molars belong to antelope or jackrabbit?"

"Both. I have been collecting teeth from the dunes around my uncle's farm."

"The school shut down, didn't it? But you're still practicing?"

"Our coach got dusted out. He left us. But the team wants to keep playing. They elected me Captain."

"Captain. A big job. You should go home and get some rest."

She followed me into my room, brazen as an alley cat. She had a burglar's curiosity, touching whatever caught her eye, picking up a clock and shaking it.

"I am tired, girl. Thank you for helping me with the horse. Come back another time, when you're ready to make a deposit."

"I want a job," she said, and I laughed out loud.

"Sounds like you have one already, Captain."

"My uncle told me what you are."

"That's no secret."

"I think I'm something like you. A Vault."

I stared at her tawny eyes in the dark. Some wound had encased her like a scabbard—that much was obvious. *Was* she something like me? Maybe, I had to admit.

She had wandered over to my earhorn and was staring at it with a strange expression. The sort of grim fascination I rarely saw on a young face.

"I had a dream about that thing," she said. "A nightmare."

"That only proves that you've seen my advertisements."

She sank into my straight-backed chair and stared up at me like a pupil awaiting a lesson. "I don't recall inviting you to sit," I said.

"I want to learn how to be a prairie witch," she said. "Let me be your apprentice."

Downstairs in the saloon, laughter rocketed up and made me jump. The moon loomed in the window, a singed orange color. I couldn't see the dust as easily at night, but I knew it was there from the warping of the light. The girl seemed to be everywhere now, reflected in the window glass and my mirror, sitting before me in my chair.

Prairie witches fly into an inner sky so vast and empty it's a wonder that we ever manage to return to our waking minds. Had I wanted a protégée, I would have taught this young trespasser how to uncollar herself from her name and her history. How to stop thought. How to numb feeling. How to close off her sensing all at once, the way two eyelids shut. "You have to find your own descending path into a trance," Kettle had told me when I was this girl's age. "Then you have to find your own path back to consciousness, cued to a customer's silence. Practice makes the path. Your body will learn when it's safe for your mind to return."

Had I wanted an apprentice, I would have told this girl to imagine crow-black wings enveloping her, and watched until I saw a blankness snowing through her eyes. Then I would have taught her how to use the rhythm of her breathing to accelerate it.

"Get out," I said, opening the door. "Or I will call the Sheriff."

She stood and ran as far from the door as she could get, wedging herself into a corner of the room. I grabbed her shoulders and tried to push her into the hall; she slid free and returned to her nook. Her eyes were wide awake in the dark. I was frightened, Son. I thought this girl must be half-mad.

"Go home before the Sheriff drags you there."

"Let me stay. Let me tell you why you should take me on."

"I do not want an apprentice."

She was padding right behind me like a puppy. I groaned and sat on my bed. Tomorrow I would locate whoever was responsible for her. Meanness was stewing in my joints, in the little cauldrons of my knuckles. I felt in real danger of slapping her.

"Are you well, ma'am? Did you come from the saloon? I can make you some lemon tea and a verbena compress. I used to do that for my mother. Her miracle hangover cure . . ."

The lightness swarmed inside me, and my vision began to pulse with dots. A voice was calling back to me from the future, my voice tinted with alarm, telling me to heed my instinct and lock this stubborn girl out. Simple exhaustion got the best of me. And perhaps I felt sorry for her. And perhaps I saw something of myself in her, and Cherry, too, and every witch of this West, in her tawny, muscular body and her dirty hair and her determination to get her way tonight, to prove to me that she had real magic inside her.

The girl told me that she was fifteen and grew up in Hubbell, Nebraska, on the border of Kansas. Two summers ago, her mother was murdered. Now I understood. According to the prosecution, the judge, and the jury, and just about everyone in Uz County, the Lucky Rabbit's Foot Killer had taken her mother's life. Had he also turned this motherless child into a witch? For her sake, I hoped not.

"Do not say another word to me until sunrise," I snapped at her.

Mysteries abound in this life, Son. In the end, I let the girl stay.

The Prairie Witch's Apprentice,
Asphodel Oletsky

The Antidote's chest rose and fell, lifting a sunny, well-loved quilt embroidered with a purple Wheel of Fortune pattern. Barter from a customer, I bet. I could guess what she'd been given as payment—the Zenith radio, the lake blue rug, a cattail teakettle that I thought I recognized from Mrs. Wirshing's kitchen. Objects with a frayed and dented liveliness that stood out against the bare room.

I was surprised at how the Antidote lived. I guess I'd been expecting something closer to a brothel than a monastery. Had she told me she'd moved in yesterday, I would have believed her. On the far wall, the painted earhorn hung like a large teardrop from its hook. Light hit the metal receiver and scattered rainbows to all four corners, where they seemed to claw at the peeling plaster.

The Antidote had told me not to rouse her before dawn. Despite what my uncle believes about me, I keep my word. I sat on the sill, studying the Antidote. She had a long, horsey face, a burnt orange color in the apples of her cheeks. Wrinkles around her mouth and eyes. She was older than I'd guessed in the stairwell. I wake first in whatever house I'm staying at. Mama and I used to sleep in the same bed, unless a boyfriend was visiting. On Sundays I'd wake up hours before her. I'd read novels or do a puzzle until close to 10:00 a.m. I loved the ritual of sitting next to her and watching her breaths lift the blanket, her mouth hanging open and her arms flung wide like a toddler. I loved her clover-scented weekday breath and the slow-surfacing smile when she woke to find me sitting beside her. We switched roles often in the yellow house in Hubbell. We took turns being mother and daughter.

At last the clock chimed seven times and the sun turned the curtains coneflower pink. I stood and stretched, all of my muscles singing their relief, and crossed the room to wake the witch.

"Good morning," I said.

One eye opened reluctantly.

"*You* are still here."

"You *think* you are disappointed to see me," I told her. "But wait until you taste my breakfast."

This was a bluff. I am a terrible cook. My mama would gobble down my eggs fast to keep from tasting the burnt edges. Hot coffee and toast dipped in egg yolk brought her back to life after a night of poisonous fun with strangers who, at dawn, she'd introduce to me as friends.

The prairie witch's small pantry had a sack of sooty onions and potatoes sprouting eyes. A quart of milk and half a loaf of rye bread. I cut two thick slices, rummaged around for butter and jam. She was better stocked than most of my friends' families, some of whom had been reduced to eating "dandelion salad." Everyone in Uz had been talking up a storm about the upcoming jack drive and the free bunny meat they'd take home. While the tea brewed, I grabbed an unlabeled jar from the back shelf. Was it eye of newt? Hell-broth? It tasted like applesauce.

"Do you take liberties like this wherever you go, Miss Oletsky?"

"I am making your breakfast. I work for you now, remember?"

"Do you get all your jobs this way? Barging in and taking your employer hostage?"

"You're too powerful to be my hostage," I said. "Otherwise I'd never want to work for you."

Was that a smile? She was squinting right at me, an improvement—at least I'd made it through the doors of her dark eyes. "I'm too tired to kick you out," she admitted.

"What am I supposed to call you, Boss?"

"Can you read?"

She pointed at the gilt-framed poster on the far wall over the chair: THE ANTIDOTE in circus lettering, underlined in a trellis of blossoming pink and red rosebuds and viny greens. It looked like a cross between the Ringling Bros.' billboard and my Children's Bible illustration of Eden. Beneath it sat a large rocking chair, the seat upholstered in fancy green satin.

"*The* Antidote. Isn't that a little formal? What do your friends call you?"

Smiling did not seem to come naturally to my mentor. I pictured a needle diving and resurfacing, stitching the witch's face on.

"We're not friends."

"No, I guess not."

I appreciated the Antidote's clarity. Both parties do need to ratify a friendship. Plenty of people in Uz refuse to understand this. My poor uncle, for example, believes that he is friends with everyone.

"What should I call *you*?"

"Asphodel Oletsky."

"Asphodel Oletsky, I would not hand my real name over to a stranger so cavalierly. That can be a fatal mistake in this line of work."

I felt so happy. Already my plan had started to bear fruit. She was talking to me like a teacher. Her angry tone reminded me of Coach. The Dangers had two more games and no money to pay for uniforms or gas or transportation or lodging. I'd seen the Uzians lining up outside the Antidote's door. We had not discussed my salary yet, but I planned to ask for a percentage of her profits. Then I'd become a prairie witch myself, and we'd never have to worry about money again.

"You have picked a dreadful season to embark on your new vocation, Miss Oletsky."

"Yeah, well . . ." I whisked three yolks into one massive sun and poured them into the skillet. "It's a dreadful season for everything."

"Here," I said, handing the prairie witch her tea. The sliced lemon bobbed inside it like a little hostage moon. We sat in silence for a quarter hour, staring out at the Uzians as they crisscrossed Main Street. Abruptly, something shifted; I remembered my mother unpinning her hair at night, shaking her bun loose across her bare shoulders. Time came swinging down around us, and I felt us relaxing into each other's presence.

"So you think you are a prairie witch. Should we test that hypothesis?"

I kept breathing at an ordinary tempo. I didn't want my new boss to hear how scared I felt.

"You gonna drop me in the Platte and see if I float?"

"I want to see if you can take a deposit."

She retrieved her earhorn from its hook. My heart started pounding, the way it does just before a jump ball. The rasp of the earhorn coming off the wall felt like a cue I had been waiting for since my first night in Uz. I believed I could do what she was asking. I was ready to enter the trance.

Put me in, Coach. Put me under.

The earhorn was lighter than I'd expected. Its color made me think of the winged dragons on the Kearney carousel, the way their scales seemed to change from green to blue with each revolution. "So you just talk into this part, and I listen? That's it?" The witch shook her head. She leaned in and tucked my hair behind my left ear, which made my face go hot—how many days had gone by since I'd drawn myself a bath?

"No. You disappear into your trance. Then I talk into the funnel—" The Antidote held the metal receiver against my left ear. She settled the funnel against the seatback. Two hooks with canvas snaps held it in place.

"Always secure your earhorn first, girl. Before the lights start flickering in there—" She tapped my forehead. "Nod forward if you can manage it. When I was first learning, my head would always loll around . . ."

She smiled at me, and I realized something marvelous: no matter how much she'd insisted that she wanted me to leave, more of her wanted me to stay.

"Should I close my eyes?"

"Let your body do what it wants to do. This is a test, remember? A diagnostic test."

The Antidote's sun-lined face hovered over the fluted edge of the earhorn. I could see the dark hairs around the corners of her lips, smell the lemon tea on her breath. Was this how it happened? Could you will yourself to black out? Using Coach's voice, I tried various commands: *Hush up. Shut up. Quit thinking. Catch the ball.*

"Ready?" She tore a little slip from the ticker on the wall. In her throaty voice, she recited the date backward.

I shut my eyes tighter. I could still hear the witch moving around the room. I remembered the number. Was that good or bad? One great thing about basketball is that everybody plays by the same rules. The test is public. The rules are clear. You never have to guess if you scored a point.

"A trance is like a waking sleep, girl. Where did you go in your mind, when your body was in terrible pain? When the pain felt shattering? Remember what you did to survive it. Do it again."

Her voice hammered into me, so loudly that I winced. Was I supposed to be conscious? If not, I was failing the test. I was not in a trance. I was somewhere else, back in Hubbell, remembering my mother's funeral.

⁂

The fact that my mama is dead is not something that I can grasp for very long. I can know it for several minutes at a stretch, before it goes sliding away again. When I say I cannot grasp it, I mean just that. I have a dead hand hanging by my side. People told me what had happened to my mother and I stared at them, watching the words as they exited their mouths. From sunup to sundown in the days following her murder, I stood under dark canopies. "Sugar, talk to me," said a woman from church. Crows scattered from some soundless explosion. In the graveyard, I watched dirt falling on a box the width and the length of a person. *Coffin*—the word came back to me, from wherever words hide when you can't find them. I thought about the Easter when we tried to bake a cake that never rose and then frosted the chocolate wreck of it, laughing so hard that we had to scoop up the dark crumbs as they came cackling from our mouths. They put the pieces of my mother they found into a box and they nailed it shut and they sent me far away from her. The coroner gave me the only picture that I have of Mama, a print of her body in the ditch.

⁂

"Five, three, nine, one . . ."

I shut my eyes and tried my best to enter a trance. In spite of my efforts to disappear, I heard every word she said:

"All right, girl. This is my deposit. When I was eleven years old, my nonna Onofria took me to the ten-cent matinee at the Orpheum for my birthday. I did not understand many of the jokes, but it felt so good to laugh with the crowd of beautifully dressed strangers. In my memory the whole theater was shaking, walls and all. I laughed so hard that ginger ale shot out of my nose. Afterward we rode the trolley car and I saw something that looked like an orchard of glowing clementines in downtown Omaha. So many tiny electrified lights. I asked my nonna if I could pick one, and she laughed and said no, they were for everyone, but I could take them home in my mind. I could remember them. This concludes my deposit."

Her voice withdrew from my skull.

"Did I pass?"

"Did you enter a trance? Could you hear what I told you?"

"Not much of a story," I said. "But, yes, I remember it."

"So do I," she said. "Goodness, I can still feel that ginger fizz in my nose. The orchard of light." She smiled at the wall, or at someone I couldn't see, maybe the nonna from her story.

"You know, I have never been back to Omaha. I hardly ever tell stories of my own, girl. It's quite the magic trick. Duplicating a memory inside a stranger."

"Does that mean I failed the test?"

"Your word for it. Others might say you dodged a bullet."

"If I am not a Vault yet, I know I could become one."

She placed the earhorn back on its hook with a firmness that enraged me.

"Stick to basketball. Nobody aspires to be a Vault, girl."

Nobody aspires to be poor either. Nobody aspires to be a burden passing from hand to hand, from Hubbell to Uz. Nobody gets to pick what they start with, and few get much say in where they go next. I wanted to learn if this hole in my heart was worth something.

"I just need to keep practicing. I bet you weren't so great when you first started out. Give me lessons and I'll get the hang of it sooner than you think."

"This isn't basketball. You can practice a thousand hours, but if you are not a Vault in the first place, there's no way to become one."

"As far as you know, ma'am."

But how far was *that*—?

This woman who spent many of her waking hours in a trance?

"My mama is dead," I said. "It tore a hole clean through me. I have been a prairie witch since her funeral, if I wasn't one before."

I drew a wide circle around my navel.

"I feel it when I play basketball. It's the reason I can run faster than any of them, and jump higher. It's the reason I can get knocked around and recover quicker than anyone."

A pounding at the door made us both jump.

"Open up, or I'm calling the Sheriff!"

The Antidote resembled my mother for a moment, her eyes glassy and bright like those of a cornered animal, her voice unnaturally low. I remembered a night when Mama had refused to open our door for a surprise midnight visitor, shouting her threats that had no force behind them, threats like desperate prayers.

"Get in the closet," the witch hissed. "Do not make a peep. If you cough or sneeze or move a muscle, you'll get me killed—"

The witch's closet was wider than it looked from the outside. I leaned back against her coats and dresses, as flat as I could go. The darkness was thick with odors—horseradish, detergent, mothballs, sweet leather.

"Mr. Boyet," I heard her say in a stately baritone, the door screaming on its hinges. "What an unexpected pleasure."

The Dryland Farmer, Harp Oletsky

I am more afraid of these clear skies than I've ever been of any storm.

Today the sky is dry and gray as chalk. The wheat is growing tall and tillering out faster than seems possible. The mercury in my barn thermometer climbs toward one hundred. I never imagined I would sweat like this in April.

Lada's girl didn't come home from her game last night. After pacing the hallway at 2:00 a.m., I finally knocked on her door. I needed another set of eyes, but all I found was an empty bed. I was alone in the farmhouse when the strange light returned.

Only God and the scarecrow, five hundred yards away, could hear my prayers.

"Heal my eyes, God. Help me see only what is truly present."

Something is developing on my fallowland. I see it during the deepest part of the night, when I stand in my pajamas at my bedroom window. Radiance pours out of the parched ground. It rises like glowing stalks that flow into one trembling sheet, stretching from the sandy black soil to the new moon. It burns in a hue for which I have no name. A color that to my watering eyes seems newborn in our world. It reminds me of too many earth colors at once. Snakeskin in sunshine. Oily rainbows. Mother-of-pearl seashells. Blue-black corn kernels. Blood rounding out of a child's cut finger. Wings shaking off water. Somehow it's all of them and none of them. The stars look dull as rocks above this blazing light. It escapes every dart my poor mind throws in its direction.

Not-earthworm   *Not-onion*   *Not-agate*

                                    Not-penstemon
      Not-sunflower   *Not-comet*

Not-rain-in-wallow   *Not-dawn*

                                    Not-blue-corn
      Not-black-oak   *Not-green-wheat*
      Not-quicksilver   *Not-blood-red*
                            Not-rabbitgray

                                    Not-moonstone
Not-hoof   *Not-wind-in-bluestem*
      Not-icicle

Shadows move behind this trembling screen. Sharpening into shapes I can almost name, scenes I can almost decipher before they collapse again. Shadows that dance behind the veil of light. Last night, I watched from the bedroom window for two hours, afraid to take a step toward or away from the dazzling color.

Is this a sign from God? Am I losing my eyesight? Suffering from heatstroke?

At four in the morning, I knotted the curtain sash and shut my eyes, waiting for the sun to restore me to sanity. I did not want to frighten my niece. Tomorrow night, I promised myself, I would beg Otto to come. I would seek the counsel of someone reasonable. Someone who can distinguish a hallucination from an omen, a blessing from a curse.

But tomorrow became today, and I cannot find the courage to ask my friend to keep vigil with me tonight. To wait with me until the light appears again, or until it becomes clear to us that I am no longer a sane person. I stopped believing in curses, didn't I? Maybe Otto is right, and I am simply not equipped to handle good fortune. Maybe the answer is sleep and aspirin. Whatever else is going on here, I don't think it's only a break in the weather.

For seven nights now, I have watched this strange light erupt from underground and blossom across my fallowland. It began the night after the Black Sunday roller. The first time it happened, I thought perhaps the dust had injured my weak eyes. Now I am not sure what

I am seeing. Or what has chosen me to see it. Whatever keeps shining out of the fallowland persists inside me well past dawn. Daylight doesn't extinguish its memory. Those flames of light go on growing and glowing in my mind while I kneel in ordinary sunshine, digging up weeds. Dust covers the western sky, but the air here is pleasant to breathe. Sweet, even.

What is happening to this land, and to me? While I'm working, I inhale and exhale almost mindlessly. It's only when I'm still that the fear seeps in.

The scarecrow smiles with his stitched-up lips. Maybe I won't tell Otto or Dell about any of this. Maybe a secret has chosen me to keep it.

The Scarecrow

*S*pring. The word returns to me out of the blue. What a gift to receive, unbidden. One of the most beautiful words in this language.

It is spring in Uz, Nebraska. The sky is loud and hot and dry. It hisses day and night. No rain falls. But something grows inside me. Under the surface of this mind. Under my thinking. Under the blue world, something is springing. Something that wants to erupt and flower.

Into the field of my awareness. Into this field where I am staked.

The man calls it fallowland. But he is wrong about that.

A seed is a funny little casket. Bury it, and something springs to life.

The Antidote's Story:
Part 1

T he girl asked me how I became a witch. Something happened, I
told her, that made me bottomless. I have never told anyone the
full story of what happened to us at the Home for Unwed
Mothers. Not Kettle. Not Cherry. I would like You to know it,
Son. It is our story.

Other places, I've learned, were kinder to their girls.

We had all heard about "the Ritz"—the Willows Sanitarium in
Kansas City, Missouri, where the daughters of prominent families
were picked up at the train station in limousines and driven to private, heated rooms in a three-story mansion. They were treated like

guests instead of inmates. Willows girls got rose gold wedding bands to wear on their trips into town. If you had money, you were never a whore. You had been *seduced*. You had made a mistake. You went to the Ritz to do your penance. After delivering your baby, you returned home alone. Your mistake would live elsewhere with a new mother and a new last name—far out of earshot of anyone who knew your rich family as prairie nobility.

The Milford Industrial Home for Unwed Mothers was not the Ritz. The word *Home* mocked us on our hard cots. The foyer had green-ferned wallpaper, but upstairs in our dormitory we were starving for colors. I hear the girls have steam baths now, but in my winter months I went weeks without bathing. The weak tea they served us tasted like drizzly rain. Nothing too strong. No thudding pleasure that might upset a fetus in the womb. Coffee was forbidden, and cigarettes; also unholy magazines and books. This made for a bustling black market run by Suzette, the disgraced daughter of a Mennonite family, although we all guessed there was an even darker story lurking behind the Milford rumors. Suzette was an "Incorrigible"— her official status in their files. A Third Offender. I was locked in the attic when they sterilized her—although I am getting ahead of myself now.

At the Milford Industrial Home, each pregnant inmate was ordered to a twelve-month confinement by the courts. A woman had to complete her full year, no matter when her baby was born. If a woman had no money to care for her child, the infant was taken by the state of Nebraska and placed in an orphanage to await adoption. A poor girl I knew from Little Italy gave birth on Easter Sunday; her baby was sent to the orphanage the following Friday, but she was forced to stay at the Home through Christmas, marking the weeks until her release with red nicks on the underside of one arm. Another mother miscarried the night of her arrival. She was still an inmate at the Home when I left.

"We will restore you girls to virtue yet," the Superintendent assured us. Malvina Dent was the daughter of a famous Baptist preacher and a social worker. She encouraged us to call her Mother, but only the youngest and the most frightened ever did.

Melody, a prostitute from Beatrice, told me not to indulge Malvina. "Why in the billy hell does she think we'd want her for a mother?

Believe me, we are queens of virtue compared to that lady." Melody had a hoarse, happy voice that made me think of embers in a grate, gray and bright at once.

"It's easy to love the babies," Night Nurse Edna told us. "*You* bitches make the job hard."

The Home was staffed by people who were hell-bent on redeeming us. Malvina Dent was an especially shameless sort of hypocrite. She ran her Home on the labor of poor single women and sang hymns with us on Sunday mornings. Her dedication to our "moral reformation" was relentless. Someone may have even been helped by it. We were often introduced to plump young mothers who had gotten jobs as housekeepers in Lincoln, which was twenty-two miles east and worlds away. One Thursday night, we were herded into the parlor to meet a thin, serious Filipina woman, introduced to us as Crystal Anne. She had given her baby up for adoption to the minister and his wife who ran the millworks in Papillion. She did not say a word to us that night but stood beside Malvina with watery, inscrutable eyes, nodding whenever the Superintendent looked her way. Later I learned that she did not speak English.

A brass plaque in the parlor, crosshatched with scratches, was inscribed with the Home's mission: BESIDES SHELTER AND PROTECTION, THE OBJECT OF SAID INSTITUTION SHALL BE TO FACILITATE ADOPTIONS FOR UNWED MOTHERS, WITH A VIEW TO AID IN THE SUPPRESSION OF PROSTITUTION, AND THE REDEMPTION OF FALLEN WOMEN. *To facilitate adoptions*. When I first arrived, I read this phrase without comprehension. Next to the plaque hung a portrait of a dark-haired White woman with caterpillar eyebrows and wonderfully kind eyes. This was Frances P. Clark, the Omaha philanthropist who had persuaded the state legislature to fund a Nebraskan Home for Unwed Mothers, and later pushed the same senators to raise the age of consent in Nebraska from twelve to fifteen. I often wondered what Frances would make of our lives in this lonely place if her warm eyes could see out. Was I one of the girls she had imagined helping—the "penitent girls who have met with misfortune"?

Misfortune had certainly met with me, I felt. When I arrived at Milford, I was fifteen years old and three months pregnant. Nonna Onofria had died of cancer of the bone in the winter of 1907 and I was sent to live with a guardian. I hated to say "my guardian," even in the early weeks, when she enjoyed playacting like a mother. The word made me think of the angel in the foyer of our cathedral, with its dopey smile and chipped, yellowing plaster. I would have preferred to shelter under his friendly, ugly wings than under the Guardian's roof. I would have liked to be made of stone myself. My nonna's soul had gone to heaven, and I was entirely alone. Like many of us, I had no home waiting for me outside the Home.

Girls never went by their real names. We were all called *girls* in the Home, never *women*—not even the oldest inmate, Ruby, who had oaky lines around her eyes and was rumored to be thirty-nine. We were given false names on our first day—to protect us, they said. "No one need ever know" is a selling point of such reformatories. Mine was Anne Fayeweather, a costume that made me sound to myself like a wooden doll with blond braids.

IQ tests were distributed, our scores filed away and never revealed to us. We were reassured by the Examiner, in his patronizing gurgle, that sexual deviance was not always proof of evil. It could also be, he said, a sign of feeble-mindedness.

That night, Stencil kicked off the sheets and stretched her long, candle-white legs into a V, making exuberant love to the air. "Oh, ladies, I am suffering an attack of feeble-mindness! One plus one equals three? Oh help me, I am too feeble-minded to understand the arithmetic of sex!"

We laughed whenever Stencil acted out their ideas of who we were.

Some of us did, anyhow. Some of us were beyond laughter.

Rising bell at 5:00 a.m.: scripture reading, singing, and prayer.

Duty from 6:30 a.m. until 5:30 p.m.—none of us "fallen women" was deemed too far down the ladder to be exempted from labor in the dairy and the fields, the kitchen and the laundry.

Chapel every night at 8:00 p.m., lights out by 9:00 p.m.

The town of Milford had donated forty acres for our confinement. Our stays were funded by the state, but our time was certainly not free. We spent the coldest hours of the day indoors, learning home industries and pretending to read from our Bibles. My fingers walked to the lilies of the field, Matthew 6:28, as if they were traveling home. These were Nonna Onofria's favorite verses. I wanted to be a lily, growing instead of toiling. A public school teacher held classes two nights a week, but most of us were yawning at our hard desks, our bodies so noisy with aches that it was difficult to make sense of the strange parade of letters and numbers.

"The formation of sound morals." "The value of a good education." "The salutary effects of motherhood on soul and body." There were so many stories that I had accepted unquestioningly until my nonna died. Values in which I had a child's uncritical faith. I became a little more critical now, listening to the nightly lectures about my own evil.

On Thursdays, we heard from esteemed speakers and reformed wayward girls—unwed mothers who had slept in these bunks before our arrival, now chaste women and docile workers:

"A most ignorant and inexperienced girl, an orphan who had not hardly any advantage in life, became a mother at sixteen years of age. Hard to handle before the baby was born, she afterward became exceedingly tractable. She was very fond of her child. After the usual stay in the Home, she secured a position with her baby in a private family, where she remained until the baby was more than a year old. After that she boarded the baby with a widow in Lincoln and began a new job as a live-in housekeeper in a stately home. Her child is now six years old. This mother is making four dollars a week as a domestic and has a bank account. She has monthly visits with her child. She has improved wonderfully and is soon to marry."

Many of the women trained at the Milford Industrial School went on to become domestics for wealthy families, leaving their own babies in someone else's care. "When you're a live-in, you gotta do everything but chew their food for them," Melody warned me. I didn't want to pay to board my child elsewhere while I cared for a rich lady's baby. I decided that I would work as a cashier at the dry goods store, as my nonna had done. Already I was scheming, you see. Dreaming of ways to keep You with me.

In the year before my arrival, the Home recorded fifty-nine live births, twelve stillbirths, forty-seven adoptions, two newborns sent to the Home for the Friendless. Now, I don't trust any of their statistics. One of my friends, Geneva, was given a death certificate to sign while she was propped up in bed with fresh blood soaking into the towel between her thighs and the placenta still inside her.

I did not want You to become a number in their black book.

"Last year," the Superintendent announced from the podium, "among sixty-two mothers, there were no fatalities. Eight babies passed away under one month of age, two under six months. A remarkable record! For statistics show us that the death rate among illegitimate children is *much higher* than among the legitimate . . ."

Several girls, like Melody, were "voluntary cases"—although often when you listened to a voluntary inmate's circumstances it became clear she'd had no real say in the matter. Who would choose to give birth in this way, like a shamed dog locked out of sight?

Not everyone approved of the Home's mission. There were often protestors on the lawn, waving signs and screaming:

"I do not pay taxes to feed the whelps of these sluts—"

The guard, José Luis, was dispatched to remove them. He was a huge Spaniard with a polished cedar club who some earlier inmate had nicknamed Cordero for his gentleness; the nickname stuck, and we all called him this. From the dormitory window, I could often see José Luis sharing a pack of cigarettes with the now-pacified crowd on the lawn. We were taught to be grateful for every breath we took behind the locked doors, every bitter sip of lemon tea and every hand pressed to our bellies, and whether or not this touch brought us pleasure, whether or not this was a wanted pressure, we were to say the magic words: "Thank you."

Thank you, Doctor. Thank you, Mother. Thank you, Father. Thank you, Stranger.

Only after Lights Out did the Home fulfill its mandate, transforming from a prison to a sanctuary. Night was the dark wingspan of time when we were unchaperoned and free to exist outside the squinting eyes of Malvina Dent and the Home Staff. In our loose nightdresses, we were sometimes able to stage an insurrection of laughter. We carried our heavy burdens of hope and dread together. I loved these women, and I loved their future children. If I owe a debt of gratitude to anyone, it is to the other mothers. And to You, the tiny stranger growing larger and stronger inside me. You saved my life in that sad place.

Love at first sight always sounded to me like somebody's delusion. But I loved You before I saw your face. Love *before* sight—which sounds even crazier.

Stencil was the veteran inmate when I arrived, and she needed to laugh the way the rest of us needed to breathe; her body—her cartoonishly pregnant silhouette—was a joke that kept getting funnier, she told me. She was an Irish giantess, nearly six feet tall in stockings, thin as a ruler everywhere but the taut balloon of her belly. "I thought I'd at least get tits out of this!" Stencil complained. Stencil was not my friend. Not at first—our dislike was very mutual. She thought I was stuck-up, and I thought she was crazy and selfish. She'd get twenty of us into trouble just for the pleasure of indulging her own oddball humor. It took weeks before our first impressions burst at the seams. Antipathy could not survive for long in the crowded dorm, where we moaned together in the same dark, our babies turning inside our bellies.

Every inmate in her first seven months worked the garden plot near the distant highway. I could see the dim shapes inside the automobiles rattling down on the road, and it shocked me to realize that I was such a shape to them, a flash of color bleeding off, a pebble ticking off the glass. Even close up, we must not have seemed quite real to these motorists. We must have looked pitiable to them. Or—*worse*—picturesque. A row of pregnant women kneeling among the beans and peas and viny gourds. We had round peach and plum faces, white potato and sweet potato faces, we were Yankee and Italian and Black and Irish girls, German and Russian and Bohemian and Mexican and Filipina and Czech and Born at Sea girls, and we came from all over the state to be cultivated on this fenced-off plot.

I felt You kicking for the first time in January. After that, I did not feel so alone.

I went running to tell the yawning Night Nurse, who replied, "You think you're any different than a sow with a piglet? Go to bed, Anne Fayeweather, or I'll kick you myself."

Four weeks. Five weeks. It was a slow race to meet Your gaze.

⚎

My full name is Antonina Teresa Rossi. My nonna called me Nedda, and I was Toni to my school friends. Little Fool and Lulu and Love to my baby's father. I was born on December 21, 1892, in the village of Prizzi, a name I know from the ship manifest framed in our parlor. My father ran a barbershop in Omaha's Little Italy, behind the Cathedral of St. Philomena and the Bank of Sicily. I am Sicilian, not Italian—we get lumped together by the American-born settlers who do not want us in their neighborhoods. Neapolitans, Sicilians, Calabrians, Lombards, Venetians—we were all Italians here. NO GUINEAS read the sign posted in the Rutlands' storefont on Broad Street. Migrants were pouring into the city, recruited by the Union Pacific and the packing firms.

Our neighbors, the Muhleys, were a Black family from Virginia, part of a great incoming wave of Black emigrants from the Southern states. A parallel wave had delivered my Mediterranean family to Nebraska. I was a baby when we left, not a year old, and yet to please my nonna I pretended to long for Prizzi. I promised her that I did remember rocking in her arms on the deck of the great ship, our village shrinking to the size of a fisherman's gray bobber, then disappearing forever. *Our village* is what she called Prizzi. By age five, I knew this was a lie; Sicily was her home, never mine. She wanted me to be homesick for a world I did not know, and I always felt that I disappointed her with my happiness. I was a Nebraskan. An American. I did not feel sick at all. I had at least a hundred cousins that I'd never met and for whom I could feel nothing but a queasy sense of superiority, and then the pity that is pride's afterthought.

Every year that I spent in Omaha, absorbing Yankee attitudes toward Italians and Sicilians, my shame and my pride grew. I was told that Americans were superior to everyone born elsewhere. From the grown-up talk around, I deduced that I'd escaped some terrible fate back in Sicily, where everyone was poor and hungry. We were also poor and hungry. I grew up nourished by a story, the story of my good fortune—I was an American citizen, I lived in the richest country in the world, where I would learn English, work hard, marry well, and improve upon my parents' great sacrifice.

I was a silent child around strangers and a chatterbox with friends. For a future Vault, I was not a particularly good listener. I was loyal like an animal to my grandmother. My older brother and my father died in a fire at his barbershop on Seventh Street when I was three years old. My mother had died and was buried in Prizzi. I have always wanted to know more of her, to see a photograph, but the thought of her hurt my grandmother, so I learned to avoid the topic. It seems that if I could have known my mother, I would better understand myself.

You would have loved my grandmother—everybody did. My nonna: rain-wet rosemary and fat tomatoes bursting like magma in the tall pot. My chubby hands helping her strong, callused ones with the windowsill harvest. She played ragtime tunes on the splintering piano. ("A piano is a machine unlike any other, my Nedda," she said, "for what it produces has no value beyond the pleasure it brings people." "Who said that, Nonna?" "Me! I did! But if anybody asks, you can name a king or a president.") She snored like a man and slept like cut lumber in the bed we shared. She wore a shower cap on which I'd drawn crude spots and sat in the yard with me for an hour one chilly afternoon when I was five years old (I had wanted to pretend that we were toadstools). Another time we painted mustaches on each other's faces and went to the Bank of Sicily together and said we were two princes there to deposit our treasure, which made all the clerks laugh.

She had raven hair, fairy-tale hair. She was beautiful until her dying day. Every year, even after the cancer began to swallow her, she was invited to march in the Columbus Day parade. She was so devout that I often felt jealous of the statue of the infant Jesus on her mantel, the way other children my age resented their baby brothers and sisters. My nonna prayed a rosary for world peace every morning, and if I interrupted her she'd throw a pillow at me and tell me to go play jacks with Bobby Muhley.

Bobby was the middle son of our Black neighbors and my best friend. Our fathers had been good friends, and after the fire the Muhleys often watched me while my grandmother was working. That sort of mixing was very common in South Omaha. "You two are like puppies with a feather duster," said Bobby's mother. When my nonna died of cancer of the bone in 1907, I packed up my memory of our friendship and took it with me.

The Guardian I was sent to live with after my grandmother's death had a kind, bespectacled son, Giancarlo, who reminded me of Bobby Muhley. He was two grades above me in school, very studious and serious and then teasing and playful when we were home alone. He was a polio survivor and walked with a cane, and his slow tapping up the stairs made my heart gallop. His kindness kept me alive. It must have skipped a generation, because his mother was one of the cruelest people I have ever known.

The Guardian was a neighbor of ours, the church secretary at St. Philomena's. She was a stranger to me, someone who I recognized from the church pews but I barely knew. I'm not sure how it was decided that I should go to live with her, but I know it was not her idea. Perhaps Father Alfredo told her to take me in; he was always encouraging our congregation to think of earthly charity as an investment in heavenly treasures. Perhaps he convinced her that a foster daughter would be a kind of savings bond, one with eternal returns. If that is indeed what happened, the Guardian quickly lost patience with my term to maturity. "Another mouth to feed and another body to clothe! Why did God send you to me? How will we live, Toni?" If something sounded like a question, it was only another instruction in how to think and what to feel, intoned with a lilt.

When she railed at me, I looked up at the Guardian and put a spell on myself. I stared past her at the black oak reaching its strong arms toward me.

Be like that tree.

Stay dark. Go blank.

My true self huddled behind my maze of bones, peering through my eyeholes. A squirrel watched me from a hollow in the oak. The animal-to-animal gaze, I did not break. Talk floated around me, above me, about me, but I did not crack a smile. The Guardian's fury leapt as if I'd doused it with kerosene. Still I held my tongue. *Here is something*, I thought. *Here is power.*

She slapped me, and this only confirmed my sense that I'd found a magic trick. A way to retreat beyond her reach. I felt the color spreading across my face. Inwardly I smiled. Outwardly my face stayed as indomitably still as the oak.

The Guardian fed me scraps. She had barely enough to fry up for her real children, she said. Giancarlo would sneak me food off his plate—he once saved me the best cut of his birthday meal, veal scaloppine. He did remember Sicily, and he said he would have given his pinkie finger for fettuccine and clams. For scallops with a squeeze of lemon. For fresh swordfish with a crust of ocean salt. He was home-sick for the Mediterranean at night. He told me about the waves swallowing the waves, and with a sweaty finger he'd trace an ocean on my naked back.

Giancarlo and I kept each other company on the roof of the house, and I was grateful to be under the stars. I was strong enough to pull him out of the window, hooking my arms under his arms. Love gave me powers. I had never felt so much at once—a longing to be swept away and tightly held, filled up and erased. I had been evicted from my childhood overnight and lost the one person who was everything to me. Nonna would have disapproved of my near nakedness on a rooftop in Little Sicily, but she would have liked Giancarlo. He wrote songs for me, strumming on his father's guitar with the same earnest zeal I recognized from his lovemaking. (Poor guitar! I sometimes stared, with sympathy, at the shocked hole in its center.)

Giancarlo and I made love all summer, and I had a few narrow escapes, startling awake beside him just before dawn and sprinting down the long hall. I slept on an itchy mattress in the pantry, where he often visited me.

After Nonna died, I lost my faith that anything had weight. Giancarlo's arms around my waist settled me back into myself. At first, I had sex with Giancarlo to earn a place in his bed. I never spent a full night there, but for an hour afterward I would lie with my head on his chest, pressed against the solid warmth of his long body. The clumsy roughness of sex was the price I paid for the tenderness that followed. Then one July night, to my astonishment, something clicked into place: he slid his hands under my hips and rolled me on top of him, in a flash of bold inspiration, and I gasped at the waves of heat that rose inside me, pleating open and shut. He covered my mouth with his hand, panicked at the sounds I was making. Surrender was by that point very familiar to me—I had learned to go limp when I was attacked, to play dead until a threat moved off. But I had never surrendered to such obliterating pleasure. When it was finished with me, I wanted to fall back on the pillows and sleep for a hundred years. Giancarlo, to my surprise, was leaning over me, staring down with concern. "Did you enjoy that?" he asked me hopefully, and when I could speak I laughed in his face. *"What do you think?"* His kindness often made me cruel, which seems unforgivable now. I loved him. I lived in fear that the spell would break. I didn't know how to accept a love like that. I don't.

Don't leave me is what I felt. But what I said out loud must have given him the opposite impression: "Get off of me, would you? You're crushing me, Giancarlo!"

In October, I noticed a new moodiness, and a ravenous hunger for bread. I ate an entire double-crust pie that I baked for myself while the Guardian and her family were away visiting a sick cousin. I followed this up with a four-egg omelet that I salted until it tasted like the ocean. A robin watched me from the sill, cocking its sleek head as I licked salt from the webbing of my palms. The Guardian returned to find me in the pantry, retching on all fours. She knew that I was pregnant before I did. She told me a lie to get me to go with her to the courthouse. I had thought she needed a witness to notarize bank documents. Standing beside her, smiling through my confusion, I listened as she announced to the courtroom that I was pregnant. She did not stop there. She told them that I was an ungrateful whore, a little witch, and that she rued the day she agreed to offer me shelter.

At her urging, Judge Hoffmann sentenced me to a year's confinement at Milford. Did you know, Son, that in Nebraska it is a crime to have a baby out of wedlock? I do not understand how it falls within the power of the government to determine if a child is legitimate or illegitimate.

"You do not wish to assist in the rearing of your grandchild, Mrs. Bianchi?" Judge Hoffmann had asked her mildly, his eyes such a crystal blue they looked almost white. They rolled around the plastered walls of the courtroom like slow marbles, very gradually moving from the Guardian's anguished, rouged face to my new belly. Our situation seemed to amuse him.

"My son is not the father. She may have twenty boyfriends for all I know. I refuse to support this girl and her baby while my own children go hungry. Pass this curse on to someone else, Your Honor."

I did not say a word. I wished she'd given me a chance to tell Giancarlo the news myself. I was still dizzy from the realization that I was pregnant with a baby, our baby.

At the Home, everyone gossiped in the same room. "Who put it in you?" was a common question in our dormitory, as you might imagine. I learned to keep my love story a secret. It was a lucky story, luck

I did nothing to deserve, and I did not want to cause anyone pain by sharing it. My baby's conception happened on a rooftop sometime in late summer while I rode the moaning boy beneath me in the trance of my pleasure. I wanted my baby and I loved his father. Happiness threatens people, no different than horror.

Section II

The Counterfeiters

The RA Photographer, Cleo Allfrey

CLEO ALLFREY'S TRAVEL STATEMENT FOR
THE RESETTLEMENT ADMINISTRATION HISTORICAL SECTION

April 15, 1935: Left Washington, D.C.
April 15, 1935: Arrived Johnstown, Pa.

April 17, 1935: Left Johnstown, Pa.
April 18, 1935: Arrived Blairsville, Pa.

April 18, 1935: Left Blairsville, Pa.
April 19, 1935: Arrived Chicago, Ill.

April 19, 1935: Left Chicago, Ill.
April 21, 1935: Arrived Omaha, Neb.

April 21, 1935: Left Omaha, Neb.
April 21, 1935: Arrived Kearney, Neb.

April 22, 1935: Departed Kearney, Neb.
April 22, 1935: Arrived Uz, Neb.

⚌

Dear Miss Allfrey,

I am pleased to hear you have reached Nebraska. We were quite concerned about you, thinking that perhaps you had been waylaid and were sleeping in a ditch someplace.

If you can do it without too much extra effort, would you take a few shots of everyday farm life and activities? Show us how, for instance, dryland farming is accomplished west of the hundredth meridian. I think Dr. Tugwell would be very appreciative of photographs of this sort to be used as illustrative material for some things the Department of Agriculture is working on.

Enclosed is a check. Please do not be too dismayed as to the amount. Our budget is in a sorry state. Unfortunately, our project is an expensive one, and I am unable to send more at this time.

Sincerely,
Roy E. Stryker

⸙

MEMO: TO ALL RA PHOTOGRAPHERS

Roy E. Stryker
General Notes for Pictures Needed for Files

SMALL TOWNS
- Stores
  - *Outside views*
    - cars and horses and
    - buggies (hitching racks)
  - *Inside views*
    - goods on shelves
    - people buying
    - people coming out of store with purchases
    - farm machinery displays
- Churches
  - *on Sunday, if possible*
- Movies
- Men loafing under trees
- Local baseball games

- Players
- Spectators
- "The Vacant Lot"
- Main Street
- "Court Day"
- Children at play (dogs)

RURAL

- Homes
- Barns
  - *representative types*
- Fences
  - *all types—rail*
  - *stone*

SPRING

- Fitting ground for planting, plowing, and harrowing
- Planting
- Trees in bud and in blossom
- New-plowed earth (early morning or late afternoon)
  - *show* "texture." *Get the feel of* "good earth" *into the picture.*
- Clothes airing on the line
- Store windows—spring clothes
- Garden equipment
- Seed stores—"plants and shrubs for sale"

WEATHER

- We need more pictures taken to get the feeling of "weather"—rain, mist and fog, snow, wind. A few *very good* cloud pictures will be acceptable.

GENERAL

- The country—show photographically, if possible, the nature of the land.

  Drop me a line as to where you are, the progress you are making, and when you are coming back.

Sincerely,
Roy E. Stryker

⚜

Dear Allfrey,

Where are the negatives for the Nebraska pictures? We are about out of prints on this material. Will we be able to get them or will we have to wait until your return?

I know you are tired of hearing me say this, but let me warn you that you must push to get your pictures done because no one knows how long we will be holding forth here. Get everything you can in as short a time as is commensurate with good work— the bureaucrat speaking. I know you artistic souls hate to hear me ranting on about quantity production.

You apologize for the "ghostliness" of your recent work. Rothstein and Evans have made work at the height of summer, and they have produced negatives that show not the least sign of deterioration. Are you sure it isn't the *developing*, rather than the heat?

Sincerely,
Roy E. Stryker

⚜

Dear Roy,

You will notice that two of the five boxes I am sending you are marked UZ, NEBRASKA. I have decided to remain in this town to continue to document an inexplicable occurrence.

Yours truly,
C. Allfrey

The Prairie Witch

The pounding grew louder, shaking the door in its frame. I never intended to put the girl in danger, Son. Once she was hidden in the closet, I hitched a smile to my face. Hands trembling, I opened the door onto an unsmiling John Boyet.

"Hello, Boyet. How is Atha? How are your girls?"

"See for yourself." He pointed to the window. "They are waiting outside in that jalopy loaded with everything the bank didn't auction off." I stood and did as he'd commanded, aware of Dell's eyes on my back. The Boyets' truck sat in the depleted shade of Main Street's lone remaining aspen. The truck looked leprous, its chassis flaking rust. Mrs. Boyet stared down at something in the passenger seat—perhaps just her empty lap. Their blond children sat listlessly among the furniture, waiting for their father's return. I was very afraid now. Boyet had been a faithful customer for twelve years, a man who came to see me once or twice a month.

"We are leaving for Sacramento and I won't go without my deposits. I know you've been avoiding me."

Boyet had aged about a decade since I last saw him, and lost thirty-odd pounds. His once-friendly jowls were pared back into a skeletal grimace. I made a slow show of polishing the earhorn, staring down at my own frightened eyes reflected on the wavy plates. *Don't look up,* I willed John Boyet. The girl's dirty white sneakers showed underneath the closet door. For ages I'd been meaning to shim the bottom hinge. Out of plumb for a decade, it was now swinging slowly open—

Dell's fingers caught it, held it shut. I could see her knuckles popping in the seam between door and wall. Boyet began to pace around me. He waved his arms angrily, as if trying to rouse some sound from the silent room. For a moment I closed my eyes and saw John Boyet as a symphony conductor in an empty pit, abandoned by his orchestra.

"You got that damn thing brighter than a hubcap. My kids are waiting in this heat. Let's get on with it."

He had a fistful of yellowing deposit slips.

Fifteen years of visits, dating back to my earliest days in Uz.

I had nothing to return to this lean, hungry man.

For the first time, I met John Boyet's eyes. I saw my terror magnified. No one who has lived an hour without a deposit feels entirely certain they want it back. Human spines curve under the weight of what a body remembers. Ask anyone returning from a war, or a hospital, or the haystack that hid a first kiss with a sweetheart. Gold is heavier than lead, Son. Even the best memories can warp a man's gait, throw a spine out of alignment. Did Boyet truly want to shoulder his deposit again, whatever it was? He seemed to be reassessing.

"Mr. Boyet," I said. "If you're having second thoughts, you can always make an appointment with me next year. Drive back to Uz from California . . ."

"All right," he sighed. "Let's get this done." Boyet's voice rattled into the drum: "Two, two, one, nine . . ."

He sat opposite my chair with his ear to the receiver. I faced the open funnel and tried to enter my trance. *Sink*, I commanded myself. *Go blank*. I knew I was empty. The only escape I could imagine was a trance—tunneling down, down, down, leaving this room. I needed to escape the pressure of the lengthening silence, Boyet's bulk groaning on the chair beside me, his breath growing more shallow with each clock tick. Ordinarily, at this juncture, I would leave my body. Kettle taught me how to time my blackouts to the patterning of air inside the earhorn; how to return to consciousness once a secret had settled deep into my body. Blinking up out of the trance felt no different than awakening after sleep, but it took me a calendar year before I could time my disappearance and my return to a customer's voice. Sometimes, as a younger witch, I bobbed back too early, and heard pieces of things I would have preferred to unknow. When this happened my first customers paused midstory, shocked to see that I was awake. I told them—"The transfer failed"—and refunded their money.

During a withdrawal, the process reverses itself. My customers read their deposit slips backward, and I regurgitate their memories. For the duration of the withdrawal, I disappear into my trance. From what I'm told, I speak in a sort of queer, mechanical rumble, an octave lower than my natural register. Into the echoing green funnel, I repeat—verbatim, as if possessed—whatever they originally deposited in me. Everything returns to them at once, or so my customers report. Not only the events, but the envelope of time that surrounds them. A week before Black Sunday, when I was still solvent and taking my trances for granted, Daisy O'Grady came to withdraw her September 4, 1929, to April 2, 1935, deposits. She was closing her account, leaving Uz forever. It was her first withdrawal from a Vault, and the experience had rattled her. "Your eyes rolled back, and you started chanting words at me," Daisy told me. "Sparks showered up and down the length of my spine, and suddenly *I felt it all again*—my favorite night on earth—the gentle night rain and the sensation of his fingers tracing my lips, the taste of our mouths and the dark red sumac all around us—oh, it remembers me too—"

What amazed her, she said, was how little the words I spoke into the emerald funnel had to do with the worlds that surfaced inside her body. "Like music, that way," breathed Daisy, clutching her sides and swaying. I could almost imagine what she meant. There are certain Catholic hymns that taste like gold in the back of my mouth and summon every Sunday of childhood. Whistles of a certain pitch release the scent of hay and grass, a lifetime of harvests. A few bars of "Rose of No Man's Land" can plunge me back into wartime. There is a lullaby I hum that resurrects our first hour together, Son.

Before my collapse, John Boyet would have recited the number on his deposit slip and listened while my body coughed up his secrets. I would have been lost to myself until Boyet shook my shoulder and said, "Wake up, lady. We're finished."

Nothing was ordinary about this withdrawal. John Boyet tapped his foot impatiently, and I was right there, caged in my body, to feel his anger mounting. I could hear his breaths coming fast and jumpy. *Sink. Sink. Escape.* I was furious with myself. Angrier even than Boyet.

My old magic had abandoned me. It felt as if my mind was repelled by the new buoyancy, the hideous lightness. A very shallow dark lay between us.

I began to plan my escape. I would have to slip past Boyet before he could muscle me downstairs. If he attacked me, I hoped the girl was smart enough to stay hidden.

I peeked once and saw Boyet staring expectantly at me down the long flaring tube. He was close enough to kiss my left cheek, or stick a knife in my neck.

"Two, two, one, nine . . ." he tried again, enunciating thickly, like someone twisting a key in a sticky ignition. I closed my eyes and waited with less and less hope, picturing a bucket plunging down the throat of a well.

"Goddamn you, *give it back*—"

John Boyet's large hands closed around my neck.

To my horror, I was awake.

The Prairie Witch's Apprentice, Asphodel Oletsky

I crouched in the closet, the witch's stiff dresses tickling my face. Through the slats in the door, I could see John Boyet choking her. She gasped for air, writhing terribly. Her panicked eyes bulged wide, staring right at me.

Two pieces of luck: John Boyet was not a particularly bright man, and I have an ear for gossip. I'd spent plenty of time on the Party Line; I knew too much about this town. All you had to do was chew some gum under one of Uz's new streetlights and you'd overhear something scandalous. Kids talk, farmers talk, everybody talks.

Three years ago, John Boyet had a love affair with Annelise Roethke. Annelise died of dust pneumonia last spring, and I went to the funeral with Thelma and a few other girls from Poultry & Eggs. Thelma had whispered to me throughout the service at St. Agnieszka, for some reason urgently needing me to know every last fact about her aunt Annelise's life. I'd felt useful and useless all at once, like the damp tissue catching the overflow from Thelma's raw pink eyes and nose. I couldn't bring her aunt back, but I could imagine a living woman with her. Later on the Party Line, I'd learned that Mr. Roethke not only *knew* about his wife's lover but claimed to feel *grateful* to John Boyet—"One less chore on my list!" he was rumored to have shouted when he found them in bed.

I am still not sure what possessed me to try it. Maybe all the hours I spent eavesdropping on the Party Line, waiting for ghostly speech to break through the static. My voice startled me as it flew out of my mouth—it seemed to come from somewhere else, someone other than myself. Like one of the voices that came bellowing over the wire:

"JOHN BOYET," I boomed from the closet. "THIS IS THE GHOST OF YOUR LOVER, ANNELISE. I HAVE BEEN WAIT-ING FOR YOU TO COME FOR ME—"

You could hear the strain in my voice, which I flatter myself to say worked pretty well for a ghost.

"JOHN BOOOOYEEEET. TAKE ME WITH YOU TO CALI-FORNIA. DO YOU REMEMBER THE NIGHT WHEN YOU FIRST SAID THE WORDS 'I LOVE YOU'?"

"Stop!" he shrieked, backing away from the Antidote and lifting his hands to his ears. "Enough!"

To my wonderment, tears began rolling down his cheeks. He looked wildly around the room—as if truly expecting to see a noon-day ghost.

"Forgive me, my dear. There is no room in my life for you now. I made a mistake . . ."

We were hearing, I later realized, a reprisal of their final conversa-tion. Excuses and apologies, blathering fear. A muscle kept jerking the corner of Boyet's mouth toward his left cheek, as if he were con-trolled by a one-handed puppeteer.

"I will treasure our nights together. But don't follow me!"

And with that, he fled Room 11. The Antidote was staring with joke-store eyes in my direction—apoplectic or speechless with grat-itude, it was hard to say. Once Boyet was gone, I dropped to the ground, sending the witch's starchy dresses down with me. My heart was going as if I'd just run wind sprints for Coach, and I felt light-headed when I stood.

We watched John Boyet racing into the gray bar of daylight below the boardinghouse window. He sprinted for the truck parked outside the Five & Dime, clapping a hand to the back of his neck. Could you outrun a ghost? Boyet was trying his damnedest. His hat flew off as he jumped into the blue truck and roared off in an envelope of orangey dust. The Antidote exhaled beside me. Even before she turned from the window, I could feel her smiling.

"You are the limit, Miss Oletsky."

Her brow touched the glass, and I could see the darkening marks he'd left around her neck. I felt a smile spilling messily all over my face. Boyet's hat was still sitting in the road.

"Boyet won't forget this visit, will he?"

Laughter brimmed in the witch's voice, lifting it a full octave. I felt a spike of game-day joy.

"Mama"—I laughed—"he believed us!"

Mama. All my happiness shrank into a tight bud of shame. It was a traitor's mistake. I was shocked to be the person who had made it.

"I'm sorry," I said. "I got confused, just for a moment."

My apology was meant for my mother. But the Antidote intercepted it.

"You can be on my payroll, Asphodel Oletsky. But you must never call me that again."

"Oh, trust me, Boss. I never will."

Her happiness dried up as abruptly as it had brimmed into the room. She looked up at me with the same huge, doomed eyes as those of the Herefords grazing on sand, staring into the future where they are meat and leather. "You have my gratitude, Miss Oletsky. You scared Boyet off, and you likely saved my skin." She tapped at her earhorn, sounding a queer hollow note. "But what am I going to do the next time a man demands his savings? Markets crash. The same has happened to me. I have nothing to return to anyone."

Then the Antidote explained her predicament to me. Her "bankruptcy." Every deposit had vanished from her body on Black Sunday "as if the whirlwind itself tore them free of me." What I pictured for some reason was not that howling cloud of dust but the stained perforated floor of the Uz abattoir. What happened to the gallons of blood that flowed through those grates?

"Well, there must be a way to get back what you lost. Sometimes I forget entire years with my mother, and they come back to me at the oddest times . . ."

The witch erupted into a coughing fit. Even after I got her a full glass of water, her voice was still a thorny sort of whisper.

"No, Miss Oletsky. It's nothing like your sort of forgetting. Maybe you lose sight of your mother for a day or a week, but she'll circle back into your awareness. I am not suffering from foggy memory. My crash is not a temporary eclipse."

The witch's voice was a steady rumble, and only her darting eyes looked agitated.

"How could I forget what I never knew in the first place?"

Her voice did not lift a decibel. But I heard the anger pounding underneath it.

"I advertise myself as a Vault for a reason," she said. "Those deposits sat inside me like jewelry in a box. Rubies and rocks are all the same to a box. I felt a heaviness, and now I feel its absence. There is nothing for me to remember—not in the way you mean."

Customers had been showing up day and night, she said. People wanted to withdraw their secrets before they left Uz. Although many, I pointed out, seemed to leave without a backward glance. I was thinking of Coach speeding off in plumes of dust.

"Why don't you leave, too? Take the train east, where no one knows you are a prairie witch . . ."

She knuckled into the dough of her cheeks. Was she trying to keep the words in or out?

"No, girl. I won't run again," she said. "I have lived half my life here, waiting to be found by someone. I've planted clues for him throughout the state. Maps that lead to Uz. I need to be here to greet him when he comes."

This was a surprise. I had never met anyone who seemed *less* anchored to this place than the witch—and that's saying something in a twenty-five-year-old town.

"Who are you expecting?" Was it some old flame? Another Vault? A customer?

She drew a long breath. As if she'd forgotten how much air conversation requires, the way I sometimes flood the Spider's tank with fuel. It was clear that she wasn't going to answer me. I started to get angry and then I noticed the web of lines around her sad eyes. The Antidote has been waiting for this person to find her in Uz for longer than I've been alive.

"Listen, I won't let anybody hurt you," I said. Tenderness rushed into my voice like blood to a cut. It surprised us both.

"Well thank you, Captain. I don't want you hurt either. You picked a very bad time to apprentice yourself to me."

She stared out the window, where across the street a group of churchgoers was pouring into the little cemetery. Another child had died from silicosis, a late arrival to the Red Cross tent in Hastings.

"And that's what you want? To be my apprentice?"

I had a feeling like my feet leaving the ground to sink a basket. It was my destiny to help her. She handed me the earhorn.

"I couldn't enter a trance with Boyet. I don't know if I can still take deposits."

"What do you want me to help with?"

"An experiment. I need to know if the power has gone out of me completely—"

She handed me a deposit slip and settled back on her chair, fixing the earhorn against the hooks that held it to the wall and leaning her ear against the receiver. Her posture made me think of a woman on a train about to nod off. My heart sped up as her eyes fluttered shut.

"You want me to deposit something inside you?"

"I want you to try."

I almost screamed *no*. You would think the witch had just asked me to cut off my pinkie finger and hand it over. I did not want to wring a drop of myself into that earhorn. I took a deep breath and turned to face her. Forced myself to cross the room to her chair. She was my teacher, I reminded myself. I wanted to become a prairie witch and this was today's lesson.

"All right," I said. "Give me a minute to collect my thoughts."

I decided to tell her about the shape of Coach's jalopy as it drove off, the way the sputtering columns of dust and the flashing fins had made it look like a sea serpent winding its way back to the ocean. I could live a long life without needing to reminisce about Coach's exit. Even now, it hurt me to recall it.

"Five, three, nine, one . . ." I read the numbers on my slip into the earhorn, my cheeks and my forehead burning. "After the black blizzard, our coach abandoned us . . ."

I felt the witch struggling to put herself under—I could see it, in her flaring nostrils and the lines of tension in her neck and shoulders. She was wide awake when I began to speak. It was the strangest sensation, to tell a story to this earhorn—no sooner did I utter a word than I forgot what I'd only just said. It felt like crossing a river and looking back to discover the bridge I'd been standing on had vanished. I spoke in a torrent without considering what I was saying, and once I'd begun, I felt like a hooked fish getting jerked along. Then the story released me and I was done. Now I understood why Valeria had suggested that I make a deposit. A beautiful spaciousness had replaced—what? I did not care a bit that it was gone. There was no shape to the blankness in my head, just a pleasant ongoing roaring. It reminded me of my single visit to the dentist in Hastings. He'd pulled a diseased tooth, and the second it was gone all the pain was snuffed. I saw that I had a choice—I could make myself crazy trying to figure out what I'd just surrendered to the Antidote. I could read the slip backward and retrieve my deposit. Slide that rotten tooth back into my mouth. Or I could enjoy my freedom from it. Whatever "it" was.

The Antidote opened her eyes. "I've never been awake for a transfer before. I didn't know it was possible to receive one without entering a trance. I heard every word you said, Miss Oletsky. But I also feel the weight of your memory. It's inside me now, isn't it? Sinking and settling—"

The witch touched the hollow of her throat and drew a line to her navel. Her heavy blue skirt bunched around her, covering the chair legs. Yellow rickrack ran around the hemline like a fence of lightning. Her eyes swept my face. "It hurts me to know something you don't."

I smiled at her, the blood rushing to my head as I stood. I had been afraid to make the deposit—I remembered that. But I had no regrets on this side of the transfer. I felt so light on the balls of my feet.

"It worked, Boss," I said. "I remember making a deposit, and nothing after that."

"Read your slip backward. Let's see if I can return your memory to you."

My heart sank—I did not want it back. Why could we not continue practicing deposits? My unburdening was only just beginning. I lifted my arms and lowered them, delighted by the new roominess inside me—under my ribs, in my throat and my chest.

But I did what she asked. Coach always reminded us that the best players take direction. I read the slip backward and held the receiver to my ear. Then I waited while the Antidote's lips perched above the funnel. Silence seemed to slosh around the room. I'd only been her apprentice for a day, and even I could tell that something was going awry. The Antidote put her head in her hands and made a choking sound low in her throat, as if she were coughing up a bone. Then she lifted her face to meet my eyes, and I saw that she was terrified.

"Dell, I still can't enter my trance. It's lodged in me, your memory." With open eyes, facing me on the chair, she described the day Coach had abandoned us. She used some phrases that I recognized as mine, and many of her own. It was nothing like the sorcerous withdrawals I'd heard about—she told me what had happened in her ordinary voice, full of holes and stammerings. It reminded me of Mama, on certain threadbare mornings, when she woke up still drunk, unsure of how she'd gotten home, the events of our long night in town barely in her mind. It wasn't magic, or not the kind I'd hoped to learn from the witch. But it was enough to send Coach's car speeding back into me.

"Enough," I said. "He's back." But I had to squint to see him behind the windshield, and as I did so I knew that I was imagining something, not remembering it. The Antidote had given me a seed packet of words, and I was using them to grow a picture of these scenes I had forgotten. A gap remained between what I'd once known and what I knew again.

"That's not how a withdrawal is supposed to feel. That was just a clumsy story. What am I going to do when men like Boyet come, Dell, and I can't enter my trance?"

With a stricken face, the witch returned her earhorn to the wall. She remained there, staring at it, and I guessed from her shoulders that she was crying. Her long fingers began kneading her scalp, her hair tumbling free of its ribbon. Silver hairs flashed like wires through the coarse black mass of it.

"I'm done for," she said in a soft voice.

"You can still receive a deposit. There is that."

"Yes. For all the good it does me. Who's going to drop gold coins into a hole?"

"Nobody *knows* that you lost their deposits," I told my boss. "And nobody has to."

I've never once cheated at basketball—I don't call cheap fouls, I don't fudge the lines. But I have excellent credentials as a liar. I used to lie for my mother on a near-daily basis, inventing reasons for her absences and delinquencies and failures to pay our promissory notes at J.J.'s Groceries. I sweet-talked J.J.'s son into giving my mother a longer line of credit. I lied to my teachers and my doctors, persuading them not to investigate my tardiness and—during a short but unforgettably bad stretch where we lived with her nastiest boyfriend—apple green bruises. I lied to conceal my unhappiness from my mother and my happiness also; I made up my lies out of caring and spite, out of everything in me. I still can't hem a pair of pants, but I can tailor a lie for anybody's figure.

"These people don't remember what they deposited inside you! You can tell them *anything*. Make something up when they come to withdraw a memory."

The Antidote peered at me over her reading spectacles. She squinted like she was trying to draw something into focus. My boss was a powerful witch, but I saw that spending half her life in a blackout trance had stunted her imagination.

"We both know what's happening in this country. The more people who leave their sections, the more the land blows. No ground cover and more dirt cyclones and these shallow towns disappear with the topsoil. Why not plant new memories inside your customers? Something to hold them against the drought and this depression?"

The more I talked, the more I began to believe it. This was exactly what the CCC men were doing on the vacant land west of the depot, I noted. Planting saplings as windbreaks. Seeding cover crops. We could do that same work *inside of people*. We wouldn't be lying to hurt anyone. No—we'd be dropping anchors inside them. Weighting them down, so they did not blow off. We could be heroes and make a healthy profit too. We could save the whole town.

"That seems a little grandiose, girl. I would be thrilled if I could save my skin."

The Antidote was staring out the window, to where a line of customers had gathered outside the Jentleman, chatting and smoking, waiting for the doors to open. "We can try it," she said at last. "But I don't expect it to work."

❧❦

On Tuesday, Wilma Wheeler arrived for her noon appointment, coming directly from church in her green silk dress; I hid in the closet. "I've come to retrieve whatever I told you on March 3, 1927," she said to the Antidote. "I don't know why, but I can't leave Uz without it."

What had Mrs. Wheeler deposited in 1927? I had my conjectures, given what I'd learned from our neighbors' chatter on the Party Line. This was Wilma the "Wheat Queen," whose last crop had gotten dusted out, who had been a wild success during the grain boom a decade earlier, when she had been a millionaire on paper. Her riches came from buying up the sections of two Black homesteaders' adjacent land for a fraction of their value after the Bank of the Prairie foreclosed on them. It was all perfectly legal. Our Black neighbors were the first to lose their farms. The loan officers rejected their applications. They were denied the line of credit that saved my uncle from foreclosure. "A crying shame," I heard people complain on the Party Line.

Wilma reached under her dress and unpinned a ten-dollar bill from her slip.

"I'd say it's been nice knowing you, but we really never got the chance to know each other, did we?"

"In our next life, maybe." The Antidote smiled at Wilma. "Will you hold the earhorn up to my lips?"

The Antidote turned out to be a better actress than I would have guessed. She'd memorized the memory I'd written for Wilma. She recited it in an underwater monotone, as if she were floating somewhere leagues away, with such a slow-bubbling voice that I almost believed she was unaware of what she was saying.

"Two, two, one, eight . . ."

Wilma held the earhorn to the Antidote's lips like a trumpet. I watched from the closet, astonished, as her eyes rolled back to their whites and her head slumped forward on her neck. But her lips, I saw, were beginning to mumble. Wilma leaned closer to the green funnel, her stockinged knees on the floorboards. The Antidote's voice sounded closer to water than speech. Like a creek after a downpour, she flumed into the speaker:

"When you were sixteen years old, you fell from the hayloft and had a vision of an angel. She told you that you were destined for greatness and riches, to take heart and persevere . . ."

I confess that I thrilled to hear the words I'd written in my boss's mouth. Was the angel part a little corny? It seemed like the sort of thing Wilma might deposit in a Vault. You wouldn't want to dull the light of your angelic visitation by reminiscing about it too often. It's easy to guess what someone might like to believe about herself.

Wilma's back straightened as she stood, her heavy black purse swinging on her shoulder. She was smiling at the Antidote with relief. "So *that's* all it was—an angel telling me I'm wonderful? And here I was thinking, *Wilma! Today's Judgment Day for you, old girl . . .* "

She was laughing like hard rain, releasing her terror.

"Goodness! I had forgotten all about that. Yes, I remember it vividly now. It's all coming back to me. It was the best day of my life!"

"Now, Mrs. Wheeler," said the Antidote, bricked up behind her smile. "You know the rules. It's your secret from here on out. I don't need to know about it. Please keep the angel to yourself."

I was not like the Antidote. I couldn't make a man forget. But I could invent a memory as easily as Uncle Sam prints money. We had all been fooled by the history exams, by the scowling teacher, Jan Castle, who seemed four hundred years old herself. By the framed surveyor's maps in the Grange Hall and the tintype portraits of the Founding Families.

The past was not so sacrosanct, I discovered. You could simply make more up.

⊣⊱⊢

On Thursday, two hours before sunset, I met my teammates on the secret court. I was still soaring from a week of victories in the witch's closet, still combing through the gossip I'd collected from the Party Line and dreaming up new counterfeits. It took real effort for me to come back to earth and attempt to be a coach. On my whistle, the remaining Dangers fell into a warm-up drill. Valeria, Pazi, Dagmara, Thelma, Ellda, Nell, and myself. Each girl looked as if she'd just emerged from a lake—hair slicked back, eyes streaming water. Dust clawed moisture out of everything, including our bodies. We hadn't played indoors since they closed the school and locked up the gym.

The hot sun beat down on us, interrupted by the wind that tunneled through our formation. We played like a team of ghosts. I felt rather than saw the others as we ran. The court was all but invisible through the slits of my eyes, but I could always hit a cutter, find Pazi open under the hoop.

I was looking forward to our championship game in Red Willow. I still feel like a foreigner in this town. But when we traveled far enough to become strangers to everyone we met—forty miles, in this case—when we won a game on our rivals' court, surrounded by hostile faces, at last I could pivot and almost believe it was waiting for me: home.

I'm not sure how the fight started, or how it escalated so fast. We had been joking during the water break, innocently enough. Teasing Thelma about her Raggedy Ann haircut. Jealous of her brothers' cool necks in the heat, she'd cut her hair above her ears, wound up with a clown's wig of two-inch curls.

"You look like an electrocuted lamb!" Val said with a laugh, tousling her head. Thelma swatted her away. *They are going to scrap*, I thought. But I was wrong. Instead of shoving Thelma back, Val shot me a pained look, as if I was the one she'd insulted. Then the whole team was looking at me.

"Captain. I am sorry about what happened," said Thelma, her voice raw with feeling.

I'd thought she was apologizing for her haircut.

"It suits you," I lied. "And it'll grow back."

"The electrocution—in Lincoln—we heard it didn't work."

Now Val spoke up. "We wanted to check on you. Only nobody was sure what to ask. None of us knew how to say what we felt."

"What we feel," Nell corrected. She was watching something happen in the sky over my shoulder. When I turned, I saw tiny birds on the horizon. Swarming like our defense.

"My family prays that justice will be swiftly done," said Dagmara. "The photograph of the melted helmet in the newspaper gave my little brothers nightmares."

Dagmara was even taller than Valeria, and far too thin that spring for even her narrow frame. Coach used to sneak her cheese and ham rolls at halftime. Her red dust mask and her skinny legs made her look like one of the thousand cranes that filled the sky over the

Platte. Now she loomed over me. Talons sunken in the dust, wings folded. Watching me with a terrible curiosity. Did they want me to feel angry that Dew had lived? Did they think I could feel worse than I already did?

"At least the case is closed," said Ellda in her porcelain voice. "Soon justice will be served."

Whose words were these? They came from the Sheriff, from the newspapers, from my teammates' parents. I pretended not to hear them. Nothing feels closed on my end. Nothing feels just. The hole inside me roars on and on.

"Pray for Dew," I said. "If you feel the need to pray. How does it help me if a stranger dies in a chair?"

"Pray for a mass murderer? That he was never born, or—"

"*Thelma,*" Val hissed. "Shut up."

I wanted my mother. She was like an echo now—everywhere and gone. Valeria crossed the small distance between me and my teammates. She pulled me into a one-armed hug. Others came and closed the circle, as if we were in our pregame huddle. If the afternoon had ended there, it would have been a memory of untrammeled happiness. That moment hums on, holding me inside it. The middle C we made together. But practice continued. We pulled apart, and got back to work.

We played three-on-three, winner stays on. Losing. Winning. Losing. Winning. Dust tinted everything reddish orange. Any human rival was just a proxy for this dust, which didn't keep score, didn't know us, didn't hate us, didn't love us, didn't have a mind to strategize against us. But dust buried everyone, in the end. I ran. Dribble. Pass. Pass. Block. Pass-pass—swish. Pain began to accumulate. By the second hour, we were all feeling it together. Split lip. Bruised left thigh. Throbbing shoulder. Free. Free. Free. I burst out of my skin and became one with them. What word exists to describe that feeling of extinction, expansion? Anybody watching would have seen seven dirty young women, tossing a ball above melting chalk lines. Only we understood what we were doing. The wonderful, terrible stakes of every pass. We were stitching ourselves together. As night descended, we had successfully remade ourselves into a ferocious, panting animal. The Dangers. One team, plural.

The stitching did not hold.

Pazi stole the ball from Thelma and won the game for her team of three with a one-handed hook shot. Every Danger has seen her make this shot a hundred times, although strangers often treat it like a wild accident. Even if she makes the same "lucky" shot four times in a row. Tonight Thelma, still clearly smarting from our teasing, called Pazi a "dirty squaw."

Pazi brought her knife everywhere she went. During breaks at games, she whittled into any surface, autographing seatbacks and floorboards. When Coach yelled at her to be respectful of others' property, she carved a heart onto his harmonica case with her initials in the center. She stared at Thelma for a long moment. Then she opened her pouch and unsheathed the knife.

"Pazi!" Val cried.

She tossed it on the ground.

"I quit," she said. "Defend yourselves."

I ran after her and found her halfway to the main road. Pazi pulled on her dust mask and so did I. She didn't say a word to me, her eyes gazing out. We walked in silence for nearly a mile, the wind dying down and the flattened brush springing up. Now we could hear prairie dogs chirping, some far-off rutting bull. We had nearly reached the road, and I had no idea how to make things right. Without warning, Pazi spun to face me. "Do you know that I am Ponca on my mother's side?"

I shook my head. I knew that Pazi looked European in some ways, Indian in others. I knew from the Party Line that she'd grown up without a mother. Her father was a German baker.

"My grandmother was stolen from her family. She was raised by a Christian family on the Loup River. My aunts and uncles and cousins live in Oklahoma. On the Ponca reservation. One day I'm going to find them."

I nodded. "Thelma didn't mean what she said. She was embarrassed."

"You should all be embarrassed," said Pazi.

Unbeknownst to us, the rest of the team had been walking behind us. Giving us distance—maybe they had a misguided faith that I was patching things up. Setting a bone would have been easier. I had no idea how to repair the harm of Thelma's insult. It ran deeper than words. But health surrounds a wound—that I knew from Coach. Healing is what a living body directs itself to do.

When Pazi realized that we'd been followed, she looked enraged.

"I am sorry, Pazi," said Thelma, tugging at her sleeve.

"Do something, don't just say something," said Pazi, her voice breaking with a desolation that I recognized, and didn't. Sharp anger rose in me, and the edgeless sadness. I was not Pazi, and she was not me. I recognized the pitch of her rage and her heartbreak, but I did not know the first thing about its source.

Thelma's eyes were red, and she had something cradled against her chest—Pazi's knife. She placed it on a rock next to a bewildered skink. Nell tossed Thelma the basketball, which she rolled beside the knife. Ellda had a bouquet of wildflowers that she let fall when she saw Pazi's expression.

"I am sorry, Pazi," Thelma repeated.

But Pazi had tipped her chin skyward.

"Good Lord," said Nell, pointing above the sunset. "Look at the birds."

No sentence I'd invented did as much to bring us back together. They came out of the west. So tiny, so dense. With their sharp little beaks, the birds looked like arrowy sleet. A shower of ancient weaponry. Loosed from the distant quiver of the grain elevator, they shot into the dead orchard. The birds drew us into one held breath. A living cyclone crossed our heads and scattered into a mist of iridescence, winking out like stars at dawn, one by one by one. As we stood openmouthed on the prairie beneath an early moon, our hands searched for one another. I felt the tension hiss out of us, shoulders dropping and eyes releasing tears.

"It's a sign," breathed Ellda. "Is it a sign, Coach?"

We all wanted the starlike birds to be a sign of victory. But I think each of us also harbored some secret wish besides. Some personal interpretation. For me, the suddenness of the thousand birds' disappearance meant that I would soon become a true witch. Perhaps it meant that Valeria was falling in love with me (the spinning flock had left me dizzy; why couldn't that be an omen?). I studied Valeria, wondering what she wanted our sign to mean.

"It means . . ." I tried to imitate Coach's reassuring growl. I stared out at my teammates' expectant, uplifted, dubious faces. "It means if we win the tournament, the dust will stop blowing for good."

Nell and Ellda looked skeptical. Pazi had turned and started to follow the disappearing birds, her eyes fixed on the moon. "We should play as if that's true," Valeria said, jumping in to help me as if this were a game. I nodded, feeling the weight of the sky on my shoulders. It was a useful pressure. Anyone watching in the stands would see some girls from Uz playing a game. But we Dangers would know that the whole future swung in the balance—not just our own, but the fate of everything blue and green, everything living.

Pazi walked back to our circle, peeling blades of dead grass from the ball. I guessed from her face that she didn't agree with my translation of what the birds might mean.

"I'll keep playing with our team. But when I get enough money together, I'm leaving for Oklahoma."

She jumped center, grabbed the ball, and bolted.

❧❧

We call ourselves the Counterfeiters.

Well, I call us that, and my boss does not object.

After that first lie, the Antidote and I became ever more skillful at passing my fakes into people. And it's a good thing, too, because in the weeks following Black Sunday, a panic seized the town. There was a run on the Antidote. Not because people thought she was a failing bank, but because they were fleeing the collapsing town of Uz. Nineteen people signed up for appointments with her in a single day, eager to make their withdrawals and beat feet. The Antidote would have been exposed, maybe even killed, had I not been here to invent shiny new memories for her customers.

Sourdough was Nebraska slang for counterfeit bills. I like to picture our work that way—kneading dough, watching it rise inside of people.

These have been the happiest three weeks I had ever lived, a time of intense labor and creativity and usefulness. I knew better than to share it with anyone, although my teammates noticed a change in me right away. "What's gotten into Captain?" teased Ellda. "Who sugared your water? Or are you in *love*?"

"Oletsky is in love with winning," Valeria said, blocking my shot. I have noticed that my cheeks look plumper in my uncle's mirror. I go to bed exhausted, with barely a hello to my uncle, and wake in a sunny mood after a night without dreams.

I have two lives now. I leave one practice for the other, moving from the Antidote's closet to the secret court at the edge of Uz. The Dangers crushed the Gordon Lady Grouses on our home court, 32–4. We have an Away game in Red Willow later this month that will decide the Region 7 championship. The Antidote is fronting me next month's salary; she is making money hand over fist. So the team will have money for gas and a night at the motor lodge.

When someone comes to *make* a deposit, I hide in the closet. I bring my notebook. My job is to spy on the witch's customers and jot down the secrets they deposit into her earhorn. She doesn't trust her own body any longer, after the collapse. My records are meant to be insurance of a kind. "We have to store their secrets the old-fashioned way, girl," she told me, "on dead trees."

DEPOSITS, 5/2
RECORDED BY A. OLETSKY

I was afraid that O'Neal would call me a coward. And so I picked up the auger and I swung, honest to God I only meant to scare him off—

I am here to deposit the first time I drank a strawberry soda. Mountains of ice and underneath a grainy pink slush, a taste like what I imagined kissing to be. The fizz rose to my brain and I heard God and God said: order a second strawberry soda, Bertie. I never want the memory of that first drink to fade. When I'm an old man and all my senses have dulled, I want to taste my twelfth summer again—

I was there when they moved on her. I didn't join in but I didn't try to stop them. Get me out of that damn field I can't stand to hear her screaming we were all just kids this happened thirty-nine years ago and I am sick and tired of listening to her begging us to stop make it stop take it out of my head some nights the sound gets so loud that I can't hear myself think—

That was the best night of my life, ice-skating under the moon with Theo near the shadows of the elk . . .

I washed his mistress's lingerie alongside my kids' clothes and hung it on the line for everyone to see—

And I don't think what I'm doing is wrong, either. I can't help it. Only I don't want to think about it anymore.

At first, this transcription seemed like more work than it was worth. I proposed inventing new memories for these people when they returned to make a withdrawal. Why not tell them a lie—something I could whip up for her as needed—and save ourselves the trouble of recording these confessions?

The Antidote has a flickery moral sense. It's either painfully bright or totally absent, like the electric light in the Country Jentleman.

"Write down what they say. Record as much as you can. I do not want to lie if it can be helped, girl," she told me.

Graciously I did not laugh in her face. What did she think we were doing in Room 11?

"If you make a peep in there," she said, "I am going to tell my clients that you snuck in without my knowing. I am going to scream and say I've never seen you before in my life."

Being a secretary in a closet is harder than you might think. My body cramps like a hand, dust tickles my nose. Some of these farmers, who can sit idling at the intersection of Main and Second for what feels like hours, speak so fast into the earhorn that I only catch a word or two. Buy an extra quarter hour of my boss's time, I wanted to tell them. Give yourself a chance to breathe.

DEPOSITS, 5/3

—A. OLETSKY

Pollina's death is the moment that my whole life pivots on. In this deep grief I cannot feel my way toward another person . . .

Then her wisdom teeth got impacted and she almost died of an infection. She's better now but we have no money and I know it's not fair but I do blame her. Sometimes I see her lying in that bed with her eyes sliding sideways and I hate her for needing more than my other five kids combined—

They beat me with sticks and bloodied my eye. Beat me worse when the Guardsmen showed up, wanting to get their licks in I guess . . .

And if they could hear me it didn't stop them any—

A ladybug landed on my finger, and that very same hour—

We danced the Tarantella!

—happens and keeps happening—

pretty near broke my heart

After a while the hot rush of the deposits blurred together, coming one after another, as steady as rainfall. Three deposits in a row were gruesome family secrets. Two deposits were like bouquets people wanted to preserve under glass (a first kiss, a last waltz). The final deposit of the day was Dick Schroeder's breathless reminiscence about winning a door prize that broke on the ride home.

When I showed my boss what I'd been able to record, I watched anger flash across her face. The Antidote held up my notebook in front of my nose, as if I might not have realized what a lousy job I'd done.

"Is this legible to you?"

"Most of it."

I was already a natural liar; now I learned to keep a record of the truth. There is no dark magic to what I do in the closet. I am the hidden recordkeeper. With a skinny blue pen, I scribbled as fast as I could—making up my own system of abbreviations, drawing pictures when their words came too fast. Later, I'd spend hours carefully transcribing each new deposit into the line-ruled accounting book, with names and dates and deposit numbers. It's a good thing for these Uzians that the witch is trying to keep honest records for them—to protect them against another collapse. They are lucky she is not actually a blackmailer, as certain gossips claim. Within two days we had accumulated years of dirt on our neighbors. In my first week working as the prairie witch's secretary, I learned more about the people of Uz County than I ever wanted to know.

The Grange Master, Harp Oletsky

We have come to the Grange, where 'tis joyful to meet.
Our friends and companions in unity sweet;
Then Patrons, in joy, come gather around.
Concord and harmony with us be found!
Down with the spite and the hate that estrange.
And long live the peace that we find at the Grange.
                                        —Grange Ode, 1877

D amn, Harp, you sound like a creaky door. Can I offer you some
water?"

"Something a little stronger, Grayson, if you've got it."

The big Welsh rabbit of a spuds farmer held his hands to his
ears, making a face.

"Anything to oil those hinges!"

The Grange used to be called the Order of the Patrons of Husbandry. Before the Civil War, before anyone in this hall was born, the Nebraska State Grange was organized at Grand Island. We Oletskys have been Grangers since our earliest days in America. When the Founding Families came to Uz, our Grange Hall was the first building they broke ground on. When I was a young man, the Grange stood up to monopoly and won—fighting the railroads for fair prices, buying seed and equipment as a cooperative. But our bargaining power has been crushed by this depression. We kept losing members. Three weeks after Black Sunday, our chorus was awfully sparse.

We'd been called in to vote in an Emergency Election, a full six months ahead of the ordinary schedule. Our chapter's former Grange Master had watched his fields torn to confetti. He'd sold his blistered land and left for eastern Oregon, where his wife's cousin had a ranch. At our last meeting, he'd presented us with a plan for Collective Action to Hold the Blowing Soils. Then he himself blew off.

It was a wonder I'd made it to the Grange Hall without crashing into a sand dune. For the third night in a row, I did not sleep a wink. I was at the window again, watching the unnameable color hiss and sparkle up from my fallowland. *Not-sap. Not-flint. Not-frost.* I am overly familiar with the bone color of winterkill. The bludgeoned yellow of wheat that's been cooked by the drought. Those are the colors in which I'd paint my life story. Not this marvelous hue. Wonder is not a comfortable place to reside, I am learning. Not for these old bones. Just before daybreak, I climbed back in bed and pulled the bedspread up to my ears like a kid. I could hear the girl's raspy snores through the wall. Asleep, my niece sounds like an idling tractor. I lit the kerosene lamp and lay in a box of man-made light, rigid in terror on the mattress. I didn't look outside again, but I still couldn't sleep.

This would all be hysterically funny, I realize, if it wasn't happening to me.

By sunup, the whole episode seemed ridiculous. The scarecrow was posted in the wheat field, his straw arms flung wide in their ordinary embrace of another clear blue day. My old mutt, Squint, was padding around out there, maybe chasing mice. A gentle breeze rippled the silver hidden in the leaves of the cottonwoods between the farmhouse and the barn. Adjacent to my green wheat field, the fallow plot was covered in a shallow stubble of clover, the sentinel sunflowers, uncultivated weeds. Every leaf, every hue, I knew how to name. It was a great relief. At 9:00 a.m. I drove in a daze to the Grange Hall in my second-best shirt.

Some men are always late and always apologizing as they burst into a room. When you're late, even your shadow becomes a disturbance. I know this because I'm an early bird, and early birds' nests are continuously rattled by new arrivals. I keep my shadow tucked neatly beneath me, inconveniencing nobody.

"Oh howdy, Harp! Didn't see you there."

I moved through the crowded hall, nodding to the faces that noticed me. People who work the land for hours and hours a day begin to look like brothers and sisters. Hammered flat by the same sun. Our foreheads are furrowed from squinting, our noses scaly and peeling. We churned slowly around the large bare floor, commiserating about the universal luck that is weather.

There are factions, of course: God Has Abandoned Us vs. We Have Abandoned Him. That's a topic of debate at the Grange. It is difficult to order the betrayals in our region, they are so numerous. The hand of Providence feels like a child's fist to me, shaking and flinging toys across a tabletop. A thousand bone-white tractors are scattered like shining jacks across the Plains. The frame houses are turning back into tinder, the old soddies smashed flat as mud pies.

All the banks within a hundred miles of Uz have closed. The Bank of Alliance, the Bank of the Prairie. Gone. Collapsed. Kaput. Although there is the story of a Kearney bank manager who ran away to Brazil, and I'm sure the bosses' bosses still eat well in Washington. I listened to my neighbors' voices bound restlessly around, trying to settle on someone to blame. Scapegoats within proximity of our fists are getting harder to come by.

"Sure, Roosevelt's checks help. But we need rain."

"Even if the rains come, what's to prevent another 'thirty-one? What happens when we grow more than the market can consume . . ."

I remembered the elevators full of unsold grain. I shut my eyes and saw a green snake stuffed with golden wheat, convulsing.

Talk drifted over me:

"Commies are striking at the chicken plant in Loup City. You read about that I'm sure—"

"We owe eleven thousand dollars on our equipment, okay? Now this government fellow has the *gall* to say, you get two thousand for the land, not a penny for the buildings . . ."

"Times haven't been good since Calvin Coolidge."

"Adams *never* strip-lists, the lazy bastard. Twice he's ruined my crops. Then come Sunday he sends over his cross-eyed son-in-law to lecture me on the angle of *my* furrows—"

Dour Eric Rasmussen took the podium, his gray peapod eyes flashing. He introduced the Agenda, "Emergency Election to Aid the

Control of Blowing Soils." He read slowly to us—for several gathered in the Grange are not able to read—from a National Grange bulletin about soil conservation.

Then Eric went off script, complaining at a bellow about the recent run on the town Vault. He had seen the lines outside the Jentleman.

"The one who calls herself The Antidote, known to many of you—"

Hisses went up beside me. Lusty and disgusted whistles. Amazing how naked air can become lewd or sweet depending on who is exhaling it. Someone hooted and said, "And how would *you* know, Rasmussen?"

"People stand outside her door day and night. Retrieving whatever they stored in her and pulling up stakes. The Kaminskis, gone. The Parkers, foreclosed on. The Leones, tractored off their section."

"Good riddance. Parker was a lousy farmer. I have been swallowing his dirt for years."

"Well, I will miss Ludwig. I am surprised to hear he was her customer!"

"Who *isn't*, these nights?"

"All things in moderation. Go once a year at most and be selective in what you tell her. Some of these fools are going twice a week!"

"Every man I know who makes a deposit triples his productivity! She is the only reason anyone can sleep . . ."

"She charges when you put it in, and she charges when you come to take it out again. It don't sit right with me, that bitch making money hand over fist while we are waiting for the AAA checks so we can eat."

I stayed silent and listened to the Grangers' spiking voices. A little robin was trying to get into the high window, disoriented by her reflection in the glass. Tipping my chin, I could see all the dust heaped on the crossbeams from the recent storm. The rafters looked dark and shiny as a beaver's pelt. I wished for wings. I would have liked to find a perch in the tall shadows. My neighbors, I realized, were now talking about my strange fortune.

"I hear it's always good weather for Harp Oletsky these days," said O'Fallon in a picklish voice, walking over to clap a hand on my shoulder.

"Three dusters in a row and somehow not a hair on your head or a stalk of your wheat is harmed. Your folks must be smiling down from heaven!"

"Some luck," I agreed.

"The luck of the Polish! Who knew? I never knew a Polack to make a success at a ham sandwich, much less dryland farming. I remember your pa planted that shelterbelt for the government cash and then he plowed all those damn trees right off again, didn't he? And then, poof, Tommy has a bumper crop the year that wheat is going for a dime a bushel. Do you remember that, Harp? He just could not catch a break, your pa—"

"I remember," I said.

"I guess you found water hiding somewhere underground! That's what Goerentz told us. A perched water table, is that so? Did you drill down to the aquifer?"

"I don't know," I said. "My well ran dry in 'thirty-two, the same as yours, Alf. The last dust storm missed me, that's all."

"Let us in on your secret, Harp," Alf Olafson said with a grin. His elbow went digging around my rib cage. He was staring up at me with his sparse shock of black hair and a child's hungry eyes, as if he wanted to spoon my luck out of me and spread it golden on toast.

"You'll have to ask the wind," I said, staring up at the robin. She was still diving at the window, although nobody seemed to notice. How long before she either broke through or fell dead to the ground?

"It's the secret of the wind, Alf. How should I know where it's going to blow next?"

STAY AT HOME—DON'T SELL was posted on the far wall behind the podium.

Folks kept coming up to ask me what I was doing to keep the dust at bay, how I was irrigating and listing and fertilizing. I couldn't convince them that I knew as much as they did—probably less—about what was keeping my wheat alive.

Right when I was in need of rescue, Urna Buczek walked over, swaying in her daffodil print coveralls. This is the outfit she wears in all seasons, six out of seven days a week. We were in school together, a thousand years ago.

"Harp Oletsky! You look like a boy of twenty! Did you dip your head in an inkwell?"

The Grange has always welcomed female members. I blushed at the intensity of Urna's stare. Urna is one of our chapter's female officeholders. She had sailed from Bremen, alone, to homestead in 1915, a plump and indomitable young widow.

"Are you goofing on me, Urna?"

"You *would* mistake my compliment for a joke. Such a humble person. Dust off your mirror and take a look—hand to God, your hair is growing back!"

Could this really be so? Even my looks were improving? I swept a hand through my hair, feeling that it was, perhaps, a little thicker.

After the box lunch break in the courtyard, everyone coughing up bologna in the thickening air, we returned to choose our new Grange Master.

Leon Leedskalin, our Chapter Secretary, took the podium and announced that it was time to nominate candidates. I pulled the pencil from behind my ear and chewed on the eraser. I wrote down the obvious choice, Daniel Ulin—a veteran Granger and God-fearing father of seven chunk-headed youngsters, all of whom have the same sweet disposition and overbite. Ulin made a small fortune before the Crash. As a farmer, he is respected by everyone. Urna came and sat beside me while the votes were counted, patting my hand.

At first I did not understand what was happening. Rasmussen began writing my name on the chalkboard in large capital letters. My heart sank, certain now that I was the butt of yet another joke.

"There has been some mistake," I murmured. "I am not running for any office."

"Ohhhhh-letsky!" someone hiccuped, breaking my name apart. People laughed and took up the chant, and I listened with horror as it echoed to the meetinghouse rafters.

"OOOOOOOH . . ." The crowd took a massive inhalation before screaming my name.—"LETSKY!"

"OOOOOOOH . . ."

"Please, friends, I like to laugh as much as the next man—"

Sebastian Alexander poured the papers out of the voting box and started counting them up. I won by a landslide. It was not unanimous, because I had cast the lone vote against myself.

OLETSKY 45 / ULIN 1

"Congratulations, Master Oletsky," said Daniel Ulin, smiling with sparkling Cheshire eyes. "If anyone can keep this town from getting blown off the map . . ."

I felt faint, and sat abruptly again as cheers flooded my eardrums. My head was ringing and my vision swam.

I had won?

My friends were clapping me on the back. Otto handed me a cigar from the Kearney depot.

On the southwestern wall of the Uz Grange, there hangs a sequence of maps depicting Nebraska's evolution from unorganized territory into the present day. I watched the lines melt and weep off the framed platte map of our county. First the name NEBRASKA began to drip ink, black beads rolling down the *N* and *B* and *K* as if these letters were icicles in early spring. Then the figure of the Sower on the Nebraska Capitol shimmered into the figure of a Reaper. A black cloak covered its face and it cheerfully waved its scythe at me. Now I felt almost happy, because I had an explanation for what was happening to me: I was losing my mind. I was still a loser, after all . . .

"Would you like a glass of water, Harp?"

"Thank you, Urna."

Her lips had a juniper berry stain that made her mouth look small and wet and alive. Up close, Urna is beautiful. She scratched at the back of her head and suddenly her silver hair came floating down around her shoulders as if she'd pulled the pin from a hand grenade.

"Say, I have fresh rolls and turnip greens and pork pie waiting at home and nobody to eat them with me. Would you like some company tonight?"

Had she slid a knife between my ribs, I could not have been more surprised. And what happened next made my arms break into gooseflesh:

"Yes," I said. "I would enjoy a night with you very much, Urna."

The stranger chose that moment to announce herself. She had been standing, still as a statue, in the back of the hall. I heard commotion behind me and turned to watch her walking slowly toward the middle of the room—toward me, I realized. A tall Black woman in a knitted green cap—a photographer of some sort—who nobody in the crowd seemed to know. She was ignoring our stares and setting up a camera. Its boxy body sat on a tripod, the glass eye staring serenely out at the Grangers, who were gaping back at it. She attached a bulb in a silver dish—it looked like an ice cream scoop of lightning. "That's the flash," said Otto, just before it went off.

"Good afternoon," she called into our astonishment. "My name is Cleo Allfrey, and I'm here to make pictures of your Grange Hall for the Resettlement Administration."

Everyone was surprised, but some took pains to hide it. She wore a wary smile under her bright cap, brushing at the yellow dust that lined the creases of her trousers. I wondered if it was fashionable for women to dress like men wherever she came from—surely some-place very far from Uz. The silence in the Grange seemed to grow in volume, and her smile disappeared. The government photographer had a thin face and wide-set charcoal eyes. Her curiosity felt gentle to me, very different from the greedy stares of the land speculators and the fast-talking rainmakers and the campaigning politicians and all the other mile-a-minute salesmen who pass through this hall. It was a pleasure to return her gaze.

I didn't see a wedding ring on the government photographer's fin-ger. *Miss* Cleo Allfrey, then. She seemed quite young to be travel-ing alone. I felt amazed to learn that Uncle Sam was hiring Black women and single women to make pictures for the Resettlement Administration.

When the all-Black colony of Audacious started losing residents, Uz had absorbed three of its families. The Millers and the Gleasons were Grangers. We prided ourselves on being an integrated chapter. But the Black homesteaders began losing their lands a good ten years before the same banks started to foreclose on the White farmers and ranchers. I felt a rush of shame, thinking about my AAA fallowing money. I wondered how our chapter might appear to Miss Allfrey. A sea of pale faces stared back at her. Most unsmiling, many shy, some afraid, several reddening with fury as she loaded film into her camera and shot at them.

"This is our new Grange Master," said Urna, stepping between us to pluck lint from my collar. A little spark jumped between us, or maybe only inside me. I might have imagined it. Either way, I felt myself flush like a kid. I turned and extended a hand to Miss Allfrey.

"Hello," the photographer said. "Have we met before? You look very familiar."

She was studying me, it seemed. I felt nervous, aware of an expectation I was failing to meet. Story of my life. You'd think I'd be resigned to it, but I will never enjoy the feeling of disappointing a woman.

"Oh, you must be mistaken," I mumbled. "Nobody has taken my picture since I was knee-high to my papa . . ."

She laughed off the awkward pause, taking my hand that she'd left stranded midair and pumping it with a sidelong look at the audience around us.

"Of course. Forgive me. A case of mistaken identity . . ."

Grayson was smiling at Miss Allfrey with his full set of fangs. He shoved himself between us until he was angling his long face down at her from a height of six foot four.

"My daddy used to cut an apple and use it for a clock. Set it on the counter and watch it go brown and sour. I guess that's what's happening in this country. It's getting browner and browner . . . darker and nastier . . ."

I knew Grayson, that old vampire. He loved attention. He would keep cranking until he got some reaction.

Some believe in poltergeists, evil spirits. Let me assure anyone who raises a skeptic's eyebrow that poltergeists are real and men create them. There was a loose and unmoored energy sweating out of everyone around me, skulking and swaying and coughing into our fists, considering the stranger with her boxy black camera. I heard what nobody was saying: why did Uncle Sam send a Black woman to make our portraits? I felt like a sailor watching a storm building at sea. Our surprise could go in any direction now. From boyhood on I have been vigilant, I have tried not to get caught up in the wind that turns the weather vane. Grayson wanted to harness and ride the waves of energy to violence. I had an unwanted epiphany then— Grayson might be the last to know this.

Mike and Matya's kid walked up to the photographer and tugged at her sleeve. "I don't like apples myself, I'm the only one of my brothers that won't touch an apple even inside pie. Did you come from the city? Do you have any candy? My cousin says there is a store in Lincoln that sells nothing but bonbons and—"

"Mikey!" his mother said, swatting him away. I felt something like a great sigh travel through the room. Shoulders fell and faces settled. The silly kid turned the tide, somehow.

"Can you kindly step outside the frame?" the photographer asked Grayson. "I would like to make a portrait of this man. Your new Grange Master. I didn't catch your name, sir . . ."

The flashbulb went off. I shut my eyes, my smile blown backward.

"Harp Oletsky. Welcome to Uz, Miss Allfrey."

The Scarecrow

ere is my beginning, I think every morning.

I must mean something—or what am I still doing here?

I try to believe that I am the one scaring the dust away, the sentry posted on this farmer's plot to hold the sky clear. If that were true—if I had a purpose—I could withstand this paralysis. I could wait in hope. Yet I cannot even scare off a single bird. The crows think I am a pushover. All night, they alight on my shoulders. Preening themselves in the tall light that grows here.

At noon, a rabbit came bounding through the clover and the stubble: *Rabbit! Rabbit! Rabbit!* Another banner day out here in the fallowland.

Black-tailed jackrabbit. The name followed on her heels. Another shape appeared in the east, moving toward us. *Meteor.* No, that was not right. *Red-tailed hawk.* It seemed to crash into the rabbit. The collision transformed them. Now they were a single creature. It soared up and off. I watched the rabbit's hind legs squirming in the air, kicking at the blue sky. I pray that something seizes me and rips me free from this hay bale.

Yesterday, the farmer ate a cheese and tomato sandwich on his tractor. I watched the old man chew and tastes flooded my memory. Sunshine and water in a fat red satchel. Cheddar and grainy mustard. Yeast building dough into bread. Salt green ocean of the pickle. Eating summer. Eating winter. Eating fall. I once had a tongue. Dry lips to lick. A yellow lunch pail with a dented lid. I remembered a scratchy voice—whose?—telling me, "Tomatoes are also called love apples, dear."

Love apples. Dear.

I meant something, to someone.

The RA Photographer, Cleo Allfrey

Dear Miss Allfrey,

    This last batch is unusable. You mention "anomaly" with the Graflex lens. Do not blame the camera for your amateur mistakes. Do not blame my lab technicians for "ruining" your cruddy negatives either. I must use my hole punch on all the blurry landscapes you shot in Neb.

Roy E. Stryker

⊰⊱

Dear Miss Allfrey,

    I appreciate the ambition of your latest work. The portrait from the integrated rural schoolhouse is quite moving to me. Your scenes of the two towns' joining for a picnic, the balloons and jubilation, White and Black children around the baseball diamond. My favorite is the group shot of the five Black and White girls standing side by side with their small hands swallowed in their mothers' leather mitts. I do appreciate such scenes of interracial harmony and simple joy. It's clear that real friendship across the so-called color line exists in rural Nebraska.

    However, the reality is that these interracial scenes agitate many of the Southern Democrats in Congress. That same Congress controls the purse strings for Roosevelt's New Deal. The whole venture rests on their support.

    In the future, please be judicious about who you frame up.

Photographs of White farmers will have much better odds of being circulated.

Yours,

Roy

⊰╬⊱

I am the eye that slid out of focus . . .

Roy Stryker didn't know when he hired me that I would mutiny. Neither did I. When I signed on with the Resettlement Agency, I would have jumped through any hoop to please my bosses in Washington. I was determined to make the kinds of pictures Roy Stryker wanted for the Historical Section. His shooting scripts gave our mission the air of a scavenger hunt. At the same time, Roy stressed that the project was of the most dire importance. We had to make the case for Roosevelt's New Deal, to the Senate and to the taxpaying public.

TELL THE STORY OF HUMAN EROSION, ALLFREY . . .

Even half a continent from the D.C. offices, Roy Stryker's voice is always in my head. I admire the man. I am grateful to him for my chance. And I find that I cannot stand him. We did not always have such an antagonistic relationship. I know Roy must feel that he is, in his way, trying to protect me. And himself, of course.

Photographs substitute for memories, he told me at our first meeting. "You must strive to become part of the environment. To be an unobtrusive presence. Our methods are straightforward here. You must avoid always the temptation to use tricks and manipulation to get a more dramatic image, Miss Allfrey. Real life will afford you with plenty of drama to photograph, if you are patient . . ."

Roy said such gimmicks and embellishments undermined our mission. We were collecting documentation. Objective data. Photographs were public recollections, "a rich fund of memories" for every present and future American. People sometimes complained that the Resettlement Administration images were removed from their historical context, their surrounding circumstances. (True. There is only so much that fits inside a frame!)

Of course they are stripped of another context as well—the context of the body. Photographs frightened my mother for this reason. Faces floated on the wall in my bedroom, miles and years away from the living people who had posed for me in the portrait studio. My mother seemed to feel she was dishonoring the subjects of my portraits by seeing them framed through my eyes. A photograph was a "misremembering," she told me. "But everybody misremembers vividly, Mama," I'd said. A memory is never the fullness of what happened. My mother is proud of me, in her way. But my portraits in particular seem to disturb her. As if I've done something obscene by making icons out of "real living people." She can't explain it to me, but I think it has something to do with her awareness that many of the people in my photographs still exist somewhere, walking around in some distant city or town. Laughing, burping, pissing, eating, kissing, screaming, aging. She'll wonder aloud if a person might have died and vanished into the ground while their eyes shine out of my portfolio. Are those eyes still blinking, or have they stopped? *He's still kicking, Cleo? She's in good health?* she asks me whenever I show her my prints, as if I am pen pals with everyone I've ever photographed. The Italian coal miners of Vollum. The striking Black farmers in Lancaster. My mother in a high-necked purple dress with golden buttons. She meets her own gaze sidelong, casting a worried eye at me.

In his D.C. office, Roy introduced me to the editor of *Fortune*. He was a White man in his fifties with guppy-like eyebrows. He glanced through my portfolio and told me, "You may consider yourself an artist, Miss Allfrey, but I don't have to agree. A photograph is merely an artifact of mechanical production."

He stopped at an image of the moon, shot through the struts of some rusty mining equipment. I thought it was the best photograph I had ever made.

Photo: *Full Harvest Moon in Vollum, PA.*
Caption: *The sense of all centuries arrested in the moon.*

"So you fancy yourself a poet too," Roy joined in. "Let's see you put the same care into your exposures as you do the captions, Miss Allfrey."

While I stood there, awaiting his verdict, he laid the contact print I'd made facedown on his desk. He then punched a hole through the negative, murdering my moon.

Later I learned he did the same thing to Mydans and Evans and Lange and Shahn. But in the beginning, it felt so personal. Depending on how much he hated the work I'd made, he might punch along the edges. He might attack the human subjects, annihilating faces.

"Do you see potential in them?" I'd asked, unable to hold a neutral tone.

"I see potential in *you*, Miss Allfrey. We must work together to develop it."

I hated to think about the hole-punched negatives, orphaned somewhere in the Anti-File. I resolved to make work so irrefutably brilliant that my boss could not reject it.

During my three-day visit to Washington, I carried my camera with me everywhere I went. People say that photographers hide behind their cameras—I live behind mine. I come alive. My lens shields me from hostile eyes. If I could lift my reflection out of them, like a jeweler lifting a glass case, I would rescue myself. When the White manager of a diner seated me in the freezing hall behind his kitchen, his anger coloring his cheeks like those of a saxophone player, I raised my camera and made a portrait of him.

At the one RA reception I attended, I met Dorothea Lange. We were the only women in the room. There were two other Black guests, including the lab manager I'd met on Friday's tour. He warned me that "D.C. is more racist than any city I've ever lived," and nothing in my three-day visit refuted his claim.

"Get Roy something for his File," Lange advised me in a low voice near the potted begonias. The flowers' small, blushing faces were turned outward, beaming at the pale men in their dark suits. "But make the work you want to make."

⊰⊱

Roy told me that we were making history. We were "introducing America to Americans." We were also making advertisements for Roosevelt's New Deal programs—including our own. We knew the faces that carried the most weight with Congress. The need that triggered avalanches of compassion was White need. The aid programs received support in proportion to voters' perception of the desperation among the rural poor. Photographs of these "Okies" were reproduced in magazines and newspapers throughout the world. People gasped with surprise when they saw how little these broke White families had. White tramps lived in conditions that were horrifying and "undignified."

Shanties are not suitable dwellings for any human being. It was not lost on me that White viewers did not gasp at photographs of Black farmworkers living in even more dismal conditions. Unable to get the AAA money from their landlords. Excluded from the new Social Security Act. White faces in pea-picking camps, in truck beds and boxes—these are what elicited shock. This was the injustice that felt newsworthy. White hunger was a national emergency. White homelessness was a tragedy. White people moving west again, no longer with the expectation of finding gold or land but looking for food, looking for work, looking for a better place to spend the night than yesterday's camp. It made many Americans sick to see it, and they voted for a President who promised relief for the common man, "the forgotten man" at the base of the economic pyramid. I too felt shocked by the desperation I found waiting for me in the farming communities of Nebraska, I wrote to my boss. Great compassion for the suffering people I met and photographed. But who else has been forgotten?

Roy told me that his rejection of my photographs of Black farmworkers at a labor strike was not artistic but pragmatic. The Historical Section, he said, could not risk getting embroiled in the crusade for racial justice.

". . . the reality is . . ."

". . . take pictures of everyone but place the emphasis on . . ."

The reality.

I reread Stryker's telegram on the stained bedspread. I could hear screams of laughter from the saloon downstairs, the Country Jentleman. Even in the middle of my fury, I felt a child's shame at disappointing my government employers. Failing, yet again, to comply with the assignment. Roy was unhappy with me, and Roy had believed in my potential. His disappointment made me feel like a child, small and afraid. I wanted to amount to something. I wanted my mother to see my work in the newspaper. I did not want my own portrait to appear there—that sort of fame has never interested me. But I did want eyes on my photographs. I wanted other people to see where I'd been and what I'd seen, the way I saw it.

⊰⊱

When I became a Resettlement photographer, Arthur Rothstein's *Fleeing a Dust Storm* had already been reproduced a hundred times in newspapers around the country. Not one picture I've made for the RA file has yet been published. I mentioned this discrepancy to Roy in one of my telegrams.

"And whose fault is that?" my boss telegrammed back.

We were sent to gather light into an argument. To convince America that the drought was real, and that the Depression had left people in desperate straits. We shot "with a social purpose," as Roy called it. Our job was to "capture the still-tensile sinews of national vigor . . ."

Arthur Rothstein was the first photographer hired by Roy, and he'd been on the road making pictures since the documentary project's inception. He was six years younger than me, a baby-faced twenty-one-year-old man with no formal art training. I wondered if Arthur had been as surprised by his lucky break as I had been by mine.

I was jealous of him. I was his admirer also, and by no means a grudging one—I loved Arthur's photographs. In one, a Black man who had the angular, dignified face of my own father stared levelly back at Rothstein's lens; in another, a shy White toddler gaped up from the porch of an Appalachian cabin that seemed on the verge of sliding free from its foundations. His work moved me to tears on my first visit to the Historical Section's D.C. headquarters, a loss of control that Roy graciously pretended not to see. I felt awed at the way Rothstein saw people. Respect communicated itself through his photographs—the framing of his subjects and the patient intensity of his focus. I cheered for Arthur, whom I'd still never met; I also felt instantly competitive with him. If this was the high bar for my boss, I wanted to clear it.

I was too shy to ask Stryker if he'd shared my portfolio with any of the other photographers, but I dreamed of my boss showing it to some new hire.

These are the photographs of our esteemed Cleo Allfrey, of course you are familiar with her work, look at her grand collaboration with the western sun and the small towns of Nebraska . . .

Yes, Allfrey's portrait went on to become the iconic photograph of the Dust Bowl era, and one of the most widely reproduced images of the twentieth century . . .

Now, it was obvious to *me*, as it surely was to Roy Stryker, that Arthur's image was a dramatization. Taken after a dust storm, or in anticipation of one. It was clearly shot at a moment of low wind and high visibility. A simple, powerful composition. The man and his children had been artfully posed. Or if they were running in earnest, something other than dust had been chasing them. My guess is that Arthur Rothstein, with his genius for storytelling, gave these characters some direction. It is an incredible photograph. It shows you what you *might* see if a camera could pierce the heart of a black blizzard. If there were sufficient light for the camera to record it. If the high winds didn't make even ordinary sight all but impossible.

"He must have posed them," I said. "I'm glad he did. What a picture he made for us. Rothstein's a true artist."

When I shared my thoughts with Roy, I did not mean to sound insubordinate. Nor was I suggesting that Arthur Rothstein was a liar or a counterfeiter. No, the opposite. He'd rearranged reality to reveal a truth that would be otherwise unknown.

Roy Stryker's boyish brows descended as I spoke. His eyes retreated behind his spectacles, joining into a single burning node of judgment on some distant horizon inside him. *This is the scorching face that his Columbia University students must get when they are too dense to understand some vital lesson*, I thought. *Nod and smile and agree with this fellow who has given you your golden opportunity, Cleo!* I heard in my mother's voice. *Say thank you and shut your mouth!* This has always been an easy instruction for my sisters to follow, but I find it all but impossible. "Once Cleo breaks her silence and starts in on something," my mama liked to say, rolling her eyes but also bragging on me, "she's on skates without a brake!"

"Rothstein is a documentary photographer," he said. "Do not forget your mission, Miss Allfrey. Reality does not need any embellishments. The goal of the Historical Section is to document the man in his environment, not to make propaganda. Do not stage your shots. Do not use props. No gimmicks. You will have the shooting scripts to guide your eye."

We'd left it there—just shy of an argument.

Sometimes we photographers have to rearrange reality to make the invisible apparent. I know of no artist who does not remake the world they see. And documentary photographers are artists too, regardless of how Roy Stryker and Rexford Tugwell sell us to Congress.

The Prairie Witch

I am always half listening for an intruder, Son. If you've spent most of your life on high alert, "relaxation" feels frightening. A tense vigil on a lumpy pillow. Lying exhausts me, and I live in terror of being found out. But I prefer counterfeiting with Dell to these lonely nights. It's strange to think that a month ago, I didn't know the girl; now we are *thick as thieves*, as she says. By day, the girl and I work without pause. The past three weeks have been my busiest in Uz. Dozens of old customers are walking around reminiscing with our counterfeits. Dozens of new customers have made deposits, enough that I can feel a dull pressure when I turn on my left side. I'm afraid to shut my eyes, afraid I'll lose the little I've built up since my crash. At 2:00 a.m., I was awake on top of the blankets when the pounding began. The knob was turning angrily in its socket as I opened the door onto the Sheriff.

"Good evening, Ant. I thought I would pay you a visit at your offices. We're full up at the jail."

"How many times have I asked you not to call me that, Sheriff?"

"It's a term of endearment." His grin greased itself, the wet lips pressing inward, then relaxed like a muscle. No matter how sweetly he says it, I picture his bootheel crushing my thorax.

"Have you two met? Percy, Ant."

A young Irishman—a boy really—shuffled in behind him. The Sheriff's new deputy. His freckles covered his entire face and neck like chain mail. A redhead, down to his stubble and his eyelashes. He had a sweet baby face. He was trying not to cry.

There was no telling how long a night with the Sheriff might last. Ordinarily he drove me to Cell 8 to absorb someone's memories. He preferred the privacy of the jailhouse to Room 11. I wondered why he'd decided this particular transfer couldn't wait another quarter hour.

"I swear I'm not going to talk, Vick—"

"The whiskey loquacity of a witness! Oh, who can risk it?"

The Sheriff operated from the assumption that every promise was a future lie, and acted accordingly. He turned to me, flashing his gap-toothed smile. The one that ingratiates him to so many voters.

"I want young Percy here to hop on a barstool and enjoy a drink or three without worry."

I did not want to take the deputy's confession and he did not want to give it, but the Sheriff stood over both of us with his hand on his holstered pistol. I have received so many forced confessions from terrified men like Percy during my stays in Cell 8. What did they tell me? Vick alone knows. The Sheriff removed my earhorn from the wall. In the same casually proprietary way that he touches everyone, everything, he pointed the funnel toward my skull.

"Down the hatch, Percy," the Sheriff directed. He smiled, motioning the deputy forward. "Let's stopper those rumors before they begin, shall we? I have to make sure everyone remains calm. Can't have voters screwing up the peace we've worked so hard to preserve—"

"You ready, Ant?" Vick tucked his thumb under my jawbone, stroking the left side of my neck with the other four fingers. I held my breath and heard the wailing of the kittens in the flour sack. Percy's reddish eyes were screaming *no*.

"I can keep a secret, Sheriff. I don't need to spill my guts to some witch . . ."

Sheriff Iscoe ignored him.

"Here's your slip, Percy. You read these numbers left to right . . ."

Percy sank into the chair, staring at the emerald funnel like he was afraid it might swallow him whole.

"How do you know *she* won't talk?"

"I've conducted my own experiments, trust me. Are you going to talk, Ant?"

I shook my head. "I won't even listen."

Percy spoke in a quaking voice for a quarter hour, describing their night in gruesome, vivid detail. But what flashed behind my eyelids was a vision of Percy at age eight or nine, dreaming of wearing a sheriff's badge. How betrayed he sounded—and petulant as well. He had set out to make this world safer and wound up shackled to Victor Iscoe. His voice broke every third word, and I heard how fear had corroded it.

Vick tipped Percy out of the chair the minute he fell silent. He plucked the cider brown deposit slip from his deputy's black fingers, rolling it like a cigarette and sliding it behind his left ear.

"Good work, Percy. I'll keep your slip for you."

Vick opened the door and shooed the stunned, woozy deputy into the hallway. We heard him banging down the stairwell and into the night.

"All right, Ant! A double feature . . ."

I must have looked startled, because he laughed angrily and said, "Why should only Percy get to sleep tonight? I deserve a vacation more than anyone in this wretched town—"

His wheedling tone reminded me of the drunks after last call, flapping their empty wallets at the bartender in the world's saddest puppet show. Pity for oneself can swing outward in a heartbeat. My stomach muscles drew in, and my fingers gripped the underside of the chair to keep from running.

The Sheriff has used me for many purposes, but he had never before deposited his own memories. I'd grown accustomed to taking deposits from frightened people like Percy. To receive one from Vick was a first. I have watched the Sheriff lose control of himself a thousand times, but never in this way. He keeps a tight grip on his own secrets. Knowledge is power—as stupid as he is, Vick does seem to know that.

"Believe me, I won't make a habit of this. A lawman needs to keep his facts straight. But I can't afford to lose any more sleep right now, Ant. What's done is done—and needs to stay done. I am delivering a speech tomorrow morning at the Town Hall, and following it up with hours of glad-handing. Kissing babies, making promises. I sure as hell can't keep my composure with this, this—" His hands drew large circles around his chest. "*All this* churning around. Get it out."

He gripped the green funnel of my earhorn as if it were a steering wheel, craning over me with a strange smile.

"I made a note on the calendar. The day after the election, I'll come withdraw it. It will be safe to know it then. After I win."

I've heard plenty of folks make promises like this, Son. I stayed quiet and nodded. I wanted only to jump into my trance, but the new buoyancy wouldn't allow it. I shut my eyes and pictured the stars winking out. I begged the night sky to open inside me, so that I could exit the room. To my left, the chair groaned under Vick's weight. It terrified me to realize that for the duration of this transfer, I'd have to stay in my skin.

The Sheriff leaned forward onto his splayed knees, croaking into the funnel. His sparse black hair smelled like a campfire. I let my head roll against the receiver, pretending to be unconscious. My eyelids fluttered. My breathing slowed. But I was awake for every word of Sheriff Iscoe's deposit. His voice echoed in the funnel, swirling through me. "Listening" is not what I did. I was drawn inside the memory—pressed up against Vick's eyeholes, crammed into his face bones. As he spoke into the earhorn's mouthpiece, I could feel the scouring wind on Vick's arm hairs, the sweat on his brow, the smell of his aftershave mixing with the prairie ozone. I have grown used to relieving the Sheriff of his problems. This time, I relived the night in question. Not with Sheriff Iscoe, Son. *As* him.

⊰⊱

SHERIFF ISCOE'S DEPOSIT

⊰⊱

It was close to midnight when Vick Iscoe and his deputy reached the top of the hill. It made him appreciate the even rise of the staircase at the boardinghouse, the prudence of the hand-hewn railings, a long oak arm to catch a wobbly man—Vick was longing for the right angles of those stairs at the precise moment he lost his footing and began to skid down the sand dune toward the parked Chevrolet, its headlights shining bravely into the unbroken dark of the blowing prairie.

Vick grasped at the clumps of dry earth that tore loose as he slid faster—scraping his pink belly raw, shrieking at an octave that surprised him. All over the moonlit, suede-colored hill, wildflowers opened their eyes. He saw purple penstemon bled of its daytime colors, little goblets of midnight. Now where had *that* voice come from? Those *voices*? He heard kittens, screaming between his eardrums. A cinched sack inside him burst. Angry mewling spilled forth. Then it was over, and Vick cursed in his ordinary baritone, his gruff voice restored to him.

Why wouldn't the dead stay quiet?

Miraculously, the chatty new deputy somehow managed to keep his mouth shut. He did not even ask, "You okay, Sheriff?" but waited patiently with the dead woman while Vick hauled himself onto his knees.

Cursing his way up the easternmost dune, Vick sank again and again, his legs at one point disappearing to their shins in a blowhole. He and Percy were soon forced to crawl forward on all fours. His flashlight hunted for the right burial spot.

Vick found his thoughts listing gloomily toward his reelection campaign. The election was nearly here, the first Tuesday in June, and his opponent was a handsome young brat, Ernie Whitson—an ex-Army lieutenant from Fort Niobrara who had worked for Doc Middleton in the northwest corner of the state. He was spending big on election placards. Last year he'd come on the scene accusing Vick of letting open cases fester. How satisfying, then, when every paper in Nebraska ran a headline that screamed back at Whitson and all of Vick's detractors: LUCKY RABBIT'S FOOT KILLER BROUGHT TO JUSTICE over the smiling face of Sheriff Iscoe.

Unsolved murders were bad for the town's well-being, he knew, and just terrible for business. Keeping the peace was not enough to get the vote. A man had to campaign for himself.

What did Percival Gander, the baby-faced deputy, make of this midnight adventure? Percy was scared half to death, and doltishly loyal. Two good qualities.

If a listener were to tune the dial to this station right now, jumping into the radio play without any of the necessary context, it would sound all wrong: two lawmen hugging the sand, panting in the oven-hot darkness of southwestern Nebraska, transporting evidence miles from a crime scene. Together they carried Mink Petrusev up the hill, her bare, cracked heels pointed at the moon.

This new deputy was a slow study. Fear had gotten the better of him, and now he could not shut up: "What will happen if we're caught tampering with the, ah, the evidence? Am I going to jail?"

Percy had not objected when Vick explained what must be done, only rocked on the balls of his feet, licking his dry lips and blinking rapidly, as if hoping his eyes might eventually settle on a different reality. Vick had asked him with the sighing frustration of a father if he would prefer to risk jail, or to be killed on the spot. Parents must absorb so many of their children's inane questions, and the same is true for lawmen and their deputies. This kid had already vomited once *inside* the parked squad car, which made Vick see red—*You couldn't open a goddamn door, Percy?*

Unlucky: a hailstorm in April, stillborn twin calves, a leaking tank five miles from the filling station.

Cursed: how Vick had felt when the new deputy rang him on the Party Line to say in a useless whisper, *Boss, you better get down here . . .*

Now how was he supposed to explain *this*? The victim was a silver-haired Russian woman, whom Vick recognized as the wife of George Petrusev, a man he'd blackmailed for years until he died of cancer of the bone last spring. A world-class poker player and a mediocre beet farmer, old George. Mink was a childless widow in her fifties who lived alone at the southern edge of Uz. What was she doing out by the depot? Had she been cutting across to the graded road? Never smart to trespass without a weapon. Mink had no protection, not even a pocketknife.

Vick shook out her overcoat and found a promissory note from the Co-op for five dollars of flax and broomcorn, a faded tintype of two pigtailed children (nieces perhaps, he hoped distant), and a carnelian rosary with glowing red beads. As if her blood had turned itself into jewelry. There was so much of it. Vick wiped the sweat from his brow. Was it possible no one would miss her? This was Vick's prayer. (What hears, and answers, a prayer like that? Vick hoped never to make Its acquaintance.) He'd pocketed the rosary for Dottie.

Had Vick believed even for a moment in Clemson Louis Dew's guilt?

This was the wrong question.

Reality was a story Vick was telling himself. The future was his possession. He'd make the past whatever it needed to be to obtain it.

Mink Petrusev, who had a pianist's long, elegant fingers and staring blue eyes, had been discovered by Percy in a clump of sagebrush two miles south of the depot. The new deputy had answered a call about tramps stealing chicken eggs and found, instead, a half-naked body and blood matting the grass. Vick's heart had sunk at the sight of fresh blood seeping through the sun-eaten green cotton of Mink's work dress. How was he supposed to wrap this up? Victor Iscoe was a hero to all and Dew was sitting in a cell. Now his standing in Uz was once again in jeopardy. All his hard work, his ingenuity, for naught. In a moment of confusion or habit, he had grabbed one of the thumb-size talismans from the trunk. He had half a dozen rabbit's feet stashed there in a biscuit tin.

But that fix wouldn't work this time—Clemson Louis Dew was awaiting his second execution, and everyone believed their town was safe again.

Vick rubbed his head, feeling agitated. It had been a stroke of genius to use the rabbit's feet to stitch the open cases together. Solving seven murders at once? It was his finest moment as a lawman. But he'd played that hand. He had no idea what to do this time. The timing couldn't be worse. Staring down at Mink's sightless eyes, Vick felt a surge of fury. *Boom and bust.* The way things always seemed to go in Uz. She could cost him the election, his newly burnished reputation. Fear of reporters closed his throat. He knew what sold newspapers. He knew *exactly* how his enemies would use this new victim to paint him into a corner. INEPT ISCOE ARRESTS INNOCENT! MURDERERS RETURN TO HAUNT THE TOWN OF UZ! The doubts that many had suppressed about Dew's guilt would now come bubbling up. Vick would have doused Mink's body in kerosene and lit a match right there if it weren't for the possibility of the distressed poultry farmer happening upon them. Had the egg-thieving tramps killed her? Had the chicken farmer? Some rogue monster?

Her skin was still warm, blood from the cuts on her arms a slaughterhouse red. "You fought hard, Mink," said Vick approvingly. "Better luck next time, honey." Between the phone call to the station and the deputy's arrival, it seemed, Mink had been killed. Vick had no interest in an investigation with polls so close to opening.

"Should we find the farmer that placed the call, sir?"

"No. Not until we have our man. Half the tramps in the Hooverville have their hand in a chicken coop, Percy—I suggest you bring one in and file a report saying the egg thief was apprehended."

"If Dew is behind bars, who killed Mink?" the stupid deputy had shouted, hopping on one foot as if trying to jostle a thought loose. "Sheriff, I can phone the coroner—"

"C'mon back here, Percy."

Vick fingered the wet collar of Mink's blouse. Nothing cleans like a fire, as Dottie liked to say. An ugly feeling was mounting in him.

Paranoia stabbed at Vick. Ernie Whitson's smug and bloated face appeared in his mind. "Maybe Whitson put someone up to this. Or killed Mink himself. Ernie Whitson would love nothing more than to ruin my good reputation . . ."

The deputy's eyes looked like hard-boiled eggs. "Sheriff, I don't think Mr. Whitson would kill someone just to win an election."

"You don't *want* to think it, Percy. Believe me, nothing is beyond the pale for a man who wants something bad enough . . ."

He turned the rabbit's foot over in his palm. It was smaller than the last one. He'd purchased them at the Emporium in Gordon. Ten for ten dollars. Every foot had come from the left hind leg, the shopkeep told him. You could buy these nasty things anywhere you found gamblers. Vick had not cared enough to ask for the reason behind the superstition.

These charms did not work very well, he thought angrily. His bad luck was back to haunt him. When the nursing students were killed, he knew he was in for a rough time. Their misfortune had infected him. People needed someone to blame, and in the absence of a killer all fingers were suddenly pointing at the local sheriff. The irony was not lost on Vick—he was in the business of cuffing scapegoats, restoring the peace. This time he was the one chained to an open case. If only the nursing students hadn't been so fair skinned, so young! If he'd had a little time to plan before the journalists came and kicked up that froth about the rabbit's foot. He might have found a way to dampen the lit fuse before it climbed the wick and exploded into headlines. If the murdered girls had been, instead of Nina Rose and Olga Kucera, some women without prospects or family in town. Those girls made for a salable tragedy—they had their whole golden lives ahead of them. But women were always going missing. That was a fact of life throughout the howling world. A young Black woman whose name Vick had not retained had disappeared from a fishing camp on the Republican River just two weeks prior to Nina's and Olga's murders, and nobody in Uz made any fuss about that. How many whores had disappeared from that brothel on the lonely road between Uz and Thedford in recent times? He'd known a few of them himself. The trouble was that *these* missing women were the wives and daughters of Grangers. Decent people. In two cases, powerful people. When Allene and Minnie had been killed within a month of one another last year, it would have been natural to panic, but Vick had kept a cool head. He could see the opportunity in a crisis. Planting the rabbit's feet on their bodies had been one of Vick's boldest ideas. High risk, high yield. Dozens of journalists poured into Uz to report on the sensational "spree," and they stayed to document the rural sheriff who put an end to the violence. He'd brought peace to the victims' families and to the town of Uz. Now what? All his hard work was about to come undone.

"We can investigate Mink's murder in private, on our own time—I am not about to plunge Uz into a panic. Our town is teetering on the edge, isn't it?"

"Sheriff . . ."

"The Lucky Rabbit's Foot Killer was brought to justice, Percival. I don't know who killed Mink, but I won't let her death destroy Uz."

"Sheriff? Do you think the man or men who killed Mink Petrusev . . . killed some of the others?"

Vick still had control of his anger then. Felt the reins slipping as the sun went down behind the grassy sand dunes. He kicked at two chickens that had strutted over.

"You think Dew was falsely convicted?"

The boy-deputy nodded slowly, his small eyes darting around the sticky hive of his face. He'd been crying, Vick realized with disgust. Crying, and probably also fantasizing about his name in the newspaper headlines. Parade floats and gold medallions. What a disappointing evening this was turning out to be for everyone.

"I'll tell you my philosophy on this one, Percy. See if it helps you to sleep a little better. If Clemson Louis Dew wasn't guilty of killing seven women? The boy was absolutely guilty of *something*. Probably something worse than what we got him for!"

He could still feel the pressure of the tramp's thin neck jerking back and sliding free before Vick tackled him. Does an innocent man run from the law? Does an innocent nearly faint from terror? The walleyed kid had pissed himself inside of Vick's headlock. Now, how else do you interpret a jet of yellow like that? It was an involuntary confession. The jury had done its duty by convicting him.

"We will find Mink's killer, I promise you. But I am not about to give my opponent the satisfaction of calling me inept. Do you really think the town is safer with Ernie Whitson in charge?"

"Well," said Percival.

The boy was slow to understand that his discovery was not going to be celebrated by anyone.

"Shouldn't I go call the coroner, Sheriff?" he asked again, with less hope.

"You should get Mrs. Petrusev into your trunk without delay. We'll be spending the night together, the three of us."

Two hours later, Vick felt they were far enough from the road. The nearest homestead was seven miles away. A single tree loomed out of the earth—a cottonwood with a scar down its trunk—which Vick took as a sign to stop. Mink Petrusev lay on the sand between the men, her red blood drying into black blotches. Vick watched the colors seep out of his cognac brown boots and the auburn sand, everything running into a uniform blue. Night shoveled the meaning out of things. Night had long been his accomplice.

You would never perceive the scar down the cottonwood if you hadn't seen it in daylight, Vick thought. It was more memory than sight that drew it out of the dark. Soon Mink's name would drain away, with any luck. The fact of Mink's life.

He should have found this consoling—he always had in the past. Why not tonight? A bad feeling came on like a wave, doubling Vick over. He shook his head to clear it. He spat into the fragrant sage. From the thin shade of the lone cottonwood, Mink watched. Vick didn't care to explore what might be causing his distress—what was the use of investigating? *You spit out rancid food,* Vick thought. *You don't keep chewing on it.*

Percival's scowl deepened, not in thought but in submission to reality. His expression changed very gradually. It was like watching a bootheel sinking into the mud, a terrible fact forcing itself deeper into his awareness. At last he gasped, and the light left his eyes.

"Oh," he said. "Are you going to kill me now, Sheriff?"

His gaze dropped to his shoes. He looked like a shy boy praying not to be cast in the school pageant.

Don't shoot the messenger and don't bury the undertaker! "Sweetheart, I can't dispose of this big girl alone."

Vick's terms of endearment grew softer the angrier he felt. An echo of his father, Victor Sr., whose voice had gotten low and syrupy the drunker and meaner he became: "Ahhhh sweetheart, sweetheart, sweetheart," he would murmur, slamming his son's small head against the far wall of the root cellar. Punishments were conducted in the cellar, a practice Vick had continued with his own boys—the sod never rattles as wood does, and generously absorbs all sound. My fault, my fault, my fault, small Vick had believed at the time. A guilt he outgrew the year he became taller and stronger than his father, and began to swing back.

"Nobody is going to kill you, honey," Vick promised his deputy. "You haven't given me any reason to . . ."

Something not-human had started calling in the dark, a shrieky music that seemed to outline the dunes in pale silver. A novel animal, with an unfamiliar call. Joined by a chorus of other nameless beasts.

Vick handed Percy the shovel.

As the sand flew, Vick began thinking about *the middle of nowhere.* How that expression made it seem as if nowhere had no periphery— you were always smack in the middle of it, weren't you? Inescapably so. By the time you made it to the *margins* of nowhere, you were *somewhere* again. On the outskirts of something. True nowhere was a pit of loneliness marooned in the middle of more nothing. It was how he felt when he woke next to Dottie and for an eternal moment could not remember his own name.

"Let's go home," the deputy chattered. "We can take Mrs. Petrusev back to where we found her and ring up the coroner. I swear I won't mention this little detour to anyone. Nobody is going to hang for a mistake."

"Ahh, young Percival, now you've gone and ruined it. I was debating this whole wild ride—is the kid trustworthy? Now I have my answer, don't I?"

The moon sulked down on them through a scrim of reddish dust. The wailing seemed to approach the pair from every direction, but without any hurry, like a trap closing in slow motion. Spiky cries drew nearer. If the clouds swallowed the moon, Vick would have it confirmed that the whole cosmos was against him. As he'd always suspected. Everything he'd accomplished, he'd had to do for himself. He brought the shovel down on Mink's head and the boy gasped— "Boss! Why did you do that?"

Vick had weaned himself off *that* question long ago. People invented their answers after the fact, and they were always self-serving. He stared down at the shapeless object below him that had once been a woman's skull. Fury began to mount in him a second time, and he used that fuel to finish digging the burn pit. He handed Percy the kerosene and watched the boy fumble with his matchbook.

"Do you hear that yowling? Are those wolves?"

"No more of those in Nebraska. Last one was shot in 1913. My daddy liked to tell the story because he had a cousin who squeezed the trigger and wore the pelt to Christmas services."

Vick leaned against the cottonwood tree and lit a cigarette. The smell was wretched, but the fire felt wonderful on Vick's hands and face. He pitched the rabbit's foot into the blaze, watching it cartwheel over the sagebrush to land on Mink. He was not immune to the old superstitions.

"Percy! Pray a little something over the body."

"God bless and keep you," the boy muttered, while Vick poured out the kerosene.

"Keep your death a secret, Mink, if you know what's good for you. George still owes me forty dollars. Let him know I have not forgotten. Amen."

Was it worse to destroy evidence, or to invent it?

He and Percy crossed the shallow creek bed and through the stand of withered shelterbelt trees some fool had tried to plant. The road was still another mile on.

Light-headed from the long walk and the night heat, Vick found that his thoughts began to turn in unnatural directions. He saw placid and terrifying scenes in his imagination. Tides of three-legged rabbits were grazing on graves, winding up their hind legs and thumping at him. Under the gasping trees, he saw the faces of the women, the ones who had been kept so beautifully hidden from sight—Enesta. Luz. Lada. Nina. Olga. Allene. Minnie. They kept flickering in and out of view, standing in a half circle around Mink, who now rolled onto her side and stood, brushing the sand from her dress, smoothing the orangey-blue flames from her hair. *Get control of yourself, you old fool.*

"Percy? Percy, are you still here—?"

Far beyond the shelterbelt, he watched his young deputy disappearing in the direction they both hoped led back to the road. *Don't look at them,* he commanded himself. *They don't exist.* He could feel the women staring at him, patiently waiting for his eyes to open. When he turned to run for the tree line, Vick groaned. Seated right beside him, regarding Vick serenely, Clemson Louis Dew was strapped to a flaming throne. He lifted the sack draped over his head and met Vick's gaze with a fathomless directness. Electric light came pouring from the holes of the boy's eyes. It burned through Vick with scalding clarity, chasing all shadows from his mind, illuminating a bare interrogation room of infinite mirrors where Vick sat before Vick. What he saw next clawed up his throat and found no exit.

"Sheriff?" Vick cried out when Percy shook his arm. "Do you need water? Or something stronger?"

He needed to get to the witch. For this infestation, a prairie witch was indeed the antidote. He'd been planning to bring the Antidote to the jailhouse to swab Percy clean. Why shouldn't he enjoy the same quiet, after such a busy night? Sleep, if it came, would be a torment. He did not want Clemson to look at him, not in life and not in his imagination, not ever again.

Yes, he would turn this unfortunate episode with Mink and its aftermath over to the Antidote tonight. Sleep it off. Certainly it was good strategy—to lay this up inside of her until after the election.

There was no room for the terror of these women mouthing his name in the dark, the terror of Clemson burning. The past had blazed to life again and he had to cast it into the witch as soon as they reached town, or risk burning alive inside his skin. Even now, he could feel the fire mounting. It decided him.

"Uh-oh, Boss," said Percy, drawing up so suddenly that Vick tumbled into him. "We got some dumb kids horsing around out here."

What were the odds?

It turned out the middle of nowhere was suddenly a crowded place.

Vick felt a furious laugh building in his chest. He and Percy had parked a mile from the road, where the lowing of Anders's cattle ended. Something had led these little bitches to the same lonely coordinates.

"Oh my Jesus, there are a bunch of little girls out here!"

They watched the group of six or seven passing a thermos around.

"They ain't so little," Vick said after a while.

"If they was *my* daughters . . ."

"I don't really want to think about my daughters right now. Do you?"

The girls were dancing and laughing in the moonlight, jumping off the rocks and rolling down the sandy slope and slapboxing one another. Vick did not dismiss the possibility that these daughters of Uz really were demonic. He recognized them now. The high school team. They'd won the Region 7 championship, big news for a sleepy town last year. He'd seen them racing downcourt with their pale and dark hair lifting behind them like claws.

"If these girls belonged to anyone, they wouldn't be out here alone a quarter to midnight . . ."

"Well, I recognize a few. There's Iverson's lardy middle girl, and the colored girl that works the register at Easter's, and that half-breed girl . . ."

One stocky girl turned sharply, staring in Vick's direction without seeing him.

There's something wrong with that one. Her mother's murder had made the papers, and Vick had recognized the name. Lada Oletsky. She'd always had a smile for him. She smiled at everyone, which of course made it almost worthless, Vick remembered with a flash of anger. He'd gone to school with Lada and her loaf-faced Polack brothers. He'd had a crush on her, a long time ago.

HUBBELL MOTHER FOUND STRANGLED IN DIVERSION DITCH

Then she ran off and got herself killed in a ditch three hours east of Uz. The location was unfortunate, because it was less than a mile from the spot some killer had dumped the body of Enesta Risingsun. Right close to the highway into and out of town, the artery of business, complained Joe Lacy. Joe had no leads, and folks were quick to anger these hot, desolate days. It had been Vick's idea to add their names to the list of Clemson Louis Dew's victims, and both the state prosecutors and the lawmen in Hayes County had been quite supportive. Vick owed his old friend a favor, and he was happy to repay it in a way that helped all parties. In the story the prosecution told, Lada Oletsky became the third victim of the Lucky Rabbit's Foot Killer. They successfully closed her cold case. In the end, it had not troubled the jurors that no rabbit's foot had been discovered on Lada Oletsky's chest. Evidence often went missing, it was early enough in Clemson Louis Dew's spree that nobody knew what clues to look for yet, and crucially: the boy had confessed. For a moment, Vick allowed himself to wonder about the night she died. Then the thought floated off, light and bright as the campfire embers behind the train depot where he'd first met Clemson.

Lada Oletsky's daughter was whirling around the fire, holding hands with a taller Mexican girl. They spun into a third girl before collapsing in laughter. When pretty women had ugly daughters it broke Vick's heart. Lada had been a looker. Her daughter was a scabby kid with a toadstool face, spotty with acne. Was she loose like her mother? Vick speculated yes. And who would want her?

"Some might say," Percy mumbled, "that it's our duty as officers of the law to escort them home to their families."

"Only if you talk about it. Otherwise nobody will say much."

⚎

Vick finished making his deposit. I waited a full minute before fluttering my eyelids. Then I stood and glided silently behind the curtain that hid my bed and vomited into the washbasin.

"Ant," Vick breathed. He sounded almost giddy. He stood up and knocked the chair over. A sound that was not laughter burst out of him. It was just physics, I knew. Like the rush of bubbles over a soda bottle. Nevertheless, a chill ran up my leg. "Is this how you make everyone feel? Goddamn. I can't believe how many nights I just stood there listening while I carted around my wheelbarrow of rocks! I can't believe I waited this long to feel this good—"

He crashed into me and kissed my neck, then bit my neck. I told Vick I had my monthlies, which happened to be true. When that didn't stop him from tearing at my dress, I slid a hand under my skirt and a finger inside myself, returning with a globe of red-black blood, which made his lips quiver in disgust. Too lazy to hit me in the suffocating heat, he returned his hands to his pockets.

There was a spring in his step as he disappeared down the stairs; from my dusty window I watched him pop onto the street, moving jauntily toward the black sedan that had transported so many dozens of us to the county jail in Vick's backyard. Galing and heavy inside me, his memory. How many deposits have I taken on Vick's orders? Dozens, perhaps hundreds. I shuddered and pictured him pouring gallons of Mink's blood into my earhorn. How many bodies has Vick rolled into my body?

Now I knew the name of at least one such person: Mink Petrusev. I saw the hill where they dragged her as if I were standing before it. I met Asphodel's sightless eyes on the night of the crime, unaware that she became a ghost forever tumbling through the haze of Vick Iscoe's memory. His story lunged up and enveloped me, and no matter how hard I gagged at the sight I would never forget Mink Petrusev's body, stiffening in the sagebrush near a poultry farmer's strutting hens. Tears won't come, Son, but I feel them building behind my eyes. I have prayed, as You know, for relief from the terrible weightlessness. For my lost ballast to be returned to me. To feel anchored to the earth again. Filled to brimming, no longer floating inside my body. Some devil is answering my prayers in the cruelest way. I have spent a lifetime swallowing the swords of this world, but now I feel them hilted inside me—all sides of the blade. I remember everything.

Monsters costume themselves in human skin and walk around telling their charming stories, and believing them. Many never learn to see the truth of who they are, the teeth inside their smiles. I am such a monster, Son. I have been one for a very long time. Now I am awake to it. I am the Sheriff's accomplice.

The Player-Captain of the Dangers,
Asphodel Oletsky

East and west and southeast a local duster blew until a quarter past 9:00 a.m. After that the sun remained the eerie color of an underwater penny, dim copper winking up from the muddy riverbed. By the time I steered us onto Highway 6, so much dust had collected on my hands that it felt like I was wearing mittens. Thelma wanted to stop and rinse out her itchy eyes but I told her she'd have to sit tight. We had a championship to win.

Our chariot was on loan to us from Ellda's creepy suitor, Pastor Robbins, a married minister who ran a Baptist summer camp, a man with a clammy grip who we all agreed did not blink enough.

"He can't come to our games, Ellda," I said. "Nobody likes him."

"Goddamn, Oletsky. I got us a free bus. How about, 'thank you'?"

The bus was a three-door red leviathan that leaked dark puddles of oil wherever she slept. Val nicknamed her Bedwetter. A nine-seater with a crank start and rheumy eyes, blackened headlights that I was constantly jumping down to clean. Val's nickname stuck, even after the rest of us voted to call our team's chariot the Pegasus.

We'd let the washing stand overnight. We left notes for our parents and our baby sisters, explanations for our empty beds that doubled as prophecies: RETURNING SUNDAY EVENING AFTER OUR VICTORY IN RED WILLOW.

I was the Captain, so piloting this bus was my responsibility. I could just reach the dust-caked pedals. I had decided not to tell the others that I had only ever driven my uncle's Dodge. They had all grown up driving steam-powered threshers and hay trucks and diesel tractors. Valeria sat behind me and whispered instructions.

We stopped for lunch at a grove of pecan trees. The farmer came outside to offer us each a scoop of tangy water. It tasted different than our water, although nobody could quite explain how. Before the collapse, he told us, he'd shipped thirty-six boxcars of pecans to a cookie factory in Illinois; last year he'd been unable to fill five. I guess this was his roundabout way of refusing our silent request to taste the meat of ripe pecans. Please, please, please, begged our hungry eyes, and his story had replied for him. Shadows, he did share freely. Green shade at noon was a wild and luxurious respite.

A thousand acres of the most beautifully ordered choreography of trees I had ever seen. On the southern plains, a single tree was famous enough to get an entire town named after her—Lone Fir.

"Who you girls playing tonight?"

"The Perkins Steelwool Princesses."

"Nobody from home in the bleachers to watch you?"

"No bleachers, either." That hit everybody's funny bone, for some reason.

"Good luck," he said wistfully. "I remember when life was a game."

⌗

On Highway 6, we passed an empty blue truck that had smashed into a culvert marker. The driver's door was hanging off its hinges.

"Not an omen," I promised my team.

I had that wheel in a death grip. The wind was blowing, then galing. I drove five miles at the speed a tall man walks. Potholes, blowouts, sand valleys, and drops. Valeria kept a hand on my shoulder until she got carsick and had to move to the back.

Around 1:00 p.m., the wind started picking up. Behind the driver's seat, I could hear my teammates' knuckles rapping on the bus windows. The bus sounded like a mouth chattering its teeth. In a quarter hour the clear sky disappeared behind a swirling crust, the sun was glowing weaker than the moon. A mutiny was brewing in the back of the Bedwetter:

"Captain Ahab here doesn't want to be late to a game that is sure to be dusted out," Nell shouted over the wind.

"It's not enough that we are playing in an ashtray?" Thelma screamed. "Now Oletsky wants to risk our lives to be punctual?"

Pazi's sharp words whittled into me: "You don't really believe your own prophecy, right? We don't control the weather, Dell. Win or lose, this dust is not going to stop—"

"This game *doesn't count for anything*!" Tiny Ellda scooted forward to be heard, grabbing my shoulder. "We should pull over and take shelter—"

The dust came pouring down between the skinny trees. I jammed on the brake pedal. I had to slide low in the seat to reach it. When the bus jumped, everyone shut up.

"It matters," I said. "We are not going to give up now, a game away from the championship. We are undefeated and we're not gonna forfeit . . ."

I was too tired to make a speech. I fixed my eyes on the horseshoe-shaped horizon, which seemed to be hurtling toward us. There are dogs in the underworld, I know from my Hubbell library books. I pictured a giant bristling dog jumping across the prairie and knocking our bus off the road. The headlights' glow weakened every minute of ticking dust against the windshield. I could barely decipher the vague shapes that rose to fill my vision. The gas pedal was flush with the floor mat. My fingers gripped the wheel and I discovered that even as my teammates screamed it was too late, I had driven past that fabled point of no return, the wide place in the road when the skies are darkening and a U-turn is still possible. The road here became so narrow and hemmed in by sand and scrub that we could only hurtle forward, or brake and wait for the dust wall to crest and cover the sky. In the side mirror, I watched, hypnotized, as the cloud rose into a roaring wall. In a few seconds, we would be inside it.

The Grange Master, Harp Oletsky

A re you scared of me, Harp?"

Outside, I heard the clatter of the ice truck. It was almost four o'clock in the morning, I realized. Urna and I had stayed up half the night talking.

"I am scared," I admitted. "But not of you."

"I've been wanting to get to know you for some time," she said. "I think we should celebrate your victory tonight, Harp Oletsky . . ."

Without warning she stood, and pulled me up from the sofa. I trailed her as she snuffed the flower-shaped lanterns along the hallway. Her house was lemon-scented, crowded with furniture and rugs and knickknacks. It felt much smaller and friendlier than our place. Urna led me through her bedroom door and let me make my own way to her four-poster bed. I sat on the mattress and hid my face in my hands. I did not understand this grace. I had accepted my lot as an old bachelor farmer, on the sundown side of the hill. God was answering a prayer I had never dared to utter. Not for years and years. Tobacco juice burned its way back up my throat. Black coffee on an empty stomach. She stepped out of her dress with the hemline of printed roses. This was no show for me—everything Urna did, down to the way she pinched out the lanterns, felt swift and practical. I stared at her bare feet walking toward me, the stockings so fine they showed the sea-blue veins running up her legs. She rolled the stockings to her ankles and shook herself free, and I was struck by how unfamiliar she seemed to me now, naked beside me, where not five minutes earlier I had felt as close to Urna as I've ever felt to anyone. Beautiful Urna—a woman with whom I have been acquainted for thirty years, about whom I apparently know nothing—unbelted my trousers and tugged them down to my ankles and guided me inside her as smoothly as if she were pocketing a bill.

"Harp, Harp . . . Honey, what is wrong?" she said, combing her fingers along the back of my head, where the hair still grows thick as river otter fur. I almost burst into laughter then—I had no idea what I looked like, did I? I could not imagine who Urna saw.

"Do you want to try it laying down?" she said in a tone that I had never heard addressed to me even in my imaginings.

I nodded.

I'd been wishing my whole life to hear such words. Urna reached a hand under my shirt and her nails felt like rain down my back. No one had ever touched me in these places. Not since my mother bathed me as a child—although I did know better than to share that.

If it sounds too good to be true, it ain't true . . .

But Urna pressed her lips to mine and they were warm and real.

So were the fingers undoing my buttons.

"May I . . ."

Another man took over. He ran his hands down the naked length of my neighbor. He knelt in front of her and drew her hips forward on the bed, circling her nipples with his tongue, parting her legs and sliding between them. Her dark eyes widened on the pillow and this new man held her gaze. Someone came out of hiding inside me, and thank goodness too, because the old timid Harp Oletsky would have broken the spell.

※

While Urna slept, I crept off and made myself a cheese and apple sandwich. I watched my shadow bloat on the poppy red wallpaper. The large rectangular window looked out across pure distance at this late hour—no Spiders dotting the horizon, a single windmill. Voile curtains hung from the brass bar. It was strange to stand in a woman's kitchen. Everything was swept and polished. Dark plums heaped in a fancy porcelain bowl. A little chip on the rim, which made me feel more at home. I have a chip on my front tooth. The collie puppy kept tugging at my pant cuffs, trying to wrestle them off my leg. I had a happy memory of doing this same tug-of-war with my old mutt, Squint. Squint and I don't have the energy for much play these days, and it was kind of the puppy to remind me what it felt like. She wouldn't stop yapping until I picked her up in my arms, knuckling her behind the ears. How was any of this happening? In the parlor mirror, I saw that Urna had bitten violet flowers onto my neck.

I started to laugh, causing the puppy to wiggle in my arms. This wasn't a comfortable feeling. Part of me wanted to gopher into the old hole of my misery. Failure is the outcome that makes the most sense to me. Birth to death, bad to worse. *From dust we came and to dust we shall return*, said my mother, linking her hands with mine in prayer. Does that console anyone? It terrified me at age four.

My parents lost their country and two of their three children and never so much as broke even on their great American gamble. Unlike my parents, who were driven out of Poland and arrived in Nebraska filled with hope, I never assume that tomorrow will be any brighter than today.

When I was a boy, I would say, "Daddy, teach me how to speak your language. Teach me Polish." And he'd say, "No. You are an American. You can teach me how they talk." He could never make heads or tails of the English verb tenses. He once grumbled to me, "In Yankee, everything I say is *today, today, today*!"

A minute before sleep, Urna had turned to me and kissed my shoulder. "Good night, Harp. I will see you tomorrow."

Tomorrow. The promise rang in my ears.

I put the puppy down and watched her run into Urna's dark room. I followed her toward the soft, strange bed that was not my own, feeling a great relief as I sank into the mattress. The puppy licked my face and Urna found my hand in her sleep. I had not spent a night away from the Oletsky place since the summer I was nineteen and working with my father in the Sandhills. I had not slept in a bed with another person since I was very small and my brother, Frank, was alive. Never with a woman.

Urna turned on her side and moaned softly, pressing heat into my spine. I felt a great drowsy peace enter my body, a happy beginning. Even the mattress seemed to sigh in welcome. I'd just completed one of the best days of my life, and to my great surprise I expected more of them. *Tomorrow, tomorrow, tomorrow*. I saw golden grain in my field, laid against the fallow strips. Carloads of wheat, bound for all parts of the world. I felt that I was, for the first time in the history of our family, speaking American.

I got back to my place at 10:00 a.m., to the baleful lowing of my neglected animals. After making the rounds with the chickens and cows, I worked until a quarter past two fixing the Spider's clogged fuel filter. When I came in for supper, I learned the house was empty. Lada's bed—Dell's bed, I corrected myself—had been neatly made. A note was propped on the pillow, the blue letters stitched to the white paper as precisely as embroidery on a pillowcase. Asphodel's penmanship is much neater than I had expected from my niece's feral appearance. She and Lada have the same handwriting, right down to the guppy tails of the *y*'s. There was Lada, alive again in the blue ink that slanted away from me, running off the paper like water. It stabbed at my heart.

Away Game In Red Willow, Home Sunday.

Your Undefeated Niece,
Asphodel Oletsky

The scarecrow was swaying slightly in the windless fields. I ignored him. I am uninterested in that scarecrow's shenanigans, his persistence. I am interested in preserving my sanity. "I am in love with Urna," I said, testing the words on the air. How does anybody know if they are inside or outside of it, love? It's another lesson I feel like I must have missed, as all the others seem to know it. X + Y = Love. Something simple to compute, if only you had learned the formula. This was back when we still had to bind and shock the wheat ourselves. A time when I was certain I would get married—it was what every boy did. Then, with each passing year, a little less sure. When I turned thirty, my conviction shifted. After that I was equally certain that I would remain a bachelor forever. I shut my eyes and tried to remember the smell of Urna's lemon-scented house. Her rough hands and the softness of her skin under the bedclothes. Were we inside of it together, love? Or was I alone in a silly dream?

Walking the rows, I saw that the first swollen nodes had pushed above the soil. I knelt and used my razor blade to split the stems—hollow, right on schedule. The flag leaf would emerge from the whorl within the next three weeks, barring some disaster.

I wondered who I would ask to help me with the harvest. In the past, Otto and I have always shared the cost of hiring an outfit. We took turns running the combine, while his wife kept everybody fed. I could pay my neighbors to help me this June, I supposed. But the thought of hiring my friends to harvest my wheat after they had lost everything turned my stomach.

Extreme luck is extremely lonely. Good as well as bad. I didn't know that a month ago. Now I'd been enclosed in some kind of bubble, set apart from the dust and from everyone who suffers. If I could extend my spell of protection to my neighbors it might feel like a true blessing. As it stands, I feel like an ant trapped under a glass. My isolation feels complete. Nobody has shunned me, or run me out of town. Nevertheless, I have been cast out of Uz.

I want to be free of it, this invisible frame that has walled me off from the others' fate. Before Black Sunday, we'd all suffered under the hammer of the same weather, and I wanted to share in the fortune of my friends.

Overhead, the blue sky looked as stiff as paper on a wall. I got down on my knees in the prickling green stalks. Across the wire, on Otto's side of the property line, three-mile-long strips had gotten dusted out. The same is true all over Uz.

"If it be Thy will," I prayed, "would you kindly forsake me again?"

The Scarecrow

The girl claims to hate it here. But her eyes go round with pleasure whenever she sees the tiny herd return. They came again tonight. Sprinting along the red line of the horizon. Fanning out as blue evening chases them. Jumping straight up from the ground. Like. Like.

Popcorn! A memory returns to me. Butter melting. Falling salt. Yellow teeth exploding into clouds. Poppoppoppoppoppop! Bursts of dollhouse gunfire. Sweet, scorched smell.

The herd springs out of the sunset. Like corn kernels popping in a skillet.

Antelope is what the farmer calls these creatures. Horns spiral through me. *Antelope.* The blank wall crumbles and a space opens. Names are spells. Names conjure skies and animals. Inside the mirror of this mind, I have begun to practice a new power. Inventing shapes out of the shapes I can recall with the high whistle of a name. Remaking names into nameless creations, flowing scenes. Yesterday I dreamed up an antelope with enormous wings. Starling green and violet, bright and muscular. Pushing the dust earthward as they flapped up and down. She carried me to a clearing as far from the fallowland as I could imagine, out of the little I remember. A very short distance.

The real herd is more astonishing than anything I can imagine. It is a blessing to watch them disappearing, returning. Happiness shakes through me like the outer winds—I feel as though I am running with them. Their beauty confounds my understanding of where and what I am. I don't want to call this prison heaven. This body of straw. But if this is hell, and I am tinder for eternal fire, why should I feel such joy?

This herd is so far south. So far from their ordinary range. How do I know this? Is it something I overheard the farmer say? He mumbles to himself as he crosses my shadow. He prays, staring down at the ground. *Look at me,* I beg the curve of his back. What I would give, to nod yes to anything. To turn and find a kind face that knows me.

The RA Photographer, Cleo Allfrey

I never intended to betray the mission of the Historical Section. I came to this so-called Dust Bowl to find what Roy Stryker sent me to see.

Two days after my arrival in Nebraska, my Contax camera was stolen from my motel room in Lincoln, along with the roll of film I was shooting on. I wished the thief had stolen the car instead. I was devastated. The new camera, the Graflex, I found the very next afternoon in a tiny pawnshop near Dannebrog. It shocked me to see it there, sharing space with a cobwebbed ruby brooch and a children's tea set; I felt déjà vu so strong it was like a kind of seasickness. Had I seen this camera somewhere before? What was a brand-new Graflex doing in this pawnshop God forgot off Highway 6? The wind had been up since 11:00 a.m. and the few trees loomed wraithlike through the dusty glass. The Graflex, spotless inside its case, looked as if it had never been handled. It scared me a little to find the exact thing I desperately needed in such an unlikely place. "Who pawned this camera?" I'd asked the shopkeeper, a red-wigged woman in her eighties who was sitting on an old church pew, moving only to turn the pages of the *Omaha World-Herald*. She rose like a mummy, striped in light and shadow from the wooden shades. She was Danish, as I had guessed from the delicious smell of baking apples and also from the Danish flag in the window. "It doesn't look like it has ever been used once, ma'am." I was thinking, crazily, that perhaps Lange or Rothstein had come through Dannebrog. I couldn't imagine how else such a fine instrument had found its way to her glass case of bartered heirlooms and oddities.

"Do you think I remember every lost soul who stops in here?" she'd snapped at me without looking up. She was reading the obituaries with the avidity of a sports fan. And right there—in the middle of her newspaper—was an advertisement for the Graflex, with its fabled focusing hood: *"where you see the picture."*

Eliminate the guesswork! A Graflex for every purse and purpose!

"For another twenty dollars, I'll throw in the box of junk that got pawned with that camera," the women offered, opening a trunk of disassembled equipment. My heart began to pound as I looked through it: an enlarger head, beakers for mixing chemistry, bed and short rail, 2¼″ by 3¼″ sheet film and holders . . .

"Fifteen," I said, trying to keep my voice from spiking. I could not believe my good fortune. I paid her sixty-five dollars—not even half of what the camera and the rest of the equipment would have cost in a catalog. It was a quarter of my RA travel stipend, but more than worth it to me. *Mama,* I'd written on a postcard I mailed in Hastings, *You will not believe what Uncle Sam just bought for me*: *my dream camera!*

I explained my work, what I was doing in Nebraska, and the shopkeeper suggested I take my new camera an hour south on Highway 11 to photograph an archaeological dig. Local men had been put to work on what the clerk assured me was an excavation of great historical importance. Something people really ought to know about, she said. They had spaded up all sorts of interesting Indian relics.

"Archaeology." She laughed. "A gloomy Easter egg hunt, if you ask me. All those dusty shards and skulls! But I know the men are grateful for the work."

I thanked her for the suggestion. The shopkeeper smiled at me. Posing, I realized—although I kept the camera snapped shut. Her red wig capped her pale face like the cherry on vanilla ice cream.

"Dannebrog has been here since 1871. This store's been in my family for sixty years. The Territory was a no-man's-land when they filed their claim. A sea of tallgrass that went on forever. Nothing but Indians and buffalo . . ."

I bought a road atlas from a rack by the window, thanked her for her hospitality. Only later in the car did parts of her speech return to disturb me. *Today, I pulled over and discovered the primitive town of Dannebrog. I discovered you here, in the Danish artifact of your chair.*

᪥

The wind picked up, and I had to slow to a crawl as dust enveloped the road. The ranches I saw sliding beyond the barbed-wire fencing held balding grass and sickly cattle, skinny as the auguries Joseph saw in his dreams. The doleful steers were percolating around the fence, framing up the horizon between their long curved horns. It was like looking at the orange sky through Nature's range finder. If a rumble of thunder could solidify into a landscape, it might look like this. Asphalt crackling over the scalded prairie.

My new camera tests my focus and my patience. *Nothing* is automated. Every shot requires at least twelve decisions. It opens outward like an accordion, and I do feel like I'm trying to learn how to play a new instrument. It took me a true eternity to set the infinity stops. I struggled to adjust the shutter speed, and then I accidentally exposed my best shot while clumsily handling the film holder. This Graflex has three viewfinders: optical, wire frame, and ground glass—I make myself crazy alternating views of the same scene, trying to compose a landscape. After a few days of experimentation, I learned to love the upside-down world of the ground glass for focusing. I see things in it that I miss when I come at my subject straight-on.

Near Webster, at Guide Rock, I found a dozen sweaty young men digging a deep pit in the earth and a man in a straw hat bounding between them, his large, serious eyes shining behind his black-rimmed glasses.

I introduced myself as a government photographer.

He did a double-take, then widened his smile.

I wrote his name and title down for the caption: Asa T. Hill, Director of the Museum and Field Archeology for the Nebraska State Historical Society.

While the crew paused to watch, I stared through the ground glass at the widening hole in the ground. Framed and focused my shot, inserted my film, triggered the shutter. I struggled with the dark slide, too aware of their eyes.

"You got your shot?"

"I won't know until I get my prints back from the government lab."

"I know the feeling," Hill commiserated. "You hardly know what you've got at first. Many ask me how I found the Pike-Zebulon site. Was it luck or instinct? It was my knowledge, of course, applied to the landscape." He winked at me, tapping at his temple. "But luck has a fair bit to do with it! I imagine it's the same in your profession, Mister Allfrey."

I did not correct him. I had stuffed my hair in my hat, and I had on my brother Elwin's shirt (it looked better on me) and a bulky pair of men's trousers. Roy had advised me to wear dresses in rural counties, and a wedding band on my ring finger. But Roy wasn't here.

"Now, it might have been lost to history, quite easily! Except that I had moved to Hastings and knew enough to guess what I was looking at when George DeWitt's son toured this site with me. When his father first plowed their section in 1872, the land was literally covered with such relics of Indian life. Mauls, axes, war clubs. I knew from my studies that this was almost certainly the true location of the Pawnee village, dating back to the time when they were ten thousand strong. George found a Spanish saddle, I can show you if you'd like to make a picture . . ."

I shadowed him, eavesdropping on his conversation with two other visitors.

"Digging up Indian bodies on Sunday is my form of golf . . ." Asa chuckled, touring them around the widening hole.

"I struggled mightily to convince the anthropologists that I'd found evidence of prehistoric agriculture out here." The sun bobbed in his glasses. "Everybody told me that no farming Indians had ever lived west of the Pawnee villages in Nance County . . ."

From Asa, I learned that the Pawnee people had been living in Nebraska between the Platte and the Republican Rivers for hundreds and hundreds of years.

"What became of them?" I asked, staring into the pit where the men's shovels flashed gem green in the hot sun.

"They live in Oklahoma now. Coughing up dust like the rest of us. The last Pawnees removed to Indian Country in 1876."

Indian Country. I didn't say anything, just snapped a picture of the Indian Country under my feet, where the men were cataloging their discoveries of Indian cookware and digging up the floor of an Indian earth lodge. I did the math in my head—DeWitt and the Pawnees had been neighbors. The government had taken their land and given it to George.

"It was a damn shame," said Mr. Hill. "But they signed the treaties."

I stood in the shade of the water tent, uneasy. Around me, half a dozen sunburned men were gulping water. I made a picture of them. Asa T. Hill stood beside me, amusing his guests. He held up a human skull and ventriloquized with it.

"Alas, poor Yorick . . ."

"Did you know him well, Horatio?" I strained to hide my disgust behind the grate of my smile. What did science have to do with this? *Roy*, I imagined writing. *Here are my negatives of a man's grave looting.*

Asa T. Hill grinned back, delighted by my recitation. "He knows his Shakespeare!" Around us, the crew had stopped working to eavesdrop, leaning on their shovels. I saw the men's expressions changing, as fast as the sun disappears. Rainless clouds lumped like coal across the parched country. I took a few reluctant shots.

"None of this is going to photograph well, sir."

"What! That's it?"

Asa was looking at me with pop-eyed betrayal, as if I were a visiting child to whom he'd offered an ice cream cone, only to have the gift smeared across his face.

"You don't want to waste your precious film on us?"

I saw that I had violated his idea of how my visit should go: I was not overly grateful. I was not dishonest. I did not remake my face into a flattering mirror of the man and his work. The needle was bumping sixty as I sped off.

I drove four hours to one of the new resettlement farmsteads. It wasn't my idea of something to photograph, but Stryker wanted pictures of the New Deal cooperatives. The houses were only a few months old, so conspicuously lacking a past. They cast thin shadows, as did the ten families who tenanted them, chosen by a local committee from hundreds of applications—Bohemians and Slavs and Germans and Irish. Black families had not been selected for this particular cooperative, and when I asked why not I was met with a wary silence that I returned in kind. The farmsteads were a bold New Deal experiment—moving poor farmers off degraded lands and onto more fertile ones. "Off the relief rolls and into the garden," as a gap-toothed young White man explained it, posing with a wheelbarrow of dirty carrots. A jackrabbit watched me from behind the barbed wire, spinning its hind leg like a clock winding itself. I made the farmers' portraits. Many of the new planned utopias in the East are sundown towns. This farmstead did not feel unsafe to me, but I did not want to test my hypothesis. My camera and I were gone long before nightfall.

I hear my boss's voice mocking me in my head: "Are you sure you would not prefer an urban assignment, Allfrey?"

Afterward I decided to drive around some of the farms on the shortgrass prairie. Part of the joy of working for the RA is the freedom of working alone, with no oversight, for weeks at a time. Two cents per mile, four dollars of spending money a day. I was on a treasure hunt for the latest request for the File:

1. Shots which give the sense of great distance and flat country (remember Lange's two mailboxes). House; barn and windmill on horizon; lots of sky.
   (WOULD ADD TO INTEREST IF WATER TANK OR SIGNAL TOWER WERE IN FOREGROUND.)

I found myself bumping down a back road, the wind chasing me, dust filming the windshield, dust coating the light. Bad luck for a photographer. I parked and climbed onto the roof of the Ford. There was only sand and tufting grass as far as the eye could see, and no nearby land in cultivation. I was nine miles from Uz, the nearest town on my atlas, but it could have been ninety. To my delight, I found something that told me it wanted to be photographed: a cottonwood that had been split in two by lightning or an ax blow, yet seemed, somehow, to still be growing. *Doppelgänger* was the word it brought into my mind. A very unlucky tree, to get hit by the lightning; a very lucky tree, to have survived it and multiplied. Each half was like a mirror image of the other, its branches shivering with identical mirth in the strong wind. Some of these western trees seem so gnarled and solemn to me, but this one looked to be laughing at its own joke.

I made one more portrait of this hardy tree, then I scrambled back into the Ford, the hair standing on the back of my neck. I thought I heard a rattlesnake behind me, and I checked the sedan twice. Images from my journey kept flashing inside my mind: the tombstone of White Buffalo Girl in Neligh, the two-sided tree. I drove down the nameless country road until I reached the highway, wondering if perhaps I had just made my iconic portrait of the Dust Bowl. Wondering if my negatives would be acceptable to Stryker—suitable for use as "loaded ammunition," as Lange put it, for the New Deal programs.

On the drive into Uz, I'd been surprised by a stretch of shimmering color. Fields greening up were an anomaly in that part of the country. Green meant water. Blue sky could mislead you, but green did not lie. It was green, and not blue, that had become synonymous with "moisture." I considered stopping and making pictures of the young wheat, the first I had seen since my arrival on the High Plains. But the light was already low, and I felt dizzy with hunger. I'd been on the road for thirteen days by that point, and driven clear across the state of Nebraska. I decided I'd have better luck shooting the green wheat field tomorrow, after I visited the Uz County Grange. In the rearview, it waved behind me like a mirage. Would it still be there, I wondered, when I returned? For a moment it seemed I might be light-headed and hallucinating green. The red eye of the sun watched me as I raced into town to find a spot to wash up and eat and sleep another solitary night.

Two taffy-colored cows and a bawling calf loose on Highway 10 caused me to skid off the road. Right at dusk, I realized it had been hours since I'd seen the reassuring angels of the telegraph poles. *Where am I?* A faded sign answered me: NOW ENTERING UZ.

In my folder I had sample captions from "the best work that's been done so far" by Roy's other field investigators and photographers. My captions were too long, he told me. "A picture is *worth* a thousand words, Cleo. It does not warrant a thousand-word caption . . ." Although he did agree that a judicious quote here and there went a long way to supplying a voice to a face, as in the portrait of Ward Pearson:

General Caption No. 87
Date: March 30
Location: Cora, Neb.
Subject: Forced Sale
Sheriff's Sale of Farm Property.
Prudential Insurance owed by Ward and Elzbieta Pearson:
$4169.85.

Sheriff Galore accepts bids at 10:00 a.m. outside the door of the courthouse. No locals present. A young bank representative from Peoria, Illinois, makes the only bid. The insurance company acquires the Pearsons' full title.

"Things will go on without us as if we never existed"—Ward Pearson.

People are wary of my camera, with good reason. Each flash ran a stake through your heart. Now you were nailed to one spot, wearing this forlorn or broken expression. The wrinkling ocean of human thinking and feeling that ripples across a face, over a lifetime—the camera cannot capture any of that. "Does my face always look so angry?" a German opera singer in Lincoln had asked me, staring at the contact print I'd hastily made for her in her basement, in exchange for free lodging. Her husband had yelped, "That gloomy old donkey don't look a thing like me!" As it happened, I'd ambushed him. I waited until the fierce sun had caught in his unshaven whiskers and pushed his features into a squint. I needed faces marred by the sorrows and the hardships of the Depression. I did not want a picture of a handsome, happy person. I sent their portraits to Washington with high hopes.

Uz was an ugly and uninviting place, although I tried to see it through Roy Stryker's eyes as a worthy subject for the File: a charming rural town. The buildings had the monochrome look of tombstones, their paint scoured off by sun and dust and wind. The grinning face on the billboard across from the saloon looked familiar to me, although perhaps I had simply seen a version of this person in other towns on my journey across the state. A sunburned White man with a golden badge pinned to his shirt and a showman's smile. A VOTE FOR SHERIFF ISCOE IS A VOTE FOR JUSTICE SERVED! I set up my tripod on the opposite sidewalk and made a wide-angle picture of it. Stryker liked photographs of rural politics.

I had not planned to stay in Uz for more than a night. The only lodging I could find was a room for rent above a saloon called the Country Jentleman. It was loud and crowded, and the landlord overcharged me. But there were no other hotels or motor lodges in Uz, and the sun was low in the sky. While I waited for my room key, I ordered a soda at the bar. I have been refused service too many times to count. Catcalled and condescended to by waiters in fancy restaurants in D.C. and fish shacks on the Platte. Commanded to exit and reenter buildings through "the colored door." I felt relieved when the bartender at the Country Jentleman took my money wordlessly and handed me my Coca-Cola. A pug-nosed White girl of fifteen or sixteen was sitting on the barstool next to me.

"Starting a little early, aren't you."

"I'm just drinking water."

I noticed that her feet didn't reach the floor, the laces dangling from her Converse sneakers. She had a celery green smell, clean and earthy, like morning sweat. She had hundred-year-old eyes in her round baby face. I was reminded, for some reason, of the intelligent, good-natured hunger in the sparkling eyes of starving hogs.

"Are you playing hooky? Is it from school, or work?"

"I am waiting for my boss to open up. She has an office upstairs. That's her—"

She pointed to a poster that looked like a newspaper advertisement for a miracle drug: THE ANTIDOTE OF UZ.

The Prairie Witch

L ast night, I caught the tag ends of the men's talk around a poker table at the Country Jentleman: a few sozzled ranchers were debating whether Sheriff Iscoe was a good lawman. I wondered what each meant by *good*.

"He got lucky with the hobo kid."

"Dew was no damn 'kid.' He was a monster."

I seized up in my chair. *He is alive*. For now, anyway, in the Lincoln penitentiary. I closed my eyes and saw the boy's gaunt face snatched away from the campfire, the silver tracks moving out into the rolling dark, the men and women at the shantytown scattering at the sight of the Sheriff's car, his flashlight pinging off the rusted clasps of the boy's suspenders.

I do not imagine things with the vividness of the Oletsky girl. But I have been trying to picture Clemson's mother, in my limited way—a silhouette somewhere back East, shot through with holes. Does she know where her baby is today?

There was one dissenting voice at the table, Charles Evans.

"You really feel safer with that touched-in-the-head kid locked away?"

He shook his head at the table, wearing the look of a shopkeep confronting his cashiers in the act of lifting dollars from the drawer.

"Let's not insult our own intelligence here, to pay Sheriff Iscoe a compliment. None of you believe that lost duckling did it. The entire proceeding against him took one goddamn day. No physical evidence. No written record of his confession." Charles's laughter sounded like fists hammering on an organ.

Around the table, the farmers and ranchers looked annoyed.

"This round is on you, Charlie," one grumbled.

Vick's plan is working, Son. Vick wants the Lucky Rabbit's Foot Killer on every tongue in Uz. Last election cycle, he campaigned on a promise to run "vagrants and miscreants" out of town. He writes scathing editorials that defend Uzians' ideas about Uz. For most of his career, promises have been enough. But this time he has a rival, that loudmouth Ernie Whitson. This election, Vick is milking the Lucky Rabbit's Foot Killer conviction for all it's worth.

A sheriff in a rural county may not sound like much power to scrap over. But taking conscious deposits has been a rapid education. I have learned a great deal more about where power flows and what it does.

"Are you gonna vote for Iscoe?"

"Probably . . ."

I did not interrupt to share my opinion. Shame burned through me, but I sat in its flames and said nothing. Several of the men were my longtime customers. What would happen if I shouted over their argument: "I know the Sheriff is a monster and a liar. I know he set Dew up for those murders." Even if they believed me, I doubt they'd welcome the news that I am awake now, listening to their secrets.

Every day, I learn something incriminating. Of me, certainly. Of Iscoe. Of my guilt-ridden customers. One by one, the trial jurors who returned Mr. Dew's guilty verdict have begun to show up outside Room 11. Five of the twelve have made appointments since the botched electrocution. It seems they are referring one another to me.

A Bohemian mechanic with a twitchy left eye . . .

A nineteen-year-old Norwegian farmhand . . .

A Welsh muskmelon farmer with nine fingers (an older story he didn't add to his deposit) . . .

A Scandinavian pharmacist who hadn't slept since hearing the verdict . . .

A Polish rancher who said he preferred his steers to people, who had no wish to prolong a trial when he had sick animals back home . . .

Reggie Nowak, the Polish rancher, whispered into my earhorn that he'd faltered when the foreman pushed for a guilty verdict. "Every day I wished I hadn't been chosen . . ." He felt he'd been conscripted into an evil pageant. "The curtain had to go down on *someone*." Reggie did not want to go home to a remote ranch with four young daughters and a killer at large. "Something is off with that kid," the foreman insisted. "Look at those big staring eyes! Look at that *smile*! He killed them without ever knowing their names!" Reggie had let himself be convinced.

Only now Reggie was not so sure. The electrocution had given him nightmares. Rumors were traveling about other women who had gone missing in nearby counties. Reggie was more afraid than he'd been before Dew's arrest. "My buddy says that after I deposit this my mind will stop playing tricks on me. It has been three weeks since I slept a wink. I listen for a killer at our door. I have these dreams of rabbits, rabbits with crumpled ears, rabbits with caved-in skulls, crushed and bleeding and still running . . ."

Peter Haage, the pharmacist, told me he never believed that Dew was guilty. He'd been bullied by the jury foreman, who he said "has something over me." He wanted to deposit the moment when he abandoned his original position. "I was the one man of the twelve fighting to save that boy's life, and I folded. Please, miss, take it out of me—"

Juror Number Seven, the muskmelon farmer, asked to deposit a song.

"Two weeks before the Sheriff arrested him, I heard Clemson Louis Dew playing his violin at the Hooverville. I was riding home from the depot right at sunset. Dew was a jug-eared kid, funny-looking. Too shy to meet anybody's eyes. When he started fiddling, his whole posture changed. His bow moved like it was stitching everything together, stars and fire and strangers like me. I remember watching him play and thinking that he looked like my mother at her sewing. His face had her sort of concentration. Well, I would like to deposit the tune he played that night. Can I do that? Put a melody inside you? It has been running through my head for months. I am roofing a barn right now and I am afraid of falling off and shattering my bones! I been wondering when they are gonna schedule his second execution? I been wondering if the warden will give Dew a violin? I been wondering if we did the wrong thing? I am worn out from all this wondering . . ."

I told Juror Number Seven that I had no idea if it would work or not, but we could try it.

"Bless you, witch!" he yelped. Into the funnel, he belted his off-key rendition of Clemson's song. I pushed my tongue against the roof of my mouth to keep from screaming. The melody now runs through me. The farmer looked a foot taller when he left, ten years younger. "Can't remember what I came here to deposit," he'd said with a grin, rubbing at his lower spine. "But good riddance!"

People talk about memories flying into and out of their heads. But my work makes me wonder if our maps are wrong. It seems to me that the seat of memory is much lower down, Son. My customers often rub at the place where their spine meets their tailbone. Others spiderweb their hands over their navel. Folks who come to me remember in their hands and their feet. Their thudding hearts remember. Their blood circulates their past. People desire with their whole bodies, and they remember that way too.

Now that I am awake, I know that my business is founded on a lie. There is no safe way to remove chapters from the book of one's life. You cannot wait until there is more time, more money, more safety, less pain to recollect the past. I hope you have never banked with someone like me.

⊰⊱

"Howdy, Ant. Mind if my friend and I come in?"

The man's face was flyleaf white. He was so loaded that he had to steady himself on the Sheriff, which Iscoe tolerated with a grimace. No, not loaded after all—was he ill? He looked at me with lucid agony. I recognized poor Al Kriska, who I have always liked. If Vick had brought him to me after midnight, the news could only be bad.

"I was having a drink with your loyal customer downstairs, and he confided something quite upsetting to me. He says he made a withdrawal of a beautiful memory last week."

"Doesn't sound so bad," I said, trying to mask my nerves.

"Well I know for a fact that memory was *entirely fabricated*."

A smile and a frown twisted the Sheriff's face around, as if two hands were wringing out a rag. His skin bunched and flattened. I swallowed back panic.

"What was it, Al? I was in my trance, as you know. I'm sure we can sort this out . . ."

"None of your business," said Al Kriska, his cheeks red as hot-house tomatoes.

"Now, don't be shy, Kriska. The jig is up. She lied to you, and she knows it."

Vick kept his eyes trained on me, pacing in front of my chair.

"Now, Kriska hears a rumor that another woman has gone missing. That the Lucky Rabbit's Foot Killer is still out there. He's been thinking about leaving Uz and that clinches it. He decides to withdraw everything. Cut and run, like so many other Uzians . . ."

Al Kriska nodded like a doll on a spring, only his wiry neck moving.

"I run into him downstairs tonight. He's humming that infernal tune I hear everywhere these days. Now, I'm a detective. I'm intrigued by this mystery. What's making Al Kriska so happy, before his first beer? He tells me that he made a withdrawal. Big daffy grin on his face. Says he's planning to leave Uz for San Francisco. He's bought *dancing shoes*—"

The Sheriff elbowed Alexander Kriska, who was certainly not smiling at the moment.

"Boy, did the witch have some fun with you!"

Kriska winced. He gave me a hurt, angry look.

"You told me that I danced with Fred and Adele Astaire at the Orpheum Theater."

This counterfeit had been the girl's invention. Her teammate Dagmara Kriska had once told Dell that her flat-footed father had dreamed of being a dancer.

"I remember it so vividly. I was pulled out of the crowd and onto the stage. Pretty girls threw roses and coins at my feet."

"Quite a whopper, Ant! You see, I remember Fred and Adele dancing at the Orpheum. My mother attended. That was 1908."

"Eleven years before my family arrived in Omaha, witch." Was Kriska's voice vibrating with rage, or humiliation, or sorrow at having to dismantle the happy memory we'd given him? I wondered what he had actually interred in me.

"You lied to me."

"I am no liar," I lied. "You read me the numbers on your slip. I returned what you gave me to store. I cannot invent, Mr. Kriska. I simply returned what you deposited. My body stays in the room, but my mind goes blank."

Without a word, Kriska stood. Very mournfully, he began to stamp and to shuffle his feet. One foot and then the other. He moved like a freshly shod horse, testing his feet, testing the ground, without any rhythm I could discern. He sat back down, and I thought I saw a small, sad smile of triumph on his face.

"It wasn't true," he said. "I have never been a dancer. Give me back my real past."

Viper-like, Vick lunged forward. He seized my wrist, dragging me to my feet. His speed surprised me. Vick is a slack-bellied, haggard man these days, graying above his ears. I can't imagine him dancing.

"Go downstairs. I'll get your deposit back for you, Al."

Flat-footed Alexander Kriska stood and hobbled toward the door. He looked back at me with wounded animal eyes. Was he troubled at the thought of how this "interrogation" would go? Or was he catching bouquets in his mind? I had loved the girl's counterfeit for Mr. Kriska. The best night of his life, at age eleven! Hundreds of people thundering with applause for his tap dancing. It had seemed like a harmless invention—even kind. His face taught me otherwise.

We listened to Kriska's heavy, uneven footsteps moving down the stairs. Only after he'd traveled out of earshot did Vick begin the interrogation.

"What did he really tell you, Ant?"

I shook my head. "Sheriff, I have not the faintest idea."

Vick locked the door. He walked to the wall and plucked my earhorn from its hook. He peered inside it, as if looking for evidence of the counterfeiting operation. Story lines taped to the metal. Paint brushed over blood.

"I don't know why Kriska would deposit a fib. But I only returned it to him—is that a crime?"

"You've changed your business model, Ant. I'm onto your tricks."

"You're calling me a fraud?"

He sat and drew his chair so close that our long noses nearly touched.

"You don't give me any credit, Ant. I am a detective. I pay attention. Your customers come downstairs grinning like dopes, making everybody listen to stories about their noble deeds and love affairs. Things that *I* know are horseshit. They smile like lobotomy patients, and talk a blue streak about the incredible things they only just remembered. You didn't think you'd be found out? Did you figure everyone in Uz would believe they were saints and heroes?"

His expression trembled between amusement and fury.

"I don't know what you're talking about, Vick."

"You'll remember I'm a customer myself, Ant, and I have a vested interest in knowing that every word that comes back through that tin-can telephone of yours is accurate."

I bluffed, then panicked. Without my assistant, I had no strategies, no stories to reassure him.

"Make a withdrawal right now—you'll see. My mouth moves alone, without a chaperone. My mind is far away."

He forced a laugh from his belly. "The way I see it, you need *me* to keep *your* secret now. And I need a favor."

A favor.

I stood and started for the door, but Vick took me by the arms and forced me backward onto my cot. Calling for help in Room 11 on a Saturday night is useless, Son. It joins the general wail from the stalled carousel of the saloon. "Whooo-oooo-oooo!" came the birdy scream of the gamblers on the ground floor.

"Ant, people really believe these lies you pour into them! *Won the state spelling bee. Survived a shoot-out. Reconciled with a brother.* Whatever you whisper into this contraption *becomes* real to them. No different than their other memories."

As I listened, I heard real awe in the Sheriff's voice. For the first time in our acquaintance, I heard respect. It was my power he respected, not me. He wanted it.

"I knew you could *remove* people's memories—you've been very useful for cleaning up some ugly messes. But you're more than just a dirty sponge, Ant. You're a *paintbrush*."

"What do you want from me, Vick?"

"Plenty of nasty talk about me at the moment. Mob opinion. We stabilized it with Dew's conviction, and now it's swinging around again."

"And what is being said?"

"A couple folks are suddenly doubting the testimony they gave. Starting to remember little details here and there. Weeds sprouting through cracks." He steepled his fingers. "There's this woman— Mink Petrusev. Her distant cousin came to visit her last week and reported her missing. Sure wish he'd stayed distant. Her cousin is a loudmouth, as it turns out. Suddenly half the town seems to feel that a killer is still out there."

"Oh? I wasn't aware."

Clemson, forgive me. Mother of Clemson, forgive me. Mink, forgive me.

But why should they? Mink stared at me from behind a wall of red flame, Vick's dime store lucky charm melting into her chest. Did Vick truly have no recollection of burning Mink's body? His memory twisted inside me. I'd always assumed Vick used me to conceal evidence. But I'd never gazed into the eyes of a woman we'd erased. I'd never kept Vick's secret from Vick himself.

"It's my rival behind it. Ernie Whitson is running for sheriff. I'm sure you've seen his fancy billboard. Paying the drunks to run their mouths about me. Telling everyone that I pinned the murders on the wrong man, that the killer is still on the loose!"

The Sheriff laughed.

"Can you imagine vicious rumors spreading like influenza and ruining *your* reputation, Ant? I bet you can. Well I have an even better strategy than Whitson. *You're* going to be my secret weapon."

Vick's face bore down on me. He plucked a purple aster from the vase on the table and began to rip off the petals, letting them flutter down into the open maw of the earhorn.

"MAKE ME A CAST-IRON ALIBI," Vick roared.

"What are you talking about?"

"We can practice on Al Kriska."

"Practice *what*?"

"Painting."

It took me a moment to understand what Vick was proposing.

"He'll come back with me to make his *real* withdrawal. You'll remind him that I'm a *legendary* lawman. Invent a memory for the day he bumped into Mink on the train platform, leaving town? We'll start with Al, then I'll bring you Mink's blabbermouth cousin, her neighbor, and so on—"

If I wasn't so afraid, Vick's face would have made me laugh. He looked like a panicked little boy who had smashed a rotten egg and was trying to fan the smell out the window.

Vick is a counterfeiter. We'd been partners, I realized. Long before I truly understood this. I shut my eyes and I could see it: the Sheriff planting a bloody rabbit's foot on Minnie's sternum, planting another one on Allene's collarbone, using the rabbit's foot to tie his story line together, stringing everyone along: "The Lucky Rabbit's Foot Killer Strikes Again!"

Sheriff Iscoe had cast himself as the hero in a sensational tale, one that was disintegrating before his eyes. "I can't have folks thinking that women around Uz County are still disappearing. I am sure you can appreciate why I need your help. Panic doesn't serve anyone, does it?"

I cradled the earhorn to my chest. Feeling somehow that I had betrayed it, too—my tin magic, my conduit. *Your mother has done great harm with this instrument, Son. I am only beginning to understand my part, and how deep it goes.*

"I won't do it."

I caught a petal as it fell and squeezed my fist around it.

The shocked stem regarded the peeling floorboards.

Could I just erase a woman from a town's memory?

Had I done so already? Who else had I hidden for him?

"Sure you will. I'll be back tomorrow, with Al, and we'll help the people of Uz remember that this town is a safe and peaceful place. Remind them that I brought a monster to justice." He winked. "And if you want to throw in a little something scandalous about Ernie Whitson—say he's been canoodling with little girls, something like that—all the better."

I stared from the purple aster to Vick's broken, red-rimmed nails.

"Tomorrow," I echoed. My mind flashed to the train schedule. Iscoe has many old cronies at the depot. I wondered if I could hitch to Kearney and catch the train there. The girl could give me a ride out of town, if I could reach her. *And where will you go?* I heard in Malvina's mocking voice. *What scheme is left for a gray-haired fugitive—a washed-up witch?*

I don't know where you are, Son, so I don't know where to run. If I knew that, I would have abandoned this cursed town long ago.

"And what if the rumor is true? What if the killer is still out there? Another woman might die while you are trying to shore up your reputation. What do you plan to do then, Sheriff? When the bodies keep coming?"

"I'll catch him, or them. I'll catch the next one. I'll catch every killer out here. But I can't do that unless I win the election. We've lost a third of our population since this drought began, we won't survive another Panic. A good leader provides a solution to the problem of fear."

"Even if I could—"

"How cute. Someone call Meachum at *The Gazette*! I've got a headline for him: THE PRAIRIE WITCH DISCOVERS A PRINCIPLE."

"I can't just pluck a woman out of her cousin like a flower."

Although of course I can and I have. What became of them, the ones I held and lost? I pictured petals spinning through the Black Sunday dust, torn loose from their stems.

"Do I have to remind you what happens to the prairie witches who run?"

Vick is a good actor. When he pretended to slit my throat with his finger, I heard myself crying out in the future, trampled by my customers, gargling blood and sand.

There are no obituaries of prairie witches, because we are not supposed to exist. We are stains on the towns that support us. The towns that we support.

"Oh, I forgot to mention that Red and I had a good long chat about you the other day."

The Sheriff tucked my hair behind my ear, as if I had reminded him that he was also a father. "He's seemed out of sorts—not usual for Red. Said you filled him up with your stories about me. He mumbled something about my 'misdeeds.' My 'romances.' At first I was put out, of course. Now I understand you better. You are a counterfeiter—stuffing him full of calumny. You wanted to turn my boy against me, did you?"

"I regret that," I said. "I wanted to hurt him with the truth, and it worked . . ."

"Worked!" Vick roared with laughter. "Who do you think my boy is loyal to, huh? He doesn't believe you."

The Sheriff began to fiddle with his buckle. His voice seemed to split from his body, warm and solicitous even as his shadow covered my face. During my stays in Cell 8, Vick has told me he loves me many times before. Hot whispers shoved into my ear. Who are they intended for? Someone he sees behind his squeezed eyelids, sweat rolling from his cheeks onto my cheeks. Some woman in Vick's imagination for whom my flesh substitutes.

Vick had the dry breath of earth still on him, panting out with his sweat, his sour odor poorly concealed by the diner's heavy odors of frying bacon and coffee, cherry pie and pipe smoke. Kittens mewled between my ears, shoveled under the water by Vick and held in their dead-alive suspension in the washbasin.

Before he left, Vick leaned down and struck my naked ear with the flat of his hand. I shrieked and winced, and he knelt on the floorboards and whispered into the smarting hole, *I love you, I love you, I love you*, breathing down on my neck, jerking my chair toward him, pulling me down from the chair and kneeling over me, fooling with his belt buckle, and all the while murmuring, *I love you, I love you, I love you*, until the distance between what his mouth was saying and what his hands were doing grew so howlingly vast that once again I felt my sanity coming apart on the splintering planks.

※

Around 3:00 a.m., Sheriff Vick Iscoe dressed and buckled up and left without a word, the door banging after him. I guess he figured I was beaten. He thought I was too smart to try and run.

Mink Petrusev, lying on a sand dune in my mind, regarded me with her quiet, intelligent eyes. Her blue lips moved. "Help me," she said. Her piercing voice, hoarse with dust, struggling up over a howling wind between my ears to make itself understood.

You can't win an argument with a dead woman in your mind. I pled my case anyhow. What right did she have to tell me how to gamble with my life? A dead woman with nothing to lose, instructing me to risk everything I had left.

For all I know, You might be on a train to Uz right now. Following the trail of bread crumbs I've left for You to find me. The cook at the Home for Unwed Mothers is keeping an eye out for You. The Vaults in the towns surrounding Milford, too. The county clerk in Beatrice receives a yearly payment from me. He's still sitting on your birth and death records from the Home for Unwed Mothers: "Baby Rossi." Should You come looking for your real mother, they have instructions to give You a letter from me and a map to Uz. What are the odds that we will find each other? It becomes less likely every passing year. I know that, Son. You are not my baby any longer. You are a grown man, whose life I can scarcely imagine.

But *unlikely* is not impossible.

Unlikely is a door ajar.

The Antidote's Story:
Part 2

O h, Saint Frances!" Stencil knelt before the portrait of Frances P. Clark, wearing her underwear as a bonnet, making me laugh until I felt dizzy. "I don't want whatever you want most for me!"

Stencil swore she had no regrets about how she'd lived—she'd enjoyed sex before she became a ward of the state, "and I'll enjoy it again the minute I bust loose." In a pique of rage, eavesdropping Nurse Elaine demanded to know if Stencil considered herself a child of God or merely "a vessel for semen."

"Bottle of baby batter, that's me." Stencil swaggered around with her belly out and the drunken gait every girl seemed to acquire in her last months.

Even when Stencil made jokes, her punch lines were shaped by the outside world's ugliest opinions of us. But we had to laugh in that place. Our backs ached and we couldn't keep food down, or else we ate and ate and never filled the hole inside us. I stooped and straightened for full workdays of Duty in the garden and the kitchen, and at night it felt like the Devil himself was strumming a red guitar on my inflamed tendons.

When we were working in the rows, our bodies occupied, serious talk came more freely. I heard such horrific conception stories in that place—rapes by family members, ministers, employers. "God must be a man, or how could She stand this?" said Nathalee, a French-Canadian girl who had whispered to me one brittle morning that she and her baby shared a father. "If you breathe a word of what I said I will kill you with my own hands, Toni. Who is going to want to touch me now?"

"Someone will," I said dully. I should have let more kindness into my voice, Son. I was shivering in the Nebraska gloom, waiting for You to kick and relieve me of the fear that You had died in the night. I suppose I am telling Nathalee's secret now. You may think less of me for breaking her confidence. But Nathalee died in childbirth, along with her baby, on the Ides of March in 1908, and I doubt she'd mind fresh mourners.

⚏

Infant corpses were taken two miles southwest of the Home and interred in the Blue Mound Cemetery. As far as I know, there were no services.

⚏

Love was never lacking in the Home. But I found it difficult to accept the love of the Nurses, particularly Nurse Edna, with her holy jewelry and her heavy scowl. A tiny crucified Lord twisted in her throat hollow. When the light hit right, He wrote rainbows on the wall. Perhaps she never judged me as harshly as I imagined. Nevertheless, I disliked meeting the welling eyes of our would-be saviors. Love reached me through the palms of the other inmates, as we massaged each other's swollen ankles and aching shoulders. We made sure the sickest of us sat nearest to the fire. We gave love and we received it. Our babies kicked and punched and cartwheeled inside us and we laughed and wept and snored in the secret symphony of our dormitory. We had kissing contests and poker tournaments. We shared whatever solutions we could find to the problem of time—the gangplank of our one-year sentence, waiting to meet our babies, waiting for freedom from waiting.

At first, I was unused to so many women gargling and coughing and giggling and farting and groaning beside me at night. "Whose socks are these?" someone always seemed to be crying. "Who used my toothbrush? Who made our dormitory smell like borscht?"

"Melody, you little thief, are you wearing my underwear?"

"If I could fit into *your* bloomers, Stencil, I'd be dead of starvation . . ."

Those first weeks, it felt like standing under a waterfall, overwhelmingly loud and powerful. Gradually it shrank away into background noise and then I could think again. To order my world, I assigned superlatives. Stencil was the tallest, meanest, funniest. Melody was the best singer, the best kisser. I was the quietest and the least understood, or so I believed until I got to know the New Girl.

If you had peered into the dormitory windows, you'd have seen twenty bellies heaving under the blue wool blankets, like a run of catfish swimming upriver to spawn.

And then one winter night, we woke to discover we were twenty-one.

"Marguerite is not the New Girl's real name," Melody told me. "Only we're not supposed to know. She is an Indian, but she was raised by a White lady. A famous one, says Opal. A *suffragist*—"

We stared at each other. I realized neither of us knew what to picture.

"For all the good it does her, a famous mother. She's still a prisoner here with us." She shook her head. "Oh pardon me, what do they tell the taxpayers of Nebraska we are? Not prisoners. 'Penitent girls—'"

"More sinned against than sinning—"

"That's from Thomas Hardy." Melody looked proud to have remembered this. "He was writing about Tess. She was an unwed mother, like us!"

She was right about Tess. But I'd read two weeks ahead of our class. I knew something troubling. Hardy got it from Shakespeare. *King Lear.* And Lear was talking about himself, not his daughter. That's how fathers and kings see themselves, I guess. *More sinned against than sinning.*

⚓

Zintkála Nuni was enrolled at the Home under the name of Marguerite E. Fox, "an Indian from Beatrice." Elsewhere, she is known as Marguerite Elizabeth Colby. We called her Zintka in our dormitory, where Malvina couldn't hear us.

Zintkála Nuni was famous, according to the nurses. Outside the walls of the Home, she was known to many as "the Lost Bird of Wounded Knee." Newspapers in the East dubbed her "the infant heroine." She'd survived not only the massacre of hundreds of Lakota men, women, and children by U.S. soldiers at Wounded Knee Creek, but a three-day blizzard that halted trains from South Dakota to Abilene, Texas. The temperature was forty below on the morning that the burial detail heard an infant wailing among the dead. They dug her out of a snowdrift, dehydrated and hypothermic and screaming for life. Her mother's body had frozen into a cutbank over three miles from Wounded Knee Creek. Soldiers had chased her that far. It was her mother who had saved her, sheltering her from the blizzard. Miraculously, ice had not covered the infant's nostrils and smothered her. She became an overnight sensation, reported on in every state in the Union. In an article that ran in the *Beatrice Express Daily*, General Leonard Colby is quoted musing on the Lakota survivors of the massacre from whose arms he stole her:

"A peculiar thing in connection with securing the infant was the remarkable reluctance with which the Indians surrendered it. Everyone . . . claimed to be its father or mother and all had a warm, loving interest in its welfare."

Before I came to the Home, I had never heard of this general, but during my time there I received many contradictory accounts of him. The General was a Civil War hero and commander of the Nebraska National Guard. He was a known con man, philanderer, cheat. He was a generous soul who had adopted an Indian orphan. He was a kidnapper and a defiler. I can tell You what I believe, Son. Leonard Colby was a criminal, and the full extent of his crimes is still unknown.

General Colby had arrived in Rushville several days after the blizzard. He insisted to the Lakota survivors of the recent massacre that his grandmother "was a full-blood Seneca." Then he brought wagons loaded with rations to Pine Ridge and threatened to withhold the food from every sick and weak mouth unless they gave the baby up. Through an interpreter, he insisted that he and his barren wife, Clara, would care for Lost Bird. To his friend Buffalo Bill, he boasted that the baby was his "war trophy." A "living relic."

Rumors spread faster than trachoma in our dormitory. Nurse

Elaine, in a tone of morbid fascination, told us that Zintka's mother had been killed while running with her four-month-old daughter. I felt sick later on my cot, thinking about how a real woman becomes a body, and then a story. Thinking about the tally of fatalities in the Superintendent's black book.

"The General rescued her," the Superintendent explained to us in the parlor. "She was born to a savage race, but he decided to love her as his own daughter. He sent her on to Clara Colby to be raised in a civilized home."

It was Zintka herself who transformed my understanding. "I was stolen from my people. But last summer, I found my way back to them. And when I get out of this place, I will find them again."

⊱⊰

We were eating last season's chokecherries on the porch, listening to music with no visible source. It seemed to come from the trembling branches and the fireflies. Sunset had been upstaged by a storm building over Milford, the air swelling with water. "That's a fermata," Zintka explained to me, pointing at the nothingness that spread between the tree trunks—the columns of darkness.

"A fermata?"

"It's a musical term. I think about it often here. It means 'a pregnant pause.'"

Zintkála was an excellent pianist and could read music as well. I played by ear, and I wondered what it would be like to look at the musical staff, all those fat raindrops caught on the skinny wires, and hear a song in your head.

"Oh, right. I knew that, I think . . ." I spread my hands in front of my face, letting my fingers web the dark. I felt a little drunk from the sedative they'd given me, my tongue fat inside my mouth. I'd been having nightmares again. The other girls complained that I was waking them. Sleep was precious—so much stolen by the dawn wake-up bells and the kicks of the children inside us. Last year, there'd been a petition to have Snoring Delores moved to the sofa. I had asked for the sedative because I was afraid of injuring my friendships while I slept.

Zintkála was stroking her belly, staring out through the rain.

"I am sorry about Malvina," I blurted out. "What she said about Indians."

"You're sorry about what *she* said? Why?"

She brushed a crust of blue and black moths from the lantern glass, and I felt as if she were swiping away my apology. I blushed in the dark. We had what felt like an endless fermata.

"I'm sorry I stood there like a stone." I paused. "I was afraid."

She lifted the light and studied my face, as if only now noticing me sitting beside her.

"Who are you?"

"Antonina Rossi," I said, surprising myself—nobody knew my true name here.

"You're the girl who wakes us with her screaming."

"And you're the girl who tried to run away from the boarding school."

"No. I *succeeded* at running away."

The last place she'd lived with any happiness was Portland, Oregon. She had moved into a rickety Victorian house with the General's divorced wife, Clara Colby. Zintka spoke about Clara with pride and love and anger. A yolky slide of feeling held in one brittle tone. In one word: *mother*.

Clara Colby, I learned, was internationally respected—a "lioness," a fierce intellect and suffragist. A close friend of Susan B. Anthony and Elizabeth Cady Stanton. But with each new fact I learned about Clara, my picture only grew cloudier. She wrote bad rhyming poetry about "the Waif of Wounded Knee." She included Zintka in speeches given to audiences thousands of miles away from the child in her care. She was often elsewhere, even when they were living in the same room, mothering a movement.

"She helped me to get a job at a lunch counter. I had my own money in Portland," Zintka told me. "It was easy to take a streetcar to the Oaks. I snuck out practically every night." She showed me a postcard of an amusement park with flower-dotted gazebos and a wooden arcade. Big puffy clouds hovered over the wide river and people strolled under a sign that read THE JOY WHEEL. Zintka pointed out a famous carousel with buck-toothed unicorns and mustard yellow lions that carried children on two axes: up and down, round and round.

"I see. Like life, that way," I said, and tried a smile.

She'd learned the honky-tonk songs she played us at the Home on the Oaks's hot piano. She went roller skating there, flying under a floating organ, holding hands with boys who were sweet on her.

"At Chemawa, I almost died of loneliness. I ran away but the police dragged me back."

I said I didn't know what Chemawa meant, and she said, "Lucky you." Zintka told me about her years at various boarding schools. Some schools had expelled her for her "indomitable spirit." Other times, she'd run away from them.

Two years before her incarceration at Milford, she'd been a student at the Chemawa Indian boarding school, an hour's train ride from Portland. She ran away during the shock waves of the 1906 San Francisco earthquake, which reached Salem, Oregon. She was brought back by the police, wearing the "loud rags of a cowgirl," according to one scandalized young officer. She escaped a second time by jumping from an open window while the Chemawa matron shrieked uselessly after her.

Imitating the matron, she started laughing, and I joined her. Tentatively and then in torrents. My tears felt like jelly because I was crying out the medicine for my trachoma. She had the same condition. Everyone at the Home did, it seemed. She stopped laughing before I did, so abruptly that I startled and nearly fell off the porch swing. "What's wrong?"

That set her off again. She blinked at me slowly through rubbed-raw eyes.

What's wrong? She stood up abruptly, and if I hadn't grabbed the armrest I would have flown from my perch.

We watched a sudden gust of hail sweep the fields and heard the rattling of the distant branches of the burr oak. My nostrils tingled at the change in the air. Rain hit my face, slap after slap after slap, the wind blowing from the east. I kept waiting for the Night Nurse to come and order us back inside, but perhaps the weather had made the weary staff inclined to ignore our silhouettes on the swing.

Thunder sounded like a bomb, and we laughed together in shock.

That night, between the thunderclaps, she told me about the General. The man who stole her from her people. Her so-called father. After yet another boarding school expulsion, an exasperated Clara Colby had sent Zintka to live with the General and his mistress—Zintka's former nanny.

"I slept on our neighbor's porch. I'd sneak out with my blanket and she'd give me buttered bread and coffee in the morning."

"The General let you sleep outside? Away from his house?"

"He said I wasn't worth hitching up a wagon."

"Is he expecting your return?" I asked after a long pause. I was thinking about Nathalee. "Do you have other family?"

"I have another family. I lived with them last spring and summer, at Pine Ridge."

But when I pressed her with more questions, she fell silent. I kicked a large piece of hail and watched it slide between the porch steps. I hated that I'd turned our conversation into an interrogation.

"My mother doesn't know I'm here," she said after a silence so long I'd given up on finding our lost thread. "I keep waiting for her to come and rescue me from wherever we are—"

"Milford," I said, alarmed. "Milford, Nebraska." Did she not know where she was? Had nobody told her? I thought for some reason of the ship manifest in our Omaha parlor and the voyage I could never remember.

We stared out across the fields to the distant water tower. Slowly, we began moving to the same rhythm, pumping our legs on the swing. Thunder shook out like God's Voice, I would have said at an earlier year in my life, but the word *God* had come to feel like a tiny hollow statuette used to bludgeon us into submission by the Superintendent. Her god of hatred and punishment bore no resemblance to the God of Love I knew at night. I prayed to that Great Love as I felt my baby kicking inside me, the black ash bench singing on its hinges, supporting our weight in the dark. I wondered what Zintka believed.

"Should I call you Zintkála Nuni? Or Marguerite? Or . . . ?"

Even with the lantern's aid, I couldn't read her expression. But our fermata felt friendlier now, and I felt braver beside her, brave enough to risk another quarter hour of freedom in the dark.

We pumped our legs harder, pushing the swing higher and higher—so high I thought we might fly off. For just a moment, I pictured the waves of an earthquake reaching us, opening the gates of the Home, releasing us into some unknown life. Who might we become if we ran? How far could we get from this prison? Then I felt You kick. My thoughts rolled to a stop. I'd scared myself with the possibilities I'd just seen mid-sky. A great fear of punishment flooded into me, with equal suddenness and intensity. I said goodnight to Zintka, and I raced to get back inside the Home.

⊰⊱

Zintka and I became, if not friends, exactly, then friendly. She gave me piano lessons and I filched matchbooks for her. Sometimes at 4:00 a.m. I'd wake to see her strike a match in the dark. A bad cough was making the rounds, and we were all miserably congested. "It sounds like a sawmill in here at night," Melody complained at Duty. "I don't know how any of you sleep. Zintka and I are always awake, aren't we, Zintka?"

"Not always," she said with a real grin. "Not on Sunday morning at church."

We all laughed at that. Just last week, the pastor had remarked on how many of the fallen women "seem to pray with their eyes shut."

Two weeks after our first conversation on the porch swing, Zintka sat beside me while I read a letter from Giancarlo. In it, he proposed to me. Zintka wanted to know why I looked like I'd been sucking on a lemon. I did not tell her that he was a polio victim who walked with a cane. I never said, even to myself, in those years, *I am afraid to weigh myself down. I am going to have a baby and I don't think I can take care of you as well, Giancarlo.* Zintka brightened when I told her that I planned to raise my baby as a single mother. "As long as you're willing to work, you'll find a way to feed the baby, Toni." She told me that she'd had many jobs in her seventeen years.

Last year, when she was sixteen and on the lam from the Chemawa boarding school—no money, no luggage, only the clothes she was wearing—she hitched from Salem, Oregon, all the way to the tent city of Lemmon, South Dakota. Just ten miles from the Standing Rock Reservation, she ran out of cash.

⊰⊱

Son, I have spent so many years carrying others' memories, without knowing anything about them. I have swallowed lifetimes, and lost them. It feels miraculous that I can still recollect any fraction of the past. I want to share with You the little that I do know, and remember. Otherwise we "fallen women" will shrink away into objects of pity, living curios. Counterfeiters like me will continue to erase us from sight. Nathalee's secret, Stencil's jokes, Zintka's courage. Please carry us with You. Please go on knowing us, Son.

⊰⊱

Zintka stopped in at one of Lemmon's four saloons to ask directions. Liquor glowed in every blistered hand. Whiskey sold for a nickel a shot. Zintka learned this when "Indian Pete" Culbertson offered to stand her a round of liquid brimstone. A career liar, Pete Culbertson! A Son of Norway, who now claimed to be an Indian. He had cut-crystal blue eyes and dyed his hair with coffee. "I was stolen from my parents when I was but a wee child, and raised by the Lakota Nation." Like his friend and rival, Buffalo Bill, he sold a deranged myth at a markup—a Wild West show shamelessly promoting fantasy as history. Indian Pete's main tent held 10,000. It drew crowds of new settlers to Nebraska and the Dakotas. Pete's wife usually played a cowgirl, but she got pregnant and was unable to perform. Zintka was hired for the role.

There were bronco busters and trick riders, bulldoggers and sharpshooters. The most popular act of the two-hour performance was a staged battle when "Indians on the warpath" attacked a prairie schooner. To get back to her home and her people, Zintka accepted Indian Pete's offer, and spent the next eight months playacting the part of a cowgirl in his Wild West show.

I felt certain that if I asked another question she'd stop talking to me. So I listened to the soft flow of her reminiscence while You somersaulted inside me.

With the money she'd saved, she was able to reach the Standing Rock Reservation. She was introduced to another infant survivor of the Massacre at Wounded Knee, a young woman whose Lakota name translated into English became Comes Out Alive. "My twin sister," said Zintka. "That's what we call each other." She helped Zintka get to the Pine Ridge Reservation, on the border of Nebraska and South Dakota. She visited the mass grave where her mother's body had been interred along with hundreds of other Lakota men, women, and children. About these experiences, Zintka told me next to nothing, except to say, "I need to get back home."

I told her our story, Son, while You drummed along. I remember pausing to hide from the sweep of a lantern. I remember how the lightning made us visible to each other in the briefest flashes, and the good smell of the rain. I remember feeling frustrated by my own shy speech, how much melted back inside me before I could utter one true word about my earlier life.

I had only been on horseback a handful of times in Omaha, and I asked Zintka what it had felt like to ride in the vaudeville show, in front of thousands of strangers. Even raising my hand at a desk gave me jitters. Zintka's eyes lit up. She had done top work, she said. Vaults and drags.

"Top . . . work?"

"Standing on the saddle of a galloping horse."

At the Omaha State Fair, I'd once seen a grown man thrown from his Appaloosa and paralyzed for life. "You weren't scared?"

"I was excellent at it. I could vault off the horse and land on my feet. I could run and jump right back onto the saddle while she was going full bore."

What Zintka was telling me was not a tragic story but a triumphant one, or else it was both and neither, it was a great braid of times and tones, it was her very life pushing at the seams of what could be told as a story. I heard her strength, her life-wish, naming itself.

My imagination could only carry me so far. I can still hear the hooting of ranchers and farmers in the circus tent, smell spilled beer, crushed cigarettes. I can picture Zintka standing up on the saddle, vaulting to her feet. But the truth is that I do not know the first thing about what it was like to be the woman known as Lost Bird.

I did know how it felt to look into the eyes of someone who thought they knew you, who had already cast you in the play inside their mind. At the Home you might be assigned the role of *Redeemed*

Woman, but you were also, inescapably, an understudy for *Beyond Hope*. You could be cast as a whore, or an imbecile, or an object of pity, *more sinned against than sinning*.

Clumsily, I reached for Zintka's hand. She gave me a wary look, and that wariness swelled unbearably between us, but neither of us pulled away. It took so much to stay in that moment together, our hands touching on the table. For the breath of rainfall between thunderclaps—which was really all that I could stand, at that time, in that place, before I retreated from the pain of the attempt, the shame that flamed through me—we both held on.

⇥⇤

I grew up in Omaha, and yet I knew next to nothing about the Omaha people. I did not know about the Pawnee, the Ponca, the Otoe and Missouria, the Lakota, the Dakota, the Iowa, or any of the many people who were living here long before my family became Americans.

I hadn't known—no one had ever told me—that I was a soldier in a war. We newcomers to the Great Plains were invited out here by the U.S. government to hold ground. The Homestead Act, the Dawes Act, all part of a battle plan. Over time, light-skinned children would grow old in this West with no memory of an earlier home, no awareness that they were the daughters and the sons of an invading army—second- and third- and fourth- and fifth-generation Americans. Putting Native lands into White hands. Putting forests and plains into production. Turning soil into cash.

If anyone had presented the history of our life in the West this way, I would have defended myself and my nonna with bared teeth. We came to this country to work hard and live with dignity. Who would blame my father for wanting what he wanted—a home, a job, a chance to care for his family? We owned nothing when we arrived. At the age of thirteen, I worked nine-hour days in the laundromat. How dare anyone suggest that we had anything to do with the murder of Indians or the theft of their lands? Had I never met Zintka, I'd have felt no more responsible than a molecule of water might feel accountable for a flood.

But I understood something, listening to Zintka play the piano. The notes converged and became new sounds. Her right foot pushed and released the sustain pedal, flooding the future with the past. Our lives were entangled in the same song. Long before we became prisoners in the Home, we'd been shaping one another's time on earth.

I did not want to be bundled into the "we" with Malvina and Nurse Elaine and the other holy rollers at the Milford Home. I hated my new understanding. My shadow on the soil of Nebraska was my father's greatest achievement, said my nonna, her voice breaking with pride and the kind of relief that made me feel instantly superior to everyone we'd left in Sicily, even my dead mother. But I was a weapon in the war. I am one. I see that now, Son.

❊

The spring thaw seemed to activate a change in all of us. On Easter Sunday, the Superintendent had surprised everyone by giving us permission to decorate the parlor and arrange an egg hunt. A kind of pagan air had invaded the dormitory, sparked by that little note of festivity. I was less than two months away, the doctor said, from meeting my baby. Many of the girls I'd become friendly with were about to burst, as Stencil put it. In every sense, we were on the verge. Stencil had smuggled in a bottle of brandy and was charging everybody in the dormitory a nickel a sip

"Aw, don't drink that! It's bad for the baby."

"A sip never hurt anybody . . ."

"A sip can do plenty! How do you think I wound up pregnant?"

In the end, Melody and Stencil and Zintka and I found ourselves drinking alone after Lights Out, suppressing our laughter in the lye-scented laundry room downstairs. I can't remember now whose idea it was to sneak off—Stencil's, probably. Although it might have been mine. I'd learned that you could introduce your dearest wish as a joke and watch it snowball into a plan, if Stencil was present. "One last bash, ladies! Before all these butterflies in my stomach come out as a baby—" Melody said she wasn't sure she wanted to risk Malvina's wrath, and Stencil began to tease her, in that crafty way of hers that got you laughing, loosening your hold on yourself.

Zintka was ready to up the ante.

"I can't breathe in this place," she said. "I want to go roller-skating."

I thought she was teasing us. Who had ever heard of four fugitive mothers escaping on skates? But then that very Thursday after the Lecture, Zintka held out a box of roller skates she'd somehow convinced the grocer's son to sneak into the week's deliveries, labeled as rutabaga.

"How did you get these!" Melody shrieked.

"Where there's a will there's a way."

We snuck out after midnight through the basement window, a tight squeeze for everyone but Stencil.

I moved clumsily behind the others, terrified that we might be apprehended and sent to the attic—the most severe punishment. "Some things are worth the risk," Stencil said, looking me dead in the eye. "If you want to die a slow death in there, be my guest."

What had convinced me, in the end, was the sight of new shoelaces. They were brighter than anything I'd touched in months. That night, the crescent moon looked sharp as a fairy-tale spindle. The fields were coming back to life, the earthworms seething across the rows.

We made it a full mile before collapsing in laughter. I felt drunk on the night air. April smells like the beginning of the world, wet and green. Our own shadows grew long and loony under the moon, stretched like invisible fingers pointing toward the woods. Zintka said she knew a place where we could skate—a secret rink.

Sure enough, a quarter mile off the main road into Milford she directed us to an abandoned barn. Its roof was partially collapsed, a large nest frizzing over the doors like the pastor's stern brow. (I'd been trained by the Home to read disapproval everywhere.) "Come in, come in," said Zintka, delighted. It smelled not unpleasantly of rotting wood and decades of rain. A shadow leapt and flew through a gap in the wall, something winged vanishing into the surrounding woods. The large hole in the center of the roof seemed like a spyglass for the moon. Silver light flooded the barn, illuminating the wide wooden floorboards. Our skating rink. I drew my name in the dust: TONI AND BABY WERE HERE. I had not yet thought of a name. It seemed better to wait. Names are the spells of protection mothers cast on their children, and I needed to know who I was swaddling.

"Lace up, you pretty whores!" screamed Stencil.

You loved to roller-skate. It was one of the first things I ever learned about You. That night, You kicked like a jackrabbit, wild under my ribs.

Melody giggled, sounding as drunk as I felt. We had finished Stencil's hooch. You might assume this would make four pregnant women even more ungainly. Would you believe me if I told you that we soared? It was a foolish risk. It was a necessary risk—one we were choosing to take. Carving up the wooden floor felt nothing like carving our initials into the dormitory walls. The fear that swelled in us at the Home had nothing to do with this round flying joy.

Shoes with wheels, I said, were humankind's most incredible technology.

"Just wait until you try ice skates. Shoes with knives on the soles."

Icarus should have hit the roller-skating rink—it would have gone so much better for him. Flying around in a circle on the wooden floor, safe from the fatal sun. We skated four across, like a single graceful wing. Pleasure, pleasure, pleasure, spinning faster and faster. Two hearts accelerating inside each of our huge bodies. I stumbled twice and never fell. Melody rolled into a wall and righted herself. Zintka's eyes, when she breezed by me, were shut.

When I saw my first electrified stars on my trolley ride through downtown Omaha, I'd burst into tears, according to my nonna. From a distance they looked like a hundred glowing clementines growing on the wooden sign. The same thing happened to me in the abandoned barn. I stared up through the hole in the roof and I saw the Milky Way. It was still there, lighting our way.

I can't remember who first suggested running. "We have no money," I said, hating myself for being the Voice of Reason—the Voice of Doubt, the Voice of Fear and Delay. What did I want more than my freedom? Safety, unfortunately. Safety for You. I could feel You turning inside me, perhaps in some kind of distress, and as we pulled off our skates and laced up our boots, my fear seemed to blot up the stars.

"Let's go back," I said. "I want to go back. If they catch us they'll throw us in the attic."

Stencil had turned in the direction of town and begun to walk.

"I'm going back," I said with less conviction. Melody, carrying high under her thin wool coat, came and stood beside me. I felt stalemated. If I went back to the Home, I'd be choosing prison. If I followed Stencil and Zintka, I'd be risking my life and my infant's also. Which was riskier? The moon with her shining poker face gave no indication of where the new path might lead.

As it turned out, it was a moot point. A moot plan. "There they are," I heard a man's voice huff. "There they are, Mack—"

We all ran then. Sightlessly, ridiculously in our new top-heavy bodies, without the grace of the skates, with the propulsion of animal terror. Now I had my answer. I did not want to return to the Home for Unwed Mothers. Too late, I learned how badly I wanted my freedom, and what I would risk to retain it. The ground had recently thawed and refrozen, and I slipped and got up half a dozen times before hands descended on my shoulders. You butted against my rib cage and I cried out, dragged along the road by a man I did not recognize.

"Mack! This bitch keeps *spitting* at me!" Something sharp hit the back of my head and I grew sick with fear for You.

In the end, our skates were confiscated. We rode home in silence in two separate cars, the four of us too large to squeeze into one.

⁂

At the Milford Home, this was the lesson branded onto our hearts, one we came to understand better than any Bible verse. If there was breath in your lungs you had not yet hit bottom. They could warp the report to make it sound as if you had died from puerperal fever, or died in your sleep. They could claim anything they wanted on these forms and nobody would ever come to discover the truth. They could leave you locked in the dark in the jacket for hours, or days, and take your sanity, your memory, your voice.

The four of us received lesser punishments on the night that we snuck out to roller-skate. We each had extra shifts of Duty for two weeks. We were not permitted to go on walks around the grounds. I felt sick with relief—I had been so terrified that we'd be sent to the attic.

The attic pressed down on me always—the possibility of being sent to that lonely place, belted into one of the straitjackets. The matador's red cape, I'm told, provokes a bull to charge. The red leather straitjacket did the opposite: the clanging of the metal buckles put a spell of dread on me. Every time I heard it, I froze against the wall. Whenever one of us was chosen for this punishment, I stared at the floor. I was aware of the girls to the left and the right of me, and I felt without looking up that they were holding their breath, rounding out their bellies like shields. I was nobody's favorite, but I was quiet—which put me in better standing with the Superintendent than many of the others. I was so afraid that their punishments would harm You, my baby. I lost everything anyhow. But at fifteen, I did not understand that the choice between doing nothing and doing something was one I shared with every other girl.

Instead I'd felt wretchedly alone, watching the firelight lick the dull red leather of the straitjacket. Each time they belted another woman inside it, I told myself my hands were tied. Perhaps even Malvina told herself this lie. *Be like that tree. Stay dark. Go blank.*

I suppose you could say I did receive a moral education at the Home for Unwed Mothers, even though I yawned through the Thursday lectures. The most important test, I failed. But I did learn the answer to the question that shuddered through our ranks every time one of us was belted into the straitjacket and taken to the attic.

Q: What is the evil this world runs on?
A: *Better you than me.*

⌁

One day in late April, I returned from Duty to learn that Zintka had been taken to the attic. The spring weather took a freakish turn, the temperatures reaching eighty-five degrees on April 22. The following morning, we learned that Zintka had gone into labor and given birth to a stillborn baby boy.

⌁

When she returned to the dormitory, she would not speak to us. I felt a shame that made me dizzy. Once I tried to sit beside her at vespers and she stood and moved to the back of the hall. As time passed, my shame became a line of fire and I cowered behind it. We floated past each other in the dim halls as if we were strangers. How did Zintka find her way through those long nights and cruel days? Who did Zintka become outside the walls of the Home? Even now, Son, in the quiet of my own mind, I struggle to meet her gaze.

The Player-Captain of the Dangers, Asphodel Oletsky

The storm opened like a mouth and swallowed telephone poles, fence posts, anvil black crows, trees, our bus. With a scream, I wrenched the wheel to the left, spinning the bus around until we were perpendicular to the road. The truck in front of us rolled twice and somehow landed on its tires. Some animal was bawling in the darkness behind me. For a bottomless stretch we were all lost inside the same whirling dust. It got inside the bus and raked over my skin; my mouth filled with a gritty paste. I was sure we were going to die. No life-saving idea came to me. *Help us, help us, help us,* I prayed. A flying tree branch hit the windshield; someone behind me screamed. I realized that I was addressing my prayer to my mother, as if she were a telephone operator who could put my call through to God, or to the storm itself. I pulled my jersey over my face. Was my prayer answered? The wind began to turn the great cloud wall to the southeast. In a quarter hour I could see out the windshield again, the sun glowing weakly as the moon through a reddish screen.

Valeria and I dug out the tires with her father's scoop. Sweat poured down our faces, and even with our goggles on it felt like trying to see through a mudslide. We spent an hour clearing out the dust, refilling the radiator three times—at last the engine coughed to life. The Pegasus crawled into Red Willow, going no faster than a person on foot. I almost crashed into what turned out to be the backlot of a roadside fruit stand, the ceiling crushed, buried under a tonnage of dirt. EVE'S APPLES CLOSED FOR BUSINESS, said the redundant sign.

At 4:00 p.m., in pitch darkness, we arrived at Red Willow.

Everyone seemed shaky on their feet. A postman with his mail sack slung over one arm came teetering toward us, rubbing at his eyes. "It's the end of the world, girls!" he said with a disoriented smile. "Save your postage stamps and toss your letters into that terrible wind!" Ellda smiled up at him politely as I pulled her out of his path. We checked into the Princess and the Pea motor lodge—we were the only guests. The lobby had a black rotary telephone and calcimine instead of wallpaper, plaid curtains so old they waved apart midsash. The radio was on, halfway through the evening broadcast: ". . . one of the worst dust storms we've had this season, heavy loss of stock, three fatalities on Highway 6 . . ."

"No chaperone?" asked the jowly clerk, riffling through our dollars. He was looking at us funny. There was a poster of Clark Gable behind him on the wall, and it was not a flattering comparison.

"He's out back," I said, taking our key from its hook. We raced up the stairs and found the door standing open. The room reeked of cigarettes and dog fur. One room for all seven of us. "It's perfect," said Thelma stubbornly. "I'll sleep with Oletsky," said Valeria, and my heart galloped so loudly in my chest that I was shocked no one turned my way. She threw our bags onto the top bunk. Nobody had eaten anything since noon and the sun was setting behind the downtown buildings. We wandered down the main drag of the new town, ravenous and giddy after hours on the bus. Stray dogs were following us, because Pazi and Ellda kept stopping to rub their bellies.

"Quit that!" I hissed. "We look like rubes!"

But Valeria, who talks to animals as if they are visiting dignitaries from a superior planet, seemed embarrassed by my reaction. "Please don't mind my friend," she said, bending to scratch their scabby ears. "She is still shaken up from the ride."

The entire downtown was electrified. Ghosts floated up poles, exploded into visibility five feet above our heads. "Streetlights," Nell whispered reverently.

We did not know Red Willow. Valeria carried her father's scoop as if it were a club. *There are too many of us to take out*, I thought. Seven is a lucky number. Whoever heard of a whole team of women going missing? But the only figures lurking on main street were the life-size dolls in the storefronts, wearing red headscarves and white fox furs.

The mannequins were better dressed than any Uzian girl has ever been. Percale, seersucker, dimity, organdy.

"My best dress is cotton," said Dagmara.

We could see our shabby clothes superimposed on the display case.

"Ma makes mine out of chicken feed sacks."

"I don't own a dress."

We lined up in the cool blue glow of electrified evening to imitate the mannequins. I tried to make my face look blank and haughty at once.

The diner we chose had a machine that cut the carrots into serrated coins. We all oohed over it. We pulled cottony stuffing out of rips in the green booths while waiting for the Daily Special. It looked more appetizing than what the sad-eyed waitress eventually served us: sugar beets and ham sitting in red drool. Thelma joked that it was the same color as her hair, getting the jump on us. The lonely green lamp on the black-and-white checked tablecloth smelled like ancient kerosene oil and singed flies. We stacked the machine-cut carrots like poker chips to see who could tower them up the highest before collapse.

"I feel like I'm eating elf money," complained Pazi.

"Don't hog the salt, Oletsky," snapped Nell. "You eat like you play ball."

"How the heck are we paying for this?"

I pulled a twenty-dollar bill from my left sock and was not met with the reaction I'd pictured.

"Is it still legal tender if its stink kills a man dead?"

"How about 'thank you'?"

"Can you buy us cocoa? The menu says you get marshmallows for a penny extra." Ellda asked in her little girl voice, wincing in anticipation of a no. Ellda is ferocious on court, gleefully blocking shots, chewing out refs, driving her elbow into her defenders' guts, but off court she sounds like a glass angel.

Nobody asked me *how* I got the money. I appreciated my teammates for that. "You girls want *hot* cocoa?" the waitress asked. "Is this some kind of prank?" The wall thermostat was at ninety. She made it for us anyway. "Don't burn your tongues," she said, shaking her head. We all did. This was not a skill we had ever drilled—waiting for chocolate to cool before gulping. I spent another three dollars on french fries and sundaes, and I felt how easy it would be to go on spending all night, as natural and effortless as touching the gas pedal to the floor mat. I had almost two hundred dollars saved up from my work with the Antidote. Soon I would have enough to move out of my mother's bedroom and into the boardinghouse.

Back at the Princess and the Pea, I listened to my teammates snoring, drooling, blinking at the ceiling, thinking noisy thoughts about losing and winning. I wondered if my uncle had found my note yet. He would certainly disapprove of seven young women staying alone in a motor lodge. When my uncle learns that I am a Vault, he will probably throw me out. I should invite the Antidote home for supper one night, just to see what Uncle Harp's face does. "Valeria?" I said, nudging the wonderfully solid body beside me. I hadn't slept next to anybody in the two years since I came to Uz. Silence opened like arms and rocked me and eventually I guess I did fall asleep, because I woke to itchy light pouring onto the ugly calcimine walls and it was game day.

⚞⚟

"Uh-oh," said Nell. "These Red Willow girls are big as houses."

They were, indeed, enormous, compared to the Dangers. Sequoia-tall players, whose girlhoods seemed centuries behind them. The Perkins Steelwool Princesses were not who we were expecting from their name. Their coach, Oramelle, was also a player, a German girl who a man might describe nervously as "strapping," a brick chimney of a center who was six feet tall and looked like she could lift a steer and toss it at the basket.

"We were sure you were gonna forfeit, Poultry and Eggs."

I mustered my authority as player-captain.

"That's not our name anymore. We are the Dangers."

"Well, we are still going to crush you like eggs," Oramelle said, chewing her lip. I sensed her retooling some of her hen-related insults.

Under our talk, I felt a deep respect. Here we were, after all. The same storm had tried to bury us. We had come here to defeat that storm and all future storms. We had come to win. We all wanted the same thing and only half of us could have it.

We shook hands and separated for a final word with our teammates. My pep talk to the Dangers started out upbeat. Close to what Coach might have told us before the battle for the Region 7 championship. I looked every player in the eyes. I told them I was confident this game would complete our winning streak. Basketball is even ground to stand on. You can use your desperation as fuel. Without a penny to your name, you can wield real power, become the champions. We had earned our victory, I told the Dangers, with a season of hard work under the most difficult circumstances. We had sacrificed so much to get here, I said. Coach left us, the sun itself went dark, the sky tried to bury us, but we never quit. We could feel proud no matter what—but the good news was that we were destined to win. *Think about the shining birds*, I said. I did not remind them that I had almost sacrificed us yesterday on the near-fatal ride to Red Willow. I did not linger on that thought myself.

A Saturday game in Uz does not draw any kind of crowd. We mostly cheer for ourselves. But these benches had filled with fans of the Perkins Steelwool Princesses: brothers and sisters and mothers and fathers, uncles and aunts holding banners, WE LUV U, SUSIE! ADELANTE, BUENA! CRUSH 'EM, CAROL. Home games and Away games feel equally lonely to me, but I could see the other Dangers were wilting in the face of all that love. Loneliness is unhelpful as fuel. I pushed that feeling aside and felt around for more useful ones— jealousy, blame, rage, contempt. These I can pump up into my body. My uncle says I live on top of an oil field of anger. Never a bad thing on game day.

As I went on, my pep talk took a violent turn. "Look at these *rich girls*," I told my teammates. "These goddamn *princesses*—" Although most were no richer than I was, and a few looked worse off—wearing threadbare uniforms, baring crooked teeth. "They go home to their castles. They have plenty of money and no cares in the world. Let's teach them how to lose. How to be humiliated. Let's show them what it feels like to be crushed—"

My words weren't landing with everybody—Ellda had jammed her fist in her mouth, which made her look like a baby. Pazi was whittling our initials into a large heart on the cedar bench, ignoring me completely. Nell was staring out the window, as if waiting for the wind to die down. But the other Dangers were nodding. Val winked at me and raised her fist. Thelma's red curls flashed as she jumped forward. Dagmara smiled with her incisors. Like me, they were out for blood. Hadn't we all been crushed, in different ways, by everyday life in Uz? You can take your revenge on any body—that's what basketball has taught me. In the stands, the pink-cheeked mothers of the Princesses were on their feet, blowing kisses, cheering for their giant daughters. My mother lay in a ditch somewhere deep inside my chest, unable to turn her head to watch me win. *I will take my revenge on your mothers too*, I thought.

"The Dangers always get what they go after—"

"Is that so?" Pazi gave me a sidelong look. "Aren't you talking about yourself, Dell?"

I laughed angrily. "Well, I am a Danger, aren't I? This is our last game of the season. Let's destroy them."

We formed our circle and piled our hands one on top of the other: "Ready, Set, Lightning!"

The referee blew the whistle and tossed the ball above me and Oramelle. She had so much height on me, I did not try for it. Instead I jumped back and deflected her tip to the Princesses' forward. I knocked it over to Nell, who passed it to Pazi, who sent it sailing through the hoop. A scowling man with a head like a golf ball changed the scoreboard: DANGERS 2, PRINCESSES 0.

The ref was someone's lanky sister, a former player who stalked along beside us with her silent whistle thudding against her collarbone. Fouls are rarely called in Region 7. It took half a gallon of blood before a ref would get involved.

We drove hard for the first quarter. Valeria can outjump anyone—the Red Willow beanpoles were unable to match her at rebounding. Nell and Ellda kept the ball rotating around the court with a crazy genius that no Princess could predict. Pazi got clear of the girl guarding her and slid into the keyhole, under the net. Thelma threaded the ball between two defenders and Pazi made the layup. I saw a shadow passing over the faces in the stands, some of whom were still loudly cheering, many of whom were seated and subdued under the awning of bright yellow balloons.

Oramelle ran into me, jabbing me with a sharp elbow. No foul was called. I took this as license to foul her back, knocking into her left side. She went tumbling to the floor holding her knee, with its fine blond hairs that looked from where I stood like a baby's downy head. The scorekeeper with the golf-ball head turned out to be Oramelle's father. He ran to her. I glanced at the sleepwalking ref, who looked back at me with glassy eyes. It was dishonorable, in Region 7, and likely everywhere, to land on your butt on the floor. She was not going to embarrass Oramelle further by calling a foul. The silent whistle winked at me, and I winked back.

Our team became a single creature, contracting and ratcheting forward, cutting and weaving, moving in a dance directed by nobody but the sun-colored ball. *Swish! Swish! Clang* and *thud*. Skulls cracked and two players howled. My left hip connected with unyielding bone. At halftime, the scoreboard read DANGERS 18, PRINCESSES 6. In the third quarter, sensing our advantage, I told my players to keep our foot on the gas.

"Don't be afraid to throw your weight around, Dangers! This ref is not going to call you on anything short of murder—these girls are too proud and too ashamed, they would rather save face than argue for a different call . . ."

Oramelle sat on the bench, holding a compress to her purple knee. Valeria got the tip-off and shot it to Pazi; I sprinted to the keyhole, my favorite place on this earth, turning in time to watch the ball arching over the heads of four Princesses and into my hands. I spun the ball off the splintery backboard and gave Oramelle a little wave as it dropped through the net. Valeria took advantage of a sloppy pass between two Princesses, sliding on her belly to knock it over to Dagmara. She bent from the waist, calm as a queen, and shot the ball crosscourt to Pazi on the baseline. Pazi put her shoulder into her defender, then—with a wide looping motion—hooked the ball over the Princesses' much taller center. I heard gasps from the crowd. Pazi kept her curved arm frozen above her head like a dancer until she heard the *swoosh* of the net. In the final moment of the final quarter, my fingertips found the rough leather in the air between two of their hulking defenders and tipped it to tiny Ellda. She made a set shot from the free-throw line. At last, with some reluctance, I felt, the stringy-haired ref lifted the whistle to her mouth. DANGERS 44, PRINCESSES 10. The game was officially over; it had been for three quarters. Once again, we were the Region 7 champions.

A low groan rose from the benches. I turned toward the sound, my heart still pounding. "WE WON!" I screamed. "ALL HAIL THE CHAMPIONS, THE DANGERS OF UZ!" A man in a bow tie looked my way and winced, shaking his head, as if I were a drunk hollering in the alley outside the Jentleman. Half the crowd had left; the stragglers were rolling up their banners and coming onto the court to hug their daughters. I could feel my teammates around me, watching these embraces, the frustrated tears that were absorbed by mothers' cheeks, the whispers of encouragement from the large families who adored these tall, stinking, sweaty, bleeding, defeated Princesses. Who were still undefeated, I let myself know for just a heartbeat. Who were in fact the winners of this life, surrounded by such love.

Our teams filed slowly by one another, shaking hands.

The bench where Oramelle had been sitting was empty.

"Where's your Captain?" I asked the guard whose bear paw I was shaking. She had a kind, round face and a wrestler's build, calves like bowling balls. She did not look sufficiently crushed, I thought. I wanted to gloat. "Is she too upset to shake hands with us?"

"My papa took her to the doctor," said the sweaty, red-faced guard. She looked at me with disgust and whispered, "You did that on purpose, you bitch. Oramelle works cleaning houses. On her hands and knees, scrubbing. If the doctor has to put her in a cast, she'll lose her job."

I stared down at my sneakers, feeling sick. The floor seemed farther away than it had been a moment earlier. "The scorekeeper . . . he wasn't her father?"

"He's *my* father. And he wanted to cancel the game, but Oramelle begged him to let us finish the season. So you can thank her for your trophy the next time you come through." She laughed, her round face shining, only her eyes shooting hatred at me. "Maybe you can sign her cast. A CHAMPION. She'll always remember *you*, I'm sure."

One of the Princesses' forwards caught me watching her over her mother's shoulder. Whatever she saw in my face made her hug even tighter, bunching the green sleeve of the woman's dress. *Taking her revenge*, I thought. But she wasn't looking at me any longer. She was leaving the gymnasium with her mother and her father. In the corner, the janitor was whistling a jazzy tune and erasing our names from the scoreboard.

⁂

The night after our victory, we made a bonfire in the thick scrub behind the motor lodge. Valeria produced a flask of moonshine and a bottle of near-rancid chokecherry wine that tasted no different than "the good stuff" she'd brought last month. We made a toast to the Inaugural Voyage of the Pegasus—our first bus ride, which we'd barely survived. "She will always be the Bedwetter to me," said Val, who had protested the rechristening of our bus. Val was a stickler for the truth. Or maybe worried that we wouldn't fix the bus now that it had a prettier name. I'd parked the Pegasus under the aspens outside the Princess and the Pea, and I could see warped rainbows of oil spreading around the tires.

We made a second toast to Ellda. Her father was an educated man with a divinity degree from a fancy Bible college in Virginia. Pastor Robbins was a good friend of his—their two families often vacationed together. "Cheers to Ellda, whose sacrifice helped us to get ourselves to Red Willow," I said, offering Ellda the first sip off the team flask. Her cheeks were burning in the falling light. "Without you, we would not be the new champions of the Western Plains!"

"Region Seven," Pazi added.

"Go, Dangers," said Ellda, choking down the moonshine.

"Why do we have to treat Ellda like such a hero?" Dagmara grumbled. "It's not like she fought in the trenches of France to get the bus. Sounds like it took all of three minutes."

Thelma pantomimed licking an ice cream cone, and she and Dagmara burst out laughing. Dagmara was our weakest defender with our biggest ego, and it annoyed her when any other Danger got to be in the spotlight.

Valeria surprised me by speaking up.

"Ellda *is* a hero. Have you *seen* Pastor Robbins? He's built like a bull wheel. His nostrils are so huge you could go spelunking in them. Ellda rolled up her sleeves and held her nose. She did what was required to get us this bus."

"I didn't hold my nose," said Ellda. "That wouldn't have worked." She rose a little on her tailbone, looking burnished from our praise. Her face rippled in and out of focus above the campfire, woodsmoke blue and less and less familiar to me. The moonshine we were drink-ing burned going down and seemed to be rearranging my insides. For a dangerous moment I felt my mind sliding toward the ditch.

"He wants to spend a night with me," Ellda admitted. "I keep put-ting him off."

"Be careful, Ellda."

"You don't want to get knocked up by a married minister."

"You were smart to do it with your mouth," Thelma said. "That way he calms down and there's no danger of a baby."

My cheeks were on fire. I could not meet any pair of eyes.

"Ellda? You don't have to keep seeing him—"

"Oh, I don't mind," she said, with the same effortful brightness I recognized from practice. "I know I can't jump, I can't rebound, I'm slow getting downcourt. But I knew I could do this for us, Captain Oletsky."

She wasn't using the title to tease me. Ellda really looked up to me. My heart lunged into my mouth. Nauseated, I wandered away from the others into a cottonwood stand where I thought I was invisible. A hand on my shoulder caused me to scream.

"Hush up, fool. It's just me."

"Val . . ."

We kissed quickly in the shadows. This time she was the one who crossed the divide between us. She kissed the way she played, expertly and unselfconsciously. I kept apologizing, panting and fum-bling around under our clothes.

"I hate that I made Ellda do that."

"You didn't make her. Is that what you want me to say?"

"I hate that she did it for me."

"No, you don't." Val's laugh had a hard edge. "You wish Ellda hadn't told you what she did to get it. But you're glad we have that bus."

I felt sick because I knew it was true. I wanted to win more than anything. More than I wanted to know what anybody suffered to make the win happen. I couldn't stop picturing tiny Ellda on her knees in front of that smiling giant. *Don't lie, Captain. You're glad she did it.* Was Valeria right? Wouldn't I have done what Ellda did myself, to help the Dangers? That line of thinking made me feel a little better. So she had used her mouth on Robbins. She had bobbed up and down half a dozen times and swallowed a sour taste. So what? Was that act really so different than the hundred other ways we Dangers sacrificed our bodies to win? Was it somehow worse than going blind running drills with sand lashing our faces? Rolling our ankles and taking elbows to the stomach? Every one of us absorbed those blows for the team. I felt annoyed at the tiny Ellda kneeling in my imagination. I wanted to banish her smiling, heart-shaped face from my awareness. Her sticky, unwashed hair and her eagerness to be a good sport, to help the team out—all things that girls are trained to do from birth. *What's done is done, Ellda.* The thought was like a loose knot I had to keep retying.

I heard footsteps behind the screen of brush and froze in Val's arms. She laughed at me, stroking my neck as if I were her spooked horse.

"Nobody's around but us, Oletsky. You don't have a team to impress."

My heart kept hammering even after the footsteps died away. Most of the girls had gone back inside to bed, but Nell and Dagmara had been stargazing in the field when we left the firelight. I wondered what they'd say if they spotted Val and me swaying in the dark like newlyweds. I wondered who else might be able to see us.

"The world is ending. What do you have to lose?"

"Everything," I said.

"That seems to be the ante lately, huh?"

My entire body was dizzy from the moonshine. If I held very still, I thought Valeria might kiss me again. When she didn't, I lifted onto my toes and kissed her, pressing my lips against her warm mouth. Was I doing it wrong? She held me low on my waist and pulled me against her, like the braver boys at school dances. Our hands went anywhere they pleased. Nobody was chaperoning them. I watched my fingers in amazement as they untucked my best friend's undershirt and slid up the bare skin of her back. We kept kissing and touching, undoing buttons and clasps. My legs were trembling from standing tiptoe. Val laughed and said it was as close to being a ballerina as I would ever come, then pulled me gently to the grass with her. I listened for the sighs that felt like gates swinging open. In her body, in my body. My own sounds embarrassed me but not enough to force me to surface from Valeria. Heat rose and spread and brought up my dead mother with it, staring at the moon with her sightless eyes, waiting under the cruel, useless sun to be found by the searchers. The newspaper headlines crowded my mind. NEBRASKA WOMAN FOUND STRANGLED IN DIVERSION DITCH—

I seemed to have frozen. Valeria rolled onto her elbow to study my face in the moonlight. The black sky rippled like water between the trees and the town, and the full moon swam the channel in her white cap. Never again would I take light for granted, I'd promised myself during the terrifying drive to Red Willow, or any breath of air that did not scald my lungs. But I'd already broken those promises a thousand times since exiting the bus into better weather.

"Are you still thinking about the game?"

"No," I said, wiping my nose on my jersey. *Not a particularly romantic movement, Oletsky*, I thought. Neither was my answer.

"I'm thinking about my mother."

"Oh." Val whistled through her teeth and stood up. Her face seemed to stitch itself back up. She was angry or embarrassed, I wasn't sure at all now. Then she looked down and met my eyes, and I watched her lips lift into a crescent. Not a smile, exactly. More like she wanted to say something. She helped me to my feet.

"What was she like?"

"She was like my child, sometimes. She was my best friend. She loved music, any kind of music—"

We walked back toward the quiet motor lodge. In the streetlight, Val's eyes looked like drenched violets. She was going to cry with me, I realized. Even this felt athletic, the way Valeria did it. She put her arms around my hitching shoulders, matching me breath for breath.

"My mama was a terrible singer and she knew it. But she sang all the time. I wish I had a recording of her singing. I am starting to forget it. She had her moods and I used to dread some of them. Now I miss even the worst ones. Her good moods touched everyone. They drew out the colors in everything—even the nails in the wall started to sparkle when Mama was happy. She could make anybody laugh. She got bounced from a funeral for making the deacon piss himself laughing . . ."

"Why did she give you such a fancy name?" Val wrinkled her nose. "Asphodel."

"It's a famous flower. It comes from a Greek myth." I heard myself getting huffy and had to laugh. "It's also a common weed. Some people call it onion-weed."

Valeria laughed with me and kissed my sweaty neck. "Okay. *Now* it's starting to make sense . . ."

"She loved books. She'd walk six miles to the big library with me in all kinds of weather. She loved flowers." I paused. "She loved me, too. And I loved her more than anyone. Although we didn't always act like it."

The line of aspens outside the motor lodge shook in a green lullaby of a breeze. It was hard to believe that this wind was related to the wind that had tried to kill us on the road.

"Valeria, can I trust you to keep a secret?"

"Of course."

"The Antidote is my boss. I've been her apprentice since Black Sunday. That's where I got the money."

"A prairie witch! Oletsky, you're gonna be a basketball star—just like me. We're gonna get recruited to a college team." She laughed, threading my braid around her shoulder. "You can practice your Dark Arts on me, somewhere far away from Uz."

"Even Babe Didrikson only has a few more good years playing. But a prairie witch can always make a living. Vaults will never be out of work."

"Is that so?" Val didn't sound so sure.

"People need help remembering. They need help forgetting, too."

"Does she let you use her earhorn?"

"No. I'm saving for one of my own."

"Can you take deposits from people?"

"Not yet. But I practice every day. You have to disappear inside yourself. I'm starting to get the hang of it. I can show you . . ."

"No! Stay with me!" Her voice jumped an octave and she grabbed my shoulders. "Stay in your body tonight, Oletsky." Her fear felt like a valentine to me in the dark lobby. Upstairs, I could hear our teammates laughing and horsing around in the group room. The clerk had gone home for the night, her little bell covered with a black kerchief. I grabbed two handfuls from the bowl of free peppermints for the team while Val struggled with the oil lamp, teasing the flame along the wick to get it burning. Her scowling face relaxed as the flame finally blossomed. Maybe mine did, too, because Val reached out and touched my cheek.

"Did she look like you, Dell?"

"Oh, no." I smiled up at Val through the blue oval of light. "My mother was beautiful."

The Grange Master, Harp Oletsky

I came back from repairing the Spider's leaking fuel line to find a stranger waiting on the porch. She was fooling with her camera, which sat on long, spindly legs like an insect from another planet. My heart skipped a beat as I stood staring at its empty eye.

It took me a moment to recognize the photographer, and my first thought was that the government must know about the strange spell on my land—they wanted to document it.

"Hello, Miss Allfrey," I said. "I was not expecting you today."

Allfrey was wearing a goldenrod kerchief wrapped around her hair and men's coveralls.

"My apologies for the surprise visit," she said. "I wasn't sure how to reach you."

Her long fingers continued making adjustments to the camera the entire time she talked.

"Good hard light out here. I was hoping I might photograph your wheat fields. I drove by your land when I first got to town, and I wanted to double back to make some pictures. You've got the healthiest crop I've laid eyes on in Nebraska."

"Oh. I see." My heart sank. "I would prefer, Miss Allfrey, that you not publicize it."

"It would be inspiring to many, I imagine. Has the AAA helped you to stay on this land?"

I nodded. "The checks I get from the government come for the wheat I am *not* growing. I appreciate the help. But it's strange to be paid for work you're not doing. I'm still trying to get my head around it. Let me show you . . ."

She followed me through the clover, waving off the noisy insects. As we approached the fallowland, she pointed and gasped. For a moment I felt certain she could see by daylight what I see here at night—the radiance that grows out of the ground. The nameless color. But it was the scarecrow that had spooked her. She started laughing at herself.

"Lord, that doll scared me good!"

"That's the world's toughest old scarecrow . . ."

"I thought I saw a man dancing in the air."

Her smile gave me a chill.

"Are *you* all right, Mr. Oletsky?"

I kept looking over my shoulder, to where the wheat shivered in the strong, dry gusts. Growing taller by the second, it sometimes seemed.

"It is easier to breathe out here than anywhere I have been since Omaha," Miss Allfrey said, inhaling a bellyful of air. "Who knew that breathing could be a leisure activity?"

Clouds parted overhead, changing the color of everything below. The green tillers looked silver in the sudden light. It was beautiful, and I felt myself soften. Cleo Allfrey did not know anything about my strange run of luck. She saw only the healthy soil and the green color that means light and life and water. Silently we walked the rows. Gliding almost, like butterflies. I loved the smell of the earth, fungal and cave cool. I turned some over with the spade for her to see and smell and feel. It was damp as cake.

"Do you irrigate?"

I shook my head. "Something is helping me," I said with a little shrug.

"Ah. I understand." She smiled at me. "A secret of the trade. We photographers also like to keep our favorite methods and techniques close to the vest."

I nodded. It was a secret, all right, even from me. The rest of the morning passed in a companionable silence. The photographer's total absorption behind the lens put me at ease. We worked in parallel furrows. Miss Allfrey spent the early afternoon setting up shots in the wheat field and the fallowland. I grudgingly agreed to appear in several of them.

"Nice work if you can get it!" I teased. "Taking pictures of people doing real jobs—"

But I could see that it *was* work. Real spooky work. She was in a kind of trance, squinting at the sky through a wire frame, choosing which clouds to corral. Each click made me happy. I don't know much about photography. The fellow who snapped our family portrait for a dollar in 1909 had tried to explain it to me and Frankie. *It's light*, he'd said, *that's all it is*. Light that writes itself on paper, waking up tiny silver crystals. Light from a star so far away that my mind ached to consider its journey to and through the lens. The same star, it now occurred to me, that was causing gallons of sweat to pour down my back as I followed Miss Allfrey.

She climbed onto the flat roof of the shed to make a landscape portrait. I watched her framing up the beige ridge of cloud where my blue skies shaded into rust brown. Miss Allfrey told me about a summer month she'd spent photographing the ocean from the Atlantic City pier—there were stark lines, she said, where the bright emerald water became a murkier sage and then a uniform blue. She described how the contrast between the shallow water of the harbor and the open sea made for beautiful black-and-white prints. I thought I understood her way of looking into things, although I felt too clumsy to put words to what I knew from the farm. How I also read tones and textures in my fields to learn about the world below the soil. How light on the surface helps me conjecture about the depths.

Around 1:00 p.m., I asked Miss Allfrey if she would like to join me in the farmhouse for hot coffee and cheese and tomato sandwiches. She thanked me and said that she was never hungry when she was working. What she was starving for out here, she said, was a *darkroom*. A place to discover what the camera had captured. "I hardly know what I have made until I get my prints back from the government lab," she said. "It's hard to wait on strangers in D.C. for that revelation."

I listened to Miss Allfrey building to a request, in that funny way that people have of constructing their own ramps: "My boss doesn't want us doing our own developing in the field—wants everything sent to Washington. He likes to have oversight, you know. Control. He worries the dust will ruin our negatives." She paused. "But the air is so clear out here. And I have the trays, the beakers for mixing my chemistry, a safelight. Everything I need in that trunk—"

She pointed to where her Ford was parked at a diagonal, facing the horses, whose dappled gray heads were both inside their feed sacks. Like me, they get shy around a visitor.

"All I'm missing is a light-tight place to get set up. A toolshed. A deep closet . . ."

She let the question float between us. And I was about to apologize, say that the house didn't offer much. I'd have preferred she snap her pictures and move along, really—before Otto noticed this government agent making photographs of my property. Before my niece came home and started asking rude questions. Before—God forbid—Urna stopped by and saw I had a visitor. An unmarried woman, half my age. But when I opened my mouth, something else came out. "Actually, I know just the place."

I knelt and opened the door in the ground.

The RA Photographer, Cleo Allfrey

I t took a couple hours to get set up in the root cellar. The dried beans hung in eerie chandeliers. Potatoes were buried in the sandy part of the floor. Walls seemed to breathe down here, where it was twenty degrees cooler than it had been on the surface. Cold moon smell mixed with a tubery richness. I flashed to a memory of playing by the river with my sisters and lifting my palm to smell a wet earthworm.

"A bit primitive for a darkroom, I guess." I couldn't tell if the farmer was embarrassed by the space he had to offer or regretted offering me space at all. "We're not on the grid out here, but I have a wind charger for your batteries . . ."

Harp Oletsky continued bumping around the narrow cellar, clearing off a table for my trays and chemicals. Every breath was an apology. I was surprised when he welcomed me onto his property, but I felt safer than I would have guessed was possible in a shallow cave with a strange man. I liked him, and I also found him to be a bit of a nuisance.

"Thank you for your help, Mr. Oletsky. I am perfectly fine alone. I prefer it, in fact . . ."

I thought about getting my flashbulbs from the car and shooting in the cellar. The preserves took on dream-hues down here, shelved and floating in a wall of jars. The longer I stared at the wall, the less familiar the jars' contents became. The red safelight turned the vinegar suspension an orangey yellow. Ten yards beyond the table, a stone wall stood between the root cellar and the farmhouse basement. A tunnel stretched from the shelving to the trapdoor in the roof, where the soil seemed to flow beyond the reach of the safelight and turn a darker ocean blue. I saw teeth smiling from the dirt ceiling—the tines and cedar handle of an ancient spud rake, suspended on a hook.

"I'd love to see the pictures you made today, when they are ready? The ones of the sky over my land?"

Down here, it was hard to remember the sky at all.

"Certainly. I'm excited to see how those exposures turn out. The sky over your land is so clear. Nothing like the muddy orange I find everywhere else."

When the old farmer spoke again, his voice was shaking. He sounded so young in the cave. I felt touched by the honesty of his tremors. Fear, in men, tends to show up on their faces as worry, or rage.

"I can't account for this run of luck, Miss Allfrey. The dust swerves around me. We've had blue skies since Black Sunday."

"Good luck must feel unfamiliar out here," I said. "I can understand that. Not wanting to trust it."

The farmer's eyes were blinking uncontrollably in the envelope of red light. His face was the color of a cut strawberry.

"Well, I am happy to share this luck with you, Miss Allfrey. It's good to find some purpose for it. You are welcome to use this root cellar as your darkroom for as long as you need."

⊰⊱

Vernalization is a requirement for winter wheat, the farmer told me. The dormant phase cannot be skipped. The seeds sleep under the snowy ground, undergoing their great change. I thought of this later that night, watching figures rise from the mist of the photographs.

Your camera is your weapon, Miss Allfrey . . .

It felt more like a spade to me. It was digging through clods of time.

When I looked at the tiny negative, I felt confused, then furious at myself. I was afraid I'd ruined the picture of the archaeological dig. All that showed up on the developed film was a milky cloud. Instead of scrapping it, something possessed me to immerse my failure into the fixing bath a second time. This time the clouds cleared. Something began to appear. It was nothing I had seen on the day at the Pawnee village site where I fired the shutter.

I made a note to tell my sister Isabelle back home in Gray's Ferry that she was right, I really *was* crazy to come out here alone, and in fact I'd lost my mind somewhere between Omaha and Uz. Had the bent infinity stop caused this? Had I used the wrong shutter speed? My head filled with the singsong claims of advertisements praising my camera: *Nothing can move too fast for the focal plane of the Graflex Speed Graphic! Its ground glass removes all guesswork!*

When I looked at the developed negative on the enlarger, I was afraid to move, afraid even to let out breath. I myself felt like something pinned to a trembling wire, waiting for my astonishment to sharpen into some kind of explanation. Trying to understand how this camera could have seen something so far outside the range of my own vision. I had made the exposure on Tuesday; the scene that spread before me was from an earlier century. I recognized the landscape by Guide Rock, but it was not what I had seen in the ground glass.

The picture I had made at Asa T. Hill's dig site did not show an open, desecrated grave. What surfaced instead was a living city. The scale of the photograph was staggering, as if it had somehow been taken from a midpoint in the sky. A bird's-eye view from far above where I'd stood behind the tripod. Native children were playing in the foreground, swinging from silver branches. A half-constructed mud lodge was filled with women taking measurements and erecting cottonwood beams. More lodges rose across the grassland, round as the shoulders of a giantess. Sunflowers and corn and beans and squash burst into lush life in the great farm that stretched beyond the edges of the frame.

The Prairie Witch

When the last of the drunks filed out of the saloon, just as the first birds woke into song, I climbed out of bed. I watched my frantic hands lace up my boots and pack my record books and my money box and a week's worth of clothes into an ancient suitcase. Had I decided to go to the girl for help? It felt more like a stone had come loose. Now it was gathering speed, pulling me toward the stairwell, rolling me into the street. I caught up to one of my pickled customers, fished the keys out of his jacket pocket, and offered to drive his truck while he sobered up in the passenger seat. "Sleep it off, Amos," I said. "I'll get you home."

It was my last lie, I promised myself. I parked a mile from Oletsky's huge, unpainted barn, noting with amazement the height and health of his waving wheat. Amos was snoring in the passenger seat. He didn't need help from any prairie witch; he'd forget how he came to be here all on his own. I left the keys on his lap and dragged my suitcase from the main road to the cow path all the way to the farmer's silent porch. My pinkie toes were throbbing inside my narrow boots. It was my first time out here; Harp Oletsky had never banked with me, and I did not expect a warm welcome. Was Asphodel awake? I could hear the cows' taut lowing, they were ready for their milking. The pink yolk of the sun was just now spreading over the surrounding prairie. Tomorrow had become today—the day the Sheriff had promised to return. I wanted nothing to do with his "painting." I would not counterfeit for him. The hideous lightness rushed from my heels to my temples, and I felt as if the slightest breeze would tear me from the ground. *Now I will learn what it means to refuse to play along with Sheriff Iscoe*, I thought. *Now the bill will come due*. I collapsed into the Oletskys' porch swing, staring at the ground to keep from retching. When a rooster crowed, I ducked as if the sound was gunfire. Every few minutes I stood again to try the knocker. Was Asphodel inside? Was the farmer out choring? There was something wrong with my plan, but I was too exhausted to figure out what. I sank back onto the swing and wrapped my arms around my earhorn's velvet case. Waiting like a cat to be let in.

I was about to stand to knock again when I saw something astonishing. The patchy grass in the front yard began to quake apart. The earth opened and a woman's head emerged. She climbed out of the ground, her hair spilling behind her, crumbs of dirt shaking from her shoulders like a disintegrating cape. She turned and saw me and we both let out a cry. I recognized the boxy black object that she held with two hands against her chest, cradled to her heart like an infant. The lens of her camera was pointed right at me, which made me grip my earhorn tighter. For a moment it felt tense as a stand-off.

"What nice weather we're having today," I said at last. "You've arrived from that cave just in time to make a lovely photograph!"

She burst into laughter, and that set me off too. She caught her breath before I did. To my surprise, she opened the black box to reveal an umbilicus-like accordion connected to the camera's single eye, made some adjustments to the tiny knobs and levers, loaded the holder and pulled the dark slide, then arched her body until her lens pointed at the sky. She fired the shutter. Adjusted, reloaded, fired. The sky looked unbreakably blue. I realized that I had not coughed once since reaching the western gate where the main road branched into a path to Harp Oletsky's section. The scientists insist that the sky is porous, they claim you can fly right through it, on and on forever to remote stars in distant galaxies. But out here, I felt unsure. The sky over the Oletsky place made me feel like a firefly caught under a glass.

"What are you doing here?" asked the photographer.

"Waiting," I said. Wasn't it obvious? I am so good at it, Son. Waiting has been the central activity of my life.

She eyed the suitcase at my feet.

"Waiting for what?"

I could have told the photographer what had been true a minute earlier: I'd been waiting for Asphodel Oletsky to come and help me plan my escape from Uz. To hide me in her uncle's truck bed and drive me to the train station in Kearney or Hastings. I'd come to the Oletsky place with hair dye and scissors and a pair of men's trousers. What choice did I have left? I wouldn't be Vick's accomplice, and I felt certain that he would kill me if I refused—if my defrauded customers didn't find me first. But running felt like another kind of dying. Running would mean giving up the dream of our reunion. The one thing that has kept me rooted to this earth, Son. Others abandoned their land—I was abandoning my hope. Moving the X off the map. I would be a fugitive for the rest of my life, and how would you find me?

That was my plan until I watched Allfrey burst through the earth. I had walked right over the root cellar to get to the porch and never guessed I'd missed a portal. Now I could easily spot the faint outline of the door in the dirt—but only because I knew where to look for it. The iron handle glinted like an awl left to rust in the soil. Short-horned grasshoppers kept bouncing up and falling back into the yellow weeds.

Allfrey was squinting at me through the wire frame above her camera.

"Waiting for who? Or would you rather not say?"

I pointed at the secret that she had just revealed to me.

"Waiting for someone to open the door."

As I gave my answer, I felt a great wind move through me. I shut my eyes and saw a fist uncurling into a palm. A small hand reaching to span an octave. The chord I heard was so beautiful. Afterward, I wasn't waiting any longer. I wasn't running. *What* are *you doing here,* *then?* A new answer began to form itself inside me.

The Region 7 Champion,
Asphodel Oletsky

The last leg of the drive home was a miserable one. The wind was down, but dust still choked us and coated the windshield. We wore our masks inside the oven of the bus. My prophecy seemed silly to me. This time I was on my own to navigate; Valeria sat in the back with Pazi and Dagmara, and every few minutes I heard a fresh eruption of laughter. Each one felt like a bomb going off inside me. As I retraced our route I could not stop seeing flashes of our journey: the cloud wall erasing the sun and swallowing the road, my teammates' screams as I steered us into the heart of the storm, ignoring their warnings, ignoring my own knowledge that I was putting all my friends at risk to win a game; Oramelle pillbugged on the half-court line, screaming in pain; the coroner's photograph of my mother in the ditch. I wished there had been someone at the Red Willow gymnasium to photograph us—a journalist for *The Gazette*, or that photographer I'd met at the Jentleman. I did not feel much like a champion.

One by one, I dropped each Danger at her home. "Ready, Set, Lightning!" we shouted at each parting, and it was hard not to feel sad as our chorus thinned. Ellda was the last to get off. Warm air sighed against my neck. Something quieter than a whisper hummed under my mind. I pressed the pedal to the floor mat and felt the bus shudder. The bus that Ellda had gotten for us, with her three minutes of effort. An excellent return on her investment. "Ellda," I told her as we drew up to her two-story house, her mother already running out to scoop her up. "Come to the boardinghouse on Monday. You can deposit that unpleasantness inside the Antidote. I'll cover it." She'd thanked me sincerely, which made me feel even more cruddy. We hugged goodbye, and I drove the empty Bedwetter to my uncle's place. A strange car was parked beside the western gate.

"Hello," I called ahead of my entry, not wanting to startle my uncle. "I'm here. I'm back." I imagined my teammates calling out, *Mama, I'm home! We won!*

But my uncle wasn't in the kitchen, and I was the one who got spooked. The witch and the photographer were sitting at the table, a game of cards spread out in front of them. My uncle's whiskery dog, Squint, a gray mutt who never came inside the house, was sleeping at the Antidote's feet. Her free hand hung drowsily beside Squint, scratching his head and letting him lick the carrot marmalade from her fingers. She was eating it right out of the jar with a tiny rusty spoon; the photographer had spread hers on soda crackers. For a full minute, I wondered if I was dreaming. Maybe my body was in a ditch on the side of the road, or in the hospital back in Red Willow.

The Antidote looked up at me and broke into a real smile.

"*Asphodel.*" The witch's voice went softer and warmer than I knew it could go. "I was so worried about you. The radio said there was a terrible storm on Highway Six—"

"What are you doing here?" I hadn't meant to sound so angry. Nothing about their calm faces in my uncle's kitchen made any sense.

The witch turned over a two of hearts.

"Losing to Cleo Allfrey at rummy."

Allfrey's laugh was low and friendly. "It's anybody's game."

"Hello . . . Cleo Allfrey. What are you doing here?"

"Taking a break from the root cellar. Your uncle is a kind man. I needed a darkroom, and he found me one."

"In the *root cellar*?"

The Antidote swept her cards up and fanned them into a paper fence. She was just playing a game, I reminded myself. But I felt shut out of something.

"Are you . . . all right?"

Her eyes flashed at me, and for a moment she looked like her old self. Cunning and afraid. A hundred years older than anyone her age.

"I am hiding, girl. For the time being."

Hiding. From what person? For what reason? What had happened while I was away?

"And my uncle? He's letting you two stay here?"

My uncle chose that moment to come in through the back door, holding a bucket of skinned potatoes. When he saw me he let out a yelp and dropped it. The potatoes rolled everywhere, gaping at us like shocked white eyes; Squint chased one under the table. I figured my uncle must have been ambushed by Cleo Allfrey and my boss and blurted out some polite invitation; women made him nervous. Now that I'd arrived, would he kick us all out? My uncle had warned me many times not to fraternize with the Antidote of Uz, or any prairie witch.

"Asphodel—"

I braced myself for a lecture, or worse.

My uncle drew me into an embrace, the wildest surprise yet. I surprised myself by resting there for a moment, engulfed in the pleasant hoppy odor of his fields. Relief traveled between us, and I felt embarrassed by its intensity in the middle of the kitchen. He was so happy that I was alive! Me, of all people, not some fairy-tale niece, some tiny Lada who I'd failed to resemble.

"She does whatever she pleases," he told the others over my shoulder. "I can't stop her from leaving, but I can celebrate when she comes back in one piece."

"Yeah, yeah, I'm here." I wriggled free and turned back to the table. "Let's keep the cork in the champagne." I looked from face to face, waiting for someone to let me in on the joke, or the secret—whatever I had interrupted. Surprise can be a very lonely feeling. Nobody shared mine. Even old Squint was yawning.

"Miss Allfrey is a government photographer," said my uncle. "She has been developing her film in the root cellar."

Cleo Allfrey nodded, as if this were the most natural arrangement in the world.

"Then this morning, I came in from the milking and found the witch on the porch."

The Antidote didn't say anything, just kept her eyes on her feet, her cards spread before her. Her face looked thinner to me, and her dark hair was unwashed. From this angle, the grays looked like a spiderweb covering her scalp. We all watched her for a moment, and it was as if the pressure of our gazes forced her head lower.

"She tells me you've been working for her, Dell."

"I ran here," the Antidote said, her head snapping up. "After a bad night with the Sheriff. I didn't know where else to go."

I stared from my uncle's dopey, unshaven face to her sun-lined one. Feeling somehow older than both of them. Like I used to feel in the yellow house—the only sober person in the room.

"All right. You're hiding in our kitchen. Miss Allfrey is developing pictures underground. The sun is setting in an hour. Should I be gathering linens, Uncle?"

My uncle turned cherry pink. "I suppose we haven't discussed any, um, arrangements."

The dog was still trying to nose potatoes from under the stove. Squint didn't give a damn where any of us slept tonight.

Cleo Allfrey cleared her throat. "I'm perfectly comfortable at the boardinghouse," she said. "Although at the rate they charge—"

"I cannot ever return to Room 11," my boss interrupted. She stared at me, and I knew to hold back my questions for later. "I need your help, girl. If I can't stay here—"

"Nonsense," my uncle broke in, more confident now. Chipper even. "Plenty of room for you both. Plenty of peace and quiet to go around."

For a second I felt sure this must be part of the strange spell on my uncle's land—the next phase of whatever mysterious protection seemed to have enclosed us. It was an extraordinary sight, with no easy explanation: three real smiles. They all seemed spellbound, even tail-wagging Squint.

"Thank you," said the witch.

"Much obliged," said the photographer.

"Deal me in, Miss Allfrey," said my happy uncle, pulling out a chair.

For a quarter hour, I sat at the table, watching the coffee disappear and the cards wheel around. Others' happiness can feel like stinging nettles when you're on the outside of it.

"Don't you want to play, girl?" the Antidote asked me. I shook my head, afraid of how badly I wanted to join them.

My uncle made us cream of potato soup in a bright orange bowl the size of a baby's bathtub. I had never seen it before—we had never once had company out here. I felt betrayed by the fact of this bowl. Where had such a bowl been all my life? He ladled each of us a cup of soup with a hand-carved wooden spoon that had KĘTRZYN etched on the handle—a spoon I doubted had been used once this century.

"We won," I told them. Maybe shouted at them. The words jumped out of my mouth, along with chunks of scalding potato. "The Dangers are the Region Seven Champions."

Everyone turned to me. I had interrupted my uncle and Cleo Allfrey's conversation about the ocean tides, to which the Antidote had been intently listening.

"Congratulations, Dell," said my uncle. "Now you can rest a little."

<hr />

After the last hand of cards, Allfrey excused herself and returned to the root cellar. We watched her lantern shrink into the ground. I got up to clear the table and help my uncle wash the pots and pans.

"Dell," he said at the sink, his forearms sleeved in bubbles. "Fancy meeting you here. My God, it's an extraordinary night in every way."

"Knock it off," I said, embarrassed. "I help, Uncle."

"You help yourself to my cooking. You help yourself to my car keys."

I scraped cold mush from a bowl. "Well, I'm helping now."

We stood side by side, settling into a new rhythm. It was more pleasant than I could have imagined. Many nights, I fled the table before my uncle took his first bite. "Thank you for helping my boss. She isn't a bad person. She's trying to save this town from blowing off the map."

"She's much safer here than in town. But promise me something, Dell: You'll quit that job. Make your living another way. There's plenty of work on the farm."

"Are you scared that the Sheriff might come here?" I asked. I certainly was.

"To be honest with you?" he said. "No. Maybe I should be. But no. Howling winds drop to whispers out here. Every dust storm disperses before it reaches us. I trust we'll be safe from that blowhard too."

He started drying the cookware and returning it to various drawers, alerting me to a system of organization to which I'd never paid a bit of attention. He was humming some dirge-like Polish tune and complaining about my laziness. He was so happy tonight in the crowded house! Smiling into the rainbow sink bubbles.

"Uncle? I might already be a witch."

His smile curved like the road.

"If you are, Dell," he said, staring right at me, "don't be that kind."

⊰⊱

Our spell of simple happiness and ease lasted until 9:00 p.m. I went upstairs with an armful of sheets and blankets for our guests. Cleo Allfrey was still in her darkroom; nobody knew if or when she might resurface. The Antidote helped me to get the beds made. No one had slept in my grandparents' room for decades, and I wondered for a moment if maybe the Antidote could stay here permanently.

"Boss? How long do you plan to hide out? We have four appointments for withdrawals on Monday."

"I quit," she said. "I am no longer a Vault. I took my last deposit yesterday." She shook out my grandmother's fan and closed it again, a sharp thwack in the dark. "You're fired, I guess."

"No," I said. "No. We have important work to do."

Her laughter made me think of the field mice that run before the tractor. I can't hear them over the whine of the engine but I can see them surging through the wheat.

"Dell," she said. "I owe you an apology. I put you in danger. I misused your gifts. But that's done now."

"We were helping," I said. "Weren't we?"

The gray tide of mice scampered up my spine. *We need each other, don't we?*

"You just need a few more months to get back what you lost . . ."

"Listen to me, girl. We don't have much time, and I need your help. I don't know what to do with what I know. There is no Lucky Rabbit's Foot Killer, Dell. The Sheriff made it up. He wanted to be the big hero . . ."

Then she told me everything the Sheriff had buried inside her the previous night. This exchange was nothing like my boss's ordinary transfers. She faced me across the table with open eyes. Her deep voice often faltered or broke with emotion. She forgot certain details and doubled back to add them. She was telling me the truth. As she spoke, I shut my eyes and watched a fire blossom. A woman stared at me through an envelope of flame on a blue dune, so terribly alone. My hand wanted to reach out to her. "How do you spell her name?" I asked the Antidote.

M-I-N-K P-E-T-R-U-S-E-V

⚎

After I left the Antidote, I went directly to my mother's bedroom. I ransacked the closet looking for any trace of Mama. I found: Frank's sketchbook; a dinky St. Francis medallion; a tooth-colored baseball with the red seam pulled out; a dozen mummified insects; a rosewood mandolin that needed new strings. Nothing that belonged to Lada Oletsky. No messages from her to me, hidden in notebooks or the pockets of old clothes. I crawled under the bed, feeling along the floorboards. I dumped out dresser drawers of coins, springs, pencil erasers, my grandmother's Polish prayer cards, a program from Uz High School's 1911 ice-skating performance of *The Nutcracker*. I couldn't give up. With groaning, swaying effort, I pulled the bed away from the wall.

Jackpot.

Behind the headboard, I found a hollow. An oval case was hidden inside it, engraved with tiny leaves and starlike blossoms. Her jewelry box, I thought at first.

Let it be my mother's ring. Something I can wear to feel her with me—
I opened the box. There was nothing inside but a scrap of paper.
"Asphodel. Where did you find that?"

My uncle was standing in the middle of the room, wearing his pajamas and his saddest basset-hound look. Disappointment is harder to bear than anger. Valeria and I had debated this once, and she proved my point for me, getting so worked up that she wrestled me to the ground. The heat of her anger had felt wonderful, so close to love. Disappointment has no warmth at all.

"You look like a wet old hen," I told my uncle. "Go back to your coop. Nothing to see here."

"That's your grandfather's pill box," my uncle said. "He hated taking medicine. He hated every sign of weakness. My father had a soft heart that he hid from everyone, even us—just look at where you found that box—"

"There was nothing inside it," I said. "Just a piece of faded paper."

Just some numbers written in bleeding ink.

In a flash I understood what I was holding.

"Uncle! I found a deposit slip!"

My uncle was suddenly wide awake, swiping at his eyes. He stood over me and pried my fist open. Gently, but with more force and directness than I knew he possessed. He took the slip and began to curse quietly under his breath.

"Go wake the Antidote," he shouted at me.

There was no need; we found her downstairs under one of my grandmother's blue shawls, listening to violins on the radio with the fake-pearl dial. She was lying on the sofa with her feet crossed at the ankle.

"Make yourself at home," I said.

My uncle held up the slip. The ink was an odd grapey color. "T.O." he read. "My father's initials. Tomasz Oletsky." The way he grimaced made me think of water breaking on gray rocks. "Witch, did you lose my papa's deposit?"

Sleepily, as if surfacing from a dream, the Antidote sat up. She switched off the radio. "This is not my routing number," she said. "This came from the Counselor of Genoa. Her purple ink was once notorious in central Nebraska."

"The Counselor," my uncle repeated. "Yes—I do remember her. When I was very young, my father took me to her." My uncle shot me a guilty look. Not a story he'd told me.

"I did not know he was also her customer. I made a deposit that day, and he burned up my slip."

He looked into the fire, as if expecting some response.

I returned to the hollow behind the headboard. I couldn't stop checking it, as if another slip might have materialized while we were all distracted, one that belonged to my mother. A splinter shot into my thumb and I wanted to cry. The Antidote stood in the doorframe, watching me. "Dell. Quit this craziness. There's nothing else in there." I saw her face, and her pain became my own. Our shame at what we'd done. We had covered up so many holes in the last four weeks. The gaps in the wall that told a person, *Something used to be here*. With my hand inside the inner wall, I felt what we had taken from her customers. The chance to wonder at what was missing. To go searching for it.

"I know where Genoa is," my uncle said slowly. "It's next door to where my folks filed their first preempt. They started out in the Polish colony of Krakow—our mother once took us to see their first homestead. But I do not know where to find this Vault."

The Antidote raised the flickering lantern, fear tensing the small muscles of her face. "Harp Oletsky. I can show you where to find the Counselor."

Her voice had grown alarmingly high and gentle. I hated this new octave. I felt on the outside of their conversation, and I suddenly wanted to return to the stifling closeness of Room 11, where I'd felt useful and necessary. *Go back to the old way, Boss!* The wires of our secret communication were down, or she ignored me. She continued to nicker to my uncle in the too-soft voice: "The Counselor was an old woman the last time I saw her. She may be long dead. Even if she's alive, Harp, she may have nothing to return . . ."

The Antidote said she couldn't predict how many other prairie witches had been affected by the Black Sunday storm; perhaps the collapse she'd suffered was widespread. I prayed the Vault in Genoa was still breathing and solvent and able to return my grandfather's secrets. The date on the slip was hard to read—perhaps my mother was an infant or a child inside my grandfather's memory. *Mama, we're coming to find you.*

My uncle was already smoothing a map onto the table. The Antidote made an "X" on a nameless spot near the fork in the Loup. I felt my pulse quickening in the presence of hidden treasure. What had my grandfather buried in the woman who lived on the Loup River?

"Ask her if she knows of other witches who have gone bankrupt. See if she can tell you anything about the whereabouts of Madame Quicksand."

Uncle Harp nodded as he grabbed his coat and keys. Part of him was already traveling, already speeding down the road. He was making a list of chores for us, pocketing his wallet and his map—he was leaving me behind.

"Take me with you, Uncle. I found the slip! I want to make the withdrawal. It might be about Mama—"

He shook his head. "If I learn something about your mother, Dell, I will share every word of her with you. But I need to know what my father never told us. And forgot himself."

I started to run after him at full bore; the Antidote blocked my path. Her hands were like iron on my shoulders. "This is his to know, girl," she whispered. "It's his inheritance."

"It's mine too!"

"He will share it with you if he finds it." The Antidote drew me closer to her, and I felt the fight go out of me.

My uncle swung the door open onto the clear night air. He pointed a stiff finger at the blue-white stars over his even rows of wheat. Across the fence line, I could just make out the flat rectangle of Otto's dusted-out fields.

"Something is protecting this land. Something more than just luck. I don't know if this is the missing puzzle piece, Dell. I don't know if there is one. I have prayed to understand why these blue skies have enclosed us while so many others suffer. Maybe, somewhere in this deposit, there's an answer—"

The Grange Master, Harp Oletsky

T he Counselor had seemed irritated but unsurprised when I knocked on the door of her dugout. It was daybreak when I reached her. Through the window, I could see her roan pony grazing by the silty river. Did she still ride at her age? She must have been nearing her hundredth birthday. She was easily the oldest person I had ever met.

The Vault beckoned me to sit, sinking into her chair. "I don't know your face. I don't recognize your voice. Who directed you to me?"

"The Antidote of Uz told me where to find you."

"Ah! That skinny guinea with the big-tent name." She shook her head, as if she were a swimmer clearing her ears. "Is she still open for business? That's more than most Vaults can say in her region."

"The Antidote is my friend," I admitted. "She's in trouble."

"She was always trouble. Working the railroads with Kettle and her misfits. Her 'Vaults-in-training.' Never worth the effort, in my opinion. Little backstabbers and thieves and whores."

"What about you, ma'am? Are you still open?"

I unscrolled the slip and felt her attention sharpen.

She let out a waspy sound that might have been laughter. "Here in Genoa, we were right on the outermost edge of your nightmare. Had I been closer to Kansas, or west of Kearney, who knows? I might have been emptied myself!"

The muff on her lap, I realized, was alive. Curled into itself, asleep I guess, its glossy belly lifting and falling. Was it an otter? A weasel? It never lifted its head.

"Others have experienced a . . . a bankruptcy? A crash?"

"Every Vault I know from Black Mesa to McCook went bust."

This news shook through me. The Antidote was right—she was part of a larger collapse.

"God, that's a crying shame. Why did this happen to them?"

She grimaced and took a long drink from her flask. "*Why* is not a question I bother with much, young man. People drive themselves mad asking it."

She laughed, releasing more invisible wasps. "Madness is good for my business, of course. Especially now that most of my competition got wiped out."

"Do you have any news of . . ." I struggled to remember. The Antidote had asked me to bring back word of her missing friend. "Cherry Le Foy? Ah, *Madame Quicksand*?"

"Le Foy hasn't been seen in two months," said the Counselor, with a gummy yawn. "Tell your witch to be on guard. Word is traveling that many Vaults in this region are empty. In Kimball, a mob of angry customers killed their young witch last week."

She dusted off her instrument, a battered blue ear trumpet. She secured it to leather straps and waved me toward the gaping hole of the receiver. "Sit," she groaned, fitting the speaker to her mouth. "Speak up. My hearing is not what it used to be—"

Withdrawing money from a bank, that's a happy affair. Withdrawing a memory from the witch nearly killed me. Her words parted me like a knife tugging through a rabbit, opening me from stomach to neck. Into that seam poured the light of my father's days. My ribs flared, trying to make room for Tomasz Oletsky's life.

Tomasz Oletsky's Deposit

Radzilowski told me about the free lands first, a full year before the Agent reached our shores. Radzilowski was my oldest cousin on my mother's side, with a voice like a bear torn apart by arrows. He had fought in the Poles' failed uprising against the Prussians in 1848 and lost his leg to one of the sawbones. His gruesome tales from the front never frightened me as badly as the puckered nub of his hairy thigh. He was the only one of us who had amounted to anything—a copyist with carbon-black thumbs who spoke four languages and worked for a German barrister in Berlin. He'd seen the advertisement in the paper: FERTILE AS THE BLACK-EARTH OF UKRAINE. FREE LANDS IN AMERICA.

GET A HOME OF YOUR OWN, the newspapers screamed in the linotype's tallest font. The promise rubbed off on our fingertips, the newsprint still damp. Who else was promising us anything?

The Chancellor publicly spoke of his wish to expel us. He planned to rid his Empire of Poles one way or another—either by forced exile, or by "germanizing" us. These threats colored my youth like ink in water. I was nine years of age when the soldiers burned our church. *Kulturkampf* was the German word for our nightmare. "The Polish Question" had one solution.

I lived in a village called Golab near "the belly of the woods," on lands cleared long ago to raise barley and hogs. My parents explained to us that we had descended from a tribe of Slavs who moved onto the banks of the Vistula River six hundred years after Christ's life, death, and resurrection. Our entire village had once been bought and sold as a block with every peasant on it, exchanged between two nobles as a wedding present. Serfdom had been abolished for nearly a century; in all but name, serfs we remained. My father farmed the same fifteen acres that his great-grandparents had farmed for the descendants of their master. We worked sixteen-hour days and often ate rotting food along with the stock. We could no more choose our own direction, my papa complained, than the mules we drove could choose theirs. "We have too little to live," he often said, "and too much to die of starvation."

Polska Ziemia is the Land of Fields.

Pole is our name for what the Yankees call a *plain*.

"You are Polish," my father insisted, and my grandfather told my brothers and sisters that we would live to see the Kingdom of Poland restored to all maps. He died in a cell, imprisoned for hiding our village priest, young Father Wojcik with the harelip that tugged his mouth into a grin, beloved by everyone, executed by the Prussian soldiers over our cries of protest. The year I turned seventeen, Prussia became part of the German Empire. The Germans did not simply want our Polish lands. They wanted to swallow us whole, until even the memory of our shadows had vanished.

Polakożerstwo—the devouring of the Poles.

I was a child when I first understood that the moment I crossed over from Golab Polska into the neighboring German village of Taube, I became a lesser being. Step by step, my value decreased. Imperial Chancellor Otto von Bismarck put it plainly:

> Hit the Poles so hard that they despair of their life; I have full sympathy with their condition, but if we want to survive, we can only exterminate them; the wolf, too, cannot help having been created by God as he is, but people shoot him for it if they can.

My oldest relatives were young children when Poland was carved up by the Three Empires—Russian and German and Austrian. To me, their Polonia was an imaginary place.

"What did Poland look like then, before the Partitions?" I'd once asked my mother's grandfather. "Like this," he said, directing my eye to the field outside the window. "Like that," he added, sweeping his

palm under the dark green wooded hills that surrounded our sloping farmland. "These trees are the daughters of trees that grew here
thousands of years ago. They do not change with our names."

Lebensraum had begun to circulate as an idea when I was a young
man. I first heard the word at the schoolhouse in Taube, where our
teacher explained that the expansion of an empire was not only natural but necessary, on scientific principles. German society was an
organism, and it needed habitat—"living space"—to grow and to
develop. Polish lands were *Lebensraum* for the German Reich.

In the spring of 1872, I fell in love with my neighbor, Ania
Piotrowska. We were eager to marry and to have children of our
own. Gulls blown inland from the Baltic Sea had come to roost on
her thatched roof. Augurs sent by God, said Ania, from the Gulf
of Gdańsk. Every six weeks, boats set sail carrying Poles across the
Atlantic.

The Agent had been born in Krákow, in the ashes of the great fire.
Now he worked to recruit settlers for the Burlington and Missouri
River Railroad Company. The railroad owned the odd-numbered
sections of land in Howard and Sherman Counties. Names that
meant nothing to me, names I struggled to repeat. English sounds all
wrong, the way I speak it. Music scored for a fiddler and played on a
dholak drum.

The Agent made his pitch to us in the village square, a summer
storm blowing in from the southwest. "Mothers' tears," the Agent
joked, wiping rain from his face. "Most of you will soon be setting
sail for America."

How does any man assess the integrity of another? The Agent
had fine clothes and black calfskin boots with rounded shanks. The
shoeblack made them glow like a December lake. He was a little
overweight and spoke in a genial, meandering tone—not at all what
I had expected from a merchant selling us America. It was his mandate from God, he said, to settle four hundred Polish families into
colonies in the West. We would be landholders and citizens at last.

The Agent would get a ten-cent commission for every acre we
bought up—a perfectly just amount, he assured us, considering the
effort it took to populate a colony on the Great Plains of America. He
compared us to the Poles recruited by Benjamin Franklin to cast off
the yoke of Britain, surely we'd heard of them? Heroes of the Ameri-

can Revolution! Count Kazimierz Pulaski! Tadeusz Kościuszko! The thirteen colonies had fought as bravely as we Poles did for their independence. Unlike us, the Agent said with a wry smile, the Yankees had won.

Zgermanizować meant that all children of the Reich must read and write in German. Speaking in Polish was banned in public. In Nebraska, said the Agent, we could speak our language anywhere we went. We could pray and receive communion. Own a homestead, and pass it on to our children. In Golab Polska, we lived and died by the whims of our landlord, who last February had decided to halve our supply of firewood and salt. None of my ancestors had ever owned an acre.

The railroad had donated the land for a Polish colony: lots for a schoolhouse, a chapel, a cemetery. Our train tickets would also be gifts of the railroad, the Agent swore to the skeptics among us. "They want new customers, you see . . ."

We craned over the table where the Agent spread out his maps and pamphlets. He passed around a tintype showing a scowling family standing against an unbroken gray expanse of grass and sky. Not a tree in sight. Not a smile in the bunch. Even the littlest girl looked like an unhappy toad removed from its pond.

"Do those fools live inside the pipe organ?" the fellow beside me grumbled. No other man-made structure was visible. Not a single right angle. We assumed the Agent must be joking with us when he said they lived inside the hill on which they'd posed.

Ania was the first to speak when the Agent completed his presentation. Her black eyes were burning wicks. She was one of the youngest women present, barely sixteen. "We will go," she said. "We will go," I echoed. We wouldn't stay and watch our Polish children become Germans.

What did we pack? A hairbrush. Jam and cheese and sardines. Four changes of clothes, a leather saddle, two winter cloaks. Ania's wedding dress and family Bible. A christening dress for our future baby. Bedding for the unimaginable journey. Ania's woodcutting of the Virgin Mary, Queen of Poland. Rosary beads of red sandstone quarried from the Góry Świętokrzyskie, our snowcapped mountains that we were leaving forever.

About the journey I have few memories. Under the floor of my mind, that horror still moves. The minutes stacking into hours, the night-blacked portholes, the terror of nearly losing Ania to fever. The stink and the dark and the certainty of failure, the death that lurched through the hold and turned our dear friends into morning corpses. The great sea seemed intent on pushing us back into the cage we'd just escaped. Yet one bright morning in late March, the silhouette of the Statue drew herself sharply against the city towers. A ghost-white gull preened on the port railing, and I imagined it was the same bird from Ania's roof—welcoming us to the other side of the prophecy. We had completed the first portion of our journey home. Ania could not stop sobbing. A storm pounded at the smooth surface of her young face. She begged me to return to our village with her at once. "It is not the fever that will kill me," she told me. "It is this homesickness. I want my mother, Tomasz."

"Home draws ever closer," I reminded her. A barge took us to the train station in Hoboken, New Jersey. I had never met a Black man before our encounter with the porter, Andrew Dawson. He called us Thomas and Anna, and made sure that Ania had meadowsweet to break her fever. He had lost his sister to fever, he told the bearded, one-legged man beside us, a Pole from Warsaw who spoke a little English and who quickly became the translator for our entire car. We watched the light-skinned Yankee passengers smoking and laughing while Andrew shined their shoes; one bony red-haired man in a fine suit touched the toe of a loafer to Andrew's forehead, muttering words that meant nothing to us in a hateful tone we understood quite well. Ania stood to intervene and was ridiculed in turn.

During the overland voyage, the Yankees called us a dozen slurs. We learned that our inferiority was assumed by the Yankees, that Poles were the butts of many jokes. A Polack is stupid and coarse and lazy and drunk. In America, a Pole is a Polack no matter whether he comes from Krákow or Gdańsk or Silesia. My heart sank, for it seemed we had fled one sort of prejudice into another. Where on Earth could we move to escape it?

I was born a serf in all but name, my language outlawed and my religion persecuted. My skin is the color of an unwashed onion. In America, this placed me ahead of many. On a low rung of the ladder, but higher than the Black porter. I felt that new height in my body, the distance to the ground. I heard the ticking pulse of a sick relief: *not me not me not me, Andrew Dawson—better you than me.* The same feeling I once had in Taube whenever one of my brothers was chosen over me for a beating.

"Shh, shh, shh," said the young mother beside me, trying to plug her screaming baby's mouth with her swollen nipple; she had stopped bothering to conceal it. By the time we reached the Missouri River, we were all out of our minds with exhaustion. Not long ago, a Yankee passenger told us, this land had all belonged to the Indians. Then it was opened for settlement, and tides of land and gold seekers came pouring into the west. "What happened to the Indians?" I asked through the red-haired translator. "You don't need to worry about them," he reassured us. "New Poznan is near Fort Kearny. The soldiers protect the Whites from the Indians. My cousin has been homesteading on the Loup since 1857. Things are much safer for us today."

Us! I smiled at this friendly Yankee.

By the time we reached Iowa, I had begun to avoid Andrew. The friendship, I came to feel, was a dangerous one. How quickly some of the passengers in the colonists' car—emigrants from Ireland and Sweden and Bohemia and Norway—absorbed the same lesson. In three weeks' time, our behavior had changed completely. We mimicked the Yankees. Ania gave Andrew Dawson her family Bible at our last stop, and I called her a fool—"Do you imagine that Mr. Dawson is Catholic? Do you think that he reads Polish?" She laughed angrily and told me, "What else do I have to give, Tomasz? That man saved my life."

Outside every window, on either side of the train, we found the same thing: a vast sea of waist-high grass. "Look for the tallest sunflowers," said our Agent. "The plants with height—that's where you'll find moisture." I saw no wheat growing anywhere. Nothing that resembled the cartoons of golden prosperity in the Agent's pamphlets. One evening, we saw two brown-skinned men on horseback who looked nothing like the Yankees. The taller man rode on, but his younger companion wheeled around to watch the train cross the prairie. He wore his black hair in braids and dressed in tanned skins with elaborate designs. Ania raised a hand as the train rolled off.

"Those are Pawnee men," said our car's translator, after asking the Yankee engineer on our behalf. "Indians. When we reach the Polish colony, those men will be our neighbors."

Everything we heard and saw required translation. My skull ached from my endless, mostly fruitless struggle to understand English. We passed towns under construction, and towns already abandoned—part of my education was learning to distinguish between them. The signs of life became easier to interpret. The surveyors' white flags meant a town was newborn. Laundry draped on the sides of hills marked the roofs of sod houses. Cavelike clouds promised water but delivered only shadows. Ania held my hand as we waded into the tallgrass prairie at a water stop, sending up swirling mists of pale blue and yellow butterflies.

The train was paused for a full day by the migrating buffalo. The great herd looked like a mountain in pieces, tumbling toward us. Hundreds flowed across the tracks. Horned beasts that rose a head above the tallest man in our party. Their thundering hooves rattled the car, their pungent stink filled our coats and our hair. We shrieked and gasped until we had exhausted our wonder. Then Ania and I watched as other passengers' bullets flew into the herd from between cars. Those men who had firearms shot at the buffalo, and dozens fell with blooming chests and terrible, unforgettable cries.

Take those cries from me. Take the memory of the great creatures staggering in circles.

The ladies leaned out the open windows and cheered. "Every buffalo dead is an Indian gone," explained our translator, who had become an expert Yankee eavesdropper. Every moving blur was a target for the men, and I was relieved when at last the herd had thinned and the locomotive rattled on.

"It is a disgrace, in my opinion," said a gray-haired Pole from Upper Silesia. "Such waste as I never saw on the steppe. The bodies pile up."

Now the great herds are ghosts. Ten years after our arrival in 1873, they were all but extinguished. The last buffalo I saw was at the Summer Moon Circus in 1911, after we had moved to our new homestead in Uz County: a captive calf bottle-fed by a chubby, sullen mermaid. The mermaid was sitting on an overturned bucket, her tail unzipped and her makeup sweating off in filthy rainbows. The mother cow, she said, had been sold separately to Buffalo Bill's Wild West Show. The calf's twin had died just that morning.

"I wish I could work one of the Wild West shows. I auditioned for Cowgirl and Indian Princess. Didn't get neither. Buffalo Bill pays three times what I get here and the costumes are better." She sighed and flicked ash from her pipe. "What I'd give to uncross my legs in summer . . ."

"Is Buffalo Bill an Indian?"

The mermaid holding the furry calf blinked at us.

"Bill is a White man. You don't know about him? Ask around. He is a great friend to the Indians. He gets real Indians for his traveling show. Pays them too.

"Come on now," the mermaid grunted, trying to fix the calf's lips around the bottle. "I can't get it to take a drop. I think this one's a goner, like her brother."

We had made up our mind to join the Poles who had already claimed lands on the Loup River. We had between us eight dollars and Ania's wedding ring. The Polish colony of Krakow could scarcely be called a town in 1873. There was a single inn, two livery and feed stables, a carpenter shop, a general merchandise store, a hardware store, a meat market, one millinery, and a saloon. Land, stock, tools, seed, house—we had, as yet, only our hunger for them.

Jescze Polska nie zginela!
Poland has not yet perished!

⁂

When we first arrived in Nebraska, I learned that our nearest neighbors were indeed the Pawnees. Something the Agent employed by the railroads had not disclosed when he described the Polish colony in Nebraska. The White man at the trading depot reassured us that we had nothing to fear from the Indians. "They need a pass to leave the reservation. They won't bother you none. We got the numbers on them out here."

When Ania and I arrived, White settlers outnumbered the Pawnees living on the reservation twenty-five to one. The Pawnee reservation lands were two miles from our preempt. The Pawnee are the people of the Central Plains, whose vast country reaches from the Niobrara to south of the Arkansas River, covering two-thirds of what appeared on our map as Nebraska and a great portion of Kansas. In my mother's lifetime, all that land had belonged to them. I applied to claim one hundred and sixty acres of it. We knew whose land we were taking, but where else could we go? What choice did we have?

Ania and I saw clearly then that the Indians who lived beside us had been made into prisoners on their homeland. What had happened to the Poles in Germany was happening here, and no settler lifted a hand to stop it. Quite the opposite. Many settlers spoke openly in support of forcing the Pawnees to leave Nebraska. "They got some of the best land, and it's wasted on them!" complained the innkeeper. The U.S. soldiers did nothing to protect the Pawnees or their lands but instead let the White settlers do whatever they pleased on the reservation. Every time I met the eyes of a Pawnee woman at the trading depot, I thought of my mother overpaying for bread, ignoring the German soldiers' taunting. Well, how could I help anyone, when I did not have anything? I first needed power myself, I reasoned. Once I had my own land and money, then I would be able to help others.

As a student of my new homeland, I became very interested in names. The secretary of war named the Territory that contained the

Platte River Valley "Nebraska," an Anglo mishmash of the Siouan words that named the broad, flat waters of the Platte River. Listening to English felt like standing under a waterfall. I ended each day exhausted from trying to comprehend who was doing what to whom. The basics of grammar overwhelmed me here. I heard my own transformed name, Oletsky, floating downstream in a logjam of words spoken by the Yankee innkeeper.

Time, a watercourse. For the first year, names such as Fort Kearny and Plum Creek sounded no more and no less foreign to my ear than Nishnabotna and Missouri. It was only as I learned more of the English language that I began to detect the Indian words inside it. In my tenth month living along the Loup, I went around a meander: suddenly I could hear how a word like Omaha was different from a word like Sherman, a word like Lincoln. On signs and maps, these names sounded in my ear with a different timbre: Nemaha, Otoe, Ponca, Cheyenne, Arikaree, Ogallala, Dakota, Kansas, Nebraska. The bluff overlooking the Platte River, which the Yankees in Fremont and Genoa called Pahuk Hill, had an older Pawnee name: Pahuku. A sacred place to our neighbors, although I never learned why. It felt like heresy even to wonder about heathen beliefs. The Pawnee Confederacy was composed of four different Caddoan-speaking nations, and living beside the reservation, I learned these names as well: the Chaui, the Kitkehahki, the Pitahawirata, and the Skidi.

Reservation was certainly a Yankee word.

Whereas the Republican River—which I had assumed had been named for the young republic of America—in fact had come from early French mapmakers' respect for the Kitkehahki political system. My mistake excited me, changing the way I viewed the map. Yet I wondered how much the French cartographers had truly understood of what they observed. Every day in America revealed more to me about my own misunderstandings.

At the trading post, a Pawnee adolescent dressed in an outfit almost identical to my own work clothes told us that the Republican River had a much older name, submerged on all the migrant maps for purchase: Kiraaruta. His English was better than mine. I asked where he had learned it.

"The school where they teach us to forget who we are. We speak their language, but we have not forgotten."

Some Pawnee children attended a small residential school in Genoa, the Pawnee Manual Labor School. The Headmistress, a White woman from New York named Elvira Platt, had taken up their cause. The boys were taught the proper habits of manual labor and agriculture, and the girls were trained to be domestic servants in White homes. She had dedicated her life to "transmuting the Indians into peaceful and agreeable citizens," she told me at the depot. "When you consider the vast tracts of land that we have taken from the Pawnees, an education is the least of what we owe them." She was vexed by the school's low enrollment. She could not understand why Pawnee parents refused to send their children to study the civilizing arts.

The Pawnee women were farmers, although not in the Yankee style. They grew squash and beans and corn and melons on the same plot, not divided into rows on separate plowed fields as we did. Although I never understood their beliefs, I knew that our neighbors had many ceremonies related to planting and harvesting. They used hoes made from buffalo shoulders, tools that resembled ours in some ways but must have been superior, for we could make nothing grow in our new home. Birdie Czarnecki told us that the Pawnee women sang to the corn. When I made a joke about this, my wife became unaccountably enraged. "If *you* respected God's gifts as our neighbors do, Tomasz," she said, "perhaps something might grow for you."

On the way to Genoa, we once spotted a mud lodge with bright orange pumpkins sprouting from the sod roof, a sight that made us cry out with surprise and pleasure. The sky pumpkins looked like

baby suns, smiling up at their parent star. I felt a stab of envy, thinking about our failed garden.

Despite their success at agriculture—to the frustration of the
Quaker Agent charged with transforming them into yeoman
farmers—our Pawnee neighbors endured miserable conditions which
even the poorest Poles were spared, for by the laws of the White government the Pawnees were now confined to the reservation lands and
forbidden from their former means of sustaining themselves. Their
buffalo hunts had been outlawed. Annuities had not been delivered.
All the Pawnees had to sell was timber. The United States broke its
treaty promises to the Pawnee Confederacy again and again, betrayals that seemed familiar to both my White and my Indian neighbors.

The innkeeper's daughter told me that she had seen with her own
eyes a Pawnee elder shot to death by a White man passing him on
the road.

"He shot the old man to test the power of his new gun."

"What happened to the killer?"

"Nothing happened to him." She shook her head with a patient
sort of sorrow. "The fellow who pulled the trigger is still living right
outside Columbus. Everybody knows who done it, too. No mystery
there. Some saw."

An officer from Kearny at the table beside me gave a rueful laugh,
or perhaps an embarrassed one. The name of the killer was not
uttered.

I tuned my ear to the swells of emotion in my neighbors' voices.
Often the teller's tone taught me more than the words did. Every joke
brought another lesson. Every sad or tragic story. If a homesteader
was murdered, Indians were always the first suspected of the crime. If
two hundred Indian women and children and elders were ambushed
on a spring morning and massacred by soldiers of the United States
Army, the newspapers called it "a battle."

Long before I could speak the language of our new country, I
understood that a White man could do anything he wanted to an
Indian.

I could still feel horror and outrage entirely then. I felt allied with
the Indians, who suffered the same injustices and persecution that we
Poles endured under German rule. I did not yet fully grasp that to
the Indians, I was a White man.

Eighteen seventy-four was the summer of the locusts, the summer of plague. Everything was boiling with insects. Entire fields had been eaten to the root. The locusts arrived with a roaring out of clear blue skies and devoured everything before them. Plow handles, fence posts. Winged clouds that consumed in an hour a family's year of work. We heard them chewing and snapping day and night. No scythe was as efficient as their hungry mouths. I would like to forget what their crushed and slippery bodies felt like underfoot. I would like to forget how we had to skim them out of the milk.

Ania and I once froze outside the H. R. Dry Goods store, listening to a sound like falling hail. Hundreds of locusts flung themselves against the windows and walls. We stared out at a ravaged field. In under three minutes, we saw an entire scarecrow consumed. The stake fell backward into the alfalfa—the locusts' weight had toppled it. I cried out: it was my own face I saw on the doll, just before he was lost to sight. My sewn-up lips.

Ania lifted onto her toes to cover my eyes.

"They are drawn to moisture, Tomasz. Let us hurry inside, before they eat our eyes."

It was not long after we moved into our dugout on the river that we woke to forking lightning and summer thunder and our first prairie fire.

We rode into town with our neighbor Dutko. The fire was a red line covering the entire horizon. Too distant yet for us to smell or feel, and near enough to fear. Imaginary heat made me loosen my collar. Cries rose from barns and houses, from the crowns of trees, a terror of fire that united everything living. Men on horseback rode out. We watched them dragging plows around to make fireguards in the sod. Already the fire had burned a strip twelve miles wide and four across. Was it coming for us? Beside me, Ania's soft body tensed.

Prairie fire is the terror of the homesteader. I have heard stories of families baked alive in their soddies. Fire pirouetting with the wind to turn a home into a tomb. Cows bawling in their barns, burned alive. Pronghorns sprinting through the middle of towns ahead of the flames.

Only the innkeeper, a man of nearly eighty who had been one of the earliest to claim lands in the region, seemed unperturbed. He yawned along with the thousand stars.

"Let me tell you greenhorns what a fire looks like. What a fire is good for—"

He then told us the story of an epic fire ordered by General Robert E. Mitchell, commander of the military district of Nebraska.

"The Indians had sacked Julesburg, you see, and the General could not let the savages get away with it."

I caught Ania's eye. How many times, growing up, had we heard the Germans tell stories like this one? Lies that justified the burning of our churches and the beating of our elders?

"The General waited for a clear day in late January with a strong wind blowing from the northwest. He knew the wind would be his ally. 'Just the day I want,' says the General. 'I will give them ten thousand miles of prairie fire.' The telegraph wires were hot with orders. Mitchell instructed every ranch and farm and outpost along the Platte from Fort Kearny to Colorado to set the prairie ablaze. Soldiers and farmers rode out with bales of straw, boxes of matches. It was coordinated arson! The order was fully carried out. The Plains were fired for three hundred miles. I guess those Indians survived the fire, but as you might imagine they had to live in the ashes after that! Everything south of the Platte and west of Kearny burned up—"

"Which Indians was Mitchell after?" someone asked in a flat voice, eyes fixed on the fire.

"Good heavens, all of them! All the murderous raiders killing and looting around the Trail."

The Indians had backfired, setting strategic fires to change the direction of the soldiers' and the settlers' blaze, preventing Mitchell's fire from spreading, the innkeeper explained. Even so, after General Mitchell's ten-thousand-mile prairie fire, their game had nothing to live on.

On our own horizon, I watched as scattered fires stitched themselves together into a hellish conflagration. The sheet of flame appeared to be moving in a northerly direction, pushing away from where we stood huddled with our lamps. The burning kerosene gave off an oily, appalling smell. Its yellow glow was as useless as the moon for showing us what the fire planned to do next.

⫸⫷

Kulturkampf
Lebensraum
Blut und Eisen

I woke from a nightmare to locusts crawling along my hairline. In the nightmare my mother had been a dying buffalo, tormented by soldiers. I saw my mother's anguished face reflected in the soldiers' reddish eyes like a cameo. In the nightmare, I was her baying calf and I was also a soldier. It took me a great while to understand that I was awake. Ania sat up in bed beside me and began plucking locusts from my nightclothes.

"The Agent should have told us about the people living on these 'free lands,'" I said.

Ania released a high-pitched laugh. It seemed to batter its wings against the low ceiling, echoing on and on. I begged her to go back to sleep. Every day, digging the well, opening the beds, seeding their land with milo and wheat, my heart grew sicker and sicker. The more we learned, the less I wished to understand who we were in this story.

From July into late September the locusts drummed on every surface, a dreadful husky thudding. I swallowed two with my breakfast porridge. "Crunchy," said my blue-eyed landlord, grinning through his mask of sunburned wrinkles; he was one of the first Poles to come to the Platte River Valley. He seemed amused by our horror. "That's what the good Lord gave you teeth for! Yes, grind them all to powder. They would do the same to you if they could, wouldn't they? You will make a fine Nebraskan. Welcome home, Oletsky."

⫸⫷

I knew *Kulturkampf* when I saw it. Even those charged with helping and protecting the Pawnee people seemed to do as much harm as good by my reckoning. Their Quaker agent, I learned from the man himself, had advocated for the death penalty in the infamous case of Yellow Sun, "the lesser evil," he assured me, "to pacify the mob." The federal government was determined to bring *someone* to trial for the murder of a White settler named McMurty. This Agent, in his sagacity, had seen the violence brewing among the angry settlers, he told me. He explained his strategy. He had refused to release the annuities owed to the Pawnee people by the government "until some Pawnees were in custody." Four men, including Yellow Sun—a doctor and a man of sixty—stood trial for this crime, sacrificing themselves so that thousands of Pawnees would not die of starvation. The Agent spoke freely to me—I suppose I was no one to fear. "Was they innocent?" I asked in my foreigner's English, and the Agent sighed and said we Poles were as stupid as he'd been led to believe, I could not see the forest for the trees.

Did everyone fear the Indians? No, I discovered. There were plenty of cynical men who knew how to use the fear of other greenhorns for their own gain. Some started rumors the way that General Mitchell had started his prairie fire.

"Who can forget the man, only a few miles from where we sit, for which Rawhide Creek was named. The poor wretch was flayed alive by Indians, and then chopped to pieces by fiendish squaws . . ."

The Quaker Agent told me the incident never happened but was an invention to divert the flood of newcomers to the fertile river valley. A story that circulates less frequently, but one that I can verify—having had the misfortune to witness it personally—is that a group of White settlers, many women among them, threw stones at the Ponca families as they were marched from their homeland through Duncan on their way to Oklahoma.

I would like to forget the day I stood frozen on the road and watched the stones fly.

There was much debate at that time about the best approach to the Indian Problem. Not everyone was in favor of Sherman's plan of extermination. Many wanted the Pawnee lands. Others wanted all Indians gone for good. Out of sight, out of mind. At present, we were neighbors, and there was no avoiding the eyes of the starving children or the sound of their hoarse coughing. No avoiding the knowledge that our new government had made the Indians' starvation part of its military strategy—annuities were deliberately withheld in the dead of winter. The Quaker Agent refused to purchase or distribute food to the Pawnees. I recalled the winter when the nobleman had punished my father for a bad harvest by quartering our rations, how my sisters cried with hunger and I tasted nothing but bile for days on end.

A broken promise by the government sounds quite removed from one's own life, but I could measure it precisely in the thinness of a Pawnee child's wrist and the phlegmy thickness of her grandmother's cough. I stood behind them at the trading company and felt that knowledge rattle into me. How was any of this my fault? I did not come to America to kill Indians. I had only just set foot on these soils two years ago. Treaty violations had nothing to do with me. I was simply going about my private business, the same as any man.

As my English improved, I began to mimic the Yankees' mispronunciations. I became less curious about what the Indian names on the Yankee signs and maps meant.

Freedom turned out to be a territory we occupied. It was not the freedom we had imagined when we boarded the ship. One couldn't let one's guard down. "Ania, Ania . . ." I felt my wife retreating from me, far away into herself. For our second Christmas, I rode all the way to Lincoln to buy Ania a blush-pink celluloid box, just to see her smile at me once. The box's uselessness made it a luxury. That I had spent money on something merely beautiful, this was the true gift. My time was our money, and every hour I spent away from the farm drew down the little we had. I found myself living in a crouch, staring out the windows and waiting for the hatchet blow. One dry autumn morning, I picked up my ax and joined my neighbors. On the Pawnee lands, there was a forest. We needed timber to build our barns and our homes. As any family living in a soddy on the treeless prairie will attest, there is no scarcer resource. The innkeeper had assured us we could take as much wood as we could carry. Wagonloads, if we could afford to hire the horses.

It is very possible to live in a house built from stolen timber without thinking of oneself as a thief. For years, I did this.

I am a Catholic who moved to Nebraska to live out Christ's teachings. Love your neighbor as yourself. Give him the shirt off your back. We took everything from the Indians. Even their children.

The last members of the Pawnee Confederacy—hemmed in on all sides by hostile land seekers and Army soldiers and U.S. courts that would not prosecute White settlers' crimes or uphold treaty guarantees—without any viable way to stay on their homelands, were forced to leave to Oklahoma. By 1876, all of our Pawnee neighbors had fled Nebraska for Indian Territory. Eventually my horror rusted over. I did nothing, and soon it was covered by the grasses of my new home.

In the spring of 1885, my wife found good-paying work as a cook at the new boarding school in Genoa, named for the birthplace of Christopher Columbus. The town had been founded by Mormons living without legal right on Pawnee treaty lands, until they too were driven off. A decade earlier, one could see the great white bonnets of the wagons like tall ships over the grass, said the miller, Janek Gutawolski, stretching in a line beyond the bluffs above the Loup. These bluffs that were sacred to the Pawnees, familiar to me because they had once been heavily timbered. Then the railroads spread their steel web, and now we had brick and lumber and glass, a good thing, because there were very few suitable trees left along the river-banks.

The Genoa U.S. Indian Industrial School was housed in the former reservation headquarters of the Pawnee Confederacy, a redbrick and cottonwood structure. Attendance was compulsory, mandated by the U.S. government. From my own germanizing education in Taube, I could guess what was happening in those classrooms. Such instruction was meant to burn the bridges between children and their parents, their pasts and their futures. The real education, as the Pawnee student had told me ten years earlier, was in forgetting.

Most of the new students spoke Lakota and came from the Pine Ridge and Rosebud reservations to Genoa by train. Some parents hid their sons and daughters when the child hunters came to collect them. Others were starved from their homes; agents threatened to withhold annuities until parents surrendered their children for reformation. A barber cut off the children's braids when they arrived. These students ranged in age from five to eighteen. They could be seen through the gates in their military uniforms, marching up and down the lawn.

⊰⊱

During the seven months she worked at the Indian Industrial School in Genoa, Ania's tears were violent and unpredictable. Three times since our arrival, she had grown fat; three times she had lost the baby. I worried that my sensitive young wife was not fit for a life on the prairie. In the fall of 1886, she became pregnant for the fourth time. A fear lived in her such as I had never seen.

One night my wife came home talking to herself, pausing every fourth step to stoop and shudder and blurt out a laugh or a word of warning. I watched all this from the open window, holding the lantern up. When she reached the door she stepped sideways, smiling at me. Behind her stood a sick Indian girl of eleven or twelve with a swollen bismuth-pink eye. Trachoma had once again swept through the boarding school that winter. "The doctor is never sober long enough for us to learn if he can cure anyone," Ania had complained. We had bad cases in the fall, but purchased drops at the pharmacy and recovered. A smile or a curse: either would have been better than the face this fugitive student turned on me. What had happened to turn this child to stone?

"Oh Ania," I said, my panic growing with my understanding of my wife's scheme. I married a good-hearted fool. "We cannot harbor this child. You will get us all into bad trouble. You will lose your job. Can we afford to live without it?"

The girl was a student in the fifth grade. She had run away to be with her family. At the school they called her Ellen. She would not tell us her real name. Ania wanted me to take her by train to the Rosebud reservation and reunite her with her mother.

"We have to help her, Tomasz."

I pointed at my wife's belly. "Come to your senses," I commanded, as if her foolishness were a spell I could break. "You have a good heart, Ania. But the school will find her and bring her back, and you will lose your position."

Ania's eyes were bottle-glass bright. She spoke as if in a dream, as if I'd said nothing. There was a new employee at the school, and what she did to the students was monstrous: "They call her the Counselor. They meet with her and tell her the things that are troubling them. She is hard of hearing, and so they speak into her ear trumpet. Tomasz—anything they tell her, everything they say into her strange instrument, it vanishes from their minds. It is evil, what we are doing at that school."

"To me it sounds like a kindness," I said. "A way to survive a long winter away from one's parents—yes, a cure for homesickness. What do you think, young lady?"

"I refuse to meet with the Counselor," she said. She turned from me to my wife. "Take me home to Rosebud like you promised, Ania."

Anger made me dizzy; I found my eyes crossing, focused on the taut cloth over my wife's enormous belly. Was she so stupid as to risk everything, when we were months away from paying the filing fee and receiving our deed? Meeting our own child?

"What can two people do against church and state, Ania?"

"We can find two more people. Two more after that . . ."

Ania heard the metal in my voice when I said, "Shut your mouth." I had no power over anyone or anything else, but I had the power to silence my wife.

I watched the way she looked at the girl and I knew something I had not wished to know: if Ania could have run home to Taube from this West, she would have done so. My wife did not want to be in this story with me any longer.

A pregnant Polack in south-central Nebraska has a hard time finding paying work.

"You must stay at the School. Both of you. Or we'll always be tenants in this land."

"I came here to pray to God," Ania screamed at me. "You pray to Money. You beg Money to grant you Land. You pray to Land to grant you Money. You are a convert to the gods of this country."

"What were you planning? To run away with the child?" My voice rose, and I began to laugh uncontrollably. "Tomorrow you will go to work and so will I. We do what we must to survive."

My head was pounding. Through a sheet of inner fire I studied the bruised stranger beside me. My wife's face, I remembered. I had forgotten, for just a moment, that I loved her.

I shut my eyes and saw the wall of flames advancing faster than a locomotive. The prairie fire that had raced to greet us outside the inn, when we were still visitors here. *Too far away to feel, and near enough to fear.* It was not a memory any longer. I was a flame in their fire. How can a single flame retreat from the conflagration?

"There is no escape," I said wearily. "We cannot go back. This is the world as it is."

I was speaking to all three of us. As I took a step toward the sick child, intending to return her to her Supervisors at Genoa, she surprised me. She turned and began sprinting. Before I'd drawn three breaths, she was out the door and leaping through the snowbanks.

She might have gotten away from me, too, were it not for her sickness. Nearly all the students at the Genoa School tested positive for tuberculosis that winter. I was riding along the wide horse trail next to the frozen Loup Canal when I heard a distinctly human cough. I told myself many things—what does it matter what I told myself? The girl was hiding behind a snowbank near the frozen river.

I dismounted in a flash and grabbed the child, who screamed and scratched at my face. As gently as I could manage, I restrained her and draped my coat over her shoulders. The girl who was not Ellen turned from the river and shook free of my hand. She stared up at me, calm and steady—one eye clear and one crusted over from the trachoma. Where did her courage come from?

"Take me home," she said.

Instead I fought to get my arms around her, fighting myself, fighting my own voice of protest, the *No!* in my head as loud as hers. We wailed together until I managed to hoist her onto my horse, and then rode double on my grumpy mare in a crackling silence along the banks of the Loup. We reached the school before noon with frozen ears and eyelids. I received my five-dollar bounty from the grateful Superintendent.

"I would like to visit her," Ania said in our bed, awake at 4:00 a.m. We were wretchedly close and apart at that hour, alive in our private miseries and tangled in the same sweaty sheets. I did not need to ask who she was thinking about.

Two weeks after I returned her to the boarding school, the girl they called Ellen escaped again. This time, no one could locate her. Ania read me the Desertion Report. She said we had to go searching for her. "Who is stopping you?" I said without turning. "Go to Rosebud. I will put you on the train myself . . ."

Only when I called her bluff did she at last sigh, and fall asleep. Now it was my turn to toss and turn, my turn to be haunted. I saw the mountain of buffalo skulls staring frankly at me as they were ground into fertilizer. I saw the many crimes to which I did not publicly object. By day I could congratulate myself on steering clear of the mob, but at night the same memory of my empty hands accused me. My arms held each other in a knot under the blankets. My tongue lay under a heavy stone.

In our home village, a crime committed at night carried a higher penalty—the darkness itself was considered a kind of accomplice, an accessory to murder. In America, everyone who stepped off the platform of the colonist car into the summer of the locusts became a part of the falling night. The long silence, which recruited our silences into it.

One night, a few weeks after I had returned the runaway girl to Genoa, I found Ania's woodcutting of the Virgin, Queen of Poland, in the grate with the firewood. A little brown spider ran across her soulful gaze. I felt paralyzed. I could neither save nor burn this holy object. If I returned it to our bedroom wall, Ania would see and know that I had done so. I did not want to ask my wife when she had lost her faith. It was the price of working at the boarding school, where she made ten dollars more each month than she had as a laundress.

I would like to forget the splintered icon of Mary smiling serenely up at me. I would like to forget what Ania's face did when she said, "They buried a five-year-old boy today. They did not tell his family he was sick. They do not mark the graves in their cemetery. When I tell them that what we do in this place is criminal, they tell me to visit the Counselor myself. Tomasz. If I keep working at the School, I will lose my mind."

I told Ania that she had to keep working for as long as she could bear it. We needed every penny that long winter. When the baby was born, I said, she could quit. In the swelling dark on our silent homestead, I heard us thinking about our lost ones.

⚌

I met my first prairie witch on the banks of the Loup River. Three Native students in their military uniforms sat under the cottonwood trees. They were waiting for an audience with the Counselor. I had by this point heard many rumors about these "Vaults," women who by some kind of occult art could store men's memories outside of their bodies. Her dugout was set back a mile from the road, and I rode past it and peered in the window. She was younger than I had imagined, no older than thirty, with reams of cascading yellow hair and a bright calico dress. Her ear was fixed to the receiver of an old-fashioned funnel, coiled at the end like a blue snail. A Native child of seven was mouthing something into it while the Counselor's golden head lolled on her neck like a daffodil on a broken stem.

My wife had prepared me for what I was seeing. The ear trumpet was an instrument of torture, not relief. One droplet of the Atlantic reproduces the salinity of the ocean in miniature. Words are similarly saturated with worlds, even in a stammering translation of an event into a story. I could feel the weight of this deposit in progress, although no words were audible to me. I felt the suction of the transaction in my own abdomen.

I did not try to stop you from stealing the memories of these children, Counselor. I saw a crime unfolding and rode on. I would like to forget my failure.

⚌

One night in late February, Ania lost the baby. When her cramping eased, she rolled onto her side and drank from the hot water bottle that she'd held against her belly, as if she could drink up all the danger. The sheets balled between her legs were a reddish purple, so dark with blood I could not believe my wife was alive.

Ania survived, but for weeks she scarcely ate or slept or spoke. At last Ania broke her silence and asked in a low voice to visit the Vault who lived in the dugout on the Lower Loup. She was terrified that if she kept these "secret horrors" inside of her, she would never deliver a live baby. "I need to get them off my chest, so that our next baby can live."

I hitched up the wagon and took her to the dugout without delay. The Vault opened the door in her nightclothes, scowling yet also unsurprised to find us standing there under the low moon. She invited only Ania inside.

"May I listen?" I asked them.

"No," they said in unison.

"Wait next to him," said the witch, pointing to a dismal-looking mule, which was grazing in the shallow moonlight along the river-bank, its whiskers tangling in the cattails. I chewed tobacco beside the sad animal. An hour later, I returned to find my wife smiling with the dreamy namelessness of an infant, relieved of her burden.

Wide awake now, the prairie witch bent and held her long, curved horn to my wife's belly. Ania looked petrified for a moment, then relaxed when the woman took her wrist. "You will have a boy," she said with a smile. "A boy with a strong heart." She turned and fiddled with the lock to a green wooden chest, removing a tiny brass harp. She plucked a little tune on the strings. When I shut my eyes I saw a tree root sinking through water, the clear river sweeping summer leaves downstream.

"Take this. It was my son's favorite toy," she said. "The instrument of the angels."

"What would a witch know about angels?" I snapped.

Her unexpected kindness had embarrassed me.

"Quite a lot, Tomasz Oletsky. More than you think."

She stared calmly at us, and it was as if her pupils came unlidded. For an eternal moment, Ania and I stared into twin wells. Bodies die, but human eyes are bottomless. She handed me the folded slip.

"What happens if we return to retrieve our deposit, and you are no longer here?"

"Count your lucky stars," she said. "Sleep easy for the rest of your life." She gave us a weary, leaden look, her pupils lidded once more. "But chances are good that I will be right here. You can bring your child to meet me. I'd like that."

⁂

Fear is a ghost. It grows in proportion to what we all know and never say. It swells on what we do and do not admit to our own awareness. I will offer up my own life as proof, because I am every day afraid. Take my ghosts from me.

⁂

We had despaired of ever having children when, to our great joy, Ania became pregnant and gave birth to a doe-eyed son, gentle Harp. Two years later, we christened yowling Franciszek, and then little Lada surprised us. "Our caboose," Ania joked. A miracle: three healthy children after all our losses. Our children's births were announced in the *Gwiazda Zachodu—The Western Star*. Each time she was with child, Ania made regular visits to the witch's dugout. Ania's tears dried up. She began to sleep until dawn, stiff as a board beside me. To protect our happiness I destroyed Ania's deposit slips, terrified that she might be tempted, on some dark whim, to retrieve the memories that had made her so ill, brought my beloved so close to madness. I vowed to carry them for both of us.

⁂

When the Kinkaid Act was passed, fourteen of us sold our sections and left Krakow to claim lands double the size of what the Homestead Act had offered. Three steeples went up a year before the arrival of the spur line. Uz was a God-fearing community on the shortgrass prairie. In those early years, Uz did not yet have a bank, or a post office, or a Vault.

The Pawnees now lived on a reservation in Oklahoma, and to the west of Uz, Kinkaiders were homesteading the lands taken from the

Lakota and the Cheyenne and the Arapaho. It grew easier to look at the framed deed on our wall.

Settlers, however, kept pouring in.

"It would be better if fewer came here," said Wojcik one night at the Country Jentleman. We were celebrating Founder's Day. The fourteen heads of households had gathered with playing cards fencing our faces. We were drinking the whiskey that the proprietor called, with a wink, "Non-Intoxicating Liquor."

"Eight families plan to settle here, south of the spur line," he muttered. "A large mixed-up clan, Negroes and Irish."

"Negroes can file for their preempt the same as you."

"I have no prejudice against any man, Oletsky. I am simply a realist. We are a one-horse town without a bank. A town without a business district . . ."

Nobody needed to ask Wojcik to make the connection. I caught the eye of my friend Caspar Petrusewicz, who gave me a queasy smile and lifted his golden glass to his lips, as if I'd made a toast instead of a coward's quiet plea. I am not sure how the pact got drafted that night. I know that in the hour before sunrise, I signed it. We all entered the agreement. Each of us took the same oath, to *never rent, lease, or sell land in Uz County to any person of Negro blood, or agent of theirs; unless the land be located more than one mile from a White resident.*

Still, the settlers kept coming. Certainly we were a welcoming community, but none of us wanted to be priced out of holding the good grazing land as yet unclaimed. I swear that I had no intention of getting anybody hurt. It was a scheme we cooked up one night while Gutawolski dealt cards and terrorized us with news from his sister in Valentine, who swore the number of Kinkaiders had tripled in the past month and that every day more land seekers were coming to our west.

"I say we start a rumor."

Whiskey shone in every glass, in fourteen pairs of eyes. My head was full of fire.

"You still hear old-timers muttering about Indians on the warpath. I say we spread word that the Sioux are planning an attack on Uz. A raid on the town."

I was born a good man. I had a good heart. But my life has given me a violent education. Straw and arson. Scorched earth. *Blut und eisen. Lebensraum.*

"Tomasz Oletsky, I like the way you think."

I remembered the story I heard outside the inn: General Mitchell's orders heating up the telegraph wires. Hundreds of settlers riding out with torches and tinder, and the flames joining into one unified sheet of fire.

My plan, I thought, was much kinder. A conflagration of rumor.

"Go to every speakeasy and church bazaar in the region, and tell them that the Sioux are planning an uprising against Whites. Say that the whole countryside around Uz from McCook to the Sandhills is filling with hostile Indians. That should stem this tide of land seekers."

Men slapped me on the back. My simple plan was a stroke of genius, said Grayson. It would purchase some time to get established in Uz. To put down a root and keep the still-unclaimed surrounding lands for our families. My lie would spread and form a wall around us. It would drive off more land seekers, without violence. A story could do this. A rumor could become a kind of invisible fence around Uz. Land speculators would invest their money elsewhere. I told a lie, and I watched it spread. It worked better than I'd ever imagined.

As I later learned from Grayson, my lie was taken up in earnest by many newcomers to southwestern Nebraska. One of them, a jumpy ranch hand named Timothy Ruskin, shot a Lakota man in the back as he passed the ranch gates. He had traveled south to visit with an aunt and was returning to Pine Ridge. The murdered man was a father of four named Donald LeBleu. His murderer was acquitted. "I saw that Indian galloping toward me," Ruskin said, "and I knew he was out for revenge." None of the half dozen eyewitnesses to LeBleu's murder would testify against Ruskin. Apparently he had taken the rumor I'd started about "Indians on the warpath" around Uz to heart. Please, Witch, take this memory from me. Ease this rumor I started, and its unintended—its *half*-intended—consequences, out of my conscience. Let the past stay in the past. Set me free into tomorrow. They call the West "terra nullius." A blank canvas. My children deserve that. I will not pass these stories down to them. Scrape the blood away from my memory, so that they may paint with sky.

᚛᚜

After we'd signed the oath that night, I told the others about the prairie witch I'd met. The "Vault" who worked odd hours and lived on the outskirts of Genoa. And haven't I brought you scores of new customers?

We entered a second pact, which was to forget.

So here I am, and this is my deposit.

᚛᚜

There is one final thing I would like to leave with you—

Fourteen years after our arrival in Nebraska, I received a letter from my mother. The date in the upper corner was December 1, 1886. The letter was in my cousin's sloping hand; he explained that he was taking dictation for Mother, whose arthritis had "considerably worsened." I felt so close to them, reading her pained words in my cousin's prim, furious penmanship. I could hear them quarreling as if they were seated across the table from me ("God and his angels have eternity, but we must *get on with it, Malgorzata!* . . .") I saw the dark blots on the paper and smiled. Drip. Drip. Drip. Yes, my mother would have refused to be hurried.

It is the last letter I ever received from her.

The letter itself, I burned to ashes long ago, but my mother's cries continue to sound inside me. Please move her words out of my body, and into yours:

Dear Son,

Somehow we are all swept away. Although we insist to the German soldiers that we have always lived in this valley, they call us thieves and insurgents. We are told we must leave—leave home and every kind of business for a fancy of Prince Bismarck. It seemed too ridiculous, too mad, too barbarous. But there was no mistake at all. Who is to thwart Prince Bismarck in his idea of destiny? Would you believe they have obliged 35,000 people to leave this province? No one is excepted, neither women nor children.

Harp Oletsky

The weight of the deposit settled itself into my chest. Seated in the witch's hot dugout, I began to gasp and thrash. I understood now why our papa had made this deposit. I did not want to know what I knew. I was the son of a thief and a murderer who I loved. My father's sorrow was no longer a mystery to me. It became my own.

Section III

All Is Not Lost

The Scarecrow

Three women live in the farmer's house now. The girl, the photographer, and the witch. I listen to them talk as they percolate around the field. Their mystery is still a mystery to me.

Every conversation is a storm of meaning. *Downpour. Uproar.* Their words rain into me, drawing life out of the blanketing white. Each word teaches me something I once knew. *Courtroom*, says the girl, and I remember the box where men's fates are decided. *Camera*, says the photographer, and I remember holding a pose for so long my face went numb. Standing for a portrait was good practice for being a scarecrow.

Who else stood inside the frame with me? Was it a family photograph? A courtroom portrait? Was I sentenced to confinement inside this farmer's doll? Or am I an accident that Nothing is looking to correct? A tongue is a muscle that can make so much happen. If I had one, I would scream my questions. Hell must be a waiting room with a one-way window. An eternity of contemplating the horizon. No neck to turn. Button eyes. Sewn-up mouth. No door for my questions to exit. Nothing hears or answers me.

The Photographer, Cleo Allfrey

Dear Allfrey,

Well, congratulations on defying every order you are given. The negatives arrived in advance of the captions—I suppose these dates are your idea of a joke? 1701? 2080? You must think I am the April Fool. I will not publish your forgeries. Your frauds will do great harm if they become public. Documentary photography is the antithesis of fiction, and that is all that you have given me to work with since arriving in Nebraska.

NO MORE OF THESE UTOPIAN THEMES!

Sincerely,
Roy

Letter of Resignation

Dear Roy,

The joke is on me. Or on us, I suppose.

I resign from my position with the Resettlement Administration's Historical Section. I will no longer be sending you my negatives. I fear that you will never treat them with the seriousness they deserve. They are not "trick photography." Or at any rate, I do not understand the trick of the light that creates them—I call them "quantum photographs" only to suggest that some mechanism is at play beyond what meets the eye. I never

know what will turn up in my developing tray—all I know for
certain, with this Graflex, is that whatever I saw with my own eyes
at the moment I fired the shutter never appears on the negatives.
How any of it is possible is a question for the scientists. You are
welcome to come and view my gallery under the earth. I have set
up a darkroom in a farmer's root cellar. I know you feel I did not
live up to my potential. For what it's worth, Roy, I feel a little sorry
for myself. My mother and aunts and brothers and sisters and
grandmother are all waiting for one of my pictures to appear in
Time or *Life* or *Fortune*. My neighbors ask my mother if I took any
of the photographs they see in the Sunday newspaper. Nobody has
to ask her why I left Philadelphia. Why I took this cross-country
assignment. The faces we see hanging in museums and smiling or
crying in moving pictures or staring back from magazine covers
do not look like ours. They imagine that I had to leave home to
become a success. They understand why I left.

I understand what you're up against, Roy. I do want to thank
you. You gave me a chance that nobody else in Washington would
have. Of course I wanted to make good on your vote of confidence.
I wanted to make a famous portrait like Rothstein, to be included
in the File. But something else has other plans.

I cannot begin to understand how this camera chooses and
channels these scenes, across the plains of time. But I know the
land itself has something to do with it. This land is teaching
me how to see it. Particles of animals, particles of vegetables,
particles of soil and sky. To put it in terms that you might better
understand: the land is making propaganda for the future of the
land. I would probably find this all ridiculous myself, if I weren't
the one developing the film. Your voice swells in my ear as I write
this letter, calling across the continent: *Be reasonable, Allfrey*. If your
voice can carry that far to reach me here, perhaps my camera can
capture light from older suns, and future ones.

I can be a little vain about my gift for framing up a shot, as
you have pointed out. I have always been very happy to take the
credit for my work. But when I watch these prints developing
in the root cellar, I must admit that my own role may not be as
central as I once imagined. When I shoot with this camera, Roy,

I am collaborating with forces that I do not understand. I am
never sure what influence I have—if any—on what latent image
will reveal itself in the darkroom. But I don't think I am irrelevant
to the process, either. I wait for the light and the land to teach
me where to make a picture. I adjust the focus, the aperture,
the shutter speed. I may have no control over what the Graflex
sees, but I develop its visions. Cutting the film and mixing the
chemistry, doing my processing by feel in the pitch darkness of the
cellar. Somehow I do think my decisions matter, Roy, although
I can't explain how. Perhaps that sounds like some vestige of my
artist's pretension to you, or bald egotism, womanly superstition.
Practically speaking, I can say that when I am lazy about the
few decisions in my power, the Graflex negatives tend to be
overexposed blurs. So I give each shot my best efforts, even if I
have no final say in what appears on the film. In the darkroom, I
am discovering the realities hiding behind or beyond or adjacent to
the shots I composed.

"Local agricultural practices" was on your shooting script.
After purchasing the Graflex, I stopped to make some pictures of
the wheat fields near Dannebrog. I remember what I saw in the
ground glass that April afternoon: an upside-down orange sky,
lonely fences around rows of blighted wheat. When my negative
cleared in the fixing bath, I was surprised to see a dense mixture of
grasses and wildflowers surrounding the ripe corn. The women in
the foreground are Pawnee farmers. Those small globes you see are
squash and melons growing on the cornstalks. Instead of barbed
wire, a fence of tall sunflowers protects the corn. It looks nothing
like the farms I drive past today.

You accuse me of taking pictures of "things that are not there."

But that's not what this camera is doing, Roy. This camera sees
things that aren't here *yet*.

The "Unborn, Reborn" print, I initially believed to be a
photograph of an earlier century in Uz County. Tallgrass covers the
prairie and there is no farm, no fencing, no windmill visible. But if
you examine my print more closely, you will find a crowd of young
people in the far left corner, wearing garments in a style I have
never seen in my life. They seem to shimmer in the light. Moving
on a gradient from sharpness to vagueness. As if they were blurs

of motion when I fired the shutter. Roy: I believe this Graflex can make portraits of tomorrow's children.

Another negative, "Bison Migration," seems to span centuries. I don't know if these buffalo are running through the last century or the next one. I have made multiple prints from this same negative, and every one looks different. The grass grows taller and shrinks away to dust, erupts into wildflowers like a children's choir bursting into song. When I make my test prints, I have a feeling that anything could happen—the herd on the paper might have multiplied, or disappeared. In the stillness of the root cellar, I can almost hear their hoofbeats leaving the frame and returning in a great circle. Crossing summers and winters. Thundering into and out of extinction.

Does this Graflex peer into "the" future, or "a" future? I prefer to believe it's the latter. Scenes grow out of the developing tray like droplets beading on a spiderweb. Some threads of the web seem to show what *has* happened, others show what *could*. The patterns that connect them feel more circular and delicate than definite and linear.

I do understand your rock and your hard place. Money decides everything for us. You want to get aid to the farmers, and you want to fund the work of the Historical Section. You need a portrait to tug at the heartstrings, the purse strings. I doubt the men in Congress will know what to do with these grayscale visions. Like you, I must make my own calculations of risk and reward. If Congress pulls the plug, you're out a job. The Historical Section will no longer exist. But I will, and so will my pictures. The people and the land will also.

I risk my life every day on the road—there are many sundown towns out here, even if officially they are all-welcoming. I accept the risk, but I will never resign myself to the conditions that generate it. The Graflex reveals so many beautiful worlds— future worlds made out of this one. Worlds of clear skies, shared abundance. But Roy: I have made exposures of other worlds as well, which I did not send you. My contact sheets look like checkerboards of possible futures: earthly heavens right next to hellscapes that make this Dust Bowl look like Sunday at the park. Firelit and fortressed Nebraskas. The Platte River, bare and dry.

Skies so choked with dust I cannot imagine anything alive beneath them. Different tomorrows unfolding on the same land. What we choose to do today matters greatly, as you always say. I believe you, Roy. I believe we have a choice in all this. There should be a word that means both "blessed" and "cursed," I have often thought. Maybe that word is "freedom." Maybe that word is "us."

What was a time-traveling camera doing in a Dannebrog pawnshop? Why was I the one who bought it? Why me, Roy? I don't know. If you widen the aperture enough, it's a hilarious joke. I promise you that I never intended to betray your faith in my potential. To be very frank with you, a part of me would have preferred to make more conventional work. But I can no more direct the eye of this haunted Graflex than you can from your office in Washington. All I can do is take my pictures, mix the chemicals, and wait to see what arises.

Sincerely,
Cleo Allfrey

⚎

At the Oletsky place, I spend most of my time underground. For the past few days, I've been sleeping in the farmhouse, taking pictures on and around the farmer's land, developing the Graflex negatives in the darkroom under the earth. Ordinarily I'd have balked at the old man's charity, but after quitting my job I don't have much choice. I have almost exhausted my travel stipend. I can't afford the boardinghouse—especially as Mr. Rasmussen charges me a dollar more than his White guests. When I signed on to the documentary project, I did not guess that I'd wind up in a remote town in Nebraska, rooming with a witch.

In the root cellar, it felt magical to watch the images drawing into view in the developer bath. The metallic smell of the chemicals mixed with the odor of the sweetly rank potatoes piled in the corner. Harp Oletsky has hidden them under straw to keep them from sprouting. Daylight could rot his potatoes as surely as it could ruin my exposures. I was making prints from the shots I'd taken on my first day in Uz County. Back when I was still hoping and praying for inclusion in the File. Two short weeks ago, I was still employed by the RA.

The speed with which my entire life and outlook had changed felt as astonishing to me as the time-bending photographs.

And yet on this prairie, life revealed itself so slowly—the longer I looked through the range finder, the more gradations I discovered. A dull beige landscape grew less monotonous the longer I studied it—dramatic textures and tonalities began to peer back at me, wild plum bushes and blowout penstemon, a liveliness brimming out of the ground, nothing like the wasteland I'd been sent to find.

I turned on the white light, gave the fixer bath a shake, and lifted the print to examine it. The eerie cottonwood stretched its branches toward a face I knew.

Thanks to the Sheriff's billboard and the posters that wallpapered downtown, I was well acquainted with Vick Iscoe. I had never made a portrait of the Sheriff with the Graflex. Not knowingly. Yet here he was—centered in the frame beside the cottonwood tree with the deep celestial scar. I knew exactly where the Sheriff was standing, frozen with his shovel hovering above a growing hole. In subsequent prints, the hole deepened and widened. Had I used the dodging tool on a ten-second exposure, I could not have shoveled the dark earth out of that corner of the print any faster. Could the woman at his feet merely be sleeping? The angle of her neck answered my question.

My overwhelming feeling was not horror, or even surprise, but a kind of bone weariness. It was as if my body sensed the work before her and sunk under that weight. I was too tired to wonder at the crime scene revealed by the Graflex. Too tired even to scream.

The dead woman stared sightlessly up at the Sheriff. This picture was not bound for fame in Washington. It looked like something one might find in the coroner's file. I wished that I could sit beside the woman. Say prayers for her. Learn her name.

The next scene that arose in the fixer bath made me cry out. It was a clear, accusing image of the Sheriff and a young curly-haired White man rolling this woman's body into the hole. Night ate the background, yet their faces were in crisp focus. The Sheriff was sweating heavily; he looked tired and annoyed. The youth's crumpled face might have been on the verge of tears. The woman lay on the sandy ground between them. In the third print, I watched a fire flowering across her.

My exposure had been an eighth of a second at f/32, 1½ tension.

In one of his telegrams, Roy Stryker had suggested that perhaps I was using the wrong shutter speed. A loony wail rose in me: *Good note, Roy. Next time I'll try half a second. Maybe that will stop the lens from digging a woman's body out of layers of time . . .*

How should I caption this one, Roy?

Burial or exhumation?

Premonition or hallucination?

Mounting evidence of what? My madness?

A crime that had already been committed?

Or one we can prevent?

I must have been truly lost in thought, because when I surfaced half an hour had passed. I'd gone through the motions like a sleep-walker: moving the papers from the fixer to the wash bath, pinning them on the sagging clothesline to dry. The woman's gray face lifted out of the paper, sharpening into focus. I could hear my beating heart. It was so loud in my ears that I must have missed the trapdoor opening; I heard somebody on the ladder and screamed.

"Allfrey! It's just me!"

"Damnit, Dell. Shut that door. And try knocking. You're lucky I wasn't in the middle of developing something—"

Ruby light pooled around us.

The dead woman held her pose on the emulsion paper.

The Sheriff could not flee the negative he'd been caught on.

Stryker's voice floated through me. Advice on how to see:

". . . But the fellow who's hiding behind a tree and hoping you don't see him is the fellow that you'd better find out why . . ."

What was there to hide, I'd wondered, in a season of drought, on the open prairie? Now I had one answer.

Dell drew up beside my shoulder and grabbed my arm.

"Oh Lord. It's her . . ."

"You recognize this woman?"

"That's Mink! Mink Petrusev!"

The girl wheeled around, as if looking for someone behind her. I don't blame her. These photographs make me wonder how alone we ever are.

"Miss Allfrey? You . . . you were there when they did this?"

"I was *there*. I wasn't . . . then."

"Whatareyatalkingabout?" I heard her frown without turning. We were both still fixated on the floating woman's face. "My camera—I know how crazy this sounds, but it makes pictures of the future. And the past. I don't always know which is which."

The White girl yawned up at me, rubbing at her dirt-ringed eyes as if that might speed her understanding. She looked like a bear cub just waking up in this cave.

"I don't understand what you mean, Allfrey. Do you want me to get you a calendar?"

Words were useless to explain it. I handed her my portfolio from Uz. She let out a low cry, thumbing through the recent prints. I felt reassured by the girl's stunned reaction.

"Look how blurry certain exposures are compared to the others. Even after I lift them out of the stop bath, they never really stop moving. They retain an underwater quality."

I turned her toward the drying line, where new scenes were still emerging.

"You think you made photos of things *that haven't happened yet*?"

"Things that *may* happen. I don't know. Things that have happened, before my arrival at the place that I choose to shoot. Or that chooses me to shoot it; lately, it feels more like I'm taking direction from this prairie." When the girl wanted to know how this was possible, I told her that she'd have to ask Einstein and Bohr.

Dell moved down the clothespinned prints, examining each in turn. She made a clucking sound deep in her throat that made me think of a fisherman letting out line. It was the future photographs that had magnetized her—the children swimming in the river, the migrating bison.

"Do you think the future is settled, Asphodel? Predestination—do you believe in that?"

She stared dumbly at me. In her left hand, she held the contact print of a mud lodge filled with men and women and children where her uncle's house presently stood.

"Miss Allfrey? I don't understand what I am looking at—"

"The future," I said. "*A* future. Unless it's the past."

That's what I wanted to believe, anyhow. That destiny is open. Narrowly open, maybe. Not infinitely open. But undecided. Unfixed.

Free. I wanted to believe that people could change direction together. If I didn't believe that, why had I joined up with the New Deal photographers in the first place?

"So you choose the dates? There's some setting on the camera?"

I laughed. "There are plenty of settings. I choose them. Then the Graflex ignores me and does what it wants. I had a mission, Dell. The Historical Section sent me out here. But this camera has its own plans for me."

"Uh-huh. Are those plans a one-way ticket to the State Asylum?"

"Look, I wouldn't have believed it was possible three weeks ago. But some of these prints look to be thousands of years in the past . . ."

I reached into the box where I kept the oldest landscape the Graflex had revealed, peeling back layers of time like an onion.

"See that? I made this one on your property. Standing on the tractor seat on Tuesday, in the middle of the wheat field."

It was an ocean. The standing rows of wheat had vanished, replaced by the calm surface of a sea. The sun hung low in the western sky, a bright gray nimbus around it. A large fin was scything across the green surface of the water.

"You took that *here*? Are you sure?"

"I am sure of only that, Dell."

"Allfrey, I am sorry to break the news. But nobody is going to believe you."

"Do you?"

"I . . ." Fear broke up her voice, and I had my answer. "I wish I didn't."

We stood shoulder to shoulder, staring at the print of the Sheriff and Mink. I felt a sadness too large for the root cellar. I waited for Mink to open her mouth and tell me what to do next, but she stayed stiffly curled at the Sheriff's feet. The timer buzzed, reminding me that my safelight was wearing out and needed charging.

The girl's shrewd face looked softer to me today. We barely knew each other. But in the cellar, I felt myself drawing near to the youngest and the oldest part of her. The wounded part of her. A scab fell away, I felt it happen. She uncrossed her arms and touched my elbow. She grew very quiet, breathing beside me in the dark. Was my everyday personality like that, I wondered—a kind of scab? Most people seemed to develop one in their aboveground lives. I had my camera lens, and my poker face behind it. A smooth wall of glass and metal and silence.

"Please. How did you really get these pictures? Tell me the truth."

"I took a picture of a cottonwood tree in broad daylight. Nobody was there."

"Did someone put you up to this? Because it's a mean prank if they did—"

"I would never trick you or anyone this way." I paused. "Harp told me about your mother."

The girl planted her left hand onto the dirt wall—started to push at the packed earth until I could see the veins standing out in her neck and her arm. She pushed like that until she had exhausted something, then let her arm drop. She walked over to examine Mink Petrusev.

"When my mother died, it made people afraid for themselves. Nobody thought it was a tragedy. Nobody but me and my uncle. I miss her all the time, Allfrey."

"Do you think that Dew killed her?"

"No."

Shadows waved on the red wall around us.

"Who, then?"

"Some old boyfriend. Someone she met on a barstool. It doesn't matter who did it. She's gone."

"Is that how you really feel?"

The girl looked at me with black holes for eyes.

"Look, if her killer is still out there, hurting people, I hope he dies or stops or gets caught. It won't fix the hole inside me. I know that much from working with the witch."

"Who do you think killed the other women?"

"A man or men the detectives haven't caught yet. And probably never will."

"No rabbit's foot at your mother's murder site?"

"No. My boss says that was the Sheriff's idea. He started planting them later. Made it seem like there was one killer. Made his job easier."

"She thinks the Lucky Rabbit's Foot Killer is your Sheriff's invention?"

"Unsolved cases are bad for his election prospects. That's what

she says. The Sheriff used Mr. Dew to close those cases and become
a hero. He took the rabbit's foot story line and he ran with it . . ."

"That's a pretty sophisticated lie for someone like your sheriff."

"It's the only thing he's good at. Covering up what a bad detective
he is. Hiding his own laziness and evil."

"How can that man live with himself?"

Dell touched the edge of the wet paper.

"Allfrey?" I could see the girl shuffling the words in her mouth.
"The Antidote and I . . . we've been planting stories in people. Just
like Vick did."

"What do you mean, *planting stories*? You're starting rumors?
Exaggerating your powers?"

The girl looked anguished. She chewed her lip a little, maybe
regretting what she'd just told me, maybe deciding how much more
to say.

"The people who bank with her?" she said. "The witch's custom-
ers? They have these holes inside them, where their memories were.
The Antidote, she lost all her deposits. No clue where they went.
Or how to get them back. So we've been filling in the gaps. When
customers come to make withdrawals, we give them a new memory.
A false memory."

I laughed out loud. It was my turn, I guess, to be shocked at what
was possible in this life.

"We don't have Vaults in the east. Not that I know about. You
two, what? Hypnotize people? Make them believe every day was a
parade?"

The girl bristled for a moment, then nodded. "More or less. I
have always been an excellent liar. I wanted her to take me on as an
apprentice—I thought I could become a prairie witch myself."

"And are you a witch now?"

"Not for lack of trying."

"Your uncle must be relieved."

"He only just learned that I've been working for her."

"Does he know that you've been . . . passing these fakes into
people?"

She shook her head.

"I told myself we were doing a good thing. Helping to stabilize
the town."

She was staring up at me, pleading with her eyes for something I did not want to give her.

I would not offer this young liar absolution, or anything else. How was it my job to treat her welling shame? *Do that work yourself,* I thought. *Don't ask me to do it for you. Find your way through the difficult feelings, then start to put things right.*

I told her so, in my own way.

"When I worked at the portrait studio," I said, "my entire job was to make the wealthy White socialites of Philadelphia look good. At the time, I thought it was harmless. Just a job I did for rent and groceries. Supplying the flattering lighting. Editing all the ugliness out of the frame. Eventually, I came to feel differently about it . . ."

The root cellar shrank on me, and I remembered with a jolt that we were inside the earth. Again the timer buzzed. The red bulb seemed to pale, as if the safelight was inhaling its glow. The girl's twisted face was staring at me anxiously. It took me another minute to understand what she was telling me, and when I did I felt so sick I could not meet her eyes.

Victor Iscoe could never have covered up the ongoing murders without the help of my two roommates. Who had sewed up an open case before anyone had a chance to solve it? Who had put an end to everyone's bad dreams of butcher's knives and rabbits' feet— swallowing those nightmares whole, replacing them with fantasies of a sleepy, peaceful town? Who had buried the truth, long before Vick buried this woman, and made it possible for the state of Nebraska to electrocute an innocent person?

He is still alive, Cleo. I did not hear this in Stryker's voice. It was my own sturdy whisper. It was not an assignment I wanted—overturning a conviction. A weaker part of me balked.

Dell listened as I put these questions to her in the root cellar, and I watched shame paint her face in the wavy glow of the lantern. It turned us different colors. My hands were a dark purple on the table, Dell's skin was a pickled beet. It felt good to see her cheeks darkening. I didn't want her to stop feeling ashamed yet. Shame is a guide, if you can direct its burning light to the next right action. We couldn't rest now until Clemson Louis Dew was a free man.

"Asphodel," I said, swallowing hard against a rinse of bile. "Do you know how many people you've fooled with these . . . counterfeits?"

"I kept excellent records," she said, with a hint of pride. "One hundred and eleven, as of last Thursday."

"Are you done with all that?" I asked her. "Or are you two still . . . counterfeiting?"

"We quit. Maybe too late."

She wouldn't meet my eyes. "I think the counterfeits are making everybody nuts," she said. "People don't remember who they are anymore. Don't have the tools in their toolshed to understand their own lives. If I boarded up your window and painted a blue sky on it, I bet it would make you nuts too."

Instantly I knew what the girl was describing. The Uzians' blank eyes above their sleepy smiles, that queer humming coming from the backs of their throats. A sound like machinery abandoned to its task. "Are you all right, sir?" I'd asked one of the witch's customers who I'd found staring vacantly down the stairwell. The dust was up that day and every face was masked. He'd stopped humming abruptly and shouted, "Never better, never better!"

Mink's hand on the sandy earth seemed to be reaching out to us. Why did I have to get wrapped up in this? "Murdered women" had not appeared on Roy Stryker's shooting script. Neither had "monstrous Sheriff," or "western town of spellbound amnesiacs," for that matter. Or prairie witches. Or blue skies and healthy wheat, spared from the blowing dust killing everything else. For a moment I felt a surge of fury at the Graflex, as if it were the camera's fault that I was now entangled in these strangers' fates. We had evidence that might free Clemson Dew before his second electrocution, and indict Sheriff Iscoe. Evidence that would reopen these cases, unsolve them. The town would have a chance to mount a real investigation. I could share my photographs with the authorities. On the heels of this thought, I heard my mother's voice chiding me: "Cleo Allfrey, what *authority* is going to help you with this problem?" Who could I ask for help? Certainly not the Sheriff's department. My mind felt sore, as if I'd just slammed my head into a low ceiling.

"All right, Dell," I said. "Help me carry these prints up the ladder."

When I mailed Stryker the first box of negatives, I knew I was risking my reputation and my job. I had never made a picture that required me to risk my life.

The Antidote

Cleo Allfrey fanned her darkroom prints before us like a dealer at a high-stakes table. Which is what Harp's kitchen table felt like to me now as I sat staring into these candid snaps of the Sheriff and Percy. Photographs from a lonely place where I'd never once set foot but which I knew on sight. I felt a lurching sensation, as if a nightmare was beginning again. Straitjacketed into Vick's consciousness, I had dug a hole in those sandhills northeast of downtown Uz. Mink stared unblinkingly back at me. My memory of his memory melded with the photographs. Mink grew more definite in my imagination, and more demanding.

It was 2:00 p.m. on the third day that I'd sheltered at the Oletsky place. Already it felt like a lifetime since I'd been in Room 11. Allfrey had driven to Uz and checked out of the boardinghouse on Monday, and she reported that the sign I'd posted was still on my door. I hoped that my customers believed it (GONE TO VISIT A SICK RELATION, WILL RETURN IN JUNE). The Sheriff hadn't come looking for me on the Oletsky property. If he did show up, I'd hide in the root cellar. The farmer had promised to ring a bell if he saw any car coming down the road. At first I had felt a joy that surpassed any I'd known since You were born, Son. A feeling of wondrous correctness. On the morning that I saw that door in the earth, the feeling had surged through me from the soil itself: I did not have to run. I could stay in Uz and change my life. The longer I hid here, the less sure I felt about my decision. How would I survive? What else could I become at this late hour?

Certainly not a photographer, I thought, staring at the stark, accusing images. Cleo had a witchcraft of her own. I could see that her camera had channeled something—different times in the same place. Now I understood what compelled her to work night and day in the root cellar. What kept drawing her underground. She had a magic Graflex, a haunted camera—she said she didn't know what to call it.

"He torched her," said Cleo. "Your sheriff doesn't want people to know that women are still being killed out here. This 'Lucky Rabbit's Foot Killer' . . ."

"He made it up," I said.

"It's quite a story," Harp sighed at last, taking off his reading glasses. "But it's hard to argue with these pictures . . ."

"It's hard for *you*," said Cleo. "Others will find it very easy to dismiss us."

Harp was nodding eagerly. "I have seen such visions myself! With my naked eyes!" He sounded like a boy to me, and I felt afraid for him. In Uz, simple enthusiasm is rarely met in kind.

"Dell, you saw the prints on the drying line. I have three more film sheets waiting to be developed, down in the root cellar . . ."

To midwife yesterday into tomorrow, to reveal something that had not yet come to pass—it seemed like difficult labor. I felt a wave of relief that this was Allfrey's work and not my own. Then I saw Mink's face staring up at me, merging with the face in my mind. I caught Dell's eye. She nodded. "There's more," I said.

When I finished telling them what Vick and Percy had done, I looked at Dell to see if she had something to add. Dell was sucking on the ends of her hair like a much younger child. Her wavy braid was stiff with dirt. I wonder if I would have been a good mother to You, Son. I felt irritated at the girl, not very loving at all. It was time to make a plan, not disappear into a shallow trance.

"So you both knew?" Harp looked from his niece to me, his sagging face made childish by fright and disappointment. "The Sheriff told you that he did this, Ant? Why didn't you say something?"

"That's a bad question to ask a Vault," said Dell. "Who could she tell, Uncle? Who would believe her?"

The girl always leaps to my defense. How quickly she must react on court. Just as swiftly, she switched to offense: "So what's the plan?" she asked. "Are we just going to hide out here forever? Or are we going to do something?"

"Call a lawyer," said Cleo Allfrey. "We could start there."

"Every lawyer I know is in Vick's pocket."

Dell stood and took off up the stairs; we listened to her crashing around. A moment later, she returned with the book of her transcriptions, those deposits from late April and early May. Beautiful and terrible things went slanting across the paper in her childish scrawl. "We have a lot of dirt on a lot of people! Some of them were jurors in the Lucky Rabbit's Foot trial."

"Excellent plan, girl. Let's ring them on the Party Line. You can break the news. Tell them they have no memory of this, but they betrayed seven murdered women and sentenced an innocent boy to die. Read the jury foreman his deposit. See how he absorbs it."

We stared at each other for a long moment. It would be easiest, I thought, to agree that there was nothing to be gained by showing these photographs and returning the deposits. What would it change? It was unlikely any good would come of it. All but certain that we would bear the consequences. This was the lullaby I sang to myself for years and years of good behavior.

The blue kettle that had been wobbling on the cookstove, forgotten, began to whistle. I felt my body bracing for a scream. Nobody else seemed to notice, so I leapt up and grabbed it off the firebox. I had been fixing tomato soup and carrot slaw for supper when Allfrey and Dell arrived from the cellar with the prints of Mink Petrusev. Dirty carrots striped the sink, wet dough lay under the rolling pin. Nobody was interested in eating now. With the exception of the dog, thudding his tail beside the stove.

"Let's have a think," I suggested. "Tea slows me down, helps me to see around a problem . . ."

I tossed the dog a stale biscuit, poured the rest of us two-leggeds black tea. We all burned our tongues at the same moment, then cursed in unison—which became the vent for an almost hysterical laughing fit. We laughed and laughed for the pure release of it, far longer than felt reasonable, long enough for the scalding tea to cool. How strong we sounded as a chorus.

"I guess the spell of protection has its limits," said Harp Oletsky, trying to keep the joke going. It had the opposite effect, and the table went silent.

"Not everyone is in bed with the Sheriff," Dell said at last. "Or afraid of him. Besides, we have the Grange Master here! There's some credibility for you—"

"Yes, that's true, isn't it?" The farmer sounded a little dazed. He kept dropping sugar lumps into his tea, staring into their fizzy dissolution as if therein the plan resided. "Founder's Day is coming up. There is a ceremony at the Grange Hall. I am supposed to give a speech. I have my predecessor's speech, which he got from *his* predecessor. It's more or less the same speech every year. The following Tuesday the polls open, and everybody votes."

He stirred the sugar into a tiny cyclone.

"Maybe we could try something new."

Allfrey blew on her tea. "Founder's Day?"

"It's the Uzians' Fourth of July," said Dell. "The town's birthday. Uncle!" She was grinning in a way I recognized. Fearlessly, if you're being generous. I never raised a child, so I don't know if this is what a mother feels when she sees her toddler swaying at the head of the stairs. "We can expose the Sheriff," Dell said in her game-day voice, a bright growl. "Show the whole town these photographs. Make them see that Dew's conviction didn't solve anything. That an innocent person is about to be executed. If people think that the real killers are still out there, they'll listen. Even if they try to pretend otherwise, they'll know . . ."

She turned to me, her voice suddenly full of apology. "We have a lot of cases to reopen. So many people have our counterfeits inside them."

Harp Oletsky, God bless him, had already pulled out the pencil from behind his left ear. His eyes swung between us like a baby following a glass mobile, happy and mystified by the whirring reflections. "Can you slow it down a little for an old man? Dell is just like her mother, she goes a mile a minute . . ."

I burned with shame while she told her uncle about our counterfeiting operation. I am always underestimating people, Son. He did not do what I'd expected—order the girl out of the room, lecture me on my damnation. He nodded once or twice, and spoke only to say, "It's good that you've washed your hands of all that."

"We haven't," I said. "Not yet." I had the feeling that our real work was just beginning. I stretched out my hands, as if they might express this better than I could. The girl was looking at the print with the leaping tongues of flame. Something under the cottonwood had fixed her attention.

"This is about a lot more than Vick Iscoe," I said. "We'll need to return as many deposits as we can."

"Yes," said Dell, still mesmerized by the split tree that the Sheriff had put out of his mind. It made me feel dizzy to see it leafing across the paper. I knew that place from Vick's deposit, although I had never set foot there myself. We could find it, I realized. Between the four of us, we could make the map.

In rummy, Allfrey is an expert at making melds. She knew how to pool our knowledge, our talents. "An exhibition," she said in her firm, quiet way. "That's what's needed. The Mayor invited me to show the photographs I've made in Uz County. You'll speak, Harp. And you two can share what you know about Iscoe."

I almost told them about you then, Son. I felt the words beading on my tongue: *I cannot risk my life to save another woman's son.* But as it turns out, I can. I am. We are risking everything together at the Founder's Day celebration. We have so little time to prepare.

⚏

We make a funny sorority in the farmer's house. Dell's practically been living in a tunnel with Allfrey, helping to prepare her gallery. She goes barging down the ladder into the root cellar to help with the developing—smacking gum, tiny wreaths of grass and blood on her bare knees—whether Allfrey wants her help or not. She leaves the basketball like an anchor in a little wallow she dug beside the cellar door. "This girl gets on my last nerve," Allfrey sighed to me yesterday on the porch. "She does help, but she asks too many questions. I get fed up sometimes and send her aboveground." It makes me happy to commiserate about the girl with her. At the farmhouse, I'm as close to being inside a family as I've come since I traveled with Kettle and Cherry.

Allfrey plans to cover her prints with dustcloths and display them in the Grange Hall. Hanging some on the wall and perching others on tables.

"Why cover them?" I asked. She looked surprised by my question.

"Timing is everything," she said. "We'll reveal them all at once—

like the sun appearing from behind a cloud. I don't want to give people a minute to grow doubtful."

Harp has been neglecting his farmwork to work on his speech. He came to me yesterday for help with his spelling, which I found both sweet and maddening—"Nobody but you will see what's on the paper, Harp. If you can read it, that's all that matters." He wanted the letters to be right all the same.

For the past few days, I've been quilting together secrets to make public on Founder's Day. The girl and I have been collecting the most damning evidence against Vick, and against the entire structure. Listening for the hollow places beneath this humming town. A hearing at the Grange Hall, with hundreds present, is going to feel very different than my midnight withdrawals.

Of the four of us, only Allfrey seems to have the right perspective on what we are aiming to do. Harp's excitement worries me. Dell seems to think the whole town will applaud us for it, poor little fool. She doesn't understand who we are exposing to the light. There is no way to tell the truth without first revealing ourselves as liars.

⊰⊱

"Lull," said Dell this morning, undoing the sash and peering through the curtains. "Looks like we got another break in the weather." Cleo Allfrey and her uncle were playing dominoes and listening to a rebroadcast of Roosevelt's Fireside Chat. Harp seems happy to offer us shelter here. I wonder if Cherry is alive and hiding from her customers, like me. I wonder if we have a future on the Plains. Are other Vaults closing permanently? Will they let us become something else?

So far, nobody has come looking for me here. If I survive Founder's Day, Son, I will have to find a way to get my new location to you.

The Sheriff is conspicuously absent from the Party Line. Campaigning hard, would be my guess. The election is a week from Tuesday.

Time is short, but time also seems to sprawl here—as if the four of us are stretching it out, each of us holding on to their corner of a blue blanket. Our days here are filled with patient urgency. At night we eat together and argue about the right things to say, the right things to do. I have not felt this simple happiness since the night that we escaped from Milford, carrying our roller skates through the moonlit forest. Believing in the existence of the rink together as we moved away from that prison and through the dark wood. Carrying a small dream to term. When we stepped across the threshold of the barn and burst into laughter, You butted my ribs.

I feel safe here, or safer than I have since early childhood. Still, I do not want to sleep in this new place alone. I keep waiting for the Sheriff to burst through the door. Dell, Cleo, and I have started sleeping on mattresses that we pushed together like so much cordwood. Nobody wanted to take a bed and consign someone else to the floorboards—which is how we ended up snoring together on this nest. When I can't sleep, I stand and sway by the window. I wonder if maybe this is what a mother feels—standing at the edge of a crib and listening to the steady breaths of the beings that she is charged with protecting. I feel like a mother in this house of women, and I feel like a baby. The house cradles us. Outside the sky remains an uncannily steady blue.

Cleo says she grew up sharing a room with her sisters. Dell has practice sleeping in a room of snoring basketball players. I remember the dream-spun silence and crowded air of the Home for Unwed Mothers. The terror of Milford was instantly replaced by a secret registry of happiness—Stencil telling her crazy jokes in the dormitory while the rest of us howled with laughter, aching everywhere. Zintka playing ragtime songs on the piano whenever the Superintendent was absent. Melody teaching me how to dance. The night we flew in circles under the moon, entirely free. I wonder often about the other women who spent a year at Milford, and about their babies. I wonder who is sleeping in our old beds tonight. We were so much bigger than any story can tell, Son. More alive than even your mother's best memories.

What would my own History of the West look like? Not Manifest Destiny, but Invisible Loss. The infinity of what might have been, and never was allowed to be. A History of Childless Mothers and Motherless Children. It would include a picture of enduring love. The love that flies with the homing instinct of a bird into and through all weathers, in search of our lost ones, our unforgotten.

In my History of the West there would also be four pregnant women, roller-skating.

❧

On the morning that I watched Cleo Allfrey emerge from the door in the earth, I had the most curious sensation. Not quite déja vù. Almost like retracing a forgotten path, finding your foot outlined by older steps—a kind of premonition. I knew this door. I felt strongly then that I did not have to run, that I could hide here and discover what I am supposed to become. How do I use my gifts, now that I am closed for business? What is this body for?

Your mother is still a powerful witch, Son. I would like to learn a new use for my emptiness—my spaciousness. Look at the rosewood mandolin in the corner of this bedroom. People string catgut over a hole, and send music pouring into the atmosphere. Maybe I can restring myself, and learn how to make music from my hollow place. There is a spot in the Sandhills where a spring fed by the aquifer lifts from deep underground, bubbling into earshot. I want to serve a song like that one.

Sometimes, counting sheep in the loneliest hours of the night, I've had something like a waking dream. I see the scarecrow come down from its cross in the field. It comes shuffling and dancing toward me. Waving its marooned arms at me from the clover. Crows appear on the slate of the sky and multiply, they circle him like a crown, a message that is almost, almost legible to me. What a mind invents in the gray of predawn. That time when the world looks like one of Cleo Allfrey's ghostly negatives. A beat before the lines harden with the rising sun. I see something growing on the fallowland: a great wave of illumination that begins to rise from the soil and take shape, tasseling light and ripening light and hardening kernels of light. It lifts and sprawls into a single trembling sheet, stretching high above the barn, burning in a color I have never seen. Pulsing like the aura around the moon. Shadows ripple behind it. At daybreak, the light shrinks into the ground. As if the earth is gasping back a dream.

The strangest part is that it does not scare me.

Over breakfast, as any sane houseguest would do, I drink my coffee and let the others do the talking.

Asphodel Oletsky

I t's nice to hear laughter downstairs. My gloomy uncle has surprised me—he loves having company. "It's not *my* fortune anymore!" he told me on the stairwell yesterday, his pupils shiny as buttons. "It's a gift to share. What we have, we have to give."

"Sounds good, Uncle. You can embroider that on a pillow."

Valeria came to visit me yesterday. "What the heck is going on out here?" she whispered. "Is this your new coven?" I was happy to hear a note of jealousy churning around in her questions.

"Don't tell anyone, not even another Danger."

We played for hours. When it's just the two of us, we play rough. "Foul!" I called. "Offensive!" Val screamed, knocking me to the ground, both of us laughing. We had a free-throw contest that Val won, nailing eleven in a row. "Queen of the Foul Line!" She did her victory dance. "Queen for a Day," I yelled back, snatching the ball out of her arms. "Enjoy it, sister. It's my crown next time." Cleo Allfrey, pumping water for her darkroom, paused to laugh *at* us.

Before she rode home, Val asked me to help her pin her bangs back. "They keep flopping in my face," she grunted. She knelt so I could do this and suddenly we were facing each other, eye level, as I fumbled with her bobby pins, still laughing—I was doing a terrible job. I held her hair in one fist and kissed her. It was a shy, clumsy kiss. I felt none of the confidence about my movements that I feel on the court. She kissed me back. I slid my arms around her waist and pulled her close, standing on my toes, and Val began to laugh. Too easily, she slid out of my arms.

"This isn't like when I'm guarding you, okay? I'm not trying to get clear of you either. You can relax a little, Oletsky."

We kissed again. This time she sat down in the dirt beside me.

"Do you think your uncle knows that we are in love?"

Was that where we were? My eyes flew from her face to the wheat field, where my uncle was taking measurements between the rows with a toothy ruler. An earthquake was shaking apart every map I had, every belief, every expectation about how my life would develop. I felt like the top of my skull was about to come off. Val's tone was flat and indifferent, as if she was only making conversation to fill the time, but her eyes were tracking my face. I said, "I love you, Val." The moment I said it, I knew it was true. She smiled at me, although her eyes looked afraid. I am certain my eyes did too.

⚜

That night, my uncle came to read part of his speech to me. I had a sense of what kind of boy he must have been, preparing for exams. It made me wish my mother was here to tease him with me. Remembering someone you've lost can feel like drinking mist. I was thirsty for more. I did not want to see a picture in my head. I wanted to hold my living mama. To be held by her. How stupid, to want the impossible. I don't know how to want what I can get.

"How did that sound?" He looked so anxious to hear my opinion. It surprised me, and I felt guilty; I'd been far away.

"Sounds good, Uncle. Ready, Set, Lightning. You can lead with that—it's what I tell my team."

"This isn't a game, Dell," he said crossly. "Lord, I know what I *need* to say, I just don't know if I can manage to get it across—"

Before he closed the door, my uncle turned and swooped his watery eyes around the room.

"I slept here, too. Did I ever tell you that? When we were small, the three of us shared one bed. We made Frank sleep by the window. One winter morning he woke up with a pile of snow on his chest."

"What was Mama like?"

My uncle's smile is like some shy, nocturnal animal, scared of its own shadow. It's always trying to burrow back into his wrinkles. But when I said Mama's name, the smile emerged without a trace of wariness. He looked truly happy. Story after story after story rolled into me, and I was happy to receive them. Uncle Harp spoke without pausing for close to an hour. When he finally stopped, he looked flushed and tired. The moon floated in the center of the sky, gold and full. Almost as close as the moths batting against the window. I tried to picture twelve-year-old Harp wearing ice skates and wheeling over water with his brother, Frank, and their daredevil kid sister.

"Lada could make an L with her skate blade," my uncle told me. "Of all the people on the ice, she was the only one who could do that." His smile made my eyes ache. Thirty years later, he was still proud that his sister could autograph the lake.

Last night I did not dream of Mama. Instead I was a rabbit, limping in a moving wall of a thousand panicked bucks and does. Men were walking in a slow line behind us, clanging metal and shooting into the writhing, streaming mass of us. In the dream, I could barely keep up, slipping to the left and right of whistling bullets that sank into less fortunate rabbits, running as fast as I could, which was not nearly fast enough, aware from my whiskers to the tips of my claws that we were doomed. Doom wasn't something to which I could resign myself. I had to keep running. Failure is the guarantee. Failure would have been so easy! To lie down and let this death overtake me, instead of lunging for a later one. To let the men shoot or club or trample me. *Life, kindly and cruelly, compels us to continue living for as long as we can, Dell.* My mother's voice filtered into my tall ears, and I swiveled around, looking frantically for her; she was nowhere to be seen on the open grassland. Deep inside, I could hear her. *Breathe and run. Breathe and run.* Even sprinting for my life, in the body of a rabbit, I had time to marvel that my mother had found me right here, that my mother was running right through me, braiding through my sinews and my bones, through the chorus in my mind that was somehow never only-me, not my singing-alone. My mother came screaming into my burning chest and legs, pushing me onward, urging me to run for the trembling edge beyond which the shapes of trees collapsed into vagueness and shadows. I leapt with a thudding heart for the cover of a distant cottonwood stand alongside tens of hundreds of does and bucks and kits. We fanned out to cover the entire prairie, from the Missouri River to the Rockies. The men's clubs swung over us. I looked down and saw that my front leg ended in a stump. This was why I wobbled here and there through the sagebrush and the buffalo grass, crossing through curtains of scent, crumpling bluestem and the powdered sun our paws stirred out of the ground. On my three legs, I ran—bunching and springing forward, trailing blood along the trampled grasses. My three legs carried me back to consciousness, where I am a human girl named Asphodel Oletsky, a two-legged animal, sweating in my dead mother's bed.

Harp Oletsky

I stood outside my niece's door, comforted to know that everyone was sleeping soundly behind it. Outside the window, Venus was a brilliant pinprick over the wheat fields. Its color shifted as I stared, from violet to sapphire to red. Gem-like sparkles reached my old eyes from the depths of space. How far, I wondered, has the light that pours out of the ground in the fallowland traveled?

My wheat waved up at me under the full moon—the best I'd ever raised. Overnight, it seemed to have gone from shin height to waist height, an unripe green to a deepening gold. I opened the window and stuck my head into the clear night air. There was the scarecrow, dancing in the winds that always blow in western Nebraska. "Hold your pose," I warned him. "Let's try to have one ordinary night."

Only lately have I begun to wonder if *Why me?* might be the wrong question. *Why?* seems to point in a better direction. Allfrey is teaching me that lesson. How to swing the lens outward. How to look and listen before you surface with a new comprehension. She is always asking, from behind her camera, *Who wants to be seen? What wants to be known?*

"Why is my land spared from the dust?" I asked God last night. I walked the rows and found no weeds, no weevils, no signs of heat stress.

When I take myself out of the question, I see a possibility that did not occur to me until my guests showed up. Maybe I'm not being punished or rewarded. Maybe this is not *my* blessing or *my* curse. There could be another reason for this clear and quiet sky. Even now, under this black awning, something is developing.

The Photographer, Cleo Allfrey

I woke to a full moon shining through the windows and felt a stab of panic. Two days until the exhibition. I am grateful for the good weather when I'm working in the darkroom, but at night the transparency of the glass frightens me. Every surface in this house is free of dust. The wind out here never screams or howls. Whereas at the boardinghouse, I could point my flashlight at the chinks in the walls and watch dust pouring in like flour. The root cellar, like this farmhouse, is somehow sealed against the weather, as well as the light. I measure the temperature when I mix, stop, and fix, and it's always an ideal sixty-seven or sixty-eight degrees. It feels almost as if this place itself is helping me—the dirt and the grass curving over my darkroom, the sky holding its breath. A great urgency fills me while I'm working, but at night the fear returns.

Yesterday I drove to Kearney, where nobody knew me. I felt like an alien visiting a different earth—no talk of rabbit's feet or spells of any kind, everyone gaunt with more mundane worries. I spent the last ten dollars of my RA funds on a hamburger with extra pickle and a telegram to my family in Gray's Ferry, telling everyone I loved them. Giving them directions. If I go missing, or if I am killed at the Grange, I want to be sure they know how to find Harp Oletsky's farm. My Graflex negatives are in labeled boxes in the root cellar, along with my undeveloped film. That's what I'm leaving to my family, in lieu of a deposit slip.

Why are you doing this, Cleo? I hear in my mother's stern, warm voice. *You quit one job, why not quit this one?* Would any of these people help me, if I was in Clemson Louis Dew's position? In this land of

mysteries, one of the most bewildering to me is my continued presence in Uz. After I sent the telegram, I sat in my car for close to an
hour, staring at the highway that led back East. What did I owe to
any of these strangers? Why not leave them my prints, and take off?
Just after sunset, I drove back to the Oletsky farmhouse. Maybe there
was a spell on me as well.

Some places and people want to be seen for longer than a moment.

The Graflex is teaching me how to recognize them. There is a
magnetism I often feel while looking into the ground glass. As if
something is gazing back, asking me to complete the circuit. When
I get that sense, I fire the shutter. Composing a shot is always a collaboration with other beings, with the light, with the whole environment. I know I have a good picture when I feel things click into
place—the balance that holds both symmetries and asymmetries.

Today I looked at a negative with daylight behind it and started
to cry—a thousand cranes soaring low over the tree islands in clear
water, although when I took this shot two weeks ago, what I saw in the
ground glass was a turbid, shallow tributary of the Platte. *I remember
you*, I thought—although I have never in my life seen sandhill cranes
before. A portrait I made last Wednesday of two hogs rooting around
a doorframe became a group of happy children in odd attire, swallowed to their knees by grass and wildflowers. I pointed the Graflex
at the Oletsky wheat fields, and when I developed the negative, the
barn and the wheat had disappeared. In their place was a crowd of
hundreds stretching across the horizon. A parade of people—every
age and every color—standing with linked arms, some on horseback,
PROTECT WATER on their banner. Yesterday, tomorrow.

The emptiness of any place is an illusion. That's what this camera
has taught me. Any piece of earth is brimming over with living. I
think this must be what the poets mean when they write *in the fullness
of time*.

⁂

Sleep abandoned me, and when the girl's snoring became unbearable
I stood and walked the house. It was a different country at night, the
dog padding silently behind me as I carried my camera around like a
colicky baby. I was afraid to go anywhere without the Graflex; afraid

that something might happen to it. In the blue kitchen, I ate a whole ripe tomato right off the plant in the window box. I made a picture of its green Rapunzel tendrils dropping over the sill. Venus was shining in the distance. The moon followed me upstairs, reappearing in window after window, posing in too many places at once.

"Why don't you let me sleep?" I asked the Graflex. I wondered if Roy had received my resignation letter yet. Soon I would be a cautionary tale in the Washington offices, if I wasn't already. Then I would be forgotten. One of the hundreds of hole-punched faces in the filing cabinet: Untitled, Unknown.

I was whispering to the Graflex when I startled at the sight of Harp Oletsky at the top of the stairs. Holding a lantern and pacing back and forth, murmuring to himself—practicing his speech, I'd thought at first. He raised the lantern and swung it like a pendulum in front of the window, as if he were greeting someone. Or practicing some witchcraft he'd learned from my two roommates. I moved gingerly up the staircase, not wanting to interrupt his speech or his spell.

"Allfrey? How long have you been awake?" He continued to stare out the window, and he asked so quietly I nearly didn't answer, unsure what the etiquette might be for this sort of encounter.

"Hello, Harp. I couldn't sleep."

"Who were you talking to just now?"

"My camera. And you?"

"My scarecrow."

"I see."

"Forgive me for interrupting."

"No. I was just pouring myself a warm bath of self-pity."

"Yes, I do the same at this hour. Can I ask you a question, Cleo? What color do you see through your window?"

"Midnight blue."

"Nothing stranger?"

"A clear night with stars. Moonlit fields for miles. That's plenty strange around here."

"I suppose it is. It's just— I've been seeing some funny colors out there, in the fallowland."

"Hmm. I don't have my flashbulb. But if you'd like, I'll open the window and take a photograph. With this camera, and the aid of that moon, you never know. Something might turn up on the film."

"Would you do that? Thank you."

I leaned out the open window. The air was cool and smelled of sage and something I couldn't place. I almost fell while trying to position the camera on the sill.

"Don't fall, Cleo!" Harp cried out.

"Why do people think it's helpful to yell that? Don't worry—" I softened when I turned and saw that he'd been truly afraid. "Just a wobble. Happens all the time. I haven't fallen yet."

"Of course," he said. "Well, let me know what shows up on your film."

It was a long exposure. I wondered what might surface inside my trays tomorrow.

"What were you waving at just now, Harp? The moon?"

"No," he said, with a note of embarrassment. "It wasn't the moon."

I closed up the Graflex. For a quiet moment we stood shoulder to shoulder, staring out the same window. The straw doll seemed to float between the moonglow and shadow. At first I saw nothing out of the ordinary, but as usual, the longer I looked, the more extraordinary the whole scene became: the dry silver sea, the man suspended in air.

"It's late," I said. "We'd better get some rest before that scarecrow starts talking back."

"Good night, Miss Allfrey."

"Good night, Harp."

He crept back down the hall to his bedroom, but I stayed by the window for a good while, watching the strange light travel.

The Antidote

On my ninth day at the Oletsky place, I told the girl about You. We were sitting on the windowsill in her mother's bedroom, combing through her transcriptions. Founder's Day was almost upon us. I could not believe how many deposits I'd taken since Black Sunday. In our short time together, the girl had filled five notebooks. Blue ink ran slantwise off the paper like rain. It gave me a pang to read the town's secrets in Dell's childish handwriting.

"I am a criminal, girl. I should never have made you my accomplice."

Dell snorted without looking up from her notebook.

"Come off it," she said. "I begged to work for you, remember? I thought I could help you—I got my mama out of scrapes all the time."

Dell rubbed at her face with her fists. It's a habit of hers, as if she's trying to smooth some bulging feeling. Or push tears back inside her skull. She usually does it when she thinks I'm not watching.

"I was good at it, too." The girl's wistful expression reminded me of the hard drinkers at the Jentleman, misremembering their worst nights on earth as great fun. "Counterfeiting for people. I did that long before I met you. Guessing what a man wants to hear, what a woman wishes she had done. That part came natural, Boss."

"You don't have to call me Boss anymore. We're done with all that."

"So what *do* I call you then?" snapped Dell. "You're not my boss anymore, you're not the Antidote—" Her toughness flaked away. She looked up at me with animal hurt in her wide eyes, the tail of her braid in her mouth; for an instant I could picture Dell at three years old.

"Who are you?"

Through the open window the eastern wheat field tossed in golden waves, touching the edgeless blue sky. It was almost harvest-time. Another week or two, and the binder would be clicking. I shut my eyes and heard the loud clock in the parlor at Milford.

"My name is Antonina Rossi," I said. As I spoke, I felt that I was placing Your warm, wriggly body directly into the girl's arms. Your living weight. There was no instrument to mediate the transfer, no sparkling funnel. We held You.

"You asked me once how I became a prairie witch, Dell. I'm ready to tell you now, if you still want to know—"

The Antidote's Story:
Part 3

Five weeks after our roller-skating night, I was belted into the straitjacket. We were shelving books in the library, which quickly turned into a foulmouthed game of Tease the New Girl:

"Oooh, watch out! I am going to Sin on you, Marcia . . ."

"Shut up, you cunt!"

We traded insults back and forth and they sang out like valentines. Our babies were already friends, said Stencil. "I feel her laughing inside me," she told me, massaging the rise of her watermelon belly—Stencil was convinced she was having a girl.

Observation was not really an option with Stencil. She'd pull you into her affairs, usually literally, grabbing you by the wrists and tugging you down the hallway. One rainy morning in the library, she snuck up behind me and flipped up my skirt, laughing when I cursed at her.

"We're not the only whores around here, you know . . ."

She lay on her back and rolled around on the library floor, lifting her brown dress over her bruised skinny legs.

Melody shrieked. She saw Malvina's shadow coming first.

"A book is a whore, splayed out for anyone—"

"Shut your mouth right this minute."

"Look at that whore of a Bible, flat on its back on the table—"

Malvina was a stocky woman in her fifties, but she flew at us at the speed supplied by rage, by humiliation, and jerked Stencil up by her braids. For a terrifying moment I flashed on a memory that was not my own but surfaced in me anyways: the gallows rope going taut in an executioner's hands. Fear froze me again. I did not intervene. Not when Malvina slapped her and not when my friend kneed the Superintendent in the chest and rolled to the far end of the library carpet. Stencil had blasphemed Malvina, and now she would pay.

José Luis claimed to hate this part of his job. His face looked like a wrinkling tablecloth, glass shards for eyes and plummy wine stains spilling across his cheeks. "Help me," he implored his audience of eighteen pregnant women and panting Malvina. None of us moved. Sighing his resignation, he walked to the closet and returned with the leather straitjacket. I crossed the room to help Stencil up, but she would not look at me or take my hand; I felt a great shame spreading from my toes to my hairline. "I'm sorry," I whispered, but when José Luis came toward us with the jacket pulled open, I stepped away from her a second time.

"Please, Stella Maris, cooperate?" José growled, filled with self-pity. "Think of the baby—" Stencil punched above her weight class. "Augh! That was my good eye, Stella!"

I began to laugh hysterically, to ventilate the terror in my chest. Everyone turned to look my way. No one had ever heard me cackle at that volume in a public space.

"You think your friend is funny, Anne Fayeweather? Is eternal fire also funny to you? She is beyond help, but you might yet be saved—"

I struggled to get control of myself, kneeling on the carpet and shaking as if possessed. While years of submerged feeling poured out of me—howls of pain and howls of laughter—I felt José's hands close on my shoulders. Stencil had been freed. Nurse Irina and Nurse Edna came charging right at me like two cowboys in a cattle-roping contest. I had become clumsy, and I no longer trusted my body as I had that day at the skating rink. When I tried to run from them, I banged into another girl and fell hard on my side.

I recognized the hard set of their lips. It was the face our neighbor made when she was about to kill a turkey. "This is for your own good, dear," said Malvina Dent. "It hurts me more than it does you, believe me . . ."

A great chill rode up my spine. I heard in her sad, resigned voice that she believed this. I began to scream then, hurling myself at the glass windows in the parlor and every onlooker's staring eyes. Nobody helped me, just as I had helped nobody.

Here is something I've thought about many nights since: if every one of us had rushed the nurses, we could have easily overcome them. We outnumbered them five to one. If we had made a coordinated movement to save Zintka from the attic on that sweltering April night, we could have freed her easily, and ourselves for that matter. But each of us made our decision alone.

To get a thrashing pregnant woman into a crawl space is no easy task. I gave myself a shiner, somehow, trying to wrestle my way free. The red leather straitjacket was a prison inside the prison. Did you know they had these custom-made to fit pregnant women at different trimesters? I have often wondered who agreed to make them. I knew that my delivery date was drawing near when I could only wear the largest size. It hung menacingly in the hall closet as a warning to us and looked like a trench coat for a circus elephant.

I was sentenced to ten days alone in the attic. I knew that if I died, or if my baby did, nobody but the other wards would call it a tragedy. Malvina would moan about the extra paperwork, and feel sorry for herself. I was afraid I'd begin my labor and that nobody would hear me. "If that is God's will, there is nothing to be done," Malvina had told us flatly after Zintka's stillbirth. While I passed in and out of consciousness, her voice rang like their heavy bells in my ear:

"This Home endeavors to keep our girls surrounded with such a cheery, congenial atmosphere, that upon returning to their own homes they find they have grown entirely away from their old environment of evil and ignorance."

This Home endeavors to keep our girls surrounded—

The straitjacket chafed so badly that I grew delirious with the desire to itch. That first night, I could imagine nothing else but scratching my skin, shredding it like tissue. Unwinding my outsides to the bone. Torture takes every desire from you until the best thing you can imagine is the cessation of pain. If I'd been given the choice that first night I would have begged God, or Anything Listening, to snuff my mind like a candle. It was only the kicking baby inside me, the clock of another life waiting for us beyond the attic, that kept me praying to live until dawn. The second day passed and I spent every minute repeating this prayer. There was a single cushion on the attic floor and ancient blankets that smelled of other mothers' sweat and piss. No bed would have fit in that triangular cell. I wormed my way over to the small window and discovered it was nailed shut.

I read the graffiti on the wall—*Mother, I do not know where I am. Sylvia was here*—another heartbroken girl. *Another twenty-four weeks in this hellhole.* Someone, or several people, had clawed the plaster from the low ceiling. Someone had prized a nail from the floorboards to etch these words, perhaps at the beginning of her labor, perhaps while pacing in the middle of a long night. I might have done the same, had my arms not been bound to my sides by the straitjacket.

It was Nurse Elaine who came to check on me twice a day, at dawn and twilight, her tawny head poking through the door like a scowling gopher. "Pray with me," I begged, hoping to convince her to free my arms. She'd tiptoe over and murmur a perfunctory Our Father or two, our hands threaded together. Gradually her hands relaxed. It felt like a rope going slack. She sighed once and went off script, saying, "This isn't right, is it? But there's nothing much I can do about it."

"You could let me out of the jacket," I suggested.

"I could do that." She repeated this slowly, as if she were trying to coax a horse out of its stall. In her shoes I imagine I would have been terrified as well. Nurse Elaine had a decent-paying job, a government job, and for a woman in Milford those were hard to come by.

"I won't tell anyone."

"You better not."

She fumbled with the wide belt, cursing softly and avoiding my eyes, then fled back down the ladder as if she were escaping a fire. I heard the bar slide shut behind her. I flexed my fingers, crying out as the feeling flooded back into my arms. I limped over to the tiny window, where I could glimpse a wedge of yellow moon. The attic prison was directly above the Superintendent's bedroom, and I'd heard stories about girls screaming for help only to be gagged by the groggy, furious Superintendent. My baby was kicking so violently inside me that I worried something was going wrong, and still I would not call for help, terrified of the gag and the straitjacket.

That night I slept on my side with my hands clasped over my navel. I still sleep that way. Lovers have told me that my fingers never loosen, even when I'm drooling on the pillow. Two years later, riding the rails with Kettle, I woke in a freezing freight car to a man trying to tug my bindle free from my arms. My eyes flew open, and he screamed in my face. "Gawd, I thought you were dead! You got fingers like claws, lady. What's in that bag, rubies?"

It was my baby's blanket and a pair of lopsided goldenrod booties I'd made for him in Milford. I had become a prairie witch, but I was still his mother.

⚎

Three days after my confinement, my water broke. None of the girls' stories could have prepared me for the joy I felt. My mouth stretched wider and wider into a song. Every spasm of pain tunneling through me was something welcome, something I'd been waiting for months to feel. Contractions dynamited through me. I was a mountain getting blasted apart so that light could pour out, so that my baby could exit my body. Pain is never any one thing, it is always moving. To my great happiness, I could tell by reading the faces of the doctor and the two nurses, my labor pains did not mean I was dying. Today was the day I would meet my child. The Nurses continued lecturing me up until the moment that my baby crowned.

"No," I said, my fists held up to my face. "No, no, no, no. I am keeping my baby."

"Is that really the best choice for the child, dear?"

"Is that the loving choice?"

Part of their strategy was to show us our own faces in the mirror and call them dirty, ignorant, incompetent, sinful. Selfish, for wanting to raise our own children. From the day we arrived at Milford— and on the planet, in some cases—we were told that our babies would be "better off with someone else, someone better equipped to give a child a good life." Some of us wished to do just that. Others relented and signed their papers. Others, like me, never agreed to give their babies up.

They treated us as if we were patients burning up with private shame, bodies *more sinned against than sinning*, souls in need of redemption. There are many happy adoption stories—women who choose to give their babies to caring families. But too many of my friends at the Home gave up their babies because they were forced to do so. If you do not have the power to say no, your yes is meaningless.

The happiest moment I have ever lived was when Nurse Jonquil put my slippery son on my chest, alive. Memory makes me our observer. I see my younger body on the bed nursing my newborn with his shock of black hair, a bird's-eye view. It is only my memory. A memory is never equal to the moment that spawned it. It tells me less and less as the years pass. His scent vanished from the cloth. His fresh-born smell is lost forever. I can conjure his dark, astonished eyes but not his tiny body's odor. In dreams, sometimes, I come closer.

I wonder now if I was drugged. The sleep came on so suddenly and did not lift until close to noon the following day. The curtains were sheets of gold when I woke. Panic shook me awake. I felt the madness of full, leaking breasts and no baby inside me or sleeping on my chest. "Where is my son?" They told me, not unkindly, that my son had died while I slept. They said his body was on its way to the Blue Mound Cemetery.

"No," I said. I watched the nurses exchange a long glance. "No. You are lying to me. Where did you take him? I told you that I want to keep him."

It was in that moment that I became a witch.

Sunshine poured through the windows of the makeshift hospital. It was so quiet in the room. I looked up at the wall of their faces, which wore theatrical looks of sorrow and pity and concern.

"I know he is alive. Bring him back from wherever you've sent him."

After that, there are many gaps in my memory. I remember a struggle with the visiting physician, a long needle, an injection and another snowy omission. When I woke a second time, I escaped them. What I recall is that I was all-body. Nobody expected me to move a muscle, which is how I got away. I pretended to fall asleep and when I heard the last nurse leave, I rose and put on Jonquil's coat and left through the back door of the birthing room, walking as steadily as I could toward the road. Someone whistled at me from a passing Model T and I kept walking. I still felt torn apart from my long labor; whatever sedative they gave me dulled that pain, however, because I must have walked eight miles in the falling dark. I was going to find the police and get them to arrest Malvina. My thoughts thinned to a moan, and after another mile the sun was nearly gone and I could only see to the next cottonwood tree, zagging in this way up and down the empty road.

The sky had turned artichoke green, as it does before tornadoes. I heard a stray baying at the early moon east of the chicken coop. *Run for your life*, said a deep voice inside me. It sounded so much older than I was. Older than humans, the voice from under the stones. Perhaps the angels were counseling me also, but I could not hear them over the tornado.

I obeyed. I ran.

To be pursued by a cloud is a terrifying experience, like trying to outrun a forest fire, a predator that could not see or hear or smell me, that would consume me without realizing it. Hunger without a body to contain it. Hunger nourishing itself with anything in its path, trees and dams and sheds and silos and entire barns. Something slid down my leg, wet and dark. My head roared as I ran, until I could no longer tell where any sound was coming from. Even after the howling was miles behind me and the sky had resumed its blue humming, I kept moving.

How long did I run before I realized that nobody was looking for me?

I saw my baby's absence everywhere. In the graveyards and the train yards and the fairgrounds. The gray spaces between tombs and trestles. Balloons were empty, knotted wombs for years after they stole my baby, blue and yellow and green and red, loosed and lifting into the empty sky. I imagine I will go on seeing that absence until I die, or until my son and I find each other again.

When I finally reached the town, I discovered that I was too afraid to ask for help. I saw my dirty reflection wearing Jonquil's stolen coat, my skirt stained with mud and blood, and my triangle thoughts returned. If I went to the police, I'd be standing in the attic again before sundown. Who would believe me? Why should they? The Home was a powerful place and the people of Milford preferred to believe it was a charitable enterprise. Many in the area had some connection to the Home, and looking into these crimes would have shown them their own faces. You can understand why an investigation was unpopular.

War is being waged in Milford at the Industrial Home for Unwed Mothers. It is a contest for the future.

They wanted to take my conviction that my son was still breathing. Not stiff and blue, but screaming his life, naming himself from that first rattling breath. My baby was taken from me, and I know this has happened to many other women. It is happening to someone today. They do more than take our children. They destroy our sanity. They twist our memories. I held on to what I could. I gave birth to a healthy son. They stole my baby. I hold on to what I know is true.

Asphodel Oletsky

"I believe you," I told Antonina Rossi.

Harp Oletsky

As we drove toward the Grange Hall, I noticed that the sky was blue on the main road. Today it was everybody's blue. I felt a great happiness. All this time, I'd had a role to play—a destiny, some big hat would call it. Some larger story was playing out here, and I was just a crumb of it.

As I kept vigil each night, I'd started to realize that I'd been asking my questions from the wrong position—from the center of the field. Imagining, like Job before me, that I was at the heart of the mystery. What did the whirlwind do to Job? It spun him around to see the breadth of the earth. Forests and mountains, rivers and stars. Whales, crocodiles, hippos, eagles. The storehouse of the snows. The green womb of water. Suddenly Job could hear the voice of God everywhere—not only in the whirlwind, but in all creation. Job got pulled out of his suffering and his confusion, out of the middle of his mind, and replanted with a universe inside him.

When the whirlwind set Job down again, he was still in Uz, but his field of vision had been transformed. My papa's deposit had spun me around too, and shown me where to throw my crumb. The bubble of luck meant something different to me now that we had found a purpose for it. Allfrey had developed her unsettling pictures. Dell and Antonina had pieced together their secrets. With their help, I wrote the speech in my pocket. It was the beginning of something. By the lights in the fallowland, I could almost make out its shape.

Dell teases me for being simpleminded. She tells me I keep repeating things under my breath "like a kid learning the alphabet." But I don't want to forget again. After I withdrew my papa's deposit, I felt shame like lead in my pockets, dragging me down. But I had also recovered a chance to put things right. It was not too late for that.

I'd practiced my speech in front of the washroom mirror. I wanted to share this new clarity with my neighbors. The story we taught our kids and dramatized with silly hats during the Founder's Day pageant—that story was killing everything. There were cavities in Uz's story that needed to be filled in, before a more permanent collapse occurred. We had to look at the real origins of this blowing soil, this degraded land. Sheriff Iscoe was not the only man with blood on his hands. I would hold up mine to show them, and make a beginning.

That morning, the kitchen had been filled with yawns and sleepy laughter. You could hear the change in pitch after the coffee was served. My niece's wild voice shouting invectives against the Sheriff. She thinks that Founder's Day will be like a Home game. A big win for our team. I don't know what is about to happen, but confetti seems unlikely.

Founder's Day always falls the week before an election. Balloons seem to flock across the sky like birds, traveling in bursts of yellow and purple and green. When I was younger, I looked forward to it all year. The schoolhouse put on a pageant, always a little heavy on the allegory—some poor kid with a rashy face would get cast as "the Scourge of Locusts" and have to wear wax-paper wings; another dressed in brown from head to foot and starred in the villainous role of "Drought Unending." The prettiest girl always seemed to get cast as "Rain." One year, it was Lada.

All of Uz turned out to celebrate, bringing home-baked pies and cakes and pickled delicacies. When I was young we rode in on wagons festooned with bright ribbons and clanging tin cans. It had felt to me like a long wedding. We gathered in the sweltering hall to sit on hard benches and applaud old Grangers telling their stories, then we'd be released into colorful mayhem, spitting watermelon seeds and bonking each other with balloons. Customarily, descendants of the Fourteen Families take turns at the podium telling the same handful of stories. As the new Grange Master, I am expected to kick off this competitive nostalgia with an invigorating speech. My slot falls right before the Sheriff. Today marks the twenty-fifth anniversary of Uz County. At the time of our incorporation and first general election, those fourteen families were the only folks on the rolls. The largest population, 636, was recorded in 1918. Since 1931, we've lost more than a third of our residents. That year marked the beginning of the end for our brief boom times—just as a bumper wheat crop reached the elevators, the price plummeted. Twenty-one pennies per bushel, down from a high of $1.50 in 1930. The war was over, the Wheat Price Guarantee Act had lapsed, and suddenly we were doing twice the work for half the pay. Prices keep falling. Dozens of towns our size have already folded. Unless there is some great change, I do not see how Uz can make it to a thirtieth anniversary.

"Do you think the Sheriff will be there, Uncle?"

"I certainly hope so," I said. "I want to see his face when Allfrey unveils her photographs."

"Do you think he will retaliate? Open fire?"

I shook my head. "Vick is a bully. But at his core, he's a coward. Besides, it's hard to win an election if you start murdering your voters."

Now that we were finally rolling toward the Grange Hall, my fear disappeared, and suddenly I was champing at the bit to deliver my speech. The truth was on my side, and perhaps more important, any fool could see from the cracked dead earth that the way we'd set things up was not working out for any of us. My happiness swelled until I could barely hear the others' voices. I guess that should have been a warning.

"Uncle! Watch out, you almost hit that pothole—"

The dust went whipping like a tail across the lot behind the Grange. I parked the Dodge and started unloading boxes with Cleo. Several of my neighbors exited their cars just ahead of us and waved at the Gutawolskis as they crossed the cottonwood bluff on their horses. I could hear the band warming up, the horn section making a big-bellied guffaw, a lone flute climbing its ladder of notes.

"Look at Harp Oletsky, all dolled up for his big speech!"

Grayson jutted out a hand, which I took reluctantly. Behind me, my niece and Antonina were helping Cleo carry her prints into the Grange. My gut twisted with a swooning sort of excitement, the way I felt as a kid looking down from the hayloft. In five minutes, the ceremony was scheduled to begin. Urna, in her flouncy hat, gave me a curt nod from the second row. My face went hot with shame. I'd intended to ring her up, and then my guests had arrived. I had no words to explain how full my time had become.

"Urna, please forgive me. I owe you an apology. I have had a strange few weeks."

"I can see that." She looked from Cleo to Antonina, and I could not for the life of me think what to say. Instead I did a crazy thing. I lifted her hand and kissed each rosy knuckle. Her laugh sounded shocked and embarrassed—but not only that.

"Urna, come to my house. Any night you like. I have a speech to deliver now but, ah, assuming all goes well . . ."

The audacity of my invitation was not lost on either of us. Asking for second chances. Asking Urna to assume a good outcome might still be possible. Not only that—to plan for it. She gave me a wary smile, her knuckles pressed to her lips.

Then someone whistled sharply right behind my left shoulder. Three brawny young ladies tugged me toward the stage. Dell's teammates, and Dell herself. They started fussing with my hair and shirt collar in front of God and everyone.

"Okay, I think that looks pretty spiffy, Uncle."

My niece adjusted my bow tie. I did not point out that her own broad face looked like a scarred pan. Long nasty scratches ran down her shins. A pluming bruise on her cheekbone, ribbons of skin around the welt.

"Where was the ref on *that* one?" I asked, touching her face gently, amazed that she'd permit me to do so. She squeezed my shoulder, as if I were one of her teammates.

"Good luck, Uncle."

At the podium, I felt light-headed. I had the feeling—as I always do when speaking publicly at any level—that I was stepping into the center of a bull's-eye. Men and women lowered their punch cups and turned to face me. Throughout the crowded Grange, I could hear children getting shushed and whacked.

"Welcome to Founder's Day, everybody. Happy Birthday."

Someone sneezed. In the distance, I heard the lowing of a disturbed cow. I looked down at my notes.

"We'll be getting the program started here in just a few minutes, but before we do, I wanted to—as Grange Master—I wanted to

introduce Miss Cleo Allfrey, the Resettlement Administration photographer sent here to take pictures of us. The folks in Washington sent her to 'show America to Americans.' Miss Allfrey's going to
share her photographs of Uz County. She's going to, well, she's going
to introduce us to a new way of, I guess, seeing—of seeing ourselves,
and this land."

Cleo Allfrey

I smiled at the sea of White faces that studied me, clearly skeptical of their grange master's claim.

"—of seeing ourselves, and this land."

The light in the hall felt syrupy and slow. Light is the first thing I notice. Even before faces and guns. Scanning the room for danger, I found plenty to fear. As the crowd prepared to move on from me to my photographs, I saw faces sour with polite unease, faces boiling with anger at my presence in their Grange Hall, faces blank as stumps. Sometimes, those are the scariest. The Sheriff was nowhere to be seen. Maybe he was practicing *his* speech, like I'd caught Harp Oletsky doing that morning in the washroom. His last chance to make a pitch to the voters. HAPPY BIRTHDAY TO UZ! read a sagging banner over the lava-red punch bowl. 25 AND STILL ALIVE! A town two years younger than I am.

I scanned the Grange for warmth and refuge too, and I got smiles from Hester Brophy, a Black woman who'd introduced herself to me earlier, along with twin girls in polka-dotted skirts. She was the wife of an Irish-Canadian tenant farmer.

"The color line is not so firm here as it is elsewhere," she told me frankly, "because we all need each other, and because there are so few of us."

I counted seven darker-skinned faces in a room of two hundred. Uz was an almost all-White town, and the commemorative pamphlet confirmed it, celebrating "the racial assimilation that has occurred since our town's founding." A column inside the pamphlet broke down the population into two categories: "Native White Americans, and the foreign-born." *Native White Americans*. The Black residents of Uz went unrecorded in the pamphlet.

Harp had barely finished talking when the Mayor came striding toward me. His big horsey teeth were bared. He wanted to show me how very welcome I was.

"Hello, Miss Allfrey! We are delighted to host you today on the twenty-fifth anniversary of Uz. What serendipity, your timing."

Displays of power can take many forms. Perhaps he truly only wanted to be a gracious host. Perhaps I was wrong to interpret the Mayor's welcoming smile as another way of showing off his fine sharp teeth.

"We've all been curious to see your photographs." He winked at me. He wore a checked jacket and a yellow cravat. His outfit was inspired, he said, by the prairie grouse. "I am sure you made many fine portraits of decent people."

He loomed over me. We stood toe to toe. Now his smile came down like a harrow.

"Thank you for the invitation to show my work," I said, slipping off.

It was a temperate day for Uz, eighty degrees in the shade. I felt stains spreading under my armpits and rubbed at the dried lavender in my suit pocket. Soon everyone would see whatever the Graflex Speed Graphic wanted them to see. Even I couldn't be sure what was happening to the photographs under their covers. These prints had held their poses for a day and a night, but I was not ruling anything out.

I had curated this show for the Uzians, but I did not feel the work was mine. Sometimes, I'd accidentally been its enemy. Overexposing the film, bungling the temperature of the developer fluid, failing to agitate the solution in the tank properly. Too hot, too cold, too fast, too slow. Often the ideal conditions only reveal themselves to me in hindsight, after I hold up a ruined print and see what I should have done for it. It is incredibly hard to make a picture that even approaches what you saw through the lens. "On your luckiest days," Roy Stryker told me, "the camera will see beyond your intentions. It will see more than you can."

My handwriting looked stiff to me on the banner we'd hung above the prints: NEW WORK PRODUCED BY QUANTUM CAMERA, ACROSS THE PLAINS OF TIME.

"Cleeeeo All-fry?" I heard a woman drawling. "Who is he? Is this his idea of a joke?"

"It's that colored woman that made them. A *government photographer*. You and me are paying her salary, Hannah . . ."

I raised my hand, and lowered my hand. Down came the curtains. Dell and several of her friends, squat and gangly girls from the basketball team, began unveiling my photographs. I stood behind a sea of heads, watching the Uzians contemplate the exhibition. People were jostling each other, gathered shoulder to shoulder in front of the wall of pictures. In the gaps between their bodies, I could see the eyes of future animals and people staring out at me. Some smiling back at me, through the finish that never quite seemed to be finished. It was almost too much for me. It was too much. I had felt crazy for so long, crazy and alone with what I was seeing in the darkroom—to hear these farmers and ranchers exclaiming over my pictures made me feel an inexpressible relief, something close to euphoria. If not necessarily sanity. Echoes of my own astonishment surrounded me, and I lifted onto my toes, up to my full height, watching the light from the high windows strum across my pictures. I began to feel less and less like a ghost haunting a darkroom and more like a seed lifting up through layers of earth, leaves and blossoms tumbling free of me. Wonder surged through my soles to my fingertips and spilled into the hall.

Although this reaction was far from universal. Even this far from their jostling, I could feel the heat mounting around me in certain bodies, fanning out to my right and my left. A large man with an eraser pink face seemed on the brink of collapse, his breathing shallow and urgent. Another kept rubbing his hand along the rim of his glass pie plate, as if some emotion inside him was filing itself to a point. What was it that these people felt, looking at the time-traveling photographs? I can only speculate. A dapper grandfather a few paces away craned around to meet my eye, fixing me with a look of pure hate. In other bodies, incredulity spilled over into laughter. Some women's shoulders shook with tears. A small yellow-haired girl beside me held her braids aloft like wings.

A humming momentum was now gathering in the room. At the labor strikes I'd photographed in Vollum, I'd felt something similar. *Heat is energy,* I reminded myself. Anger had a purpose. Anger could remake the world, redraw the lines. Without my anger pumping through my veins, I might have slid out of the Grange Hall and disappeared down the road. I felt the atmosphere around me changing, murmurs swelling into a low roar. I tried to stay hopeful. I was afraid, but there was something larger than my fear.

While putting this exhibition together, I had spent hours considering each photograph. I wanted to help free Clemson Louis Dew. That was our shared imperative in the Oletsky house. But the Graflex was using me in another way—or that was my feeling, as I was sorting through the prints. I saw into what could happen next. I'd taken dozens of photographs of the skies over Uz, my attempt at an homage to one of my heroes, Alfred Stieglitz. The contact sheet felt like a grid of tiny windows onto heavens and hells here in Nebraska. Fiery skies torn apart by explosions. Gentle prairie sunsets. Cemetery skies like gray voids. Morning skies alive with soaring cranes. The Graflex exhumed memories of the land where I'd made them. It also seemed to produce visions of the land's future. The land's dreams and nightmares of what might happen here.

Standing over the fixing bath I'd mixed, I'd watched ghastly scenes come into focus. Mink Petrusev's murder and disposal was only one of many atrocities the Graflex captured. I'd made contact sheets that showed horrors that left me reeling, undid my conviction that I was beyond surprise. I'd made blurry landscape portraits of what appeared to be the end of the world, or close to it. Tents sprawling for miles around a fortressed building. The dying grass crumpled under dying people. A wasteland where Uz stood today, bodies piled amid rubble. I could have put together an entire second exhibition with the prints I left in the root cellar. But these were the visions that I could see with ease in my own mind when I couldn't sleep. Not far off from what the townspeople saw when they opened the curtains. It took no effort at all to conjure a hellscape, not with dust raining from the sky. I wanted to show people that all was not lost.

I'd asked the farmer for his advice—he knew this town, after all. He held up a print of his own property, in which the barn and the wheat and the fence line had vanished. "I'd know that tree anywhere"—he smiled—"the burr oak. Look at that. It's full of kids." He laughed. "They don't look related, do they? Or do they? An unfenced future. Show them this one, Miss Allfrey."

I thanked him for taking a look, and he surprised me. "Miss Allfrey, I know as little about the future as a closed furrow knows about the harvest. But you can show us the seeds to cultivate. What can grow out here, in spite of everything we've done."

So, I chose to build my exhibition around the most beautiful scenes. The photographs that provoked me to reconsider my beliefs about what was possible in this life, what was true. That rounded out my understanding of what the past had been and contradicted my own darkest predictions for my future, our future. It was an impossible task, organizing the dozens of prints into anything coherent. I wanted this town to see clear water and intact prairie, healthy, intact people. What I made, in the end, was nowhere close to a complete record of what had happened on this land, and what might someday be. My selections are biased in ways I know about, and ways I surely don't. Even when—especially when—I myself could scarcely believe in them.

I felt the holes in what I put together, and wanted to share it anyhow. Here I found myself, curating my own propaganda for the future. *Roy Stryker*, I thought, *I understand you better.*

While I was observing the viewers of my pictures, I felt something brush against my shin and nearly screamed. An enormous tabby had gotten into the Grange Hall. It was purring like a thunderhead. It looked like one too, its belly taut as a basketball. The rumbling cat threaded between the legs of the farmers and sauntered right into the center of the hall, the patches on its fur telling some terribly incomplete story. It walked underneath the tables, casting a pointy-eared shadow, and then bounded straight for Antonina.

Antonina Rossi

Certainties can be transformed. Convictions can be overturned. We must believe this, Son, or else what are we doing here? I'd seen the twelve exposures of the Sheriff burning Mink's body in the sandhills, but I was as clueless as these Grangers as to what other visions from the past and the future might be hidden under Cleo's dustcovers. Unlike Dell, I'd never climbed down the ladder to the root cellar. I'd been too shy, or perhaps too self-protective, to ask Allfrey to show me her prints. I heard several gasps around me as Asphodel and her teammates removed the pins. These basketball girls had theatrical instincts; they lifted the silver dust-cloths at an angle, as if they were mouse-size curtains. I might have laughed if I did not feel suddenly dizzy with fear. Daring to look was all that the photographs required of us. Yet for whole minutes, I could not bring myself to do so. Instead, I knelt and rubbed Gladys Iscoe's cat between her ears. "Where have you been, Cat?" I was happy to see an old friend.

The girl touched my elbow. The cat and I both bristled.

"Come look at this one—"

Cleo Allfrey's "quantum photographs" took my breath away with their beauty. That was the first surprise. I had expected to see photographs of suffering and evildoing. The lynchings that went unrecorded in any newspaper. The mass graves and mountains of skulls. But when I forced myself to look, the first picture I saw was a peaceful scene on the Loup River. A spring day of good weather, the leaves furled tight as sleeping bats on some trees and shining flags on others. Pawnee women were watering their horses outside a huge lodge. Children were playing in the grass, and the clear river held tall reeds and a thousand swimming clouds. These exposures were full of ordinary, extraordinary things: sisters were cultivating squash and corn and beans, babies were yawning, sunshine swam along the gray river.

The last thing I had expected to see was joy. It struck me that this was a real problem. One photograph showed a table loaded with food under a stand of quaking aspens. A potluck, or so it seemed to me. Everything on the table reminded me of what the land gave to us—ears of roasted corn and loaves of bread, glistening berries and pitchers of water. Who was sharing with whom? The seats were empty, waiting for the guests. Allfrey had captioned it *Plenty*.

More words were unnecessary. Every eye around me was blown open. I saw things that were unthinkable a moment earlier. Surprise is a good teacher. The Graflex Speed Graphic had made portraits of an abundance that looked nothing like the old boom times in Uz—no carloads of wheat next to the shanties and tents of Hoovervilles. Allfrey's shots were panoramic, but these were not lonely vistas, single farms set against the dying prairie. They were crowded with lifetimes.

Happiness and beauty and peace accused me just as forcefully, from the opposite direction. The enlarged prints were black-and-white but my mind supplied the color. Every face in the frame—whatever age, whatever race—looked relaxed and well nourished. Complex mosaics of prairie wildflowers exploded in the tallgrass, the beautifully varied and hardy crowd of perennials. The mystery of kindness.

What made me gasp were the images of the children, swaying from the overhanging willow branches and jumping into the river. Laughter boomed between the future and the past, ringing in my ears.

Behind me, I overheard Cleo fending off the Grangers' anxious questions:

"I don't understand. Are these photographs of what did happen? What will happen?"

"I don't know myself," she said. "But I'll tell you this much: I suspect we have more choices than we know."

"This is just more New Deal propaganda then! Ghost photography, like those Spiritist frauds! You're just trying to scare up votes for Roosevelt!"

"You are free to draw your own conclusions. For my part, I think the camera is showing us possibilities that could develop on this land."

I had expected to see horrors. Instead I saw laughter shining out of the eyes of a family gathered for a Black child's first birthday. The round cake blossoming with tiny pink and yellow flowers. Tidy writing that said *Happy Birthday Ann!* A single candle emitted a shimmering silver plume. *Audacious* read Allfrey's caption. Nobody was mugging for the camera. Nobody seemed aware that a photograph had captured the depths of their happiness, from what must have been—based on the old hussy lamps, the grandmothers' clothes—a distance of seventy years. They were free to celebrate the beautiful, living shadow of Ann's first year on earth. Another print showed what appeared to be a strange city, rising out of what I recognized as the Sandhills to the north of Uz. The print was black-and-white, but in my mind's eye I imagined every manner of blue, from midnight lake to mistflower. Plants I had never seen before surged heavenward, with leaves wider than the bridge over the Republican River, as big around as the beanstalk from a fairy tale. Giants lifting out of the soil. Each stem branched into platforms that supported small dwellings. Yes, it was a city, spawning vertically, circular rings stacked in the middle of the sky, a supple, living city on the Plains that rose into the clouds. Staring at the undulating photograph, I felt somehow certain that the plants themselves were its architects—some collaboration with human minds and hearts and thumbs.

The woman beside me began to cry. She was looking at a magnified photograph of a water droplet on a wide gray leaf, moving skyward as her eyes rode over it, drawn toward the rising sun behind the rows. *Lifeward* read Allfrey's caption.

I wish we had recorded the Uzians' reactions. They made a crazy music as they percolated around Allfrey's exhibition. Little gasps, terrified laughs. The large red-bearded farrier beside me had a coughing fit. Some responded with hiccupy jokes edged with confusion; some stared blankly forward; others seemed pink and shy with awe. Behind me, two men's incredulous voices were thickening into ridicule.

The Dudley family crowded in around the eight-by-ten-inch

print of a buffalo migration. Hundreds of bison were crossing what was clearly their farmland—we all recognized the landmark of the crooked centenarian oak. The Dudleys stood shoulder to shoulder, linked in a deepening silence. Mr. and Mrs. Dudley broke it to bicker—they couldn't agree on what they were seeing. Was it a picture of the land before their births, or after their departure?

I was mesmerized by two photographs that Allfrey had mounted side by side: a print of a pioneer family's dugout next to a Pawnee mud lodge with forty-odd people milling around it. I had not realized until this moment that a sod house—the symbol of the pioneers, proof of their courage and their ingenuity—was in fact a tiny copy of the Pawnees' architecture. The mud lodge had a round ceiling with a smoke hole, a single eye staring at the early moon. For a blissful window of time, I forgot myself. When I looked up, it felt almost like surfacing from a trance.

Sheriff Victor Iscoe was standing in the corner of the Grange Hall. He didn't seem the least bit interested in Allfrey's photographs. His face looked like his badge, blank and shining. He was staring right at me.

The Cat

You didn't think you'd hear from me again, did you? Believe me, I had no intention of returning to Uz. Had I not heard the voices of my children calling me home, I'd have jumped into a truck bed and found my way to another story entirely. You never travel out of earshot of your children. The foursquare, the prison—those awful places, I only thought I had escaped them. They traveled with me.

Sometimes I think: *What would my life be like if I didn't give a damn about anyone?* After a month on my own, crisscrossing the towns along the shallow river, I fell in with a migrant family on their way to Oklahoma. Good people, bad drivers. And I might have continued with them had I not witnessed a tragedy. A truck sent a clumsy land turtle spinning onto her shell. The turtles all seem clumsy to me, which I know is unfair. We cats must look like reckless lightning to a turtle. The truck swerved—not to avoid the turtle, but to knock into her like a bowling pin. I jumped out of the truck bed and came to her aid. Her hard yellow toenails could not find purchase on anything. Click! Click! Click! the toenails begged for help.

I butted at her shell with all my strength. It took three tries before I got her back onto her clawed feet. Gently, with my mother's skill, I removed the foxtail and oat beard matted to her scales. I spent the next seven days helping my new friend to get across the highway, up no less than seven embankments, through a sweltering field of withered alfalfa, and into the low water of a lake. One step per century. A rest every ten paces. "Goodness is its own reward," the turtle said, yawning and then disappearing under the water. I did not kill her. I do feel good about that.

It took some doing to get back here to Uz, Nebraska. As it turns out, our town is not a popular destination. But cats can be haunted, as surely as people. I discovered, very unhappily, that I could not escape. I have unfinished business with the man who drowned my babies.

The girl is my amanuensis. The farmer's niece. She is a little too pleased with herself. She thinks she is making me up. Look at her smiling in the front row of the Grange, taking a break from her fear, jotting this down in her green notebook.

What a funny idea! the girl is thinking to herself. *I wonder where it came from?*

It came from me, you idiot! The Cat!

Asphodel Oletsky

It was always disorienting to see my teammates costumed as ordinary girls. Valeria was dressed like a nun, in a black cotton dress, dark stockings, and pointy shoes. She was seated between Mr. and Mrs. Ramos a few rows from the stage, quietly reading the commemorative pamphlet, and I almost didn't recognize her. Thelma was holding her wild red hair hostage in a bun on the top of her head. Ellda, I saw with a stab, was wearing a polka-dotted dress and white dress gloves. She looked like she'd let candy melt on her face—"She looks pretty," Val had informed me while we were setting up the exhibition. "That's makeup, Dell." Ellda was seated between Pastor Robbins and her father. Her hands were trembling, holding a glass of fruit punch. I caught her eye and she waved me away; either she did not want my help, or she believed I'd make something worse. Dagmara was still standing with a rapt face in front of Allfrey's wall of skies. Some were perfectly clear and some almost opaque with dust—it burned your lungs just to look at them. These sky photographs were the least anchored in time and place and still they'd startled me with their variety. The cat was swaying between the rows of chairs, her tail held aloft. Only young children seemed to notice her. Most adult eyes were on my uncle, waiting for him to make sense of the exhibition. Near me I heard a man whisper, "If this is some kind of joke, Bert, I am not laughing." The hall felt like a held breath.

Cleo and I took careful steps up the old ramp to the oak stage, with its black and gold drapery. It makes every event here feel like a bumblebee coronation. I carried the photographs of Mink Petrusev and Sheriff Iscoe and his deputy, smudging the silver cover with my sweat. The plan was that I'd hold them up onstage when my uncle cued me.

"This will be a challenge for you, Dell," he'd told me. "I know you like to mouth off. But today you are furniture. Stand there, and hold the pictures. Today, I have plenty to say." Valeria and Thelma were going to help me, walking the rows with additional prints and making sure that nobody present could fail to see them. I scanned the room: no Iscoes. Where was the Sheriff? My shoulders rose, expecting hot air on my neck, hands around my throat. I waited for my cue.

Harp Oletsky

The whole room tensed like a body. Row after row of Grangers craned forward, fists on knees. A memory found me—my queasy father leaving the harbor, clutching his empty stomach. A sour, hairy taste rose in the back of my throat.

"We have all seen Sheriff Iscoe's advertisements," I began. I scanned the sea of weathered faces, half expecting to see my brother and my sister and our parents out there. Allfrey's photographs made my family feel alive to me. The dead were closer to the living than I'd guessed. But it was my niece who locked eyes with me, holding Allfrey's print and waiting for her cue. Her teammates were sitting in the front row, some wearing their ugly jerseys, others costumed as polite young women. My neighbors blinked at me, ruddy and vexed.

"Our sheriff's face plasters every window from the depot to this Grange Hall. But I, ah, I wonder where he is this morning— I sorta hoped we could invite him onstage to look at a few candid portraits made by Miss Allfrey—"

Was the Sheriff seated in the audience? Heads swiveled, searching for the Iscoes. The corner where I'd spotted him a moment ago was empty. When I'd practiced my speech, I had imagined staring right at Vick. His rival, Ernie Whitson, was sitting in the second row, looking like the happiest man in the Grange Hall. Ernie needed no persuading that Vick was an evil and lazy lawman.

"Get on with it, Harp," shouted that old bear Luther Hotchkin.

"Right. Okay. Vick—Sheriff Iscoe—as you all know, he campaigns on a certain claim, that a young violinist living in a hobo camp, without a job and without any kind of education—seventeen-year-old Clemson Louis Dew—is the Lucky Rabbit Foot's Killer."

The crowd started to murmur. I looked from my niece to Urna, from Otto to Antonia. I tried to swallow, but my mouth was as dry as these men's farmland.

"If it weren't for that Black Sunday dust storm, Dew would already be buried six feet under Grasshopper Hill. I'm here to tell you the kid is innocent. He had the misfortune of playing music near the depot on the evening that Vick was out looking for a scapegoat. If a Lucky Rabbit Foot's Killer exists at all, you can be certain he is not Clemson. We have proof . . ."

Dell held up the photograph of Mink Petrusev's body on the sandy ground near the lightning-split cottonwood. Sheriff Iscoe and his deputy, Percival, stood beside her, their faces blank as their shovel heads.

"The rabbit's foot—it was a magic trick the Sheriff used to stitch up half a dozen open cases. A trinket was found near the body of Nina Rose and Olga Kucera, and Vick turned it into a grim totem. That detail made the papers, and it gave our sheriff a wicked idea—one of the few original ones he's ever had. He started planting rabbits' feet on every unlucky woman whose murdered body was discovered in and around Uz. He pinned all those unsolved cases on Clemson Louis Dew. A tramp without money or family, just passing through."

The Grange Hall was silent now.

"Clemson Louis Dew's confession was coerced. There is no Lucky Rabbit's Foot Killer. If you have any doubts about that, I want you to study these photographs—"

Dell slowly walked between the rows of chairs, showing the photograph of the Sheriff digging the burn pit with Mink's body beside him to the crowd. On the opposite end of the stage, Cleo Allfrey held up a copy. A man in the front row began to laugh at a hysterical pitch. A sound like helium exiting one of the children's balloons.

A few people joined him.

More people joined *them*.

"How much is Ernie Whitson paying you for all this, lady? Just days before the election and you drag Vick's name through mud—"

Antonina chose this moment to walk onstage. Was it good timing, or bad? She moved behind the podium, taking my place in the slash of light from the high eastern window. She wore an out-of-fashion dress with a heavy lace collar and faded navy stockings that she'd spent half a day darning. Garments on loan from Ania Oletsky. Her brooch looked like an old bar of soap. "I want them to take my testimony seriously," she'd told me when I questioned why she was rifling through my dead mother's trunk. I don't know that the witch really succeeded in convincing anyone that she was ordinary. Her black braid was already unraveling. Her inky eyes seemed to drink up the room. Briefly, they passed over me; I felt the pull of the deep place inside her. Her lips moved soundlessly, rehearsing the words before she finally spoke.

"My name is Antonina Rossi. You know me as the Antidote. Officially, I am not supposed to exist. For many years I have banked your memories. I am here to confirm what Harp Oletsky just told you— the Sheriff has been covering up murders in and around Uz County. He wants you all to think the case is closed, but an innocent man sits on death row and these murders continue—"

The laughter died down.

Something more dangerous than ridicule began to prowl around the room.

I stood at her shoulder, staring nervously out at the Grangers. Half her face was hidden by the sheaf of papers. But as she read on, we all heard her voice growing in power. She began with the transcription of the jurors' deposits. She moved on to the deposit of the greenhorn deputy, Percival Gander, describing the very scene from Miss Allfrey's photograph. Then she shared the Sheriff's lies, and the number of times she'd taken forced deposits for Vick in the jailhouse.

Anger crashed into the Grange. Smoke seemed to fill the Hall, swarming bees. I could not believe how fast the change came. How completely the feeling among us transformed.

"I thought you said you couldn't hear a word! That you blacked out what we told—"

"Liar! Why the hell should we believe you now?"

"Is this legal?" someone called nervously.

"Don't let this witch drag our sheriff's name through the mud!"

In a middle row, I spotted Percival Gander. He looked like he had seen a ghost. I suppose he had—he was staring at his face in the firelight in Allfrey's exposures. He stood up and raised a hand, as if he were still a schoolboy.

"Yes, Percy?"

"I visited the Antidote that night," he said, in a voice like a slow pour of oil. "With Sheriff Iscoe. I remember that much. I found a box of those little feet in my trunk, and I got a chill. It makes more sense now . . . what we were doing, what we . . ." Like a dog surfacing from a lake, his whole body shook. ". . . what we'd done."

Suddenly it looked like young Percy was going to be sick.

"I can show you the rabbit's feet! Don't let them pin this on me! It was all the Sheriff's idea! I was just following orders—" Percy turned a full circle, maybe looking for someone to agree with him.

One of the jurors, Peter Haage, looked like he was having a seizure. Another walked onstage, with a face as tight and blank as a balloon, and without warning drew back a hand and slapped Antonina. I took him by the shoulders—it was my old friend Elwin McPhee. He stared at me with wounded eyes. "Don't let this bitch stand up here telling lies about me, Harp!"

He sounded so convinced of his innocence that, for a moment, I questioned her testimony myself. When I turned to Antonina, her terror credentialed her. Her business prospects in Uz were forever ruined. She was risking her life. *Oh dear,* I thought, staring into her lined face, her sad horsey eyes. I had come to care a great deal about the former prairie witch. I knew what she planned to say next, and I almost stopped her.

April McPhee, a sturdy mother of six and Elwin's wife of thirty years, came onstage to help Antonina up. She cussed out Elwin at the top of her lungs. "How long have we known Vick?" she asked. "Would anyone here be shocked if he did what he's accused of? We ought to get that young man a good lawyer. It's Sheriff Iscoe who belongs in a cell!"

In her clear, calm voice, she did what I had been unable to do. She got the room on our side. The speed of it frightened me. A mob swings like a fist. Many times I have experienced the fickleness of the crowd's support. But I had always been part of the crowd, riding the pendulum composed of my fellow Grangers. Never once had I been on this side of the podium. Staring out at the familiar faces in the

Grange Hall, I felt a cry rising up in my throat. It lifted me onto my toes and everywhere I heard it repeated:

"Justice for Clemson!"

"Jail for Iscoe!"

"Justice for Clemson!"

"Jail for Iscoe!"

The Sheriff was nowhere to be found. I glanced nervously at the rafters, as if he might be hiding there, ready to swoop down and tear out my throat. There was only a frizzing, ancient nest.

People seemed excited by their fury. They were out for Iscoe's blood. They were with us, even the ones who had originally seemed ready to hang Antonina. For the moment, we were a chorus. But I had more to say.

Antonina Rossi

An eye can reject what it sees, just like a stomach retching. A pupil can contract violently and gag back tears. When Harp started talking, I braced myself. But they believed us when we exposed the Sheriff. Our plan was working.

Harp Oletsky

My parents claimed their land here in Uz in 1904, moving west from the Polish colony of Krakow. So did many of yours."

I saw the faces of men who I'd known since boyhood, beaming up encouragement at me. Big-eared Henry the harness maker and his sons in the second row; my little goddaughter, Nancy Goerentz, beside my best friend, Otto; Frank's first boss in town, Paul Easter. Friends who had voted for me to deliver some inspiration today. It was better, I found, to look down at the paper.

"We all know the same facts about the founding of Uz. Our parents left Krakow to homestead the free lands available to them as Kinkaiders—six hundred and forty acres! More land than most had ever owned. These Founding Families were quickly joined by other newcomers from Europe, by Americans from the Southeast, the Northeast, the Midwest. Two years after Uz was first platted, the town had tripled in size and become a spur line on the Union Pacific. Uz officially incorporated on this day twenty-five years ago with 215 residents. About the number we have standing in this hall today—"

Murmurs passed around the room. We'd lost so many since last year's celebration.

"But you may not know that those original families made a promise to each other. The 'Founder's Pact,' they called it."

I recited the words to the Grange Hall—as best as I could recollect from my father's deposit—the pact of exclusion.

A low grumbling filled the room as my neighbors took in the ugly words. I pressed on.

"Later, they made a second pact, which was to forget . . ."

Without fanfare, stammering when I hit a pothole in my own understanding, I shared the memories I had recovered from my father.

"I understand why he chose to put all this out of his mind, friends. He couldn't live with what he'd done to get the land. He kept his deposit a secret from us. A private affair. But when many thousands of us decide to forget the same truths, what happens? Look at what is happening to the soil without roots. We are the children of these crimes of memory, and we go on committing them."

"*We!*" someone shouted, with a mockingbird laugh. "A man talking nonsense should speak for himself—"

"We Poles," I continued, "we 'people of the Plains,' know what it means to be carved up by Empires. Well, the land on which Uz is built belongs to the Pawnee people."

I looked over to my new friends for encouragement, but the women's faces made me even more nervous.

"My Polish father," I continued, "grandson of the Partitions, understood his new role in America on his very first day in Nebraska. He found himself living a horror story—a gentle man who had fled the German persecution of the Poles only to find himself a soldier in an invading army. Not every attack comes in the form of a military ambush. Not every battalion is made up of trained men. The U.S. government mustered so many things. Armies of cattle, armies of pale children. Fence lines crept from sea to sea. Forests of wire. Railroad spikes were hammered into the grassland."

I told them how we were planted in the arid western lands by the Kinkaid Act, while Natives were removed or forced onto reservations, their lands divided and sold and given to light-skinned newcomers. How the goal was to turn "wasteland" into profit, to transform grassland into steaks and leather and wheat for export. *To turn Native lands into White ones.* Our grandparents and our parents settled across Native lands like a snowbank, and when the spring thaw came, there was a crop of kids like me, like us, with no memory of anything but our childhood on the prairie.

"My papa knew all this," I said. "He had lived a similar story. This knowledge swelled in him like a bruise for years, shutting up his eyes.

When he could afford to do so, he paid a Vault to hide what he saw so clearly in 1873."

My voice cracked as I described the conflagration of rumor, started by my father—his idea to keep settlers from coming to take the unclaimed lands west of Uz. I explained how it had led to a man's murder, and may well have provoked other violence I did not know about. The cradle that I slept in, I told them, was built of stolen Pawnee timber. My father cut down his Pawnee neighbors' trees, I said. Then he clearcut his own memories. He died without the knowledge that he, along with the other founders of our town, had set aside.

Otto was waving frantically at me. He wore the same face I'd seen when I'd been dragging cable unawares on the Spider, in mortal danger. I watched my niece walk over to Otto and take his hand. *Settle down*, she mouthed. Not the phrase I would have chosen today, but it seemed to work. Otto rolled his eyes at me, let his arms drop.

"We share a responsibility," I said, "as the children of the Homestead Act, the Dawes Act, the Kinkaid Act, to right these wrongs. If we don't, we'll grow as soul-sick as this dusty air we're breathing."

The room was quiet. *Should I leave it there? Open the floor for discussion?*

"I have been searching my own conscience," I said. "I may be your grange master, but as you folks know, I barely finished my schooling. Even so, a child of five knows the right thing to do—if you steal something from someone, you give it back."

"A five-year-old is a helluva lot smarter than you!" someone yelled. I tried to ignore them, although heat pushed into my face.

"Now, I don't know exactly what it's all going to look like but, well, the Pawnee reservation in Oklahoma is a six-hour drive south of Uz—"

"Everything the Founders did was perfectly legal," Mr. Unger cut in. "It's a shame, what happened to the Indians, but it's over and done with."

"If we give everything back, we'll have nothing!"

"All right, Willa. That's a fair point. What about, 'something'? There's a lotta room," I said, "between 'everything' and 'nothing.' I wanted to open up the conversation . . ."

Dell was nodding at me with a ginned-up enthusiasm; I got a

sense of how she must coach her teammates. I can't say I felt much encouraged.

"What my father's deposit taught me is that there are many alternatives that we have never explored . . ." The paper was shaking in my hands. My train of thought kept jumping the tracks.

"There's got to be another way . . ."

Asphodel Oletsky

Sitting in the middle row beside Otto and his frowning wife, I watched my uncle's mouth moving. A buzzing in my head grew to an intolerable volume. Whatever he was saying was changing the faces around me. Flattening them into blanks, pinching cheeks, thinning eyes into angry slashes. The temperature in the Grange seemed to have dropped ten degrees since everyone was happily denouncing the Sheriff. Could my uncle feel the change inside of people from the stage? I felt proud to be his niece. And very afraid.

Harp Oletsky

Most of you saw Pare Lorentz's documentary film, *The Plow That Broke the Plains* when it played at the Aladdin last month. *Settler, plow at your peril!* I know that line ruffled some feathers in here—"

"It makes quite a difference if you're *actually from here*," Beth Lamb called from the back, to cheers. "And not some so-called experts scoring sappy music for our struggles in a Tin Pan Alley back East!"

"Well, sure. Although I will admit, Beth, I enjoyed the score. Bring your tissue box to the theater, haha . . ."

My niece was giving me a worried look.

"Right, well. That film, which comes from the same New Deal agency that sent us Miss Cleo Allfrey, blames our so-called Dust Bowl crisis on us, more or less. We plowed up the native grasses and nothing was left to hold the soil in place. Four hundred million acres, up and blowing! The Great Plains seemed inexhaustible. Yet in fifty years—my lifetime, friends—we lost all that tallgrass and shortgrass prairie, all those root systems holding the soil in place, all that fertility in the ground."

I suppose we were back on a familiar subject. I had their attention.

"Soil erosion isn't new," I said. "It was a problem for Jefferson. What was his solution? To send men west. To take land that belonged to Indians, and to give it to homesteaders like us. What happens after we run a spot dry? Get more land, and do it again. We don't have anchoring roots either, do we? Nothing strong enough to hold us steady when the market changes and money gets scarce. The stock market, as you all know, does not exactly harmonize with nature's cycles."

Something was helping me, I felt. My arms looked like gnarled branches, stiff and steady. The sheet of paper no longer trembled in my hands.

"Allotments carved up this huge rolling prairie—a grid of boxes fell on the Plains. Every man working his own furrow, for his own gain. Each of us striving to pass down safety to our children's children, each of us failing or succeeding in our separate boxes, with disastrous results for every living being now choking on dust. I grew up on the Oletsky section, trying to scratch out a living. What choice did I have? None—that's what I grew up believing. What choices do *we* have? That's a different question."

There was a little boy gaping up at me from the middle of the Grange, his head cocked like a clay-colored sparrow. He reminded me of the boy I'd been, listening hard without understanding much beyond tone. Staring over his head to the rest of the crowd felt like panning a stubble field.

"Most of us feel driven to continue. To feed our families, to stay ahead of debt. Some of us also wanted to get more money, more land, more power than we had at birth. I understand that. Nobody in this room set up the rules of the game. We win by them, or we lose by them. Pare's argument is hard to contradict—farmers plowed up too much land and opened it to the wind. Markets drove us. We can all admit that, right? Greed and fear and debt. Ignorance of the science, the conditions of the Plains, that 'high wind and sun,' the right farming techniques. Don't they think of us that way in Washington? Poor and ignorant, the college professors' words for dirty and stupid? But listen, friends—that movie, it starts in the middle of the story."

Crickets out there. In the front row, Urna coughed, somehow flirtatiously, and I felt encouraged; at least I had not lost everybody.

"I guess, the way I see it, you could tell the story of the Dust Bowl another way. You could widen the lens and say: this land is blowing because we stole it from the people who know how to care for it. Before we uprooted the prairie, we uprooted human beings. With our cooperation, the United States waged a war against the Indians, who were farming these lands long before our arrival, and—I think we can all admit—with much better results. Our war created the conditions for the dust clouds that swallow the sun. Now we're the ones forced to leave our homes—tractored off, dusted out, foreclosed on. It was a great collapse of memory that paved the way for our collapse."

"*War?*" shouted Orren Bledsoe. "Don't be so naïve. There were wars aplenty going on out here. The Indians were scalping each other long before *we* showed up . . ."

"Look around you," I said. "Some of you have lost your kids to this dust. All over Uz, people are losing everything dear to them, begging by the roadside—that is a tragedy. I'm not saying it ain't."

"So what exactly are you saying, Harp *Oletsky*?" called Karol Kaminski. Shouting my name like a finger-snap, like he was trying to wake me up. I heard the panic in his voice. He wanted me to get my spinning wheels back onto the road and out of danger.

"Just that, it's interesting to think on: *whose* eviction is a tragedy, an emergency? Ask Miss Allfrey here who she's supposed to take pictures of. Ask her bosses in Washington whose lost land tugs at America's heartstrings? Who makes lawmakers weep and approve the budget for our relief?"

"Say what you mean, Oletsky. What are you getting at?"

What exactly was I getting at?

What I *wanted* to say was that these so-called Okies who lost the lands they'd farmed for a generation, maybe two, were set up to fail. If the Pawnees had been permitted to stay on their lands—if the Ponca and the Omaha and the Otoe and the Missouria and the Lakota and the Dakota and the Cheyenne and the Arapaho and the dozens of other tribes had not been forced from their homes, "removed" to reservations—then maybe the Dust Bowl would never have happened. What color would the sky be today, if our government had respected treaty rights, instead of handing our parents this "free Indian land"? Drought would come—no doubt—but grass would anchor the sod. Healthy soil would hold rain in the ground. This dust would not be burying houses up to their windows, choking dogs and cows and horses, turning the sun a drunken red.

What I *wanted* to say was that now, now that we settlers are being moved off this land and resettled ourselves, we can see clearly what this system of ours produces: end-of-the-world weather and dese-crated earth.

What I *wanted* to say was that I'd soared as the crow flies inside my father's memory, and I'd seen more than he was able to see: the plow that broke these plains was the plow that broke my family back in German-occupied Poland: the plow of empire. The plow that displaces and murders people, tearing them from their homes. The plow that levels more than tallgrass. The plow pushed by people like me. Like my papa, I grew up believing that there was no other way for us to survive on this arid land. Could I imagine another way? Until my strange luck began, I had never even tried.

What I said was "Does it feel right to live as we do?"

The room went silent. Or not exactly. A humming rose from every corner. I hoped I was imagining it. People's lips were sealed. The vibration seemed to come from the center of their throats.

"This is a little hard to swallow, Oletsky," called Grayson. "Com-ing from the only one of us whose fields were *not* destroyed on Black Sunday."

Once, Wynne Jenke—the sweetly daffy pipe organist at St. Agnieszka—suffered a stroke midhymn and fell face down into the keys. I thought of her now as an alarming droning filled the hall. A toddler on his mother's lap plugged his ears and winced. I didn't know if this humming was something deliberate, my neighbors taunting me, or a sort of reflex. Maybe the humming people were communicating with each other, as insects are said to do.

"Stop that, please. Just a few more minutes, and then we will break—"

I shouted to be heard. At the podium, for just an instant, I had a vision: everyone in the crowd was wearing a bloody rabbit's foot on a collar around their neck. I was wearing one myself. I rubbed my eyes, and when I looked again I saw my neighbors and friends, their shirts tucked in and their pretty dresses ironed into sharp pleats, staring blankly back at me.

"Okay," I said, "let me try again. Can we continue like this?"

"Shut up, Oletsky."

"You want me to feel like a criminal? We proved up in 1881 and we've been ranching in Uz for three generations. Fair and square."

Waldowko's son shook his head, evidently disgusted with my speech-ifying. His father and I used to go fishing for walleye near McCook together in the old summer weather. The Waldowkos were one of the Fourteen Founding Families, and they always tell the same stories, dealing them out like a deck of playing cards. *There was no one when we got here, just grasslands and buffalo and Indians . . .*

A few men in the crowd were standing and turning uncertainly from the stage to one another, as if awaiting some command. It was not quite noon. In the corner, pies were oozing. I saw apple and chokecherry filling leaking onto the tablecloth. I saw a big cat with her hair standing on end, bright as a burning cinder in the doorframe.

"I am not singling out anyone in this room!" I shouted. "I have plenty to atone for myself, and I am only beginning to understand how deep my own part goes. I am saying we can start to take responsibility, we can change direction, together, we do not have to wait for our government—"

"You figure out how to make one wheat crop and suddenly you think you can tell us how to live? Go to heck, you old windbag!"

"Get that Bolshevik offstage!" Grayson called.

"Get the hook!"

I was beginning to suspect I might not be the Grange Master for much longer.

"We have chewed this soil to powder. The way we farm has to change. But so does the way we live, friends. Private failures make for these great catastrophes that hurt all of us, kill everything—like these dust storms."

I wobbled a little, staring out at the crowd. The feeling in the room felt like a fist ratcheting back. I cribbed from Roosevelt's Address to Congress on the AAA:

"I tell you frankly that it is a new and untrod path, but I tell you with equal frankness that an unprecedented condition calls for the trial of new means to rescue agriculture . . ."

"What new means are you proposing, Harp?"

"Yeah, enlighten us, Oletsky . . ."

Other jokes were sharpening into threats. I couldn't make out every word, but I understood what was happening inside my friends.

"I grew up believing that if you held the deed to your land, you could do whatever you pleased on it or with it. But dust doesn't stop at your property line, does it? It blows right over to choke your neighbor. What I do on my land will have consequences for you. Surely there's a better way to, to . . . We could get our pencils out, share some ideas?"

Asphodel and two of her teammates were moving through the crowd, holding up the prints from the darkroom under the earth: the photographs of the future, the landscapes with the strange metallic finish that never quite settled.

I was distracted by the blimplike cat. Out of the corner of my eye, I watched her walk the ramp; a moment later I felt her arching against my shinbone. Christ alive, how many times can a man lose and regain his composure in the span of five minutes? Was this damn cat going to upstage my speech by giving birth onstage?

"You don't have to take it from me. It may still be possible to retrieve what your relatives did, and knew, and saw—"

People were standing up with fists raised. Flying from the Grange, like dust shaken from a blanket.

"Hunt in your houses. Look for deposit slips—"

"Quit slandering our people! Get off your high horse, Oletsky!"

"Who does it help, to get everybody's blood up with these fake photographs?"

"It hurts to see the future," I heard Urna tell her friend Maureen. "We won't be here, will we? What good is all that beauty?"

Lips pulled back from teeth. I thought of land curling up before the plow.

"What precisely are you suggesting? That we give the land back? And then what, you idiot? What do we live on then? How will we live?"

How will we live?

It was a good question. Had it been intoned like a genuine question, it would have been the best one of the day.

"Did you notice that a third of this town has pulled up stakes and driven off? Half this room is about to get blown off the map—"

The outrage swung at me now. How easily the mob exchanges one target for another! Sheriff Iscoe was no longer circled in the bull's-eye: I was.

The faces of my neighbors became bubbles convulsing on the surface of a pot. Bubbles screaming as they burst. A chair came flying at the stage, falling a few yards short. I recognized the man who'd launched it as my old classmate Wayne Yeager, a veteran of the Great War who had fought in the same battalion as my brother. He was so angry he couldn't speak. The blue cords in his neck looked like reins that some cowboy was jerking.

"It's all right, Wayne," I said uselessly. "Please let me get to the next part of the speech—"

"Oletsky," he screamed at last. "I never would have had you figured for a traitor. You hate the country that your brother died for—"

I flinched at that, which made Wayne shake his head.

"Wayne, all I'm asking you to do is hear me out . . ."

"Shut the hell up, Harp!"

Cheers and curses. A nightmare scored for my neighbors' voices.

"Who does it serve, to dig all this up?"

"Liar! First you slander our sheriff, now you want to make a mockery of Founder's Day . . ."

"We got little kids in here, Oletsky! Watch your goddamn mouth!"

The Edmonson brothers lifted the table and dumped Allfrey's prints to the floor, while others tore them from the walls. I watched my neighbors rise to their feet, the people I'd grown up with, kindhearted people, hardworking people, frightened people, humiliated people, forgotten and forgetful people, who seemed to think they were the butt of my cruel joke. Many folks I loved, in their Sunday best, started stomping on the photos in a crazy dance, grinding their heels into the faces of people and animals, the full rivers and the clear skies. The buffalo migrating through time, circumambulating our ruin.

My niece—where was she? Panic squeezed my chest as I scanned the room and found only more furious faces. Antonina and Cleo were still beside me, watching silently as the photos were shredded. Four Grangers who I'd known since I was knee-high were standing at the building's only exit, blocking the doors.

"She's a fake, Doreen, don't be fooled by this hokum—"

"She painted the negatives!"

"It was vibrations that did it!"

"Burning and dodging. You can see where she manipulated the process, it's quite obvious—"

"I followed the Mumler trial, I can see your darkroom edits—"

"A cloud is forming outside—"

"Honey, a crowd is forming, get the girls to safety—"

"That coward Iscoe snuck out! I seen him driving off—"

"What is that sound? Did somebody shoot a cannon?"

I felt something thread between my legs and almost screamed. It was the cat. She looked up at me with rolling golden eyes and I'll swear before anyone that I heard a voice sound inside my head, a low purr across the floorboards of my mind. It said: *Farmer, run.*

I bent to stare at her in amazement. Time seemed to slow, or else my eyes sped up; I was aware of the spokes of sunshine turning inside the cat's pupils, the clear tube of each whisker. A second later I heard a crack that made my skull ache. A bullet had put a hole in the wall where my head had been a moment earlier.

Asphodel Oletsky

I thought they would kill us then and there. Even before the bullet hit the wall, I realized our lives were in danger. Fury flew at us from every direction. Several men rushed the stage and backed Antonina against the wall. Screams from other parts of the echoing room joined theirs as the crowd pushing toward us thickened: "I want my deposits back!" "She has been awake and listening all along—" "We can't let that bitch leave without paying for what she did!" This was what a bank run looked like.

The first man to hit her was Ellda's father. I tried to intervene, wedge myself between them. He looked down at me with disgust, furious that I had seen him hit a woman, which was when Ellda, Nell, Pazi, Valeria, Thelma, Dagmara attacked from opposite ends of the stage. It was nothing from our playbook. We kicked and elbowed our way into the knot of men, breaking it apart with our bodies. We ambushed them with shame—we were living mirrors, flying at them. We had the faces of girls they knew, the daughters of Uz, and when they recognized us some dropped their arms. Antonina got spun right in front of me for a moment, near enough to mouth "Thank you, girl." She slipped offstage through the space between Valeria and Pazi. I took off in the opposite direction, leading the men toward the open doors, running alongside the other Dangers, fanning out and threading back together, pursued by these men who had decided that old-fashioned decorum would not stop them from knocking young girls to the floor, trying to catch a witch.

Cleo Allfrey was just ahead of me, already outside the great doors and sprinting across the bare lot in the wrong direction, away from the truck. I could not blame her—there was no time to strategize an exit. A crowd of dozens poured out of the Grange Hall behind us, hurling curses. Stones would come next, and more bullets. I felt resigned to it, even as I vowed to keep running. It was like the heavy sense of defeat that overwhelmed me as the clock wound down in a losing game, when I felt a compulsion to press on anyway. We were going to fight for our lives, and we would lose. Someone grabbed me and pinned my arms behind my back. I thrashed and kicked and tried to bite—I recognized Red Iscoe's voice, calling to his brother that he had me. So easily, these might have been my last thoughts.

Antonina Rossi

I knew enough to follow the cat. She leapt from the stage, not very nimbly, given the pendulous live cargo in her belly. My mind had slowed and I had so much time now, it seemed, even as another shot was fired and the crowd burst into shouts and screams and a baby started wailing. Through an open window, I watched bodies pouring from the building and stopping dead in their tracks. Men and women with faces locked in fright, children with sleepy looks of shock, as if they'd been pulled from a dream into a burning building. It was such a curious sight that for a moment I forgot that I was fleeing for my own life and paused to watch. My God, what was happening? Why was everyone stopping?

People were looking straight up into the sky. An angel might have been descending.

The cat, who had already pushed her body through the window and emerged on the other side, looked back at me, clearly annoyed.

Jolly red-haired Art Cotter—a baker and a loyal customer who always brought me sand cherry cookies, who joked that he'd never met a lemon he couldn't turn into dessert—led a group of my former customers. He pointed at me and screamed at the top of his lungs, "Get that lying bitch. Stop her before she makes off with our deposits—"

I felt them coming for me without turning. Their shadows reached the far wall first. I scrambled onto a table and pulled myself through the window, falling gracelessly to the ground beside the cat and losing Ania Oletsky's shoe in the process. Cleo picked me up by my armpits, and with one bare and bleeding foot I ran and hopped toward Harp's truck. The cab was empty.

Across the lot I saw Red Iscoe dragging Dell toward a brown sedan. Jed sat in the driver's seat, watching with that granite face while Red and Dell fought each other. The wind picked up and lashed at us, seaming our eyes and our mouths. I raced to help her. "There you are," Red spat at me. "Everybody knows you're a liar now. You have some very unhappy customers waiting to get their lives refunded to them, Witch . . ."

There was a boom so loud it caused us all to jump. Lightning snapped green and yellow between the silos. Somewhere a rooster was crowing at 3:00 p.m. The dark came down and spread over the ground. Ozone flared our nostrils. The Iscoe brothers stared at the sky with open mouths.

"Dell," I breathed in the sheeting water. "It's *raining*!"

The men and women pouring out of the Grange Hall halted in the middle of the vacant lot as if running into an invisible wall. The huge sun-colored cat ran up the hood and the windshield to the car's roof and, with claws extended, jumped toward Red's upturned eyes.

Everywhere dust was becoming mud. We watched it rolling down rooftops and windshields, brick walls and striped awnings. Every gaze was on the cloud bank. Every chin tipped toward the storm. Even babies in their mothers' arms craned up. Red's screams did not cause a single pair of eyes to turn from heaven.

Dell managed to free herself and tumble loose through Red's passenger door. Together we ran for Harp's truck. She was fumbling with the keys while the Iscoe brothers stumbled behind her, a losing team desperate to recapture their advantage. When I looked behind us, the orange tabby was curled in the truck bed, grooming the staticky fur on her belly.

Rain! Rain! Rain! Were people chanting that word, or did I only hear it in my head? Falling onto my scalp and sliding into my eyes, changing the way I saw everyone around me. The meanest old men I knew were laughing. Children were sticking out their tongues and running in circles in the rearview as the engine roared to life.

Harp Oletsky

When the second shot was fired, I was too stunned to move. Someone was trying to kill me. People were screaming and shoving into one another, trampling those who fell. A golden balloon popped and people dove for the floor. Crawling on all fours, I reached the edge of the stage and jumped down to join the crowd pushing for the exits. A child who had been torn from her protector was wailing alone in the center of the Grange, and this was the last thing I saw before I blacked out. Someone or something had sent me sprawling—a luckiness I guess, because nobody had noticed me lying face down on the ground beneath the Founder's Day table. The hall was empty when I came to consciousness, a soiled tablecloth and shattered punch bowl on the ground and bits of shiny paper everywhere, scraps of past and future. A triangle of prairie dawn was stuck to my shoe. My head throbbed and it hurt to open my left eye. I groaned and rolled onto my side.

Thunder shook the windows, through which I witnessed a miracle.

In the yard of the Grange Hall, on a carpet of dying brown grass, a crowd of dozens stood in silent prayer. People were fanning out, catching the water on their outstretched tongues. I stood, then walked outside to join them. Single droplets became an even sheet. Everything was running paint. The dry air became moist skin. We were all united inside the rain. Something broke loose inside my chest and came rolling down my cheeks. I stood anonymously in the middle of the crowd that had wanted me dead only moments earlier. Every face seemed to bloom. To dilate in water. Just as quickly as my neighbors had turned into grimacing strangers, they now shook out of one state and into another, their faces wrenched around by cries of wonder.

The rain was falling down, down, down. Water returning to us from the sky is always moving lifeward. Rootward. Leafward. Thirsty earth welcomed the water home, bringing the rainfall down to the roots. The people around me broke into applause between peals of laughter.

Now I have seen everything, I thought.

A mob snuffed like a candle in the rain.

Cleo Allfrey

Harp Oletsky was standing in the downpour with his head tipped back. He heard Dell honking and turned to us, slowly, a nasty peacock blue bruise on his left temple. Dell swerved and screamed for her uncle to get in the truck. Relief waved through me, and I could feel how afraid I'd been that we would not leave this place alive. I'd reached the Dodge just after the heavens opened, astonished to spot Dell behind the wheel, amazed to watch the rain sheeting down the windshield as we sped toward her uncle. Harp stumbled up to the driver's side door. "Let him drive, Dell," I said—and to my relief, she slid into the passenger seat. Harp looked concussed, and still I preferred him behind the wheel—although to be fair, every face we'd passed looked similarly dazed. The same four men who'd been chasing us not ten minutes earlier now stood arm in arm in the rain, swaying and singing. "Customers of yours?" I asked Antonina as we sped by them. She nodded.

Harp drove with an arm stuck outside the window, the flat sail of his hand turning in the rain. "I owe you ladies an apology," he said. "That did not come off like I planned it."

Saved by the rain. Of all the things we'd failed to predict.

The low river had already risen several inches, and the cottonwoods were drenched and shining. Fantastically dark and swollen clouds raced toward us and seemed almost to converge above Uz, the two granaries staring straight ahead as they were half-erased by rain.

We made it back to the Oletsky place just before full dark. I felt so happy to be alive, happy to think of my negatives in the root cellar, safe from the mob. Wedged beside me, the drenched girl held a basketball on her lap, rolling it under her fingers. It was covered in mud, thin watery dirt that had transferred to her palms and the vinyl seat and the door handle. Another miracle: she could hold this ball under the sky to clean it when we got to safety. The wipers were frenzied, blindfolded in gushing water. A slow-blinking Harp Oletsky pushed his nose almost to the windshield, trying to find the road. I realized I was holding my camera in the exact same way that the witch held her earhorn and the girl held her filthy ball, using it to anchor me to my purpose, and I smiled. This life will surprise you. A month ago, I knew none of these people.

Harp parked the truck, and we ran for the covered porch. The cat went bounding out of the truck bed and disappeared into the wheat. The ripe stands were tossing like a great inland ocean. I tracked her ears and tail poking up in the spaces between the rows, then lost sight of her. She reappeared in the center of the field, using the scarecrow's hoist as a scratching post, her claws ripping at the fabric of his trousers. His wilted legs sputtered straw. I swear the cat swiveled her head and looked right at me, her yellow eyes glowing in the rainy dark. It spooked me good.

"Ca-at . . ." I murmured. "What is it?" She was arching like a copper wire against the scarecrow's blowing legs. The hairs rose on my neck. His silly grin above the cat's small, intelligent face made the straw man look even more lost than usual. A castaway in the middle of the field. Lightning seemed to harmonize with the cat's claws, shredding through the black sky. In the flashes between the rolling thunder, I saw the Sheriff's car. It was parked at a crazy angle beside the farmhouse, the door hanging open.

"It's all right," I whispered. To my mother, to the Lord, to the wind, to my death, to the cat—I don't know who I talk to in such moments. "Whatever happens now, it's all right. The pictures exist and people saw them. Someone will find my negatives underground . . ."

Was this true? I tried to imagine a young person in the future, climbing down the ladder, developing my film. Magically unruined, thanks to the spell of protection that I now felt eager to believe in.

Harp's headlights were still on, tunneling through the rain and up to the porch. A runway of light down which the Sheriff walked, stretching his arms behind his back, skipping the last step that hung like an overbite above the eroded soil and jumping down into the wild weather, waving us in with his pistol pointed at our foreheads. How had I believed that these pictures of mine could convince anyone of anything? I could not even get one man to holster his gun.

"Don't be shy, now," the Sheriff called to us. "Come in out of that tempest."

When none of us moved, the Sheriff continued his approach. He walked with his elbows pointed outward like the yards on a ship's mast. Windswept wheat tossed left and right. It felt like we were watching the Earth's turbulent dreaming. Everything looked blue around the weakly glowing lights.

Where was the spell of protection now? I don't know what I expected to happen. Maybe a hole would open up to swallow him. Maybe all the fury of the swerving dust would return to crush his skull.

"Get off my property, Vick," Harp cried out. He was rubbing his eyes with his fists, like a big child, as if he could banish the Sheriff the way you might clear your head of a sparkling heat mirage in the middle of the road. When the Sheriff did not budge, he turned and tossed the flashing ring of keys to me. "Get back in the car, everybody—"

"Now, what's your hurry? You've only just arrived!" The Sheriff followed us with his gun, beckoning us away from the rain-lost Dodge and toward his fortress on Harp's porch.

"How long have you been operating a brothel out here?" The Sheriff barked with laughter, and I saw that he was shivering in the rain, his shirt pasted to him. Vick Iscoe was much older than he looked on the posters.

"So you've all been staying at Hotel Oletsky. What a nice surprise. This makes my job a lot easier! Road conditions being what they are—"

For a moment all that could be heard were the dueling sounds of Iscoe cocking the hammer of his gun and me opening the camera and removing the dark slide.

"Don't shoot," we said at the same moment.

The Sheriff sprang at me. He fought me for control of the Graflex, toe to toe in the slippery fallowland. With a grunt I freed it, stumbling backward into Harp Oletsky. He caught me, spun me, and gave me a push in the direction of the root cellar. "Run—" he said needlessly. I ran and ran. Through the sheeting water, through the tall stalks that slapped at my legs. Losing my bearings in the wheat field with the rain on all sides. The Sheriff I heard crashing behind me, and I might have gotten away if I hadn't slid and fallen, twisting around to protect the open lens. I lay stunned on my back with the Graflex on my chest, water running into my eyes and mouth. "You can see the sky through a bull's legs out here," a farmer had told me at the Grange Hall. "What we have in abundance on this prairie is sky, sky, sky. Nothing to block heaven from reaching you, until this dust blew up . . ."

Through the triangle of the Sheriff's spread legs, I saw the storm that had enveloped all of us. He knelt and tugged the camera out of my grasp. I felt a ripping pain in my chest, as if he'd torn my heart itself loose. "Give it back!" I screamed, and the lightning seemed to echo me soundlessly. *Give it back!*

At first I thought I'd been killed by thunder, struck by lightning on the ground. The Sheriff pointed the gun at my camera and squeezed the trigger. Sound burst between my ears and rattled every bone in my body, the earth below me. Twenty yards from where I was lying, the camera exploded. Glass and metal came raining down around the field. I hid my face and tried to crawl, thinking I might disappear into the wheat as the cat had done. The Sheriff came and jerked me to my feet. My shattered lens lay in pieces on the ground. I saw shards flashing as the Sheriff pushed the gun into my spine and marched me toward the others.

Antonina Rossi

Rain lashed at us and made it almost impossible to see out. When lightning flashed, I recognized the grief on Cleo Allfrey's face as Vick marched her toward us through the muddy field. She picked her way around the fragments of her broken camera, skirting an old rut that had filled with water.

The Sheriff's boot plunged right into it. He lost his balance and a creature chose this moment of weakness to attack, leaping out of the bending wheat. We watched Vick scream and kick at—what was it, a jackrabbit? A rusty blur, its long ears torn off. No, not a rabbit, after all—the pregnant tabby, who flew before Vick's boot toe could touch her. He did not recognize the cat as his family's pet. His former hostage. Or if he did, this knowledge did not lower his gun. The bullet clipped her ear and buried itself in the ground.

"You're a lousy shot, Vick," I said. "I wish I'd known that sooner."

To our collective astonishment, the cat stood and ran straight for him a second time. She pushed the blood-wet triangle of her ear against Vick's leg, smearing herself across his fine gray Founder's Day trousers before bounding off into the wheat field. In the middle of my terror, I was impressed. The mother cat had left her autograph. Part of the blown off orange ear clung to the fibers of Vick's pants, adhered by red glue. I was awed by the grace of her escape, with all her living cargo inside her. The wheat field thrashed beneath the forking lightning; its golden ears drummed against the ground.

The Sheriff motioned me forward with his free hand. He used

his gun to trace a line between Cleo, Dell, and Harp. Out in the
fallowland, the scarecrow danced wildly on his stake. Its sackcloth
face turned translucent for an instant, like cornsilk pulled in a clear
shroud over its milky kernels. Something was shining behind the
doll, inside the doll. Something distinctly Other than sackcloth and
straw. I saw it for an instant, but there was no time for marveling.
The Sheriff was a humiliated man. We had exposed his evildoing
and his incompetence; I felt certain the latter had angered him most.
The Sheriff threw his arms wide open, advancing slowly toward
me—as if we were at a family reunion picnic, as if he could not feel
the wind and the rain. It was coming down so hard now that Ania
Oletsky's iron yellow dress was clinging to my skin, soaked through
and heavy as canvas, a perfume from the last century revived by the
water.

Where would the bullet enter me?

What would Vick do with my body?

"Don't think I won't shoot, Ant. You know better."

I made my way toward Sheriff Iscoe. He seemed to be uncon-
sciously imitating the scarecrow, his arms flung open, a crazy grin on
his face.

My body remembered the Home in Milford. The nurses with the
red leather straitjacket pulled taut, waiting to push my arms through
its empty sleeves. The attic above me that swallowed our screams,
my own cries and those of a hundred other mothers. Our voiceless
babies kicking like rabbits.

Red's blank stare flashed into my mind, the swirl of freckles reminding me that he was really just an overgrown child. Small Gladys with
her scalded eyes and her thick ankles, trailing a mother who thought
other people's sadness was imaginary. *Forgive me, Gladys*, I prayed
in my head. *I am going to try and kill your father. Forgive me, Son*, I
beamed to You, wherever You might be, while the black sky released
gallons of water.

"Here is an offer you can't refuse, Ant. Why not make a fresh
start? You made a sorry mess of things at the Grange Hall. But you
have the power to clean it up. Get your earhorn, and get situated in
the jailhouse, and I will bring you some folks who need to unhear
what they heard . . ."

"Too many have heard and seen. If I were you, Vick? I'd get clear of Uz tonight."

"If only you had heeded your own words, eh? You could be half-way to Garden City. Instead, you're one more *no* away from a bullet in the brain. This whole town wants you dead, Ant. And if I let them get to you, it won't be quick. They have time to kill as well . . ."

"For a man with secrets, you sure love to hear yourself talk."

"A mob rarely exhausts itself on just one death," he said. "Remember Kate Bender? They'll be looking for you, Ant, and for every unwed woman that resembles you. They'll want to kill you more than once. I pity any tall, mousy-haired spinster living in western Nebraska."

"Everybody knows that Clemson Louis Dew is innocent."

"You think *your* testimony will hold in court? Do you imagine that hoax photography is evidence of anything?"

We could barely see through the rain. The scarecrow danced in and out of focus, a ghostly shape behind Vick's left shoulder. He moved the gun in a slow circle, pointing at my chest, my ear, my face. Lightning struck, so close to us I smelled burning sweetness on the air. Fear cut my sight to pieces. Vick's eyes. Vick's slouchy stomach. Vick's finger on the trigger. Vick's teeth.

"I hear the Chair is on its way back to Lincoln—"

He screamed to be heard over the booming thunder. Gloating again, growing more and more certain that he had won.

"We know where you disposed of Mink's remains. Your young deputy deposited that night, but I bet he remembers plenty of other ones. Percy looked like he found our exhibition quite convincing—"

I could picture what would happen next: men digging around the dunes where the Sheriff dragged Mink; the young deputy Percy's tearful oath on the stand; that shopkeeper from Gordon, identifying the Sheriff as the man who purchased a box of rabbit feet; more lies unraveling. The closed case opening up, just like the door in the earth.

"Why not run, Vick? Use the weather as your cover. Get far away from here. Grow a mustache, change your name."

"Now, why would I run on the eve of an election that I'm bound to win?"

"It's over for you here. People may want to deny what they saw and heard about you, but they won't forget it. Go ahead and shoot. I am closed for business, Vick. I won't be around to help them put their doubts aside . . ."

"Goodbye, Ant. You won't be around to help anyone. You leave me no choice."

The Scarecrow

It was such a little thing that I was able to do to help her. Such a small contribution to the drama unfolding. I inclined into the wind. Ever so slightly, I felt a wall yield. A shift like a bead of rain rolling down a leaf. With all of my will, I urged the hat forward, and the wind met me in this endeavor. The hat soared off, somersaulting on the gale. How far did I succeed in my aim? A tenth of an inch? Less? A miracle. It was enough.

A hat is not a scimitar. It is a very unlikely weapon. With the wind's assistance, it became one. I watched it bump along an updraft and fly into the large man's face. The straw brim scratched his open eye. *Cornea* is a beautiful word. The hard snap of that *kuh* and the elemental vowel sounds. *Cornea.* The name returned to me as I listened to the large man cover his eyes and scream.

Asphodel Oletsky

D ell against the Dark," Valeria liked to tease me, watching me shoot baskets after midnight on the secret court. "Do you think Coach is going to make you play blindfolded?" This was back when we were fourteen and still played for Uz Poultry & Eggs. I'd convince her to sneak out with me after dark (it didn't take much: a running engine and a basketball, the liquor I'd found buried in the root cellar).

Dell against the Dark always made me smile. If I survived, I'd have to tell Valeria that I'd remembered her joke as I sprinted through the driving rain toward the Sheriff. Almost sightlessly, I ran at him, my ears ringing with gunfire. He groped on all fours, cursing at everything, feeling for his gun, which I saw shining in the muddy field right beside him. I threw the basketball at the side of his head, hard as I could. It sent him sprawling forward, shrieking in terror more than pain.

Up until the final buzzer, Coach used to tell us, you can always turn things around. Play like that. Play like you believe it's possible, even when you're down twenty. Squinting into the rain, I saw my opportunity. It was crazy luck, crazy timing—although no crazier than anything else that had happened to me. Just kinder.

Defense to offense. It's my favorite pivot. The scarecrow's hat came free and flew directly into Sheriff Iscoe's face. The way he howled, you'd think it gouged his eye out. So easily, as if I were stooping to pluck my namesake flower, I picked up his gun. I threaded my finger through the trigger.

"Let me escort you to your car, Vick."

He was staring at me with a look of pure terror. I confess that the power felt good. I pointed the gun at his chest and motioned at the road. It was only when I saw Cleo and Ant and my uncle wearing almost identical expressions that I realized I had not caused the change in him. I turned to follow their gaze to the fallowland. What I saw—what we all saw—made the Sheriff scream and shield his eyes.

"What madness is this?" the Sheriff cried out in a tone I'd never heard from him. He buried his face in the crook of one arm. "Where is it coming from?" He began gibbering something, taking lunging backward steps away from the waves of light pouring out of the ground.

I didn't need the gun, as it turned out. The Sheriff went running for his car. Out of the corner of my eye, I watched him fling open the door and speed backward down the cowpath. The rain opened like a tunnel to absorb him, then shut quickly behind him. He drove with his headlights off, and a minute later he was lost to sight. The sky was like Vick's injured eye, streaming violently. Night had fallen and it should have been impossible to see anything. But we could see each other's faces. For a long time we stood together in the same sheet of rain, Cleo Allfrey and Antonina Rossi and my uncle and I. Drinking in the same wonderful, terrifying vision.

Cleo Allfrey

Not-gray   Not-pink   Not-flame

          Not-blue   Not-snow

                                                Not-fawn

Not-mist   Not-sea-green

   Not-moon   Not-snakeskin

     Not-rainbow

                              Not-eggshell

    Not-gold   Not-silver   Not-amber waves of . . .

Rays of light came shooting out of the ground, shivering and tangling and tasseling out from burning stalks, blooming and melting into one unbroken sheet. Radiance danced across the fallowland. The way light slides around the skin of a bubble. But what we saw together was even stranger. I wish that I'd had my camera. A color from outer space, I thought at first. But that was wrong. What is the word for a color before it is born? It was all the colors of this Earth, bleeding and blending and mixing.

It looked like nothing so much as the unborn light in my developing tray. I stared at the shape of things to come. *Make the work you want to make.* In the darkroom under the earth, I had left a dozen prairies shimmering in utero on the drying line. *Which one*, I wondered, *will develop? What will be growing on this fallowland in ten years, twenty years, fifty years, five hundred?*

I don't know how long we stood there shivering in the rain. Whole lakes were crashing down around us. Summer thunder, after such a long hiatus, sounded like the kettledrums of the apocalypse. The nameless light leapt like a fire that the falling rain nourished instead of putting out. Something spoke to my heart. But I am a photographer. I transfer light onto film, not into language. There's no use trying to translate what we saw growing in the fallowland into English. What fool would perjure her vision that way?

Antonina Rossi

Watch your step," said Cleo in the middle of the soaking field. She sounded shocked. We were all still dazzled by the light show in the fallowland. "Do you think the Sheriff will come back?"

I could barely hear her over the wind.

"I don't think so. Did you see his face as he ran off?"

She shook her head. Speech was returning so slowly. Words had vanished from my mind also. Something had dilated inside us and was now contracting; the rain slanted steadily on. Everything was dark again. I had a vision of the Sheriff swerving sightless in the hard rain and careening off the drowned road, his body crumpled against the wheel. Perhaps we would find him in that position tomorrow. Or maybe he would escape the storm and return to Uz. Would the town reelect him, given what they now knew? Would they arrest and investigate him? I am not the sort of witch who knows those answers. Cleo and I reached the porch first, and found the bloody cat scratching her back against a post. If the cat had witnessed the miracle in the fallowland, she'd recovered her composure.

Cleo turned to watch Harp and Dell staggering toward us.

"Why would anyone run from a color like that?" Cleo asked.

I knelt to stroke the cat's belly, like a witch in a storybook. "Vick did not want to change his reflection in the mirror," I said.

Dell and Harp had only just reached the porch when we heard the telltale whistle. The rain pushed the night up to our noses. The sky had a greenish cast in the east. On the edge of the wheat field, a saucer of darkness had suddenly appeared; another miraculous visitation, I thought at first. My ears rang as they had on Black Sunday. The whistle swelled to fill the world. A tornado danced toward us on its single toe.

"The cellar!" screamed Harp. "Run!" I bent and scooped up the cat. We all held hands to avoid losing one another. Outside, we couldn't hear anything but that bottomless groan. If it weren't for Allfrey's battery-powered safelight, I don't know how we would have seen anything down there. The nameless color was still dancing in my memory. None of us seemed as afraid as we probably should have been, as the twister danced overhead. By the clock, we heard the rumbling for ten minutes. But as all Vaults know well, a clock is worthless to measure how long some sounds continue.

Harp Oletsky

L et me tell you about spellbreak. It rained all that night and well into the next day. The Republican River became a four-mile-wide whitewater monster, thrashing its long tail from eastern Colorado to Oxford, Nebraska. Twenty-four inches of rain fell in twenty-four hours! Bridges split and splintered apart. Hundreds of miles of road got washed out. The river poured forward with enough force to carry cars and rooftops. Walls floated away. Friends became cadavers in outfits we recognized, floating beside tractors and drowned cattle. Bodies were seen riding on the crest through the middle of towns, their shy faces staring underwater even as we screamed their names. The carcasses of horses and hogs and cows were packed in the driftwood, lying on sandbars, and carried off by the current.

An hour before dawn, when the howling winds had subsided, I climbed the ladder and periscoped out of the root cellar door. My farmhouse was one of those destroyed. My wheat crop was gone—torn from the ground, as if a giant's fist had done the weeding. The bubble around my house and my harvest had burst.

I stared at the caved-in barn with the greatest relief I have ever felt—relief to be drawing breath, relief to have a chance to build another kind of life. I thanked the heavens for unsealing us and allowing us to rejoin the general fate, to endure together the drought and the dust that challenged all other living beings on the Plains. Anything that is yours alone can become a curse, even good fortune. This understanding hit me with the force of revelation. Words alone won't do it justice.

What these Vaults stored for so many newcomers to this West is more than horror. More than the hugeness of our sorrows, our losses that we can only absorb with the stupefaction of our animals, soft-eyed and uncomprehending.

So much of what we have laid up in these Vaults turns out to be happiness. Scrolled maps to other worlds, the dreams we forgot, the unthought possible. The kind, laughing hearts that we had as children, we can recover. Our strong and soft and generous hearts. I saw this, and like Job before me, I saw more than I can tell.

Many songs have been lost. But not all songs have been lost.

I breathed in a lungful of dust at the top of the ladder, sinking my fingers into the wet soil. Job ends his interrogation of God in a great quiet. When I surfaced from my whirlwind, I heard a lot of noisy, irreverent chirping. Meadowlarks darted around the ruins of my house, skimming the tires of the truck the twister had flipped onto its back like some colossal beetle. Goldfinches were swooping in and out of the roofless barn like indecisive stars. Grassland songbirds chorus every morning on the prairie, rain or shine, drought or flood. Singing at the tops of their tiny lungs and stitching the world together, waking everyone to the work ahead. But rarely do I pay attention. In the Book of Job, what God reveals inside the whirlwind cannot be written down. The omission made more sense to me now, listening to birdsong. Already, God has translated the answer into everything living. It was Job's ears that needed tuning. The whirlwind gave Job a powerful instruction, and so did the great quiet it left in its wake. The silence of God is not so silent after all. It is teaching me how to listen.

The tornado, I later learned from Otto—who had watched in horror from his hayloft window—had spun across his land and onto mine, skirting the root cellar where we'd sheltered. Allfrey seemed dismayed that she had missed a chance to photograph it, even though I pointed out it might well have been her last shot. No harm had come to any one of us, not even the cat, who birthed her litter of kittens at 4:04 a.m. The scent of afterbirth and kerosene oil mixed with the rooty breaths of the potatoes. The chemical tang from Allfrey's trays. Rich life, new life. Milk and blood. We all watched the slick kittens drinking thirstily from their weary mother. A litter of seven.

My niece naturally wants to keep all of them.

I said we'd have to let the cat decide. I won't interfere with this mother's plans for her young. I saw the intricate scratches she clawed into the Sheriff's skin—the cat has her own designs.

Asphodel Oletsky

Next to the buried potatoes, under the bent clothespins that held Allfrey's prints over my head, their edges curling in the cool cellar air, I knelt and waited. Somewhere in the near darkness, my uncle was listening intently to the static from the shortwave radio. Nobody else seemed aware of the drama unfolding right here under Allfrey's table of trays and potions. The cat stood and stretched, her yawning mouth a tiny cave inside a cave. I could see her unborn kittens squirming inside her. It was almost her time.

Mama, where are you?
Are you still . . . ?
Anywhere?

You know, if you sync up your breath with the thing breathing behind you, you can barely hear It at all. I have fought so hard to keep from thinking about It. The absence of my mother, the way It swells to fill everyplace and the entire future. All day and night. Every minute since they told me she was dead. I learned something in the root cellar, riding out the storm, something that sounds very obvious but came as a shock to me: A thing doesn't hurt you so much if you draw it close as it does when you keep pushing it away.

"Mama, help me not to be afraid of this. It is a time I need to remember. It is a part of my life."

I plunged into It then. I stopped fighting shy of It. It shuddered through me and poured out of my eyes. Grief, although that name for It does not feel complete. Love, I guess. "I remember you," I said, turning toward all the mothers in my mind, hidden and waiting for me to find them behind the coroner's lone picture. It felt bottomless. It was going to drown me, the pain that flooded through me. The Antidote was standing beside me, and I fell into her and let her rock me in the root cellar, both of us swaying as if we were dancing. I guess I should have been embarrassed but I wasn't any longer. Some thunderhead inside me burst and I cried until I felt delirious, hungry and thirsty and weak, emptying my eyes onto the Antidote's dress—my grandmother's yellow dress, I remembered. My uncle's and Cleo Allfrey's hands touched the base of my neck, my shoulders and cheeks, so that I knew I was not alone with It.

"Do you think your mama wants you to get vengeance?" Allfrey asked me, once I was breathing evenly again. "To find her killer?"

"I am not going to spend my whole life chasing down my mother's killer," I said. "What kind of life would that be? She's gone and I can't bring her back by killing the man who did it."

Only when I said it, I felt that she wasn't gone. A little sun rose in me, warming my bones from within. Like the sun on the rocks teasing greenery up, small white flowers. *Mama. Is this you?* There was no answer but the spreading warmth. A very powerful warmth. I still have no idea how to talk about it.

When I was calm again, Allfrey handed me a black-and-white print. It did not shimmer or undulate like her photographs of the future. It was matte and still. Relative to some of her photographs, very ordinary seeming. I recognized my bedroom in Uncle Harp's house.

"I made this the other day," she said. "I was testing out my flashbulbs in the bedroom. That's not you, is it?"

I shook my head.

"Thank you, Cleo."

I was too happy to say much. Yes, it was our bedroom. I recognized my mama's face, although it was also a complete surprise. She looked younger than me, ten or eleven. Baby fat filled in her cheeks. She had wide-set eyes like Uncle Harp, thick, unbrushed hair, and bushy eyebrows. If the Earth had rolled on its axis after an eclipse, unlidding the sun, it could not have felt any more astonishing to me than Allfrey's portrait of Lada Oletsky.

"Uncle," I said. "Look who Cleo found."

Everybody gathered around the photograph. Above the root cellar, the trapdoor vibrated. Rain and thunder were stampeding aboveground. We *did* look alike. Not in the obvious ways—but there was something in the set of her jaw, the wild explosion of her hair around her tiny frame. Nothing looked posed in Allfrey's portrait. My ten-year-old mother was sitting by the window, drawing her finger along the glass.

Dear Mama, What does it mean that I am certain you are with me? Sometimes I doubt God, but never you.

The Cat

I do miss the sun. I have made a bed for us in the warm, dark corner. It is a pleasure to lie here on my belly, letting my children devour me. The relief of milk flooding out of me into my children's warm mouths is indescribable—in your language, or mine.

You might go on thinking that we cats are supporting characters in your human dramas, instead of souls in four-legged bodies with our own compelling destinies. *Pet* is a word I have always detested. Anyone who truly loves a cat must admit that it is a love between equals—it does not fall from a great height like rain, or pity.

Some sentimental idiot will imagine me nursing my newborn children in the root cellar and say that "all was restored" to me. Make no mistake, these newborns are not my dead children. That loss cannot be reversed.

The Scarecrow

Memories came racing toward me. I watched them massing on the horizon: the feathery, skeletal outline of my life. Hail flashed in wild slants across the prairie, and in that fractured mirror I glimpsed scenes I recognized. So much blew into my awareness at once. Great chunks of time began falling into and through me: my big brothers wrestling in the new snow behind the church. The dark purple lampshade in Grandma Alba's house that my father said looked like a whore's lacy underwear, but to me was the color of safety and peace. An entire prairie dog town blinking back at my sister and me one warm afternoon on our walk home from school. Dad's knotty fist covering mine as he taught me how to work the clutch. Our wedding day in fennel-scented July. The night of the meteor shower over Valentine, Sara and I climbing onto the roof to watch the wide tail of stars shake across the Plains. A small yawning face doubled in my mother's pupils. My face. I had a life. An extraordinary, ordinary life. I recognize the woman crossing the fallowland. She carries something that looks like a large metal teardrop. A green raindrop. Even before she reaches me, I feel a door opening—

The Antidote / The Scarecrow

When I heard the wind dying down, an hour or so before dawn, I found myself climbing the ladder out. I don't remember deciding anything. Harp and Cleo and Dell were all asleep. The cat had just given birth, and she was lying in an exhausted heap in the corner of the root cellar, watching me with glassy eyes while her litter nursed. I moved with the strange certainty of dreams.

The rain was still falling in waves, blowing at an angle from the east. I turned and could not believe the sight before me: Harp's house had been destroyed, ripped from its foundation. The windows were blown out, the roof in splinters. Whatever spell of luck had put a frame around this land was well and truly broken. Although a moment later it occurred to me that perhaps this wasn't true—we were all alive, weren't we? Cleo's camera was shattered; the Oletsky homeplace had been flattened by the fist of the sky; I had no livelihood; there would be nothing to harvest this June.

But hadn't we been the beneficiaries of some mercy last night? The strangest luck in its latest permutation. The Sheriff was nowhere to be seen. We were still here, breathing. Many of Allfrey's prints were hanging on the drying line in the root cellar, and her negatives were safely in their boxes. My earhorn was under my arm, giving off its emerald glow.

The scarecrow looked much the worse for wear, bedraggled and coming apart on the posts. But by some miracle, like us, he had come through the storm intact. He had not blown off.

What I did next felt like an ancient reflex, although to my knowledge I had never done anything like it. I tipped the earhorn up at the darkening sky. The receiver pinned my lobe against my skull. I stood in the center of the field and I listened intently to the storm. Water ran into the funnel. Water drummed directly into my brain. Rain, rain, rain. Down, down, down.

Instantly, something began to grow.

I held the earhorn to the scarecrow's chest, to the square pocket of his overalls, where a human heart would be. What possessed me to do this, I'll never know. But crouching there before the scarecrow, pushing the fluted edge of the funnel to the ragged clothes like a doctor's stethoscope, I heard a sudden roaring in my left ear. It sounded as if I were in the path of a locomotive, and I nearly screamed and dropped the horn.

Up swirls the light from the bottom of the world. Up swirls the water. I hear a voice say, "Mama?" I know You, Son. In an instant I had to learn more than I could have borne in a long lifetime—I saw your death first, your body flying through the windshield. I saw the car roll backward to your home in Rushville. Your family's old sheepdog limped through the open door and licked your small cheek. I watched You decorate a Christmas tree with your brother Auggie. A shudder passed through me and it was You, it was You, traveling through the straw wall and into my body. Somersaulting through me, with the same solidity and vigor that You had as a baby. It was nothing like falling backward into a trance. You were wide-alive inside me, passing through me on the way to someplace else, moving in the opposite direction you had during your birth, up up and away like a dewdrop on its journey to the clouds. It was You, shaking my skeleton like birch limbs, flaring my ribs. Braiding through me came everything at once, your death and your life, the weight of your suffering, the dragonfly skimming the water one summer, a fight with your brother, a kiss on the lake, the farmers' holiday strike in Sioux City, the pronghorns running at dusk. Your other mother, holding your hand in the line for the penny juke. You lived a good life, a hard life, a short life. I felt so happy to find You here, hidden right in front of us, needle in the haystack, scratch on the negative, glint in an eye. I felt like my knees were about to collapse.

Wind pushed right through me, swelling behind my face-bones, battering my chest, my ribs, my tailbone, the hourglass of my pelvis, a symphony of wind crashing into me. My baby, You came home. I watched You grow into a man. My eyes were shut against the rain and I could see You standing in the doorframe. Was it wishful thinking? I do not think so. In years of trying, I have never succeeded in conjuring any face so beautiful into my imagination. I have never seen a face I loved more. Or a face that I recognized, as surely as I know my own. I saw your father, Giancarlo, in your long Sicilian nose and high cheekbones. I see myself in your dark eyes and your full lips. My young nonna's inky curls. The halved hearts of my large ears. You wear them so well, Son. You looked nothing like I pictured. You are a man. You are a boy. You are my lost infant. All your faces were shown to me in the whirlwind of our reunion. Circling the funnel came more and more memories that had traveled from your lifetime, that were braiding through mine. I never got a chance to name You. The woman who raised and loved You named You Benjamin. Squeakie was your nickname until you turned twelve. Then your voice dropped three octaves. You died in a car accident in Rushville on Black Sunday. The wind brought you here. You waited for me to find You. You stayed.

Little whirlwind, brilliant constellation. My baby. This is not the reunion that I have dreamed about since I was fifteen. It hurts to hold You and to release You in the same breath. You are not lost anymore. A part of You I feel moving into and through me, expanding beyond me like a stem breaking through soil, and a part of You remains with me here. Always I have thought of a soul as something indivisible, but now I am not so sure. Welcome home, baby. Thank you for filling in the silhouette I've carried inside me, wondering who You became. Thank You for filling my heart with your days, pushing your arms through these empty sleeves. Thank You for waiting here for me to find You. Our long separation is over. I will go on knowing You.

⚏

I stood with my son in the field for a long time, and when we were ready, I dropped the earhorn. Somehow I know all his ages at once, collapsing and expanding like accordion pleats. I don't pretend to understand it. But I know that my son lived, and died. I believe that he is free now, and that he knows me.

I heard a noise behind me and turned to see the girl climbing out of the door in the earth. She was clutching her basketball to her chest, wearing a troubled expression. She turned to the flattened house, and I watched her register the shock of its destruction with her body.

"The season's over, I guess."

"When the ground dries out," I said, "we can start practicing for the next one."

There are many ways to be a witch. And there are many ways to be a mother. I am still learning how much is possible.

She pushed into my arms, a little rabbit launching from her hind legs. All squirm and sinew and thudding heart. My hands settled on her back and pulled her close. Dell is so fierce. I forget she is only five feet tall. Her hands were clasped at the nape of my neck, mine at the base of her spine. We swayed like that for whole minutes, the storm intensifying and ebbing off. After such a long wait, the rain felt like a violent gift.

Dell's wet hair hung in her eyes. She let me brush it away, staring up at me.

It does not feel like a betrayal of You to love someone.

She looked from me to the slumping scarecrow, which was just an empty husk again.

"What happened to the scarecrow?"

I shook my head. "More than I can tell."

Why write a story about something beyond what words can name? There are many beautiful facts about You that I can put down on paper, but not the fundamental one.

Coda: Restoration

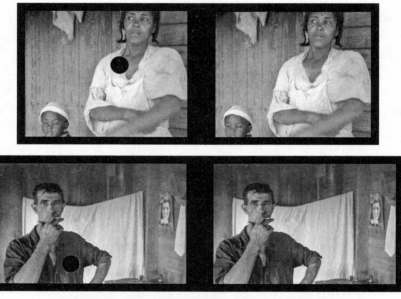

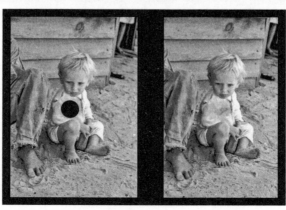

The morning after the storm, we emerged into a changed world. At daybreak, I climbed the ladder. The others had already fanned out to survey the aftermath of the rains and the tornado. The scarecrow had somehow managed to stay upright on the post, but half its stuffing was gone. A gap in its hay bale chest released straw into the wind. I felt a pang for the animals—I could hear a loose cow crying out. Any wheat that the twister hadn't torn from the ground had been lodged and flattened. Dust blew across the ruins of the house, dimming the pink sun. I was a zero-yield man again. My spell of luck was gone. Blessedly, the heavy clouds were moving. The great consolation of difficult weather is that we live in it together.

Just as the rising sun shook free of the ground, a prickling began at the base of my spine. The air around me seemed to bend and wave. There was a drop in the thermostat, a salt-heavy taste. A feeling like the sandhill cranes returning, first as specks on the horizon and then as a many-winged flock, turning against the red sun and descending to the branches of our town.

I opened my eyes and felt it enter me: my first memory. I was six years old at a jackrabbit drive near the Loup River. These jacks were pests, Papa told me, eating up all our fodder. The town was banding together to rid itself of rabbits. "You'll understand when you're older," he'd promised me, but then he'd burned up the slip and robbed me of that chance. Here it came, lunging into me again: the frenzy of the drive. The madness of the falling clubs, the screaming of the rabbits. The club has always been in my hand. I had only forgotten I was holding it.

Gradually I feel something buoying me, drawing me out of the pen and into the morning light. *You can put it down now,* my father sighs inside me. I don't want to live this way any longer, swinging in a sightless panic to defend the box into which I was born, repeating the story that it's necessary. I wonder what other memories are coming home to the people of Uz. I wonder what might happen in the wake of such a restoration. We are full of days again.

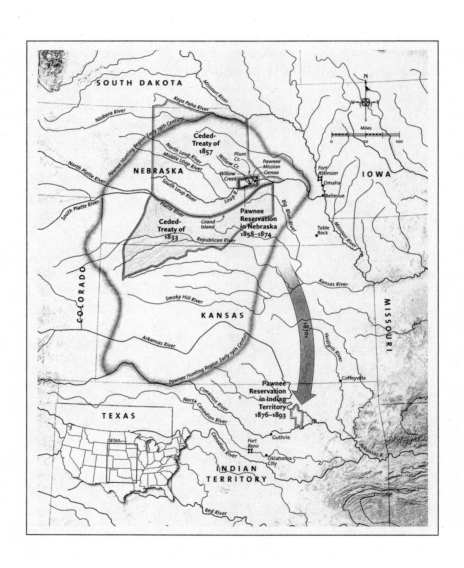

Land Lost Acknowledgment

With James Riding In

The Antidote uses fantastical conceits to illuminate the holes in people's private and collective memories, the willful omissions passed down generation to generation, and the myths that have been used by the U.S. government and White settlers to justify crimes against the citizens of Native Nations and the theft of Native lands. One of the most destructive of these is the myth of *terra nullius*. There were dozens of Native Nations hunting and farming on the Great Plains long before the arrival of European colonizers. Although Uz, Nebraska, is an imaginary town, every non-Indigenous American in our country is living on American Indian homelands.

This novel takes place in the nineteenth and early twentieth centuries on Pawnee homelands on the Central Plains between the Platte and the Republican Rivers in what became Nebraska. The Pawnee Confederacy, then as it is now, was composed of four autonomous nations: the Chaui, the Kitkehahki, the Pitahawirata, and the Skidi. The Pawnees have a profound spiritual and cultural bond to their land. Their tenure on the Plains predates the arrival of foreign colonizers in the Americas in 1492 by at least a millennium.

Living in permanent mud-lodge towns along the Platte, Loup, and Republican Rivers and their tributaries, the Pawnees followed a seasonal round of life-sustaining and ceremonial activities. They planted corn, beans, and squash crops in nearby river bottoms. They conducted two buffalo hunts annually, covering a vast area while living in tepees. Their architectural, hunting, and agricultural practices were rooted in their spiritual beliefs and reflective of a millennial relationship stewarding the prairie ecosystem.

The Pawnees loved their lifeways and did not want to lose them. They kept a covenant with their creator, Tirawahut, requiring living and worship in specific ways in return for the gifts of life, including corn and buffalo. With the spearhead of westward U.S. expansion penetrating the Central Plains in the early 1800s, they became engaged in an unprecedented struggle to protect and defend their cherished independence, land, and culture against overwhelming odds. They battled other Native Nations who were pushed westward by European and American expansion and infringed on their hunting lands, while suffering dramatic population losses from smallpox, cholera, and deadly diseases spread by emigrant overlanders. The White travelers en route to the Pacific Northwest and California also slaughtered buffalo for sport and food, destroyed crops and timber, and polluted the water. Weakened by the onslaught, the Pawnees lost most of their Nebraska and Kansas homelands through treaties in 1833, 1848, and 1857 and gradually fell under federal domination as wards. Under the terms of the last treaty, the Pawnees retained ownership of a fifteen-by-thirty-mile reservation with rich soil and timber along the waterways. In return for the land, the federal government established schools, farms, and an agency of the reservation near Genoa.

Meanwhile, the Kansas-Nebraska Act of 1854 opened millions of acres of Native land ceded to the U.S. government for settlement by its citizens, who mainly attained land titles under the Preemption Act of 1841 and Homestead Act of 1862. Building farms, ranches, cities, and towns scattered across the landscape in places crucial to the Pawnees' economic pursuits, they changed the countryside to conform with White American rural life. The Pawnee reservation soon became an embattled cultural enclave surrounded by aggressive settlers, including many who advocated an Indian-free environment by extermination or removal.

The Pawnees nonetheless entered a military alliance in 1864 with the federal government. Hundreds of their finest men fought in special U.S. army units known as the Pawnee Scouts. Although the Pawnee Scouts' bravery and heroic feats made life safer for settlers and protected the transcontinental railroad's construction, the alliance did virtually nothing to improve Pawnee relations with land-hungry settlers. Overwhelmed and demoralized by intensifying settler pressure and federal ethnocide initiatives, the beleaguered Pawnees accepted a small reservation in the Indian Territory in a desperate bid to preserve their culture and escape White settlers.

Their move to the reservation on Black Bear Creek had devastating consequences for the Pawnees. Malaria, poor health, despair, and hunger soon killed hundreds. By the late 1890s, their population had declined to less than seven hundred people, living under the heavy hand of U.S. domination. Federal policymakers simultaneously ramped up their campaign to Americanize Indians using more coercive measures of assimilation to erase Native languages, cultures, and freedom. That genocidal campaign mainly targeted children for cultural transformation in on- and off-reservation boarding schools, where students were forcibly removed from their families and communities by government agents, often sent to schools hundreds of miles away from their homes, and harshly punished when they spoke their Native languages. In 1884, the Genoa U.S. Indian Industrial School in Genoa, Nebraska, began in a one-room schoolhouse that the United States had originally built on the Pawnee reservation as part of its treaty obligations, and became a 640-acre campus that operated for fifty years. There are few American Indian families that did not have a relative who attended one of these schools, and today American Indian families are still living with the legacies of the schools.

In 1887, Congress responded to incessant settler demands for access to more reservation lands by enacting its infamous Dawes Allotment Act. This law divided reservations into individual allotments ranging from 80 to 160 acres in size to accelerate the Natives' expected assimilation into U.S. society as farmers and laborers. It opened the so-called "surplus land" on reservations for non-Indian settlement. Between 1887 and 1934, the Dawes Act stripped Native Nations and their citizens of ninety million acres.

Through all the adversity, the Pawnee Nation has shown remarkable resiliency. During the unfolding of this history, the Pawnee people never consented to eradicating their traditional way of life. The U.S. genocidal and ethnocidal policies inflicted considerable harm without destroying Pawnee culture. Today, the number of Tribal enrolled members is more than 3,200, and Pawnees can be found in all areas of the United States, as well as foreign countries, within many walks of life. Pawnees take much pride in their heritage. Still viewing their ancestral Central Plains homelands with reverence and respect, they endeavor to overcome the consequences of a destructive past. The Pawnee Nation is experiencing a vibrant language and cultural revitalization movement with scant fiscal resources. Recently, its citizens built a mud lodge, the first in many years, on the grounds of the former Pawnee Indian boarding school on the Pawnee Reservation in Oklahoma. It also established its Digital Library, Mukurtu Portal, and Research Library project, with federal grant funding, as a crucial component of this undertaking. This project will provide Pawnees and others with valuable information about Pawnee history and culture. This effort entails establishing partnerships with repositories and the laborious process of collecting, creating metadata for, and digitizing massive materials, including treaties, government documents, maps, recordings, photographs, court cases, firsthand narratives, scholarly studies, unpublished manuscripts, newspaper articles, and works of fiction.

With the project's funding ending in 2024, the work continues through the efforts of dedicated volunteer help. The Mukurtu Portal, still under construction, can be accessed at https://mukurtu.pawnee nation.org. For more information about ways to support this project, contact mukurtuportalinfo@gmail.com.

James Riding In is a Pawnee Nation citizen, historian, husband, father, grandfather, disabled Navy Vietnam veteran, and retired Arizona State University professor, where he cofounded and directed the American Indian Studies Program. He is the founding chair of the Pawnee Nation College Board of Trustees, past editor of *Wicazo Sa Review: A Journal of Native American Studies*, and the project director of Pawnee Nation's Digital Library, Research Library, and the online Mukurtu Portal.

This photograph shows a recently built mud lodge standing near the former boys' dormitory of the defunct Pawnee Indian boarding school on the Pawnee Reservation in Oklahoma. It symbolizes the cultural resiliency of the Pawnee people to withstand and outlast harmful federal policies of ethnocide and coercive assimilation. Photographer: James Riding In, April 22, 2023

Author's Note

The Antidote is bookended by two extreme weather events that happened within months of each other on the drought-stricken Plains in 1935: the Black Sunday dust storm and the Republican River flood, during which this gentle river received twenty-four inches of rain in twenty-four hours. For the most part, the historical events in this novel hew closely to their real chronologies. However, in some cases, I adjusted dates to fit this compressed timeline:

- The Resettlement Administration (RA)—a New Deal federal agency—was created on May 1, 1935. The first photographers employed by the RA's Historical Section began making work in the early summer of 1935.
- Pare Lorentz's government-sponsored documentary, *The Plow That Broke the Plains*, was released on May 10, 1936.
- Arthur Rothstein's iconic photograph—*Farmer and sons walking in the face of a dust storm*—was taken in April 1936.

While researching *The Antidote*, I visited two Progressive-era institutions in eastern Nebraska that operated during the same period roughly sixty miles from each other: the Genoa U.S. Indian Industrial School and the Milford Industrial Home.

There were more than 523 government-funded, and often church-run, federal Indian boarding schools across the United States. These institutions were designed to break Indigenous children's ties to their families, their nations, their languages, their ceremonies and beliefs, their cultures, and their homelands. Between 1884 and 1934, the Genoa U.S. Indian Industrial School enrolled more than 4,300 children, representing more than forty Native Nations. Today, the Genoa Indian School Digital Reconciliation Project is dedicated to these students' descendants and communities, who have survived and persevered despite the U.S. government's attempt to eradicate Indigenous cultures and sovereignties. To learn more and to support the Genoa Indian School Digital Reconciliation Project, please visit https://genoaindianschool.org.

The Milford Industrial Home for Unwed Mothers operated from 1889 to 1954. It was the first such state-funded institution in the country. As many as four thousand babies may have been born there, and part of the Home's original mission was to "facilitate adoptions." Several years ago, while I was drafting this novel, I reached out to Lakota/Nebraska historian Broc Anderson, who introduced me to the history of Zintkála Nuni—also known as Lost Bird—an infant survivor of the Wounded Knee Massacre who was stolen from her Lakota family by General Leonard Colby. I learned that Zintkála Nuni was imprisoned at the same Nebraskan maternity home in which I'd set "The Antidote's Story." The biographical facts of Zintkála Nuni's early life, including the dates of her incarceration at the Milford Industrial Home and the stillbirth of her child, come from published letters and secondary sources. The characters, dialogue, and scenes that occur inside this fictionalized Milford Home are my invention.

I hope that I've been able to honor the qualities that shine in Zintkála Nuni's letters and in the facts that are known about her life, but please do not confuse the character in these pages with the real woman known to many as Lost Bird. She is at home in the hearts and alive in the memories of her relatives and the Lakota people.

Several other characters in this novel share names and biographical facts with real historical figures, including Roy Stryker, Dorothea Lange, Arthur Rothstein, Asa Hill, and Elvira Platt. This novel is an act of imagination, based on research I've done and conversations I've had, but fundamentally fiction.

Roy Stryker was a complex figure who helmed an unprecedented government-sponsored photographic project, one that created a rich archive of images of American life between 1935 and 1944. My fictional correspondence was inspired by real telegrams, memos, "shooting scripts," and letters between Roy Stryker and his photographers in the field, including Dorothea Lange, Walker Evans, Marion Post Wolcott, and Gordon Parks.

The collection compiled by the Historic Section consists of 175,000 black-and-white film negatives and transparencies, 1,610 color transparencies, and around 107,000 black-and-white photographic prints, most of which were made from the negatives and transparencies. Thanks to recent digitization efforts, everyone can also view a shadow archive of unprinted and hole-punched negatives, available online at the Library of Congress website: https://www.loc .gov/pictures/collection/fsa/.

The hole-punched images from the Resettlement Agency/FSA project are included to give a sense of the aims and ambitions of the documentary photography project, as well as the artistic curation and political calculation that shaped the file and people's understanding of the Dust Bowl. These photographs are not meant to be illustrative of any character in this novel. The people in these images have their own names, families, and histories that did not unfold in this fictional Nebraska.

The Graflex Speed Graphic is a real model of camera, favored by press photographers and used by several of the New Deal photographers in the field. To my knowledge, there is no such thing as a quantum camera. The only similar technology I know of is the one we each come installed with at birth—our inner eyes that can see beyond our own lifetimes. Our long memories and longer imaginations.

While I was writing and revising *The Antidote*, I left a space open in brackets that read, optimistically: **[provocatively beautiful photograph of a future tk]**. I held that space open for draft after draft, waiting for this final vision to surface. Eventually I turned in my manuscript, with the defeated feeling that I'd failed to conjure something necessary, something vital this book had wanted me to share. Now I see that space a little differently. If *The Antidote* has taught me anything, it's that I cannot imagine a future alone. The lens cap is off, the camera is pointing at the horizon. So much remains to be seen.

Acknowledgments

Writing *The Antidote* has been a deeply collaborative experience, and I am overwhelmed with gratitude to the many kind and brilliant people who helped me along the way. It's humbling to write a novel about the holes in people's memories while aware of the many gaps in my own understanding. Thank you all for patiently answering my thousand questions, for pointing out mistakes, and for sharing your knowledge and in some cases deeply personal connections to the people, places, and events that inspired this novel. Thank you for helping me to see and to imagine so much further than I ever could alone. This book, in some form or another, has been with me for nearly a third of my life. I could not have written it without all of you.

Thank you, James Riding In, for answering my cold call years ago, for your extraordinary kindness and generosity to a stranger, for your brilliant and bracing scholarship, and for sharing your deep knowledge of Pawnee culture and history with me. Thank you for inspiring me and so many others with your commitment to justice and truth-telling, and your ongoing work defending American Indian sovereignty, self-determination, cultures, homelands, sacred places, repatriation and burial rights, and human rights. Our friendship has changed this book and my life for the better.

Thank you, Electa Leigh Hare, for the myriad ways you cultivate the seeds of change, and for introducing me to the amazing work of the Pawnee Seed Preservation Society. I'm so grateful to be your friend. Electa, James, Ida, Tawali, and Signy: thank you for including me on such a meaningful journey to Pawnee homelands in Nebraska, and for sharing so much laughter. Ida, a special thanks for your patience with my terrifying driving down "Country Road Z." Getting to know your family has been one of the greatest gifts of writing this book.

Thank you to Judi M. gaiashkibos, Margaret Jacobs, Susana Grajales Geliga, and the members of the Genoa Indian School Digital Reconciliation Project for inviting me to witness your important work.

Thank you to Nancy and Jerry Carlson, Kirk Budd, and Richard and Cherrie Beam-Calloway, for sharing your historical knowledge and your family stories, and for your kindness to a visitor.

Broc Anderson, thank you for your friendship and your encouragement, for our illuminating conversations, and for your invaluable contributions to "The Antidote's Story." Thank you for helping me to better understand the past and present of the Lakota Nation and the United States in what became northwestern Nebraska, and for the work you do to globalize history.

Thank you, Denise Walker, for speaking with me about the rich history of DeWitty/Audacious.

Thank you, Mimi Casteel, for helping me to envision what a verdant future might look like and how to get there, for educating me about social change and soil ecology, and for your commitment to rebuilding our soils and restoring balance to our ecosystems. Thank you for sharing your conviction that "moving from conventional to regenerative agriculture on working lands is the most powerful tool humanity has to reverse climate change," for teaching me and many people what's possible when healthy, biodiverse soils with living roots store water and carbon underground, and for working to help transform agriculture on a global scale while there is still time.

Thank you, Andrew Moore, for climbing down into this fictional darkroom with me and helping to mix the chemistry, for sharing your knowledge and your creativity with me, for your enormously helpful notes, and for your awe-inspiring intimate and panoramic photographs.

Thank you to Marie Howe for permission to use lines from "Gretel, from a sudden clearing" as this book's epigraph, and to Michael J.

Bennett for permission to share images from *Countering Stryker's Punch: Algorithmically Filling the Black Hole* as part of the coda.

I'm tremendously grateful to Hannah Holleman, whose *Dust Bowls of Empire: Imperialism, Environmental Politics, and the Injustice of "Green" Capitalism* enriched my understanding of the global soil erosion crisis caused by colonial capitalist expansion, and the ongoing "decimation of lands that is predicated on the domination of people"—not just on the drought-stricken Plains but all over the globe, not just in the 1930s but today.

Rebecca Clarren, thank you for your kindness, your support, and for mapping a pathway toward material redress and repair. Your work has helped me understand that to wait for federal leadership on reparations and restorations is "to delay the wait for justice indefinitely."

To my incredible agent, Denise Shannon, and my brilliant editor, Jordan Pavlin—it would take another novel for me to even begin to express my gratitude to and for you. Thank you for believing in me and in this novel from the very beginning. Thank you for helping me and this book in a thousand different ways.

Kaveh Akbar, thank you for being such a wonderful friend to me and to this novel, and for the gift of your transformative notes. Thank you to Morgan Talty, Ellis Ludwig-Leone, Rivka Galchen, Dinaw Mengestu, Tommy Orange, Lauren Groff, and Nana Kwame Adjei-Brenyah for such generous and insightful early responses to my novel, and for giving me the confidence to send it out into the world.

Thank you to the many institutions that have given me the gift of life-changing support, including the Guggenheim Foundation and the MacArthur Foundation. A special thanks to Mary Ellen von der Heyden and the Cullman Center.

Thank you to Emily Reardon, Emily Murphy, Kathleen Fridella, Cassandra Pappas, Kathryn Ricigliano, John Gall, Izzy Meyers, John Ingold, Susan M. S. Brown, Maggie Carr, Alisa Garrison, Tess Rossi, and the amazing team at Knopf. Thanks as well to Rose Tomaszewska, Molly Slight, Asia Choudry, Priya Roy, Katrina Northern, and everyone at Chatto & Windus.

Allison M. Long, thank you for finding and sharing such excellent resources, which changed the shape of this story, and for our nourishing conversations. Bea Crook, thank you for sharing your beautiful home with me. Emily Chenoweth, thank you for getting me unstuck, cheering me on, and for the deep magic of our friendship. Lori Pollock, thank you for helping me to listen better.

Carey McHugh, Christina Rumpf, and Cowbird Creative, thank you for helping me to organize my tornado of images and resources into a beautifully designed website.

A huge hug and thank you to my friends and my family for years of love and encouragement.

Tony Perez, this book wouldn't exist without you. Thank you for being with me when I was lost in the dust, for helping me to find my way to the ending, for pouring so much of your time, energy, attention, and creativity into this story, and for your brilliant edits to every iteration of our novel. Thank you for your all-weather, all-terrain love.

Oscar and Ada, I love you so much. Thank you for making this earth a heaven for your mama. Thank you for everything you help me to learn, and to remember.

So many books, articles, photographs, and films informed not just my thinking, but the characters, details, and texture of this novel. Some of these are included below, with gratitude to their creators:

Native Historians Write Back: Decolonizing American Indian History, ed. Susan A. Miller and James Riding In

Nation to Nation: Treaties Between the United States and American Indian Nations, by Suzan Shown Harjo

"Six Pawnee Crania: The Historical and Contemporary Significance of the Massacre and Decapitation of Pawnee Indians in 1869," by James Riding In, *American Indian Culture and Research Journal* 16, no. 2 (1992):101–17.

The Pawnee Seed Preservation Society Revive Ancient Ties to Ancestors | *Seed Warriors*, dir. Rebekka Schlichting

Return of the Pawnees, dir. Charles "Boots" Kennedye

Violence Over the Land: Indians and Empires in the Early American West, by Ned Blackhawk

Like a Loaded Weapon: The Rehnquist Court, Indian Rights, and the Legal History of Racism in America, by Robert A. Williams Jr.

Lost Bird: Spirit of the Lakota, by Renee Sansom Flood

The Lost Traveler, by Sanora Babb

Lakota Nation vs. United States, dir. Jesse Short Bull and Laura Tomaselli

Ghostly Matters: Haunting and the Sociological Imagination and *The Hawthorn Archive: Letters from the Utopian Margins*, by Avery Gordon

Dust Bowls of Empire: Imperialism, Environmental Politics, and the Injustice of "Green" Capitalism, by Hannah Holleman

The Likes of Us: America in the Eyes of the Farm Security Administration, by Stu Cohen

A Choice of Weapons, by Gordon Parks

The Learning Tree, dir. Gordon Parks

Fields of Vision: Library of Congress (five volume series)

Daring to Look: Dorothea Lange's Photographs & Reports from the Field, by Anne Whiston Spirn

The Cost of Free Land: Jews, Lakota, and an American Inheritance, by Rebecca Clarren

After One Hundred Winters: In Search of Reconciliation on America's Stolen Lands, by Margaret D. Jacobs

The Homesteader, by Oscar Micheaux

Farming the Dust Bowl, by Lawrence Svobida

Dust Bowl Diary, by Ann Marie Low

Dirt Meridian, by Andrew Moore, with Doug Dean

Dust Bowl Girls: A Team's Quest for Basketball Glory, by Lydia Reeder

The Book of Job

A fuller account of the true history of *The United States v. Yellow Sun*, alluded to in "Tomasz Oletsky's Deposit," can be found in "The United States v. Yellow Sun et al. (The Pawnee People): A Case Study of Institutional and Societal Racism and U.S. Justice in Nebraska from the 1850s to 1870s," by James Riding In, first published in the *Wicazo Sa Review* 17, no. 1 (spring 2002) and anthologized in *Native Historians Write Back: Decolonizing American Indian History*, ed. Susan A. Miller and James Riding In.

You can also find this and other supplemental photographs, documents, photographs, and resources connected to *The Antidote*, as well as more information on some of the people listed above and ways to support their work at karenrussellauthor.com.

PHOTOGRAPHY CREDITS

4   *Rabbit Drive in Western Kansas,* 1934 or 1935, Potter, Kansas State Historical Society.

5   [Untitled photo, possibly related to: *Homesteader's children. Penderlea Homesteads, North Carolina*] Photographer: Carl Mydans. Library of Congress, Prints & Photographs Division, Farm Security Administration/ Office of War Information Black-and-White Negatives.

20   [Untitled photo, possibly related to: *Mr. Tronson, farmer near Wheelock, North Dakota*] Photographer: Russell Lee. Library of Congress, Prints & Photographs Division, Farm Security Administration/Office of War Information Black-and-White Negatives.

24   *Scarecrow, North Carolina.* Photographer: John Vachon. Library of Congress, Prints & Photographs Division, Farm Security Administration/ Office of War Information Black-and-White Negatives.

96   A picture postcard of the two main buildings at the Nebraska Industrial Home, Milford, Nebraska, Nebraska State Historical Society.

109   *The bleached skull of a steer on the dry sun-baked earth of the South Dakota Badlands.* Photographer: Arthur Rothstein. Library of Congress, Prints & Photographs Division, Farm Security Administration/Office of War Information.

152   [Untitled photo, possibly related to: *Transients clearing land. Prince George's County, Maryland*] Photographer: Carl Mydans. Library of Congress, Prints & Photographs Division, Farm Security Administration/Office of War Information Black-and-White Negatives.

152   [Untitled image, unidentified photographer. Taken between 1935 and 1942.] Library of Congress, Prints & Photographs Division, Farm Security Administration/Office of War Information Black-and-White Negatives.

152   [Untitled photo, possibly related to: *Girl picking cranberries, Burlington County, New Jersey*] Photographer: Arthur Rothstein. Library of Congress, Prints & Photographs Division, Farm Security Administration/Office of War Information Black-and-White Negatives.

152   [Untitled photo, possibly related to: *Young Indian mother and baby, blueberry camp, near Little Fork, Minnesota*] Photographer: Russell Lee. Library of Congress, Prints & Photographs Division, Farm Security Administration/ Office of War Information Black-and-White Negatives.

156 *Farmer and sons walking in the face of a dust storm.* Cimarron County, Oklahoma. Photographer: Arthur Rothstein. Library of Congress, Prints & Photographs Division, Farm Security Administration/Office of War Information Black-and-White Negatives.

186 Camera from the studio of H. C. Anderson. Collection of the Smithsonian National Museum of African American History and Culture.

241 Hans Ehlers farm, Root Cellar, F Street, Papillon 18 Damsite, Millard, Douglas County, Nebraska, 1933. Photographer: Harry Weddington. Library of Congress, Prints & Photographs Division, Historic American Buildings Survey.

258 [Untitled photo, possibly related to: *Pupil in rural school. Williams County, North Dakota*] Photographer: Russell Lee. Library of Congress, Prints & Photographs Division, Farm Security Administration/Office of War Information.

267 Man stands on top of enormous pile of buffalo skulls; another man stands in front of pile with his foot resting on a buffalo skull; rustic cage is at foot of pile. Handwritten on back: "C.D. 1892 Glueworks, office foot of 1st St., works at Rougeville, Mich." Courtesy of the Burton Historical Collection, Detroit Public Library.

270 Pawnee students at their reservation boarding school, Nance County, Nebraska, circa 1871. Shared with permission from the Pawnee Nation of Oklahoma.

288 *Homesteader George Barnes and his children in front of their sod house in Custer County, Nebraska.* Photograph by Solomon D. Butcher, Custer County, Nebraska, 1887.

288 Pawnee lodge. Kansas State Historical Society, shared with permission from the Pawnee Nation of Oklahoma.

289 Untitled photo, possibly related to: *Planting locust root cutting, Natchez Trace Project, near Lexington, Tennessee.* Photographer: Carl Mydans. Library of Congress, Prints & Photographs Division, Farm Security Administration/Office of War Information Black-and-White Negatives.

396 *Cat and her kittens, Canyon County, Idaho.* Photographer: Russell Lee. Library of Congress, Prints & Photographs Division, Farm Security Administration/Office of War Information Black-and-White Negatives.

402 Images from "Countering Stryker's Punch: Algorithmically Filling the Black Hole" (https://journal.code4lib.org/articles/12542) by Michael J. Bennett. The article is licensed under the CC BY 3.0 US license (https://creativecommons.org/licenses/by/3.0/us/). © 2017 Michael J. Bennett.

404 Map of Pawnee lands, from *Nation to Nation: Treaties Between the United States and American Indian Nations* (National Museum of the American Indian and Smithsonian Books, 2014). © Smithsonian Institution.

409 *Recently built Pawnee mud lodge next to defunct Pawnee Indian boarding school on the Pawnee reservation,* Oklahoma, 2023. Photographer: James Riding In.

A NOTE ABOUT THE AUTHOR

KAREN RUSSELL is the author of five previous books of fiction, including the *New York Times* bestsellers *Swamplandia!* and *Vampires in the Lemon Grove*. She is a MacArthur Fellow and a Guggenheim Fellow, a finalist for the Pulitzer Prize, the recipient of two National Magazine Awards for Fiction, the New York Public Library's Young Lions Award, the National Book Foundation's 5 Under 35 award, the Shirley Jackson Award, the 2023 Bottari Lattes Grinzane prize, and the 2024 Mary McCarthy Prize, among other honors. With composer Ellis Ludwig-Leone and choreographer and director Troy Schumacher, she cocreated *The Night Falls*, listed as one of *The New York Times*'s Best Dance Performances of 2023. She has taught literature and creative writing as a visiting professor at the Iowa Writers' Workshop, the University of California–Irvine, Williams College, Columbia University, and Bryn Mawr College, and was the Endowed Chair of Texas State University's MFA program. She serves on the board of Street Books. Born and raised in Miami, Florida, she now lives in Portland, Oregon, with her husband, son, and daughter.

A NOTE ON THE TYPE

This book was set in Janson, a typeface long thought to have been made by the Dutchman Anton Janson, who was a practicing type-founder in Leipzig during the years 1668–1687. However, it has been conclusively demonstrated that these types are actually the work of Nicholas Kis (1650–1702), a Hungarian, who most probably learned his trade from the master Dutch typefounder Dirk Voskens. The type is an excellent example of the influential and sturdy Dutch types that prevailed in England up to the time William Caslon (1692–1766) developed his own incomparable designs from them.

Composed by North Market Street Graphics,
Lancaster, Pennsylvania

Designed by Cassandra J. Pappas